THE
Ha-Ha

THE
Ha-Ha

A NOVEL

DAVE KING

Little, Brown and Company
NEW YORK   BOSTON

Little, Brown and Company
Time Warner Book Group
1271 Avenue of the Americas, New York, NY 10020

The author is grateful for permission to reprint the description of a
ha-ha from *The New York Botanical Garden Illustrated Encyclopedia of
Horticulture* by Thomas Everett, copyright 1981. Reproduced by
permission of Routledge/Taylor & Francis Books, Inc.

ISBN 0-7394-5371-8

Book design by Brooke Koven

Printed in the United States of America

For Frank

The dark threw its patches down upon me also . . .

—WALT WHITMAN, "Crossing Brooklyn Ferry"

A ha-ha is a boundary wall concealed in a ditch so that it does not intrude upon the view. Much employed by the great nineteenth-century English landscape gardener "Capability" Brown, its original purpose was to make possible uninterrupted views from the lawns and other more neatly cared-for areas surrounding the mansion, of more distant trees, copses, lakes and meadows grazed by cattle and sheep. . . . The name ha-ha derives from the exclamation that a stranger might make upon coming upon such a ditch unexpectedly from the top of the wall. An experience of this kind could, of course, be highly dangerous to the unwary.

—Thomas H. Everett,
The New York Botanical Garden
Illustrated Encyclopedia of Horticulture

I

1

W<small>HY AM I HERE?</small> Is it only that Sylvia telephoned so desperately after midnight, and I stood listening by the answering machine as she asked me to take Ryan? Or something bigger? Because before the sun has burned the dew from the grass, here I am. I pull into the driveway and turn off the engine, and Sylvia, who's been standing on the stoop waiting, steps toward the truck. Her sandals slap the flagstones as she approaches.

I should have realized only a truly serious binge could force Sylvia into rehab, but still, I'm shocked by her appearance. Her blonde hair is slicked back so tight that the waves seem painted on her skull, and her face is puffy, especially in the soft patches under her eyes. She has lines where I don't remember seeing lines before and a sore budding on her lower lip. Nevertheless, she's made an effort to clean up. Her white shirt's freshly ironed, and as she leans in the window of the truck, I can smell mouthwash.

"It won't be that long," she says flatly, and licks her cracked lips. Beneath the pale skin of her face, the muscles look clenched, and I wonder how long it's been since she slept. "Just a tune-up, get me on track. I doubt I'd even do this except my harridan of a sister is making it *so* — and I'm sort of at my wits' . . ." She shakes her head sourly. "And if it is for the better — who the hell knows? Because for a week I haven't *left* the house for fear of being away from my — not to take a *walk* or get him to a *movie*, let alone work. I couldn't bear to crash. But I mean it absolutely: a tune-up. I'm not looking for a makeover, and I really don't plan to impose him for long. I don't — I don't think I'm a hard case." At this, her eyes well, and I take her hand. She sighs irritably. "After all, Howie, isn't it your problem, too, in a way? Who knows if I'd even be in this spot, but for you?"

I drop Sylvia's hand. I'd love to tell her her pressed shirt has done nothing for her disposition, but instead I just glower at the shut garage door. And Sylvia knows, even through her come-down haze, that she's blundered. She stares glassily at the asphalt driveway until at last I shrug curtly and bark out, "Sh-cke!" It's the best I can do.

"Okay, fine," she says. She knows the score. "Well, I appreciate your coming on such short notice. And we're almost ready. Hang on, we'll get this show on the . . ." To head off another silence, she goes back in the house.

I get out and wait on the fender. It's neither true nor fair to say I'm to blame for her predicament, but I have a long history of letting Sylvia call the shots. And it's not an unappealing notion, her falling apart over me, though in truth, I don't think her situation is so bad. Sylvia's one of those small-time users who does a fair job of managing her cocaine and keeping her kid fed and clothed, and even if she has missed a day or two of work, I think she might be satisfied with the life she's got. I suspect that for a lot of people coke is like a chronic disease or a handicap or injury from which they don't fully recover; if they're smart, they patch around it and keep on going. So my bet is Sylvia will be home the day after tomorrow. She'll realize it's her lot to love getting high, but there are worse afflictions, and the minute she realizes this she'll call me to bring Ryan over. By the time we get there, she'll already be buzzed, and maybe I'll stay awhile. Maybe she'll be grateful or affectionate or dismissive, but nothing will change. Her life — and mine, to the extent it revolves around hers — will start up again at virtually this same point.

I watch a delivery truck pull in next door, and a couple of dogs bark. Over the years I've done my own share of recreationals, primarily hallucinogens, but I never liked snorting for the way it made me aware of my head. Finally I abandoned the drug realm altogether. I don't think Sylvia's forgiven me for not developing a habit myself, but she wouldn't change places with me.

There's an eruption of shouting from behind the screen door, then silence. The houses in this development are pastel-colored boxes, and I remember a remark of Sylvia's the day I helped her move in. She said she never thought she'd be living in a Silly Putty–colored house, and I wondered if she remembered how the corn used to cover this area when we were kids, and how we once drove out this way for a picnic. Now there's a red Chrysler parked in the street by her mailbox, with a jumble of ratty suitcases and shopping bags alongside, and as I look at the car and the bags, I wonder why Sylvia even bothers keeping track of her expectations. *The world takes a shit in your mouth*, I could tell her, *and you swallow it whole*. If you're waiting for compensation or payback, forget it — or else I've got a lot due for what happened to me. I think again of her saying I'm part of her problem, and I glare at the screen door. Hell, I'm not even to blame for Ryan, but here I am.

Sylvia reappears, accompanied by a gray cat and a well-groomed social services type. They don't look up when I stroll over, so I touch Sylvia's shoulder, and she darts me an anxious glance. "You two know each other," she says. "My sister Caroline, my intervention*eer*."

I put out my hand. It's perhaps fifteen years since I saw Sylvia's little sister, and in those days she looked like an overgrown cheerleader. Now she's a dressy woman in stockings and a silk scarf tied in a Windsor knot. She takes my hand and drops it, then gives me a smile that's no smile at all. "Could I speak to you?" she says to Sylvia, and the two of them step away. I stare at Caroline, refusing as much as possible to grant her her privacy, and after a minute she turns her back on me. She keeps her voice low, but any idiot could guess what she's saying.

Actually, I'm not a bad choice when it comes to child care, even if no one's asked me before. There's nothing wrong with my intellect or judgment, and my steady gig, maintenance at the convent, makes for a flexible schedule. Living on disability, I'm home a lot, and I run a stable household and keep my nose clean. So I'm a poster boy: a drug-free, contributing member with no record of violent episodes. I'm practically a hero. If I don't utterly love life, so what? I don't know anyone who does. Of course, with my scar, I'm not most kids' preferred associate. I decided years ago I had nothing to hide and threw all my caps away, and as my hair's thinned, the dent in my skull has grown more noticeable. Then there's the language thing, but people learn to deal with that. Anyway, it's my impression that kids like talking but care less about being talked *to*.

These are my thoughts when the front door opens and Ryan steps onto the stoop: a brown-skinned, lanky guy of about nine, with wide-set hazel eyes, tightly curled hair, and a few dark freckles across his nose. He's wearing a clean white T-shirt with long basketball shorts and big white basketball shoes. I've never known who his father was, but it's not me: his dad wasn't Caucasian. And of course, my time with Sylvia was long, long ago, whereas Ryan was the surprise of Sylvia's mid thirties. I watch him bend to scoop up the gray cat, and I notice that his hair, which was a fluffy halo last I saw him, is cut now in a sharp fade. He's more a black kid than a white. I walk over to pat his head, but he flinches when I raise my hand, so I stroke the cat's chin instead. He doesn't greet me.

Sylvia steps toward us. "Caroline doesn't think I should leave him with you," she says unnecessarily. "Like I have so much choice." She eyes us as though we'll disagree, but it's true. Sylvia's circle is barely larger than mine.

Ryan says, "Why can't I go with Aunt Caroline?"

Sylvia snorts derisively, and for a moment this seems to be her total response. Then she snaps, "Don't bust Mama's chops right now, you mind?" and in the silence that follows, I'm embarrassed for both of them. "*I'm* the one who's out of control," she mutters. Caroline touches her elbow, and Sylvia says, "All right, all right," and places her hands on Ryan's shoulders. "Don't you want to stay in school here with your friends? Rather than having to make up a lot of work? Hmm? Isn't that a good idea?" Kneeling before him, she puts on a smile. "Howie has a great big Victorian house and a nice spare bedroom you'll have all to yourself. And there's *lots* of interesting people living there. So let Mama get her act together, then we'll have *such* a reunion, 'kay?"

Ryan frowns. He looks down, mumbling something no one can hear. Sylvia says, "Hm?" then "*Speak!*" and for a moment he looks defiant. He kicks at a leaf that's fluttered to the flagstones, then carefully flattens it with the toe of a sneaker. In his arms, the cat twitches her tail. At last, he leans against Sylvia and whispers.

Sylvia sighs. "Please don't do this. Howie's known you all your life. He loves you a lot." She speaks so Caroline and I can hear, and I smile at Ryan, but I'm relieved when he keeps his face to her shoulder. It's true, of course, that when he was born I went to the hospital, and I even wept as I held him in my arms. But Sylvia knows I wasn't weeping for joy, and she can't think he and I have much of a bond. I see Ryan when his mother calls me — she wants a couch moved, some wood chopped, the cat brought off the roof — and with a task involved, she makes an effort to be cheerful. As for Ryan, he's polite but aloof with me, and I'm carefully polite and amiable toward him. But love? We don't go beyond neutral.

Sylvia says, "You and Howie will do all sorts of *guy* things. Whatever *guys* do." She's being comical, but when he remains impassive her voice hardens. "Anyway, buster, it's what's happening, and it's not open to discussion. So let Caroline take Bindi back to Chicago. That's the most she can handle with her great big job." Caroline steps forward, and Ryan shrinks back, hugging the cat. Sylvia says, "Sweetie, there's *dogs* at Howie's —"

"Not!" I say. This is one word I can dependably force out. The only dog at our place is Laurel's French bull, who's too chubby and placid ever to mix it up with Bindi, so I nod and reach for the cat myself. But Caroline only hands me an envelope she's fished from her bag. I think I recognize "Sylvia Mohr" written on the outside, but I don't take time to puzzle out all the letters: the address and phone number of the facility, I suppose. Inside the envelope, a business card is folded between three hundred-dollar bills. I wonder how they came up with the figure.

I offer the money back to Caroline. I can cover the kid's meals, and I won't have it thought that my friendship's for hire. But Caroline tucks Bindi under an arm and waves the bills away, flapping her hand as if I might not understand. Ryan and Sylvia observe this spectacle, then Sylvia snorts again. "Caro," she says. "Howie's not *deaf*. If you spoke, I bet he'd hear you."

Caroline reddens. "In case of emergency," she says, but now I'm mad. I fling the money at her, and the bills and business card flutter to the ground. The cat yowls, and Caroline winces. As she plucks up the money, a red scratch appears on her forearm. "You can call me anytime," she says grimly, handing back the business card. I'd like to tell her I don't make phone calls.

Sylvia runs her hands down Ryan's brown arms. "You do everything you're told, now. I called the school, left Ms. Monetti a message." Ryan scowls at the road. Sylvia wraps her arms around him, holding him tight for several minutes, and at last he softens and murmurs into her neck. Sylvia sighs, glaring at Caroline. "Satisfied?" she says. "It must feel damn good, storming in here, uprooting our lives. Because you sure don't give one shit about the cost to me. Or my child."

At this, Ryan pulls away. "Nn-*nnng!*" he says, and stomps the two steps to the door. He slips into the darkness without a look. As if a gust of wind has blown it, the door slams, rattling the knocker.

"Ryan!" Sylvia wipes her cheek as she stands. She flexes her fingers, then suddenly embraces me, too. "You're always there for me, Howie," she mumbles, and as I touch her waist I feel how thin she's gotten. I doubt she's been this thin since high school, and I remember the bus station when *she* saw *me* off. I tried not to cry because she was already sobbing harder than I'd seen anyone cry in my whole life, and I wanted her to remember me strong, in case she never saw me again. But that was all teen swagger; I never really imagined what could happen. The last thing I said was "I'll come back soon," and who knew it wasn't a *quick* return I should have wished for, but a slow one? A full year's tour of duty, unscathed.

I can't be mad at Sylvia. Touching a hand to her hair, I offer a quick peck to say we'll be waiting, but she's already stepped away. Caroline stands beside the red Chrysler, and with expert gestures she folds Bindi into a cat carrier and places the carrier on the back seat. Sylvia piles the crumpled bags in the trunk and slams the lid, then looks at the house, her hands on her hips. "Ryan!" The door does not open. I scan the three larger windows, plus the small, pebbled window of the bath, and I can see various decorative objects — a dried flower arrangement, a souvenir doll from Central America — but no movement within. Sylvia calls out again and takes a step toward the house.

Caroline says, "Maybe I should get him." She looks at her watch.

"No, let's go." Sylvia's mouth twitches, and dark blotches color her cheeks. She looks truly haggard. "Before I change my — Let's just *go*, goddamn it. If he can't —" She blinks as Caroline starts the ignition, then she slips in on the passenger's side. For a moment, once her door's closed, it looks as if she might call out again. She opens her mouth and leans from the window, then turns abruptly, chin up, and scowls straight ahead. The Chrysler inches forward, and I give a wave nobody sees. Then she's gone.

I turn toward the house, wondering if the boy has locked himself in his room, and what Sylvia expects me to do if he has. But the front door opens, and out he comes, lugging a suitcase with a panel of embroidered flowers on one side. He's put on a dark blue Indians cap, and the visor makes a tight curve across his brow. I take the suitcase from him, checking as I do to see if he's crying, but his face is a single, concentrated frown. He runs back to lock the front door, slides the key under a flowerpot, and climbs silently into the cab. I pull out of Sylvia's road, and when I turn right, toward home, Ryan points to the left. "My school's thataway," he says.

"Not," I tell him. The day his mom enters rehab is one day a kid should be permitted to play hooky. "Na," I say, without meaning to speak at all.

Ryan gazes noncommittally from across the seat. "Are you a retard?" he says.

2

My main injury is to the left temporal lobe, which is where I landed when I came down in the forest, and where my hematoma was situated. Most of the doctors who've examined me — army doctors and battalions of others since — classify my condition as a form of anomia, the inability to recall the names of objects, but that's not how it feels in my head. From my standpoint, it's not the *recalling* that's the problem, so much as the physical manufacture of words, any words, with my lips and tongue. I can *recall* Laurel's name at any instant I need to, but with all its crazy *L*'s and *R*'s I will never, ever succeed in spitting that word out. Most of my speech is unintelligible, anyway: prolonged drawls that do indeed make me sound deficient, plus shorter pops of expelled effort.

Also, anomia is generally accompanied by alexia, the inability to read or write, but I'm not sold on that, either. Sure, there are many times when reading mysteriously deserts me, but on occasion, rarely, it flashes in very clear. And these are joyful, if short-lived, moments of revival, because through my teen years I read avidly. The fact is, my condition waxes and wanes, leading one doctor to suggest it might even be psychogenic, another notion I discount. But my capabilities do deteriorate under stress or prolonged recreational drug use, which is why I quit that nearly ten years ago. (More than the drugs, though, it's the companionship I miss. Acidheads don't care if a person can't speak; they figure he's as wrecked as they are. The same with shouting out some kind of wrong word or off sound — if you're high enough, it's just part of the trip.) Though quitting pot and acid didn't, to my disappointment, do much for my speech, it did lead me to take on faith the one statement every doctor, VA and otherwise, eventually came around to making: there's a lot about the brain we just don't know.

There are other factors, too. Some memories came back slowly, and I don't always act on what I know. An early struggle with adynamia hindered my speech therapy, and I still process slowly when under duress. Also random numbness, phantom sensations. Often my feet will tingle for days at a time, and sometimes I feel hot coffee being splashed down my arm and over my fingers, but I'm so used now to my nervous system's glitches that they pass like traffic, with barely a notice. And most guys — most *people* — in my condition are emotionally volatile, but I'm the king of control, so at merely moody I'm a success story. No doubt about it.

I'm carrying Ryan's bag upstairs when I hear Laurel explaining my condition to him. He's asked again about me, though I'm sure Sylvia's provided explanations over the years. I wait on the steps while Laurel describes the difference between retarded and impaired, then I go up and put his stuff in the room next to mine. And maybe Ryan's just making conversation, because when I come down he's asking if I'm Laurel's husband.

Laurel Cao is about ten years younger than I am. She's rented a room in my house for seven years, and rather than cash rent she helps me with paperwork. Depending on her as I do, I sometimes forget how odd it once seemed to be sharing my home with someone from Vietnam; but after my mom died, all sorts of basic tasks became much more difficult, and responsible people were not clamoring to join my clubhouse. So I took what came. Laurel has a company called Soupe Toujours, which supplies gourmet soups to a dozen little places all over town. She needed a place to cook, and this house has a nice stove and a big refrigerator from its days as a union hall. I turned over my parents' big front bedroom, too, since I sleep in the room I had as a child. And Laurel grew up in Austin, Texas, and has a southern accent, so it's easy to forget she's Vietnamese; and I saw very few Vietnamese anyway, and all at a distance.

But there's nothing between us. I had a period, when I first came home injured, of picking up hookers, but in my reformed years I keep love and sex in a tightly closed box. I'm better off without them. And who would have me? If I still care for Sylvia more than her behavior warrants, it's because she was my life's romance. She's who I have left and the only one who remembers me as I was. So I do her bidding when she calls, then I go to work for the nuns. Whatever desires I brought to our lovely early days have gone so long untapped that they must have dried up, and one torch is more than enough to carry. I'm fond of Laurel, and there's no doubt she's attractive: long legs, long hair, and a long, slim waist. She's tall for an Asian woman, and in her cowboy boots she can seem more Texan than anything else. Her face is a long oval, too, so that her mouth, which is full and broad and a surprising flower-colored pink, is a small contradiction to all her slim angularity. But I keep it light. I'll eat Laurel's soup if I'm around at lunchtime, but I don't need complications.

Now Ryan's at the kitchen table, dragging a spoon through a bowl of spinach Florentine. Ruby, the little bulldog, is on her stomach making snorting noises, and when I cock my eyebrows Ryan says, "Yeah, we met," in precisely Sylvia's flat, flat tone. At least he's cottoned on to how I communicate.

Laurel pours something into the Cuisinart. "Howard, your nun called. She wants her grass cut," she tells me, then steps to the table and gives the visor of Ryan's Indians cap a tug. "Gonna be nice for us, having a kid around the place." Ryan doesn't move. After a moment Laurel returns to pulsing the Cuisinart, and I help myself to a bowl of the soup. Spinach Florentine is one of Laurel's ten-strikes, but I'm not sure it's child food. I'm wondering what else to feed him when he suddenly digs in.

There's a small dining room opposite the kitchen, and as I eat my soup I hear our other housemates calling out names, a few I've heard of, others I presume are celebrities. This is the type of thing they're always doing that gets on my nerves. I sigh pointedly, and Laurel shrugs. "Some game. People they'd like to have at dinner, I think." Stepping to the doorway, she says, "Boys, come in here a minute," and their chairs scrape as they stand up. In this house I may be nominally the C.O., but Laurel's sergeant at arms.

The boys come and slouch in the doorway. There's a bigger one and a littler one, but to me they're identical, hovering around thirty, with goatees and visored caps and insolently easy physiques. One or both of them has a tattoo. They paint houses for a living, but the littler one's trying to be a screenwriter and the bigger one a music promoter; I pretend not to remember which does which. I also pretend not to know their names. In my head, I call them Nit and Nat, but the fact is it doesn't matter what I call them since I'm incapable of calling them anything at all. Like Laurel, they went to the university and then stayed on, and they're here because I depend on the rent. Laurel knows I don't like them, but she doesn't care — and to tell the truth, I don't care much myself. When I was their age I'd had a decade of war and hospitals. My hair had gone gray, and my skin was slack and puffy from painkillers and other stuff. I didn't do college. But the world is filled with people I resent because their burdens are lighter than mine, and if I drew the line at living among them, I'd be all alone.

Laurel says, "Guys, this is Ryan." In her Texas accent the name sounds like *Ran*. "Who's here for a while as a guest of Howard's. Ryan, meet Steve and Harrison." Nit and Nat lurch forward and slap Ryan's palm, wrapping their fingers around his small thumb in some kind of trendy handclasp. Then, for some reason, they do the same with me. They're not bad people, just stupid and untested and younger than they deserve, and that's sufficient to curry my disfavor. They linger in the doorway, gawping at Ryan until I glare at them; then they slink back to their game.

The day turns sultry in the afternoon. After finishing his soup,

Ryan shifts to the back yard, and when I peek out, he's twisting a stick in his shoelaces. An hour later he's barely budged, and his inactivity unnerves me. What the hell can I do with him? At last, I beckon him to the truck and drive to the zoo, and as we shuffle from enclosure to enclosure, Ryan seems to forget he can talk. He spends a minute or so with each somnolent creature, a small frown creasing his brow, then we move on without comment. Around six, we go to the snack bar for supper, and I point with my fingers for a burger and fries. He does the same.

It's still light when we come home, and the others are away from the house. Ruby waddles up, wheezing over a rubber ball, and Ryan scoops her up, just as he did earlier with Bindi the cat. She grunts and settles against his chest. I realize he hasn't yet been upstairs, so I lead a tour of this house, which has been my home since I was younger than he is now and where my family was a happy threesome until I came home injured. Wordlessly I open doors and indicate each self-evident room, starting on the fourth floor, the empty cupola. Then the third — the boys' two sloppy bedrooms and inexcusable bath — and the second, Laurel's closed door in the front. Two back bedrooms, my own and the guest room where I've set Ryan's bag, and the big tiled bathroom we three will share. Downstairs, the parlor and dining room, seldom used; the couch, the TV, the broad dining table still littered with lists of Nit and Nat's fantasy dinner guests; and finally, the cellar. I wave at the furnace and the washer and dryer, at Laurel's pyramids of five-gallon containers, and at Nit and Nat's ladders and drop cloths and *their* five-gallon drums of paint. Half a dozen suitcases in a corner, beside an old wooden medicine cabinet and a stack of red flowerpots; glue traps around the edges of the room. And under the stairs the most interesting item: a huge, tripartite Gothic window frame the nuns let me cart off when the convent was being renovated. I brush cobwebs from the air and move one wooden sash, just to show him how it's hinged, and Ryan nods silently, still stroking Ruby's belly.

So that's the place, typical of older homes of the Midwest, I guess. Perhaps other places, too, though I can't say I've traveled much. There's the old backyard stable yet to see, with a tack room at one end and even a privy, and I'm thinking *here's proof you didn't expect. Yes, I've known tragedy, but I live in my own house. I work and sleep and carry on, and my tragedy doesn't govern me, no matter what you may have imagined.* But these are things I can't put into words, and Ryan says he's tired, so we go upstairs.

At the door to his room he carefully sets the dog on her feet, and I wonder if I'm supposed to kiss him. He and I don't have a kissy relationship, and I'm not wishing to start one. But I believe I'll do whatever's right. The first few hours have gone well enough, I suppose, so I point at the futon on the floor of the spare room. *Mi casa es su casa*, I'd like to say. If I could talk, I'd tag along into the room, remind him to brush his teeth, and ask if he's brought his pj's. We'd drift into empty conversation, and I'd admire his Indians cap and ask about favorite players. By the time we finished chatting, he'd be in bed. I could leave with a brisk wave or read him a story while he drifted off. But instead, here we are, in the square landing between the bedrooms, searching for some way to say good night. And even if the day has passed well, I'm tired, and I don't have much in reserve for the morning. The truth is this boy is a little stranger, despite my history with his mom, and perhaps the best option is for Sylvia to take him away. Perhaps the house tour's depressed me, too: all this looking into corners. So I stare at the floor, asking myself what on earth I was thinking, and at last, the stranger puts out his hand. I look at it a moment and give it a small shake, and he gazes at me squarely and manages a flat smile. Then he goes into his room and shuts the door.

3

"I'M JUST CURIOUS where this is heading, Howard." Laurel's leaning against the kitchen counter, and I'm at the table, fooling with a vegetable peeler with a red plastic handle. All the rest of the house is dark, and the room floats, lit and solitary, under the overhead lamp. "For example, he's got school, right? You can't just let him take early summer vacation." I clank the vegetable peeler on the tabletop, and she adds, "Well, he didn't go to school today. And a full-time child is not something I can take on."

I clear my throat. One, today was unusual for Ryan, and two, no one's asked her to take on any child. And I'm not in the mood to be scolded right now. But Laurel only reaches for a small pad she keeps on the counter. "Just *try*," she says, and sets the pad and a Bic pen on the table. "I don't give a hoot how good you do. Shorthand, code . . ." She looks at me another minute, then says, "I'm gonna go fill the feeders," and steps out the back door.

I know she means to give me some privacy, but the little pad sits before me like a test. And I was given batteries of tests during my recovery. Reflex, cognition, reading speed, reading comp, reading retention, short-term memory, long-term memory, large- and small-motor function, on and on. I think of the testers — meticulous explainers, never certain how much I understood, white-clad or blue-clad or dressed in carefully selected civvies, excusing themselves discreetly or sticking by me while I struggled — and I know I won't pass this. The instant I touch pen to paper I'll be lost in a quagmire of visualizing and correcting and juggling the letter shapes with the patterns of sentences. I'll be wondering which way to turn a *C* at the same time I'm trying to navigate between two thoughts, and I'll end up tearing the pad in two and thrusting the vegetable peeler into my palm. The truth is that though I occasionally read adequately, I can't write at all; that's one of the mysteries. And because I had a few small breakthroughs at the start, some doctors have said that with steady practice I might manage some improvement; but I can't. I just can't. I won't work harder than I do already.

I hear a rattle outside as Laurel pours birdseed into the clear plastic tube of a feeder. It's a sound almost like rain. There's a pause, then the softer whish of the thistle seed for the finches. I wonder if she can see me through the window, so I pose as though lost in thought; then I hear her dragging a step stool toward the catalpa at the back of the yard, where a third feeder hangs from a branch. I get up and open two bottles of beer.

Laurel comes back, and we clink bottles and each take a sip. She picks up the untouched pad and pen and puts them away without comment, and for this small consideration I'm immeasurably grateful. She says, "Okay. Let's start with how long he might be here. A couple weeks?" In the hubbub this morning, neither Caroline nor Sylvia mentioned a time frame, but if Sylvia lasts a week in that place, I'll eat my hat. And she said just a tune-up, so I waggle a finger. Laurel says, "Oh no, Howard. This stuff takes time. Didn't his mom tell you? So like how long you think? Maybe six weeks . . . five weeks . . . ?" I pick a number, and when she reaches my number, I tap her arm. "Two, then? Two weeks? I don't know — let's say two to four. 'Bout a month, I guess, give or take." It's a huge overestimate, but Laurel doesn't know Sylvia.

Laurel takes a long swig from her beer. "You know, I don't know shit about babies," she says. "And I've got all the work I can handle as it is. I mean, I don't know how to say it without being the big bitch." I think I know what's coming, and I give her a smile, but she's squinting into the neck of her bottle. She looks ashamed. "Just that I'll pitch in all I can, but I'm not one of those gals with untapped maternal instincts. You probably know as much about this as I do, even if you know nothing at all." A strand of dark hair falls over her face, and she twists it between two fingers. "Which is not to say he doesn't seem like a perfectly nice, good, well-behaved little —"

I step in front of her and slap my chest. I'm rarely in the position to reassure anyone, and I want to say *hey: me. This is* my *thing, and I've started.* With Ryan tucked in his room, my spirits have lifted, and I was cheered by that handshake in the upstairs hallway. I can tend to this kid, despite Sylvia and Caroline and even Laurel, and I slap my chest again and spread my hands. Laurel smiles, peering bemusedly down her flattish nose. She looks especially Asian tonight, I think.

And suddenly I'd like to make her laugh. How hard can it be to keep food on the table? Get a nine-year-old to school? Even having him around for a day or two: hell, one thing I *do* is endure, and compared to other shit I've been through . . . So I do a little frug or twist and shake my ass, and the corners of Laurel's mouth turn up. Sylvia used to love it when I clowned around, but Laurel knows me as the somber landlord. I slap my gut, doing a broad double take at the hollow, popping sound it makes.

"How*ard!*" She gives my shoulder a shove. "Seriously, now. Here's a kid who's only ever had a mom, and now his mom's gone off. He comes into a house where there's all these *men* and one woman, who you think he's gonna gravitate toward? Just as like a surro —" She rolls her eyes.

I haven't quit my clowning: I'm bobbing my head and making air noises with my cheeks. I clomp around the kitchen like a playful gorilla, scratching my underarms, and besides creating a distraction I don't know what I'm getting at. If anyone else ever compared me to an ape I'd go wild — but I'm out of control now, I'm letting off steam. And at last Laurel starts to giggle; she gives an inadvertent little snort and covers her face. "Howard!" she says gaily. "Stop it! Shape up now, really! You're gonna need to be this child's *mom!*"

4

Sʏʟᴠɪᴀ's ɴᴏ ᴇᴀʀʟʏ ʀɪsᴇʀ, so it's a safe bet Ryan can fend for himself, breakfastwise. I don't mind mornings, but for years I've left the early hours to Laurel and the soup trade, and I usually stay in bed until she leaves for the day. But when this morning comes I'm awake at the crack. I've slept lightly, listening for wails or quiet sobbing from Ryan, and I lie in bed wondering if we have Cocoa Puffs or Froot Loops or even cornflakes in the house. I figure today I'll help him get started, and tomorrow, if he's still here, he can rustle up anything he likes.

Downstairs, soup is in high gear. Pots are steaming, and the smells of beef and miso and tomato stocks take a little getting used to. Laurel, in flowered pants and black high-top sneakers, is draining beans in the colander. She gives me a distracted glance, and as I watch her move from sink to chopping board to flame, I realize Ryan and I will be in the way. But Laurel says, "Oh, need a burner, Howard?" and in an instant the pots are shifted on the stove. There are eggs in the refrigerator and bagels in the freezer.

Ryan slips in while our backs are turned, and when Laurel and I notice him we stare as if we've forgotten why he's come. Then Laurel grins. "Well, *hell*o, hon. You sleep okay?" He nods minutely. The Indians cap sits low on his brow, but he hasn't yet learned to peer out under the bill, so when he looks up we see his entire face, expressionless and a bit ashen. Laurel says, "Pillow, blanket? Everything comfortable? I want to know if there's anything you need, awright?" To each question, the slightest nod. "Did Howard give you a towel and washcloth?" Nod.

I make a teeth-brushing gesture. He says, "Yeah, I did that." I scrub my face with my hands, and he says, "Uh-huh." At last, I pantomime soaping up all over, washing under my arms and behind my ears and scrubbing my back with a long-handled brush, and he smirks briefly, showing his big, square, nine-year-old's teeth. But after this I have nothing to say. Laurel's back at her stockpots, and Ryan watches me another minute, then frowns at the tabletop; and though I'm willing to move the conversation beyond hygiene, my mind's a blank. When he doesn't generate any remarks of his own, I begin scrambling eggs.

I make breakfast for three and place the plates on the table. Laurel says, "Oh, Howard, mmm. Isn't this a surprise," but she takes hers to the counter so she can eat while working, and Ryan and I are left facing each other. The morning paper, which either Nit or Nat subscribes to, lies between us, but we don't touch it, and as silence falls I'm reminded that in other homes people are discussing the day. When my mom was alive, she had a gift for keeping mealtime conversation flowing. She'd ask leading questions to which I'd respond with nods and gestures, and in this way we managed some subtle exchanges. Of course, a child can't be expected to emcee in the same way, and as Ryan and I dig into our eggs, I suppose he's discovering the burden of my dullness, and food alone isn't enough to create cheer. This is why generally I eat by myself. I wonder what I'd say if I could speak with Ryan, but I can think of nothing, and as the passing moments get under my skin, I guess he wonders what his mother ever saw in me. With this, the quiet grows thunderous. Even the birds cease their outside twittering, the pots quit bubbling on the stove, and I begin to suspect I can't do this for long. Laurel runs the tap briefly, and when the water stops I try not to listen to the scraping of forks.

At last Ryan whispers, "This is good." Maybe he means it, though for my own part I can't agree. One thing I liked about the army was how everyone pitched in, and in boot camp I was considered a pretty good cook. But today, when I should be irreproachable, I've made the eggs too soft, and if I were alone I'd chuck it all in the garbage. I nod, though, at the show of politeness, and then we endure some more minutes of unease. Pushing my eggs around, I wonder if this would be easier with a chatty kid, and I try to remember if there are children in the nearby houses. But it's been years since I paid any attention to the neighbors, and in my current mood I can't think how I'd approach them. I watch Ryan wipe his mouth on the neck of his T-shirt, then he frowns, perhaps unconsciously. *Well*, I think, *it's no picnic for either of us.*

Laurel must sense the discomfort, because she turns now with exaggerated brightness. "Oh, *I* know, Ryan. What do y'all do for lunch?"

He looks shiftily at her. "Nothing."

"I mean, does the school have like a hot plate you can buy, or does your mom make you something to take in a brown bag?"

He weighs his response as Laurel and I stare at him. He looks invaded. "Usually I make like a sandwich. Or Mom does. Like peanut butter and jelly or . . . anything." He shrugs fiercely. "Whatever."

"That your favorite, PB&J? Because I've got some nice ham and a little Havarti, or I could make up a batch of tuna. How's any of that sound?" I shoot her a look, wondering what the hell happened to her reluctance to play mom, and she snaps back, "Well, I can make a *sand*wich, Howard," then bends to rummage in a cupboard. "Drat! If I had a small thermos, I'd give you some soup. How 'bout cold soup? Do you like vichyssoise?"

Ryan says yes to tuna, no to Laurel's vichyssoise. "Want me to do the dishes?" he asks. I shake my head and hand him the funnies, just so I don't have to wonder what he's thinking, and when the plates are draining I lean over his shoulder in search of a strip that's all pictures, no words. But the one I find isn't very funny, and I don't have the patience to work out the other captions.

The staircase creaks, then Nit's standing in the doorway. He's barefoot, and his open bathrobe shows his bare chest and cotton briefs, which are ragged at the waist and look none too clean. He stares at Ryan a moment, then murmurs, "Fuck, man. Forgot you were here," and turns on his heel. But a moment later he's back. "Hey, anybody make coffee?" I step over and jerk his lapels closed. He barely notices, though he does fumble for the belt of his robe.

Ryan watches Nit pour a mug of coffee and methodically dose it with five big spoonfuls of sugar; then he frowns primly at the table-top. "Um, Howie," he asks, "did Aunt Caroline give you money? Because —" He stops, and I suppose he remembers how I threw back those C-notes. "'Cause if I wanna get milk it costs sixty cents."

In an instant, Laurel's reaching for her purse, and I'm digging for pocket change. But it's Nit, the jerk, who beats us to the punch. With a flourish, he drops a crumpled bill to the tabletop, just like a magician producing a dove from thin air. "Keep the change, yo," he says, then he yawns and slurps at the rim of his mug. I could strangle him, but he's already shuffling toward his own dank lair. And what kind of knucklehead keeps money in a bathrobe?

Ryan slings on a backpack, and I take him to school. Halfway across the city I turn the radio on, and he taps his feet and looks marginally less glum. We pull up to a one-story building with long class-room wings and a blacktopped playground, and as I put the truck in park he says, "Where should I, um . . ." He trails off, then says, "Oh," and stares up past the curved bill of that cap. I raise my eyebrows. In a small voice he asks, "How do I get home?"

I'll pick him up, of course. Could he imagine otherwise? I pat my chest, then tap the steering wheel, and to be extra clear I wave a finger at the ground. Ryan nods doubtfully. I snap my fingers, and when his head jerks up, I point to my wrist. Though it takes a minute, he says, "Well, the bell's at two-fifty . . ." Gazing bleakly at the glove box, he adds, "Because I don't think I can take the bus."

I pat the steering wheel again: *I'll be here.* But Ryan's staring at the glove box; he doesn't realize he has to look at me when we talk. "I mean —" he murmurs, and he's forlorn in his uncertainty, "I don't think these buses *go* over where you live." I remember an old joke about people who live out where the buses don't run, and I don't know if those stranded souls are me or him or both of us together, but of course all jokes are beyond my command. So I tap his visor to get his attention, then point again to my chest.

At last, he shuts the door slowly, without saying goodbye. A girl and two boys have stopped to peer at us, and the girl stares through the windshield at my scar. Ryan walks toward them and slaps palms with the boys, and a moment later they all take off running. I watch him barrel toward a tetherball game at the corner of the playground, raising his arms as he approaches the blacktop. He drops his backpack at the edge of the turf, then leaps right up and into the game, swatting the ball from the players. His T-shirt flies up, revealing a long, brown belly. As he returns to earth, a kid shoves him, and to my astonishment Ryan laughs, his mouth hugely wide. Then the game resumes, with Ryan at the back of the line.

I head off to my job, not sure how to take this, but for the moment I'm relieved to be free of him, too.

5

THE CONVENT WHERE I WORK lies on a beautiful stretch just east of the interstate. There's a stone wall with iron gates bordering a residential area, then a curving drive and a large structure that looks like a VA hospital done up in Gothic garb. The nuns have made a conference center within the big building, but no school or hospital, no vegetable garden or bread bakery or any other amenities of a self-sufficient community. But self-sufficiency may not be these nuns' thing; besides me, they have a gardener to take care of the Contemplation Garden and the flower beds and a bus driver named Alain to shuttle them downtown on a regular schedule.

Alain is just pulling out when I arrive, and Sister Amity is watching Robin, the gardener, poke pine bark under some rhododendrons. I'm earlier than usual — Ryan's school starts at eight-ten — but even so, Sister Amity gives me the hawk eye. "I expected you yesterday, Howard. The grass in the Long Field is *quite* overgrown." She's a short, square-faced woman of about forty and far more vigorous than her life requires. Tapping her fingers on the hood of my truck, she sings, "Lots to do, now that spring's here."

I don't bother telling her something came up. I gave up explaining years ago. But the Long Field looks fine to me, and in confirmation, Robin rolls her eyes. "I know it's easy for you to lose track of things, but we mustn't let nature get too firm a hold," Sister Amity says with a grin, and I clench my fists under my overall bib. "After the mowing, I want you to come around the side, please, and have another look at the novices' shower drains. Though I'm sure it's just hair." She grins again and strides off, pumping her arms, and I go the other way to get out the John Deere.

Whatever the nuns' place in the world at large, their little spot of terra firma is extraordinarily pretty. The south acreage, especially, is a delicate arrangement of trees and hedges placed just as you'd arrange them if you were laying out a model train set. A slate walk leads from the main building to an enclosure of cedars, and inside the enclosure six iron benches stand surrounded by ferns, hostas, and clumps of aromatic herbs. This is the Contemplation Garden, which is open to the public and locally celebrated; it's a place all of us were taken as schoolkids. I rarely go there — I already have all the contemplation I need — but when I do, I'm amazed by how lovely it is and by how much Robin accomplishes with a small range of plain green plants. Beyond the Contemplation Garden, the property rolls on for eight or ten acres, all filled with surprises. There's a small chapel in a stand of willows; three isolation cabins used only in the summer months; and at the foot of the Long Field a bit of stream that runs prettily through a woods, then disappears under an arch in the stone wall. But my favorite area is on the north side, behind the main building. Tucked in a crux between two ivy-covered walls is a sitting area where small white stones surround an oblong reflecting pool filled with carp. This is the nuns' private refuge, only steps from their living quarters, and often, as I'm heading to the garden shed, I see the cook, Sister Margaret, leafing through recipe books or her missal as she catches the sun. I could imagine bringing a book here myself if reading weren't so difficult for me. It's a spot that seems always to be sheltered from the breeze, and in winter it's where the snow melts first, with a bundled-up Sister Margaret the first sign of spring. Beyond this lies the garden shed and an open lawn, then a row of pines and a stone wall, with the subdivision beyond.

Only one thing belies the sense of a landscaped Arden, and that's the interstate, which curves quite close to the big main building. On days when the wind is right, you can hear the highway from the little sitting area, and the whoosh of cars makes a sound like the roar of surf, though the coast is a thousand miles away. But the wave sound is the sole hint of traffic; where it passes the convent, the road cuts a trough through the grassland, and in the days before I was on the scene, the nuns had a steep, grassy berm built at the edge of the trough. It's a clever device which creates an optical illusion: from the main convent building, the land seems to roll on without interruption, and if you don't go right up to it, you can't tell there's a roadway there. Sister Amity pointed this out to me the first time I came to mow; she called it a "ha-ha," and I didn't have a clue what it was she meant. "Mind the ha-ha, Howard," she said. "It's too steep for the riding mower. You'll want the push one." And only when I was actually crossing the berm and felt the uneasy grip of the wheels on the incline did I climb down and see the railroad ties and steel reinforcement that had been used to create a retaining wall. I looked down at the curve of little whizzing cars, as dizzying and seductive as a cartoon of vertigo, and only then did I realize that this — this small trick of landscape — was what she called a ha-ha.

The most ethereal moments of my life were the seconds before I crashed down on my head. I'd been overseas exactly sixteen days, and we were climbing through a rocky, forested area, the little lieutenant on point, me and Rimet following too close behind because the three of us were chatting and we were all a little stoned. And the lieutenant stepped on a mine and blew us all sky-high. The lieutenant died instantly, whether from burns or shrapnel or surprise I'll never know. Rimet got burns and a broken shoulder, but escaped serious injury by landing on me; I managed not to die. And though I still have trouble with just what I was telling the LT that was so damned important, and though there are weeks after my fall of which I have no solid memories, only pain, I remember the floating feeling as the ground fell away. The orange dust grew warm around me and filled recognizably with bits of life: the lieutenant's netted helmet, a few leaves clinging to its brim; a spray of pebbles, like an asteroid belt. Rimet, a shadow through the golden haze, waved loosely like a beauty queen as he tumbled toward me, head over heels, and above us I could see the forest canopy and blue tropical sky, untouched by all the bright, warm dust that was raising me up. Then one more moment of astronautical weightlessness, like a scrap of dream in the instant before waking, and the brightness flared out. I remember turning, lithe as a gymnast, and snapping a palm frond with my face, and as the sky clouded over, I suddenly touched down.

I think of this each time I take the mower up the ha-ha; it's the sudden infirmity as the big John Deere loses its purchase, the heedless ribbon of traffic below. Mowing the slope sends a clear wind blowing around in my skull, and as I hover at the edge of imbalance there are moments when my old eighteen-year-old self is still practically within reach — as though all the years since were no more than a blink. And it matters nothing the risk to me or the John Deere; we might both tumble to oblivion for all I care. But that high, weightless moment! That long shiver of sensation! This is my break in the succession of unvaried days, and I save it for last as a kind of treat. And often, as I edge further up the incline than is technically safe, Sister Amity will come out the back door of the convent and begin yelling.

I look up. I can read her lips mouthing my name, and I wave back cheerfully, just to get her goat. Then the blade strikes a rock, and the whole apparatus quivers on three wheels for an instant, and the instant stretches out forever. For a moment, I'm just a fresh-faced, unshaven American kid taking a hike on foreign soil with two guys I barely know. We're chatting, which is something I'll never do again, and I've got Sylvia's school photo in a plastic sleeve in my breast pocket. The LT's interested in botany; he's been making little drawings of the flowers we pass, and I'm still too green to resent his lack of vigilance. I'm thinking we have a year together and might become friends. I could use a buddy. And in spite of the gun and ammo belt and heavy boots, I feel weightless and even happy, and if it weren't against regulations, I might start singing. Then the air turns bright.

I bring my hands back to the wheel and turn downhill. I'm nonchalant about the danger, but I can't help flinching, and Sister Amity begins to run. She crosses the lawn with her skirt held high, like the granny in some old-time tale. I stop the motor and climb down, and Sister Amity scolds, "You can't *take* the ha-ha like that, Howard! I've told you before! Now come inside and wipe that smirk off your face. No more mowing for you today. I don't know *what* you think is so funny!"

I go inside, and Sister Margaret gives me lunch, as she does whenever I work past noon. Sister Amity takes me to the drains that are running slow, and I unscrew the grates and dig out several handfuls of hair and a tampon, and as I'm wrapping the mess in newspaper, Sister Amity pretends I don't know what the tampon is. Then she accompanies me outside.

There's more mowing yet, plus Weedwacking and trimming, but I leave them for tomorrow, just to occupy another day. Usually, this would be the end of my shift and I'd head home, but now I have Ryan to think about, and I'm closer to Sylvia's neighborhood than my own. So I help Robin with the pine bark for an hour or so, and at two-thirty I zip down the interstate to Ryan's school. For a few hours, I've succeeded in forgetting he exists at all.

6

IN MY DARKEST DAYS, after I quit speech therapy, the two poles of my life were *wasted* and *hung over*. It wasn't always possible to score hallucinogens or other exotics, but hash and Jack Daniel's I could easily acquire, and under the influence of those anesthetics I learned that the whole world was as damaged as I was, and I began cruising streetwalkers. There were times I was so wrecked I could barely get hard, but you don't have to be a hundred percent erect for a blow job — or even alert. Occasionally, when my dick finally spasmed into whatever mouth I'd purchased for the night, I couldn't be certain if I was coming or pissing.

If I could, though, I preferred to fuck them, either in the back of my dad's car or in some apartment or motel room they took me to. But the working girls saw me as a dubious character, so it was largely open-air action. I remember once fucking a blonde girl in a parking lot behind a 7-Eleven, and I had to stop in the middle to throw up. The girl was leaning on a pipe railing at the side of a loading dock, and I was behind her with my hand tight across her mouth, pumping away, and I pulled out abruptly and heaved on the asphalt. She jumped aside with a squeal, and I stumbled forward, clutching my gut, the clump of my pants as constraining as shackles. I even dragged my trousers in the puke. On the street beyond the store a car sped past, playing "Compared to What" very loud on its radio, and I plunked my bare ass on the concrete steps of the loading dock, spread my thighs as wide as my dropped trousers would allow, and waved my dick at the girl, just to see if she'd carry on. And she must have been terribly hard up that night, or she'd have told me to go to hell. But she knelt down and finished me off. When I was ready to come, I touched her spiky shag with my fingers, and with all the tenderness I had left I wished this was *my* blonde, the long tresses of her girlhood cropped cute and close while I was a fighting man overseas. The girl I dreamed of was the girl who responded — not to my cock, but to me — and who above all stayed loyal, no matter what I'd become. With this, I came hard and bucking, then fell back across the concrete and passed out cold. When I awoke, I couldn't tell how much time had elapsed. My pants were still around my ankles, and my wallet was several feet away, emptied of money. I stood up and covered myself, then picked up the wallet and drove until dawn, searching for the restitution not of my cash but of my chances. But that was long ago, and I remember it with grief. Now, of course, my best friend is my right hand, and my sex life occurs in the five minutes before rising. At the first hint of consciousness I roll over and get started; then I remember Ryan, and I can't continue.

In the shower, I wonder about Sylvia, who still hasn't bailed on rehab. Last night, while we were out having pizza, she left a message on the answering machine, her voice so jovial that I was certain she was home and high. But after a burst of introduction — "Hi, boys, inmate seven here" — there came the long drawing of a breath, and like a kid calling home from camp, she launched into a description of some people she's met there. She didn't mention the grim scene of her departure. As the message rambled, I saw Ryan's face darken, and I wondered how long before she asked about us; then she said, "Anyway, I sure do miss you, my big darling boy. A line of *X*'s and *O*'s to you from Mama, and a nice hug to Howie, too," and clicked off. Is she supposed to enjoy it?

I'm still not betting on Sylvia's completing her treatment, and it would be easiest, certainly, to send Ryan home. I'd like to see Sylvia myself. But last night, in the pizzeria, a broadcast basketball game forestalled any talk, and I think he enjoys the rides in the truck. Perhaps Sylvia's sticking to her project even goads me a little, because I consider what kind of parent she's been and wonder what kind I'd be. I don't want it said I do a bad job. So I hustle into the kitchen with shaving cream in my ears, and this time there's a burner waiting. Ryan wanders in just as breakfast is ready — he's got excellent timing — and he seems to take this as our customary morning scene. I wouldn't mind his being a little impressed; I don't picture Sylvia bothering with French toast.

I make Laurel's breakfast, too, but she eats at the counter, just as yesterday. It's Ryan and me at the table again, and when the silence descends, my exasperation is like hives. Ryan digs in, clumsily shoveling with his left hand, getting stuff on his shirt, and today he forgets to compliment the food. We're almost finished before he looks up. "Hey, is that guy — um, is Steve gonna come in again and get coffee?"

I shrug. Nit's not a topic I find worthy of discussion. I hand Ryan the dollar for his milk, and with a wave I say *keep the change, yo.* He falls quiet again. Ruby settles herself by his chair, looking up with cereal-bowl eyes, and glancing around sneakily, Ryan feeds her a bit of bacon behind Laurel's back. The poor dog will fart all day, but Laurel's decent enough not to scold us when she turns suddenly and asks about the phone.

In this house, Nit and Nat have cells and private landlines, and Laurel uses her cell phone primarily. I don't make phone calls, though I do have the answering machine; but only two people phone me, or maybe just one. Once in a while, Sister Amity will telephone from the convent, but Sylvia calls any time she's got a problem, and if it weren't for her, I'd have disconnected the service. And this is how she got me to take Ryan, of course. She called after midnight, sounding very strung out, and I came downstairs in my boxers and stood listening to her voice. Sylvia said her sister was bullying her into rehab: "She actually put me in a cold shower. Was anything ever so trite? And I really can't *take* it when she lights into me like that, Howie. It's not so easy to just *go away* when one has a child; you have to — But I was thinking, possibly, if you came over in the morning, we could, I don't know, my mind just swings. But could you stop by anyway, maybe even just for moral support? Because she's wearing down my resistance here — and oh, *Christ*, if I did go someplace I might just manage —" She sniffed loudly. "Though maybe it would do Ry-Ry some good to spend some time with a man. He sees an *awful* lot of me, and God knows I could use a break from him. And you're so . . ." And in the morning, there I was, as she knew I would be. She was waiting on the stoop.

Now, though, Laurel says, "Ryan, you know you can use the phone whenever you want. Did Howard tell you?"

Of course I did. Last evening, after we listened to Sylvia's odd, cheery message, I tapped the old yellow rotary phone with my finger. I took the envelope with her phone number from my wallet, but when I handed it to him he flung it toward the living room, where it slid under the couch. I suppose I looked thunderstruck, because he suddenly barked, "*What?*" and when I picked up the receiver he stomped upstairs. I found him curled up on the futon, and I squatted down, making the phone-receiver gesture. He gazed up with broad indifference. "What?" he repeated, a little less truculently, and when I stood to leave him he mumbled, "No, thank you." This is exactly what he says now to Laurel.

She comes over and leans on the table. "Because I was thinking your mom'd be pretty glad to hear from you. And I bet early in the morning's a good time to reach her. Before they all get started with their day?"

Ryan says nothing, and Laurel and I stare at him. I suppose he thinks we do nothing but stare. I think of his running inside at Sylvia's departure, and I wonder how thoroughly he was briefed; it's one of Syl's tactics to leave things unstated. Ryan picks up his fork and scrapes the tines down the wooden tabletop, making four parallel grooves in the surface. "No, *thank* you," he says aggressively.

Laurel runs her fingers over the damage. The table has plenty of scratches already, so I can give this a pass; but when she clears her throat, Ryan jumps like he's been shot. "Ry," she starts, and he juts out his chin. I take the fork from his hand.

Ruby grunts from under the table, then clacks to the screen door and whines at Puff, the ancient tomcat from next door. Laurel lets the dog out, and when she turns around I tap her arm and shrug. I don't worship the telephone; in fact, I disdain it. Sylvia will survive without a call-back, I think; so I shrug again and gather our dishes.

Laurel follows me to the sink. "Howard," she says. "I'm sure you mean well, but you know I was raised to honor my elders." The hell! Does she think I didn't honor *my* parents just as much? I turn the faucet on loud and wave her to her simmering pots, and she leans closer. "We've got some discussing to do." But I'm just the guardian, not the pastor or social worker, and there were times I waited plenty for Sylvia to contact me. And Ryan's temporary here, so why sweat it? I hunker over the frying pan and refuse to look up, and Laurel steps off a little sulkily.

When I was drafted, and then when I was sent overseas — and even when I first woke up wounded, so far from home and indescribably frightened and with the sense that my head had been caved in like a Ping-Pong ball — even then, the only philosophy I knew was to hope for the best. I believe I sustained that attitude my first years of being home, but as we head toward the school it seems a long time since I mustered much hopefulness. Then Ryan's gone. He murmurs, "Bye, Howie," and climbs from the truck to join the stream heading for the playground, and I notice several children wearing jackets and wonder if he's dressed himself warmly enough.

7

I PULL OUT OF THE SCHOOL PARKING LOT and drive to my job, and as I move through the morning traffic I consider the time I've spent puttering around Sylvia's life. For years, I've been the guy she calls when she's in a pickle, and though Ryan's often about, it's always Sylvia absorbing my attention. And I have to ask myself if this is normal: should a live human being have made so little impact? I once heard his mother tell him to watch me working because someday he'd be the man of the house, but even then I didn't pay him much heed.

I try to remember what he was like at six: round face, soft Afro of hair. No sign of the lanky guy he is at nine. I think of a day several summers ago when Sylvia wanted a cat flap, and I took her back door off its hinges. I laid the door in the center of the kitchen and carefully installed a pre-made kitty entrance, and it took a long time because I didn't want her to see me struggling with the instructions. I was seated on the linoleum, puzzling over diagrams, when Ryan, who must have been in about first grade, suddenly began reading aloud. He'd been sitting by me all along, while I ignored him, then with quiet seriousness he sounded out one word and the next. Remembering, I see myself turn gratefully, though I did nothing of the kind. Then Sylvia was in the kitchen, talking and talking while I was trying to listen! In high school, she was a quiet girl, and I took that for serenity, but now she fills up my conversational void. If she's on anything extra, she chatters extra.

I stop at a traffic circle, waiting to merge. On the curb ahead, a tall man in a ragged coat gestures at the traffic. I've seen this guy before. I once let him wipe my windshield, and he smeared it with something that was hell to get off, and Nit and Nat have made him the object of jokes. Now a spring breeze gusts at his long hair, and he waves a homemade sign over his head. Of course, I can't decode the sign.

The guy shouts at the driver before me, and I inch left to slip out of the lane. He spots me immediately. I glance at the traffic, and when I look again he's marching toward me, chest out, like a soldier. I hit the accelerator, then somewhere a horn sounds. A Cadillac slams to a halt; someone calls me a dickwad. The ragged man's face is giant now, and he squints at me, showing his teeth, and his large, dark pores. His dirtiness fills the open passenger window as I stomp on the gas. Then the face slides away.

Later, mowing, I ponder Ryan's refusal to telephone his mom, and with each turn of the John Deere his rebellion seems more bold. Perhaps it's simply that *I* jump whenever Sylvia beckons, but suddenly what I take without question — the ups and downs, the sulks, casual affection, petty slights, delicious flirtation and lavishly bestowed favors that have been my lot since I returned from overseas — seems unsuited to the life of a child.

I never objected to Sylvia's getting high. I wouldn't sully our togetherness with police work, and I think I assumed she was a good enough parent. Her kid went to school and was not obviously troubled, and Sylvia drew a paycheck and put meals on the table. So when things slipped, the change was gradual. Besides, I don't like confrontation. I depended on some natural corrective, perhaps Syl's own conscience or strength of character, to bring her back.

I think of my dad, whose drinking didn't start 'til I came home injured, but it distressed me anyway, even as I sought out medications of my own . . . and *I* was an adult! Abruptly, I picture the ragged man's squinting face, and when I shake off that image it's Sylvia who rises before me, the day of that cat flap. A little tense and frayed, as she often is, her voice and even the snap of her footsteps interrupting my concentration. I wish she'd shut up and let me listen! And I'm suddenly angry; three years later, I'm angry. I'm stunned by her failure to notice I can't read!

The motor noise hangs like a dome over the John Deere, and as I head for the ha-ha I contemplate life in that Silly Putty house. I picture the entry, with the living room straight ahead, and Sylvia's stuff: the club chairs from her parents' home and rows of framed photographs and knickknacks on every surface. A glimpse of green yard glows through a curtained window. But it's all dark, as if no one's home, and when I place Sylvia and Ryan in this environment, they fade like ghosts. What life might be like when I'm not there, I have no clue. And I'm on my way down before I realize what's happened. I've missed my moment of floating! I mowed the ha-ha yesterday, too! How long have I been repeating work already done?

What was I thinking while I was not paying attention? I was wondering what it's like to be around her constantly. To be her kid, to have requirements and expectations for the future, to need her more than a wounded, full-grown ex-boyfriend could imagine. I was reliving Ryan's determination as he worked at his reading; also his refusal to call Sylvia, the leap into the tetherball game, his cuddling Bindi and Ruby, and almost everything else. What this tells me about my own obligations I'm not at all sure, but as I cut back toward the garden shed I'm strangely unsettled.

8

FOUR DAYS NOW, and the fourth night. I've got a roasted chicken from the supermarket, plus frozen peas and small red potatoes. I seem to be caught in a loop of meals, but with a second mouth to feed, my customary shortcuts strike me as slop. Next time, I'll roast the chicken myself. I heat a pan of water for the peas and another for the potatoes, and I think of the calm years before my mother died, and of longer ago, when there were three of us and I still spoke. When my family moved into this house, the place needed work, and for the first year we camped out. Our table was a pair of plywood-topped sawhorses adorned with my grandmother's silver candlesticks; I thought it was cozy, and I'm glad now for the time we had. Tonight, of course, some sparkling dinnertime conversation would round out my chicken and vegetables, but certain things can't be helped. Ryan barely speaks without cause, so it's plan B: tray tables and TV.

We're not finished eating when the phone rings, and we both freeze. The actors in the broadcast go on reciting their scripted lines, while in the hallway Laurel's voice says to leave a message. Then there's Sylvia, and though I can't make out what she's saying, my blood rises just at the sound. I wave to Ryan to jump up and grab the phone, but he pretends not to notice. The television scene ends and a commercial begins, and Sylvia continues for another ten seconds. She blows three kisses and hangs up.

I do the dishes and put away the tray tables. Laurel's kept a low profile since we disagreed about the phone calls, and tonight she's off again with friends. But she asked Ryan to give Ruby her supper, and this he does, squatting by the bowl as the little dog grunts and gobbles. Nit and Nat appear out of nowhere, take beers from the refrigerator, and disappear in different directions; Ryan returns to the parlor. He's flipping channels when I beckon him to the entrance hall, where my answering machine sits in an alcove by the stairs. Sylvia called last night, too, so that's three days of phone messages! Laurel's right: this has gone on long enough.

He frowns at the floor, hands in the pockets of his shorts. I tap the phone machine, and he looks up as if I've scolded him. But at last he touches a button, and we hear what we couldn't discern before. Sylvia's getting used to her surroundings, she says, and she hopes Ryan's happy, too. "But I haven't heard from you, my mean, mean guy. I kind of expected you'd give Mama a call by now. If you're having trouble getting through, just tell them you're Sylvia's little boy and it's an emergency. Even if it's not, okay? And something's happening in a couple weeks that you have to come to, but I'll tell you about it when we talk. So call me, Ryan honey. Remember how lonely it is for me here. Love to Howie." Then the kisses.

Ryan stands motionless through Sylvia's discourse. I've taken a seat on the stairs, and when she's finished, I'm breathless with the wish to see her. Then he sighs loudly, and I suppose he's embarrassed by his neglect. I point to Sylvia's number, which I've propped by the phone. He doesn't budge, so I hand it to him; he shoves my hand away. "*Howie!*"

I lean over the banister and turn the phone so I can see it. Enough foolishness! I pick up the mouthpiece and jab at the rotary, dialing the number I've memorized with some effort. I place the mouthpiece by Ryan's head. He struggles against me, but I hold his face to the phone, and if I'm a little rough, that's not important. He should be grateful he can *use* a phone.

I hear rings, then the hum of a voice. I loosen my hold on him and nod encouragingly. *Ask for her!* Ryan opens his mouth but says nothing, and when the receiver-voice hums again he takes a breath and shouts, "Abalabalalalabalaba-ba-ba!" Jumping back out of my grasp, he hollers more nonsense while I grapple at him through the banister. And though Sylvia's name is beyond my capability, I'm trying to speak when he tugs at the phone cord. The receiver slips from my hand and knocks a cup of pens and pencils to the ground. Another jerk, and the phone flies from the table, sweeping the answering machine with it. The receiver falls heavily, and the disconnect recording begins.

I don't know how this would play out if we weren't interrupted, but I'm reaching for Ryan's hair when Nat clunks down the stairs. "Making crank calls, little spaceman? Time-honored American pastime."

I swivel my butt to let Nat pass, then pant at him as he does so. His long hair is damp but carefully combed, and he's wearing a loose tie-dyed shirt, like a fashionable hippie. He surveys the downed telephone and scattered pencils, then tugs at an earring. "Pick up your toys when you're done."

"I'm not *playing*," says Ryan. He looks Nat up and down. "Are you going on a date?"

"A date? I should be so lucky. Just a couple guys I know, their band's playing. Though hopefully it's not just guys." He grins wolfishly, smoothing his shirttail. Not a care in the fucking world. "Hey, chief. Maybe *we* oughta go out sometime," he tells Ryan. "Coupla lonely bachelors living in one house, *hell*. We might round up some fun. Grab a few beers, cruise chicks. You, me, Stevie . . ." He scratches his ear, adding, "Howard, man, you can come too, 'f you got the time." Then his eyes flicker back to Ryan. "Awright, buddy?"

Ryan nods slowly. This may be the first time Nat's addressed him directly, and he seems to be contemplating his response. But the moment's already over. Nat says, "Grrrr," and claps Ryan on the shoulder, then takes off, leaving the screen door open. A fly buzzes in; I step over and shut the screen, and Ryan comes and stands beside me. He's as close as he can get to my body without touching.

Together we watch Nat climb into the boys' old white van. He adjusts the radio and seat, then smiles at himself in the mirror and backs off without a glance. Ryan bends to pick a scab from his knee, and though I should scold him for the telephone nonsense, I've an impulse instead to put my arm around him. I'm too shy, though, to do either, and a minute later he shuffles away. I hear him gathering the pencils and returning the phone and the other stuff to the table, then he goes to the living room, and the television starts up.

I remain in the doorway, watching the fading light. The street fills with shadows, and at last the house opposite is a mere silhouette, sharp and black against a peacock sky. A squirrel scurries around my front yard, trying to accomplish something in the last of the day, and a car moves up the street, the driver reaching to flick on his headlights. The squirrel picks up something in its mouth and disappears under a shrub, and in one of the nearby houses I can hear women laughing. And I feel . . . *what?* Inconsequential, I suppose. This house is less cozy than it was at suppertime, and Nat really is an asshole.

9

OURS IS A DOMICILE of grown-ups. Even Nit and Nat, for all their slackerdom, maintain schedules and pay bills, and as Ryan sleepwalks from futon to TV, I wonder if we deliver what a kid needs to stay happy. I cast around for toys to make the environment fun, and on Friday, while he's at school, I check his room. But I find only schoolbooks and clothes and shoes. Evidently, that embroidered suitcase was for strict necessities. I'm leaving the room when I spot a bright pink paw, half hidden by a pillow, and I picture some beloved floppy animal, threadbare and limp. But when I move the bedclothes, I see the thing isn't Ryan's at all, but mine: a stupid, plush Energizer Bunny I won in a street fair years ago and never thought of again. I figure if he's dug this terrible item out, there must be other stuffed thingums he's accustomed to sleeping with, and I begin to contemplate a supply run back to Sylvia's. I wonder what kind of toys a nine-year-old plays with, and I imagine them scattered around my house. Erector sets, jigsaw puzzles, battery-operated racing cars. In the supermarket and out on the street, I've seen kids fooling with little handheld video gizmos, and I suppose they're fun, but I wonder if anybody still plays Parcheesi or Risk. If we set up a board game on the parlor carpet, would it pass the time until Sylvia's return? Sports equipment. Different clothes. A bike, a skateboard. He'll appreciate the thoughtfulness.

I pick him up after school. The radio's up loud, and we roar through the streets like a couple of teenagers. When a familiar song comes on, I even hum a little; that's one thing I can still sort of do.

Ryan doesn't ask where we're going. He's made only so-so progress at communicating with me, so I let him discover for himself what's in store. Then a glimpse of her house, and my chest tightens. Propped on her bedroom sill is that souvenir costume doll from Honduras or wherever, and the silhouette speaks of the rushed tensions of her departure: Ryan disappearing inside, Sylvia reddening and saying, "Let's just *go*." And suddenly I feel a spasm of sympathy for Sylvia. I think how hard it must be, doing what she's doing, and I consider how much she must truly love cocaine. For a moment, I recall those spectacular arcs of time when *I* was the solitary pinprick of sensation in the whole wide world, the one heroic lawbreaker in our dutiful universe. I remember the mingled glory and hostility that are just not possible to describe, and I think how long I've been away from those feelings. I know I've grown accustomed to believing I don't miss them, and perhaps I don't, but as I gaze at the back of Sylvia's Honduran doll I have an instant of exquisite empathy for what she's taken on. It's not an interesting burden.

Ryan shoots a dark look from across the seat. "What are we doing here?" he says. The little putty house has a certain serenity, occupying its plot under the warm sun, and I think coming home should make him happy. But he says, "No way," and pulls down his Indians cap.

On the stoop of the house next door, a sandy-haired kid in headphones is reading a comic book. I point a finger at the kid and say, "Cuh," by which I mean *go on: say hello*, and I believe Ryan understands. In a perfect world, he gets what I'm getting at.

But Ryan says, "It's Fartin' *Mar*tin, Howie," and his tone's so snotty that I give the seat a smack with my hand. He jumps at the noise, then his mouth sets. "I don't *think* so." This is his mom at her worst.

I get out and take a breath. Ryan doesn't look up. Is he going to just sit there? I can't *drag* him to the house, but I'd expected him to hop out and gather his stuff. What's the point in any other behavior? Looking up, I catch Fartin' Martin eyeing us, so I walk the short distance to Sylvia's mailbox, looking around at the grid of one-story box homes. With its flat streets and meager trees, this is not a neighborhood I'd care to live in, but today, as the bright sky arcs from rooftop to rooftop, it seems like a place where things aren't too unpleasant. Across the street, two smaller kids shriek as they jump through a sprinkler, and in the yard beyond that a girl pumps furiously on a swing. A well-kept, tidy world, though Sylvia's grass is shaggy.

Ryan doesn't say anything when I open his door, and when I set the mail on his lap he looks away, barely budging. One of Sylvia's tactics is the silent treatment, and I think if he starts this I'll drive off and leave him to fend for himself. And I don't know how a simple errand got so charged. Twenty minutes ago I felt generous, bombing through the bright streets, but now I wish I had five minutes — *one* minute — of clear speech to say we came here for him.

Ryan kicks the dashboard, interrupting my thoughts. He eyes me uncomfortably and wipes the scuff with his fingers. "Can we go now?" I frown at him — *pushing my buttons, fella* — then walk off, leaving his door open. I think I might as well run the mower around, and in the meantime Ryan can consider what he wants from this place. The house key, I remember, is under the flowerpot; I unlock the front door as an enticement.

I start in back, to put some distance between us, and when I push the mower around the house, the Fartin' Martin family Rottweilers circle their chain-link enclosure. Sylvia's property lines are planted with hedges of some translucent, weedy shrub, and in the yard behind, a man in a lawn chair is drinking a beer. The man waves as I start the back border. I nod, and he gets up and slips through the hedge, still carrying his can of beer. He's about seventy, and I pause when he gets close, but I don't stop the engine. I don't want to encourage him.

"Where's Syl?" the guy says. He's dressed in sandals and one of those terry-cloth swim sets I used to give my dad for Father's Day. He's too polite to stare at my scar.

I cup two fingers behind an ear. There's the noise of the machine and the barking dogs, so I make a hell-with-it gesture and start to move on, but the man leans closer. "Haven't seen the boy around, either," he shouts. "Little colored child. We're wondering if everything's okay."

I point to the strip that leads from the back yard to the driveway. The guy stares blankly. I make a swooping motion over the house, but the old fellow doesn't get it. "Look," he says carefully, and sips his beer. "You know Sylvia, gal that lives here. The blonde, right?" I nod and push the mower forward, but he won't go away. When I turn, he's still there, scratching the frizzy chest hair in the V of his little jacket. He reaches out to pluck at my arm and says, "I could call the cops, you know," then draws back suddenly, as if *I've* threatened *him*. His lips are white.

I take the guy's elbow and lead him to the driveway. I don't mind pulling harder than he likes. Ryan's still slumped in my truck, but he sits up when I send the old guy ambling toward him; then the guy points to his forehead, and Ryan bats his hand away. They're discussing my scar. I go back to work, and when the old man passes through again he stares like he's onto something. Story of my life, these encounters.

I'm starting the front when the motor coughs and runs out of gas. Ryan looks up; he must think we're taking off. I pantomime pouring and raise my eyebrows, but he only shrugs. I glare at him as I head for the garage. The gas can's on a crappy, pieced-together workbench, and I have to move some old picture frames to get to it. But as I pick up the first one I realize it's not a frame at all, but a painting on stretched canvas. I turn it around; it's an art-school self-portrait from Sylvia's college years.

The canvas has slackened, and the whole thing's gotten grubby, but in an instant I recall a day when I was much worse off than I am now, though we still held out hope for a full recovery. A song we liked was playing in the art studio at the college, and as Sylvia held up one painting after another I decided she had a tendency to make herself homely, and she always got the mouth wrong; and I noted these observations to myself with the idea we'd talk about them once I could speak. Now I notice how the head's a potato, and the shadows of the face are a dark, purplish green. I suspect by any objective criteria this isn't an *accomplished* painting, but as I hold it before me I feel Sylvia's gaze so completely that I put the thing down as fast as I can. I'm stumbling toward the driveway when I see a bat and ball inside the door.

I'm not thinking of Ryan. For the moment, I'm blind to his existence. I'm no longer hoping to lure him out of the truck to gather the makings of a contented kid, and I'm not trying to be his friend. I'm just remembering his mom. And it's not as though I swing well, but I do get a piece of it. With an unfamiliar aluminumy *thuk!* the ball binks over the hood of the truck, then slowly descends into the next lot.

In an instant, Fartin' Martin is off his porch. He's charging like a spaniel, but Ryan's up and running, too. Fartin' Martin's chunkier and somewhat ungainly, and Ryan's so swift that they reach the ball at the same time. But as Fartin' Martin picks it up, Ryan cocks a fist under his nose. Fartin' Martin drops the ball at their feet.

I let go of the bat. I run over and grab Ryan's wrist, and I know I've got a hard grip, but I won't stand for bullying. "Not," I say and shake his hand. He pulls back, glaring furiously. I go on shaking, and I say, "*Not!*" again, louder, and then again. Shake and "*Not!*" Still he pulls, and I get in his face like a drill sergeant and say it again, or maybe several times, until I'm roaring. When I let go, he falls back on his butt.

He looks up. "You can't do that," he says. His eyes are watery, and there's a darkness where I gripped his wrist. "You can't —" But I'm at the end of my rope. *I can't what?* I want to holler. *I CAN'T WHAT?* I've always — even before I was injured — hated all teasing and harassment, and if Ryan's mother hasn't schooled him in fair play, I sure as hell will! I give a pitiless look and gesture for him to get to his feet. He doesn't move. I reach down to help him, but he pulls back his hand. "I'm telling my mom," he says. "She'll take me out of here." *Oh, yeah? You're not even speaking to her.*

Fartin' Martin's staring at me, his mouth open. When I'm flushed, my scar whitens to a puffy handprint, and I know it must look awful now. Still, I reach for his small, soft paw and offer it to Ryan, and he permits this without protest. I want the boys to make up like gentlemen, but neither one moves, and at last Fartin' Martin withdraws his hand. Ryan says, "Cock*suck*er," not loud, but loud enough. His lower jaw is out, and as he digs his fingers in the grass, my blood boils. Then, very deliberately, he tears out a fistful of lawn. "Baldy damn . . . asswipe dumb shit *re*tard," he says huskily, and flings the torn-up grass at my shoes.

I turn as fast as I can and march back to Sylvia's yard. Across the street, the two neighbor kids are like wind-up toys, cavorting in their bubble of mist. My T-shirt is itchy and my lips parched, and I lean against the mower and pinch the bridge of my nose. The air around me is filled with hot, sparkling dots, and as I wait for Ryan to return to the truck, I find I'm panting. But the street has screeched to a halt, and he stays where he is. The dogs are still, the crickets absent; no wind plucks at the weedy shrubs. A trickle of perspiration slips down my nose, and as I peek through my fingers I see the two boys still standing together. Ryan's tossing and absently catching the ball; he looks suddenly jaunty. I'm humbled to note he's just a boy, and I'm grateful no harm's done. But a moment later he starts back across the lawns and gives me a look of pure, boldest indignation. Then it rushes back: how we came here for *him*, how this is not my notion of fun. I don't need it, I tell myself, and grip the mower handle with my fists. I don't need Mr. Neighborhood Nosy or a nine-year-old with attitude or Fartin' Martin's fucking Rottweilers or pudgy Fartin' Martin himself, and I *don't* need to be called names. That's not why I'm here, I think, not why I ever came home from a war. In an instant, I'm furious, and what small remorse I'd felt has fled. I watch him saunter toward the truck, and now *I* want to go home. But at the edge of the driveway, Ryan picks up the bat and smacks a nice, bouncing grounder across the two front yards.

Fartin' Martin makes a leap and misses the catch. He lands on his belly, rolls over, and grapples for the ball, which comes to rest not far away. Ryan stares for a moment at this display, then calls out dryly, "Go on, man. Go get your glove. Grab one for me, too, while you're at it, 'kay?" And the dogs once again take up their cry.

10

Ryan says nothing on the way home. I don't like this, but I'm not speaking to him either, whether he realizes it or not. When we pull into my driveway, I hop from the truck and go inside without another look. I take a long shower, then shut myself in my bedroom and lie down on the bed. When I wake, the room is dark, and it takes a moment to realize it's evening, not early morning. My window glows with the last tone before black, and as I pull into consciousness, I hear my neighbor yelling at his wife. My own house is still. I stretch a little, running a hand over my torso, and tug gently at the hair on my belly. I'm just drifting off again when I remember Ryan, who'd slipped utterly from my mind.

Downstairs, the parlor's dark. The kitchen lights are on, but no one's around. Dishes are stacked in the drainer, and a rock magazine lies open on the table. I go back upstairs and peer into Ryan's room, flicking his light on, then off. He's not there. I glance in the bathroom, and because Laurel's door is open I look there, too, then continue up to the boys' floor, where I never go. Ruby greets me on the landing, sniffs the hem of my robe, and pads into Nit's room, where a desk lamp shines dimly on the unmade bed. But that means nothing; Nit never turned off a light or made a bed in his life. A shabby, rose-colored wing chair sits in one corner, with a pile of papers on the seat and a pair of white u-trou clinging to an armrest. Ruby settles on the nest of papers, grunting expectantly, but I cross the landing to knock on Nat's closed door. No answer. I knock again, then peek in; Ryan's not there. He's not in the cupola, either, nor in the boys' grubby third-floor john, and by the time I'm heading back down the stairs I've gotten anxious.

In the guest room, I stare at the pink Energizer Bunny as if Ryan might suddenly step from its skin. I look in my own room, where my own body-shaped indentation still wrinkles the quilt. Then a glance at the darkened parlor, then the kitchen again. The dining room — a place I haven't looked . . . and the cellar. By the third step I know I won't find him here, but I charge down anyway and peer behind the furnace. No.

The cellar door faces the door to the yard, and I run back up the stairs and burst onto the back stoop. The sky's now fully dark, with a few stars and a lopsided moon, and the next street over seems very far away. A river of contiguous back yards courses darkly between the lit-up houses, eddying in deep shadows around shrubs and swing sets, but hitching my robe around me, I wade right in. I know if I could only call out, he might respond to my panic; but of course I can't do that, so I begin with my own yard: the tack room and long grass behind the stable; the catalpa, with two woody lilacs clumped at its base. Just over the property line stands a weeping willow, its branches like beaded curtains. I slip in and out of the dank room they define. Then I really set off, moving back yard to back yard, checking clubhouses and plastic pools and stumbling over scooters and dog toys in my way. Three houses down, I snag my shin on a croquet wicket and almost fall, and at the house after that a voice calls out, "Hello?" Turning, I see figures on a back stoop, with two red dots of cigarettes. I wave silently and keep going. But a yard or two later I wish I'd stopped. I could have *made* myself understood, I think, though I press on anyway, pausing at each playhouse, stable, and garden shed, then finally running headlong toward the apricot glow of the main boulevard.

Here I stop. Cars are speeding in both directions, so I can't continue in the same furious fashion, and anyway, I'm faced with more choices than I can weigh. I don't know which direction Ryan would have turned if he got this far, and I don't even know if he came here at all. Staring into the headlights, I'm considering my next move when a teenager leans from a passing car and yells, "Aaayaaaaah!" — whether at me or the glory of night, I'm not sure. Looking down, I see I'm still in my boxers and robe. I've lost the belt to the robe, and I'm barefoot.

At the corner of my own street, the moonlight's eclipsed by the canopy of elms. I turn toward home, and though I ought to keep running I'm suddenly exhausted, so I pad along as briskly as I can manage. The old slate sidewalk feels good on my feet. I try to think clearly, to decide if Ryan's run off or is simply hiding, if he has a destination in mind and what it might be. Would he go back to Sylvia's place? I don't know enough to be sure. Try for Caroline's, in Chicago? I can't remember if I saved that business card or tossed it to the ground with her money, and I have a sudden flash of shouting "Not" at her over the phone. But it's funny what you can do when the options are limited. When my father was dying, I dialed 911 and howled into the receiver, and an ambulance arrived in no time at all. With this, though, I hope I'm jumping the gun — the boy's not missing, merely misplaced. Still, I pick up the pace.

I must have been the only kid who never ran away from home. It's not that I never got angry with my folks, but even as a youngster I was even-tempered and cautious. Later, though, when I was about thirty and we were learning that I wouldn't improve, I jumped in my mom's car and drove and drove. I got as far as a cash machine outside Denver, where the text on the little screen was different from what I was accustomed to. I stood for a long time in the glass box of the ATM, pressing my knuckles to the Braille lettering of the countertop. This is how to become one of those *frightening* vets: demanding, insufferable, unmoored and unloved. Then a woman arrived with a small girl of about six. The woman was holding the child's hand and fiddling with her wallet, but she hesitated at the sight of me, and as she hustled the child back toward the safety of their car, I rushed past and drove straight home.

I break into a run, cutting away from the sidewalk and onto the grass, and I come down heavily on a broken branch or some kind of stump. But I keep going until I thump up my porch steps. Just the old rattan glider and some dead leaves cowering in a corner. I scramble back down the steps and around the narrow side yard and across the back, glancing again at the darkened stable. As I come up the driveway side, I see figures by the vehicles.

"*Howerrrd!*" Nit's leaning against my truck, chatting with a heavyset guy and a light-haired gal. I charge toward them, bathrobe flapping, and he holds up his hands and says, "*Down*, boy." To show it's in fun, he adds, "Heh-heh."

Pulling my bathrobe around me, I blink at the gravel, and as I stand there panting I recognize the smell of pot. And I can't help myself: I breathe deeply. Nit says, "What can I do for you, man?"

I hold my hand flat in the air at Ryan's height. They look intrigued. I gesture more specifically, and my robe falls open. The girl steps forward and finds the belt hitched behind me, and she pulls my robe around me and knots the belt, giving the lapels a straightening tug. Just a tiny thing, with honey-colored hair that smells of peaches, but she could fuss with me all night, I think. The reminders of Sylvia have gotten my blood up. Then the heavyset guy suddenly holds out the joint, and the girl steps away. I wave a hand: *no*.

Nit says, "Uh, Howard. We came out here because . . ." I glare at him. We have no rules against pot in the house, but I've no patience for nincompoops. "Well, I didn't know how you felt about, like on account of the little guy . . ."

I point at him. *The little guy!* I do the height thing again and raise my eyebrows, and this time it transmits. "Oh, him? Like watching TV, last I saw. Inside, in the, uh . . ." He blinks meditatively. "I gave him a coat when he dozed off." As I rush toward the house I hear Nit mutter, "Keep in touch."

Ryan is indeed in the darkened parlor. He's curled up on the couch with a green fatigue coat pulled over him, and it looks like he's inside a giant sock. An empty soup bowl sits perched on an end table — some kind of gumbo, from the small pile of rejected okra — and at the sight of this I'm filled with relief: he's here, not gone, and someone's fed him. Still, I'd credited him with independence, and it's shocking to find him waiting to be put to bed. What a sorrowful lack of options! I take the bowl and spoon to the kitchen and give them a wash, but in no time I'm back in the parlor, staring at the sleeping form.

I say, "Hoon." *R*'s are hard for me, and this may be my first attempt at his name. He doesn't move. I give him a nudge, then squat down and slide an arm under his bent knees, and I'm getting the other arm around his shoulders when he wakes with a start. Our faces are only inches apart, and as his eyes find my scar he gives a cry. With a struggle, he frees himself from the green coat and shoves me away, and I stand up, clutching my robe. He kicks twice, still partly asleep. Only then does he recognize me.

For a moment, something crosses his face; then that moment passes. He remembers we're in the midst of a quarrel and pulls the coat to his chin. "I'm sleeping," he announces irritably, and squints at the dark room. I put my hands on my hips. Ryan says, "I can sleep here," in a tone that suggests someone gave him permission, but I won't have him crash in the living room like some passed-out party guest. I wave at him to get up, and he struggles to his feet and precedes me upstairs, stomping a little on every tread; when I flick on the overhead light he whines, "Ow!" and disappears into his bedroom. Five minutes later I'm back in bed, too, though it takes me a long time to fall asleep.

11

B Y MORNING I WANT to put yesterday behind us. When Sylvia and I quarreled as kids, I apologized whether I was wrong or not, but nobody's expected an apology from me in years. I'm hoping to bury the hatchet in routine, so I mix up western omelets, but when I show Ryan the bowl he declines coolly. He's being civil but aloof, and he doesn't seem to realize how prissy this is. Laurel offers the phone again, and he says, "No, thank you," a bit starchily. I concentrate on my cooking and avoid Laurel's eye.

A box of cheap chocolate-covered doughnuts has materialized on the counter. Ryan takes two and a glass of OJ to the table. Nat appears, flashing his pearly whites, and says, "Ooh, my *man!* You don't want to *know* how long those bad boys sat in the truck." The yellow cake looks like packing material under its waxy brown frosting, but Ryan testily pronounces it good. Then he picks up and exits the kitchen, and Saturday cartoon sounds float in from the parlor. I glare at Nat — why the hell couldn't he toss his damn trash in the bin? — but he only pours what's left of my egg mixture in the frying pan, and when his omelet is cooked he takes half in to Ryan.

I haven't had many close relationships in my life. Sylvia and my parents, of course, but three's a low total for a man my age. Looking back, I remember childhood friendships but few high school buddies — once Sylvia and I were an item I was devoted to her. In the army, I met fellows from all over the country, with different backgrounds from my own, and I loved that; I was finally in the world. The first time I heard Spanish music was in basic, and the first time I had friends who'd been raised in slums or on farms. It was the first time I lived away from this house! Then basic ended, and we got separated overseas: different specialties, different platoons. Then my sixteen days. The men in my unit were good guys, I suppose, but I barely got to know them, shocked as I was by so much that was new: the weather, the landscape, the impossibility of phoning home. The heat, the smells, the way I missed my mom and dad and Sylvia and everything American and familiar, and even the bunk I'd had back in the barracks, and some of the boys I'd gotten to know there. The horrifying, defoliated landscape I'd flown over on the airlift in, and the very presence of live ammo, suddenly inescapable: ours, theirs, rounds and clips and grenades and mines and flashes of light over distant trees. Some of the seasoned soldiers had been together for months and were wary of newbies: we were bad luck — ignorant, unskilled, naive, hopeful, frightened, and error-prone — and everyone knew we couldn't all make it through. So it was a while before I could tell one grunt from the next, and the first person I grew friendly with was Rimet, who also was fresh meat. He just cracked a joke one morning in the chow line. But even on that last day, as we humped through the hills, I suspected Rimet and I weren't lifelong friends. I had more in common with the lieutenant, I thought, and I hoped to get to know him better. We'd gotten stoned, and the LT was looking for orchids, and I felt as good as I'd felt since my arrival. The sun was out. So some men have war buddies they keep in touch with for years afterward, but not me. And I never know what to do when someone's angry at me.

All morning, Ryan keeps himself occupied. I figure the hell with him and go out to polish the truck, but when he helps Nit and Nat load up their van I think he might pitch in here, too. He pays me no attention. I go inside and stretch out on the parlor couch, and when the house empties, I hear Ryan tromping upstairs. I'm not unaccustomed to being alone, and for years I've spent my time exactly like this. But it's harder to feel comfortable about being excluded, so I stare at the ceiling and wonder if Laurel's detected my exile. I have my reasons for manhandling him yesterday, but when I imagine defending myself to her, I foresee the verdict. In the Court of Laurel, I'm a condemned man.

Around one, I tap on his door; he opens it a few inches. I'm here to reconcile, and I pat my stomach. *Come on, it's the weekend! Let's go somewhere for lunch.* "I'm doing my homework," he says, but something's funny in his expression, so I push the door. Inside, sunlight streams across the unmade bed, and clots of white fluff cover the floor. It takes me a moment to spot the pink bundle, like a flocked bathrobe, cast in a corner, and I realize he's demolished the Energizer Bunny. A strip of torn wallpaper lies in a wedge on the far side of the bed. I push past him to pick it up.

The hell with him. *The hell with everything!* My dad papered this room himself, with my help, and to avoid another regrettable outburst I take off, slamming the downstairs door. I buy a tuna sandwich and head to the nun's private sitting area in back of the convent building, and I eat my lunch and listen to the roar of the ha-ha and scowl at the gravel between my feet. Sister Margaret appears and says, "Why, Howard! What brings you here on a Saturday?" She opens a fat book and starts to read, and I go back to my truck in the parking lot and sit there awhile.

When I get home, Nit and Nat are in the back yard. The heavy guy from last night is there, too, and they've got a small fabric pouch, like a beanbag, which they're knocking around with their heads, elbows, and heels. Ryan's playing right along. I stand by my truck and watch them dart about in the sunshine, and I wonder if anyone will toss me the little pouch, but only Laurel seems to see me at all. She leans on my hood and says, "That boy was all by himself when I got home, Howard. I don't think that's right. And I *want* him to call his mother." I go inside and turn on the TV.

As evening falls, Laurel comes looking for me again. "Howard," she says from the parlor doorway, "there's a few things we need to —"

I jump up — perhaps too quickly, because the house shifts, and the room's all stuffy. Somewhere there's conversation, and I remember I left Ryan with Nit and Nat; the world of talking is just out of reach. I wonder if I've been asleep, and as I reach out to steady myself, I swat at a standing lamp. Yellow circles flash over ceiling and floor. "Bot," I say, and wipe my brow with my arm.

Laurel looks at me a moment, then puts up both hands. "Well, I told you I wouldn't get involved," she says. I wait for the inevitable — *but Howard, blah, blah, blah* — but she only stares contemplatively out the window. And suddenly I wish she'd just go ahead. I'd *love* to know what's on her mind, if I could only respond. Because hell, I've got some thoughts of my own. We could hold a seminar — Laurel, Sylvia, those idiot boys — on handling Ryan during his stay, and I'd tell everyone within hearing that this wasn't my best week, but I did what I could. And how about a little warning if I'm to be someone's dad? How about respect, too — from the kid, from everyone. Or forgiveness! Love! Oh, once I got started I'd never shut up. I'd make a case for myself: *Yes*, my Boo Radley act yesterday was in all ways uncool, but how fair is the freeze-out? I'm getting my bearings, not just with Ryan, but going back decades, my whole life. Sylvia, too. I want a chance at something! And I'd tell Laurel to quit looking at me fishily. I stood up fast and got dizzy, what of it?

But I only steady the lamp, then fold my hands under my overall bib. Laurel says, "Harrison and Steve were talking about a movie later," and after a moment she saunters to the kitchen. I follow because it seems we're in the middle of a conversation, and I know I've been glaring at her, but when we get to the kitchen I just peer through the screen door. Outside, Nit and the fat friend are lying in the grass, their hands on their bellies. Nat's looking at the newspaper, leaning close as the light fails, and Ryan's teasing Ruby with the beanbag. Nat lifts his shirt to wipe the sweat from his face, and I realize summer's here.

Laurel fans her face with her hand. "Anyway, a movie sounds

good to me, and if you like, I could take Ryan." *Ran*. Sure, I'll stay home with the dog. She sets a tray on the counter and gets out six glasses, then opens the freezer and finds a can of frozen lemonade. I watch her strip the lid from the can and dump the contents into a pitcher, and I take three lemons from the fruit bowl and place them on the counter. "Thanks," she says.

Out on the main road, a car radio waxes and wanes. Somewhere a girl squeals. Ruby gives three short yips, and one of the boys shouts, "Hey, hey, hey! Don't give her that thing — what's the matter with you? It ain't good for a dog, man, and she'll fuck it up with her saliva."

Laurel frowns, her knife bisecting a lemon. She glances impatiently toward the back yard and says, "Is that what you want? Turn him over to the frat house? It's fine, but I mean . . ." She stirs the lemonade, making the ice cubes clink. "Because maybe you oughta just come on along to the movie yourself. You're supposed to be in charge." She looks up, raising her eyebrows, and again I wonder what she knows of my disgrace. I've never before been to a movie with Laurel. "Hmm?" she says, as if anticipating a response. Truly, I'd love to respond.

Laurel picks up the pitcher and tucks a bag of Fritos in the crook of her arm, then turns and opens the screen door with her butt. "Howard, things happen sometimes, and we go along with them. This placid life you've got going, your routine. It works great for you, but isn't there space to fit a boy in there somewhere?" In the other room, the TV is still yammering, and I don't know whether to go back to the parlor or follow Laurel outside. Does it seem I haven't made adjustments? I don't move, and the corner of her mouth turns up a fraction. "Start by bringing out those glasses."

12

YEARS AFTERWARD, I saw a film about the war. The opening credits rolled over a shot taken from the air, and I could see brown, bony ridges of hills and sparse trees spaced out like shaving stubble. There were rice paddies, too — neat corrals of shimmering gray set like panes of glass among black frame divisions — and the complicated coastline, with its many inlets and small streams, grassy fields, and pretty, orderly villages. This was nothing like what I remember from my sixteen days, and it wasn't until the story moved inland that I saw a landscape I recognized. Where I was, the trees bled together into four walls of foliage, and base camp was a cluster of dark tents on a slope. Below us, only a few klicks off, lay a yellow plain that had once been a plantation, but the plain was surrounded by lumpy hills and was invisible from the places where I passed my days: my tent, shared with three other guys; the mess and service tents, with latrines and showers tucked further away; and the dirt squares and spaces between, where men smoked, played cards and makeshift basketball or lounged on sandbags, cleaning their guns. Of that nearby valley I caught only fleeting glimpses when the platoon humped in or out of camp, but two days before my injury I climbed a lookout tower for the whole panorama, and I could see how a third of the valley had burned in a long, dark crescent of destruction. A few blackened trees rose from the toast-colored underbrush, and the sight of that two-tone basin, its scorched portion and its golden portion nestled together like phases of the moon, filled me with dread. I was foolish enough to pray I'd never set foot there — and I never did. Instead, I had the cover of the jungle's big leaves. The wet season was beginning, and strange things were blooming, and in my loneliness I took time to look closely at my surroundings, and to imagine that by sticking to this protective concealment I could avoid the danger waiting afield. I think there are lots of things that in this way are just like the war: you can understand them by examining them up close, like leaves, or construct a whole based on tiny, tiny glimpses. Or you can climb up for the broad view, with its stark truths and lost details; but it's almost impossible to comprehend all ways at once.

By Sunday, Ryan's begun to thaw. Reading the funny papers on the floor of the parlor, he shifts to let me squat beside him, and before turning a page, he asks if I'm finished reading. Of course, I'm only looking at the drawings.

Last night's movie excursion succeeded largely because Nit and Nat ran into some fellow dude and disappeared, leaving Ryan to share a supersize popcorn with Laurel and me. And Sunday's dawned warm and full of smells. I watch a pair of cardinals flutter from the peak of my stable to the grass below, and I wonder what all the fuss was about; I remember the same feeling after quarrels with Sylvia. Still, the week has convinced me it's a mistake to guess at what children want, and I resolve to back off. I'll put a roof over the boy's head and see that he eats well and goes to school. I'll keep an eye on him, but I'll stop there. His happiness is his own business until Sylvia returns home.

Almost immediately, though, this resolution falters. In the evening, Ryan and I are heading to the market when the radio plays a promo for a Golden Gloves regional championship match. I'm thinking of groceries, yet when Ryan says, "Cool, man. The *fights*," I turn abruptly downtown. I haven't forgotten Sylvia's promise that we'd do *guy* things, and I don't want him thinking only Nit and Nat have fun.

Curtis Hall was where the circus played when I was a kid, and once, when I was fifteen, Mom and I heard the Metropolitan Opera here. Ten years later I heard it again, with a speech pathologist who believed being in a place where the lyrics didn't matter might augment my healing process. But now, as I purchase our tickets at the door, it's not opera I'm thinking of, but a Led Zeppelin concert I heard with Sylvia before going away.

The ring is on a little platform in the center of the room. It has red and white ropes and gold bunting on the sides. Ryan and I drop our jackets on our seats, then go to graze at a food court along a side wall, and at a pizza booth I give him money for a slice and a Coke. I step to the next stall and signal for a pair of franks.

In my wallet I keep a sheaf of business cards explaining my situation, but I rarely use them. I don't like the wording: the term "mute" is embarrassing, and at the bottom of each card a line reads, *Please remember: I am of normal intelligence!* I don't blame Laurel for this: I know she sweated the best way to put it, and I've never come up with better phrasing myself, though it's one thing I think about on nights I can't sleep. And if I did somehow devise the perfect text, what difference would it make? If I could describe my changes, I wouldn't need the cards at all.

But tonight my little cards would be useless, even if I bothered to dig one out. The woman behind the counter is separating hot dog buns, and she calls out, "Next," without looking up. There's a Plexiglas grease shield at the front of the booth, and I rap on it with my knuckles to get her attention, but suddenly the hall is deafeningly loud. On a shelf behind the woman, a radio is tuned to tinny country music, and other booths have music, too. Overhead, a speaker is making an announcement about a car with lights on, and the guy behind me is saying, "Hey, buddy. Next!"

I press the Plexi, and the structure shifts. I could slam it forward and send the frankfurters flying. I rap again to catch the woman's ear, then the guy behind suddenly sidles in front. I move roughly to shoulder him aside, and in my haste it's not "Back" that I manage to bark out, but "Beg!"

The woman looks up. I aim two fingers at the rotating franks and knit my lips; I've lost my composure, and my neck's hot. I wonder what my scar looks like. Beside me, the other guy's figuring his reaction, and I remember this is, after all, a boxing crowd. I glare foully at him, wondering if I could deck him, and he steps back, giving the crowd a look: he's not about to fuck with the fucked-up guy. Then Ryan's at my side. With a mouth full of pizza he says, "He wants two hot dogs. You like mustard, Howie?" I nod. "With mustard, please. Coke?"

"Condiments to your left," the woman says, jerking her chin as she slides the dogs over the counter. She glances with dull curiosity from Ryan to me.

"Some people ought to . . . keep their mind on their *job*," Ryan ventures as we step off. It's his first voluntary remark in an hour, and something his mom might say — though Sylvia would make damn sure the woman overheard. He catches my smile and throws a few air punches, then looks sheepishly away.

We return to our seats, and the bantams enter down corner aisles. They climb through the ropes and tap gloves before the white-shirted official, and in the pause before the bell I wonder how much they're just playing at fighting, how much they're overwhelmed by their trainers and robes and this big-time setting. Boys in over their heads, again. Then the bell sounds, and the two tiptoe forward. It's more than a minute before they clinch, and they seem to be bargaining to keep the damage light. I watch, but I think of army brawls. I think of rage and recklessness, of flailing fists and ripped clothing and the howls that set torches alight and summon stoned, half-dressed compadres from their tents and barracks; I think of that feeling of being bigger than your skin, of going crazy in full knowledge and in public, of going crazy enough to fight dirty, of continuing to rave while you cast about for an axe handle or a tent peg or a fat piece of wood.

I look at Ryan. He's following each punch as he wipes his greasy fingers on his pants. I'm surprised to see him so engaged, and for once it's good not to be able to speak; I wouldn't know what to say. I glance again at the impervious boxers and see that a dribble of blood has appeared beneath one fighter's nose, and I picture tents bordered by darkness. It's not really a particular site I'm recalling, nor even any particular fight, but a composite of pieces from my two weeks' tour, plus boot camp before that and maybe a childhood fistfight or two, cobbled together like a ball of trash. It was never me, anyway, with clenched fists in the clearing, parading my irrationality; it was never me. I was usually still stumbling toward the circle when the first punch was thrown. Pulling an olive tank top down my gut, skipping around the fracas's edge, sometimes holding someone back if I could reach him, but trying not to get hurt; *always* trying not to get hurt.

The bantams battle to a draw. A fleet, narrow-chested black boy wins the next fight, and a taller kid the one after that. The fourth contest is the middleweight, and from the rising energy in the room I think this will be good. The lights that come up between fights have dimmed, and as a spotlight skitters over the crowd I see a figure in the archway that leads to the changing rooms. The boy wears a black robe with white lining under the hood; as he brushes the hood back, light falls on his upturned face. The crowd cheers. Ryan climbs on his chair to get a better view, then stands on tippy-toes, balancing against my arm. On impulse, I pick him up and settle him on my shoulders.

The fighter waves a gloved fist and breaks into a smile. He's got a politician's poise and one of those very pretty Hispanic faces: olive skin, plump, russetty lips and short, bright teeth. It's clear he's a crowd favorite, and he moves toward the spotlit ring as flashbulbs pop and spectators reach out for high fives. Far off in the shadows, a whole section of audience is in black-and-white hoods, just like his, and when the boy spots them and raises a glove I figure he's got a fan club. Then I, too, feel swept up by the enthusiasm. I add a pulsing "ha-a-hah" to the crowd's cheers and hope the kid's as good as he looks.

Ryan squirms on my shoulders. He doesn't quite kick his legs, but he readjusts his butt so I know he's too big for this. I place him back on his chair, and he cranes self-consciously, as though absorbed in the scene he can no longer see. There's a dent in his face where he's sucking on his cheek, and inside my head I think the word *sorry*. I'd pat his shoulder if I knew he wouldn't shrug it off.

The other fighter's a big block-headed kid with hair so short I can see his scalp. He enters quickly, before the spotlight can find him, and the cheers are nothing like the Spanish boy's ovation. Each boy raises his arms as the loudspeaker announces the names — Perez and Nagy — and unlike the other teenagers, Nagy's as hairy as a bear. There's a line of shaving demarcation around his neck, and he even *seems* bearlike, grumpily throwing punches as he waits in his corner. Perez looks more amiable, bouncing on his toes. Then the bell, and in an instant Nagy makes contact. He's across the ring before we know how he got there, and a punch catches Perez under a nipple. At the flash of movement, I pull in my chin.

I watch Perez maneuver Nagy toward the center, his gloved fists constantly re-establishing the fight zone. I suppose he's chagrined at having taken that first punch, and I watch him deflect a swing from the left, then, with a shoulder blow, force Nagy back. He connects again, hitting Nagy's helmet, but Nagy scores a mean blow to the gut, then they're locked in an embrace. This is tougher than what we've seen so far, and though I don't want to take my eyes from the ring, I glance at Ryan and see him wince. The ref moves in, prying at the intertwined arms, and behind me a voice calls, "Work him over, baby!"

And suddenly I'm rooting for Nagy. He's fast but not jumpy, neither butterfly nor bee. I think of his entrance: the halfhearted applause, the fire-hydrant head, now upturned by a blow from Perez. The crowd cheers Perez's rally, and Nagy lands another blunt, chopping punch. Maybe he likes it when the room's against him. I've felt that way myself, on occasion: just one more reason to give the bear the cup.

I watch Perez. Bing! He connects. His lips, monkeyish over his mouth protector, have lost their brightness, and I want him beaten to a charismatic pulp. Nagy lunges, fist across, and Perez dances. The crowd roars with elation. I think of the hot dog vendor and the guy behind me and the terrible look he gave the crowd. May every last one of them go home disappointed.

We leave before it's over. Both boys are covered in sweat, Perez shiny, Nagy matted. I'm feeling pretty overheated myself, sitting here wishing for a bloodletting. Ryan nods, struggling to remain wakeful, and I like the feel of his head on my arm. But at last I nudge him, and he struggles to his feet, peering around without recognition. We pick our way out of our row and start toward the exit, and when I turn for a last glance I see Perez knock Nagy down.

On the way home, I stop at a minimart for milk and eggs. Ryan's awake now, blinking out at the light rain, but he says nothing, and I remember it's a school night. I leave the motor running when I step into the store, and from inside I can see him silhouetted behind the windshield wipers. It looks like he's fooling with the cigarette lighter or the ignition, and I hurry to the truck. But when I get there, he's back in the shotgun seat. We're on the road before I realize what he's done.

What he's done: he's changed the radio from the oldies station I've always listened to to the one he and Sylvia prefer. The song that's on has jangly guitars and a singer with a hoarse, youthful voice, and it's hardly different from the music I customarily play; but the unfamiliar melody feels fresh, and beside me, I can hear Ryan singing along.

13

H E'S SLEEPY THE NEXT MORNING. It takes him forever to get his shoes on his feet, and Laurel says, "No more late nights for you, buster." I offer a wink, but even now he doesn't look at me much.

He does perk up, though. Turning in his chair, he describes the entrance of the fighters, then the blow-by-blow. "The one guy made the other guy's *nose* bleed," he announces. But Laurel's chopping kale and tending to something in a pot, and after a while he says, "You're not a boxing fan, are you?"

"I'm not much of a sports fan, hon. Except for equestrian."

"Neither's my mom." He pauses, and she turns expectantly. "I am, though. That fight was *bad!*"

The staircase creaks, and Nat appears in the doorway, dressed in T-shirt and pajama bottoms. He gestures grandly, as though acknowledging the paparazzi, and says, "Carry on, carry on. Stevie and I got a early morning client." As if on cue, Nit steps up behind him, his hair on end. Nat says, "Guys got coffee? *Ex*cellent!"

I could do without this element, and I'd love to pretend they're not here at all. But Laurel's rule is "Pitch in and share, pardner, or watch your ass," and I don't dare oppose her on something so basic. And in roughly a minute they've taken over the kitchen. They're yawning and slurping coffee and rearranging their balls as they flop down at the table, and Ryan's edging the newspaper in their direction. I dribble more pancake batter onto the griddle, and when I set the platter on the table Nit and Nat say I'm the greatest.

Laurel squats by Ryan's chair. "You oughta call her," she says as he reaches for pancakes. "You know, your mom. Don't you want to tell her 'bout your big night at the fights?" Ryan shakes his head and goes for the syrup.

Laurel says, "Howard —" and I look at her. The oval face, the pink mouth puckered in consternation. I want to say *yes* and *of course* and *I'm sure you're right. But I've tried, in my way, and I'm invisible here. Can't you see that?* Maybe I'm overtired, too, but I miss my old lonely life, with doughnuts and Dr Pepper for breakfast, the housemates indifferent, and no baffling child in my sights. *I'm a chauffeur and cook*, I want to tell Laurel, *and as dutiful as a soldier. But what I get in response . . .*

I watch Laurel calculating how to handle me, and at last she laughs. "Where'd you find this kid, Howard? Pretty hard nut to crack." She taps her fingers on the Indians cap and takes her plate to the counter.

Ryan's silent again, but Nit and Nat can commandeer any subject, and when I sit down, the talk is roundhouse versus uppercut. Idle chitchat gives me a headache, so I stare at the unfathomable front page of the paper, only peeking up to watch Ryan gawk at the two loud know-it-alls. When I point to his plate, he scoops in a mouthful.

The definition kids agree to disagree, then one of the boys begins to whistle. The other takes more pancakes, and I think it's time they were on their way. But Nit says, "So, Ryan, you a champeen of the fisticuffs, man? Let's see your muscle."

Ryan hesitates, then stands and rolls his T-shirt to the shoulder. He flexes his biceps, chin jutting at the effort, and a nice little bulge forms under his brown skin. He smiles tautly, glancing at Laurel. I clap my hands, and Nit says, "Not bad, man. Not too shabby." But Laurel's chopping again and doesn't turn around.

Nat looks slyly at Ryan. "Pretty buff, man. You work out?" The notion that Ryan's one more prowling bachelor is Nat's small, tired witticism, which he seems determined to run into the ground. "Have a lot of luck with the ladies?"

"Hey!" Laurel turns around, still holding the large knife. "Don't make him the butt of your jokes."

Nat's face reddens. *"What?"* he says. "I'm not, I'm not. It's my li'l buddy, right? I'm saying he's a chick magnet." He looks at me, but I stare at his red face, and for a moment he looks helpless. "So, listen, Ryan. What about, uh . . . Oh, I know, hey. How 'bout your teacher? She nice or a old bag?"

Ryan stares a minute, then smiles wickedly. "Ms. Monetti? She's a *fox.*" The boys hoot.

Nit shakes the hair out of his eyes. "Hey, Ryan. Ryan, lookit." Sloughing out of his bathrobe, he, too, flexes a biceps, ringed by an idiotic Celtic tattoo. For a runty guy, he's got some muscle. Laurel nods appraisingly this time, and I suppose Ryan digs the tattoo.

I'm rolling up my own sleeve when Nat guffaws. *"Wow,"* he says, and swats Nit with the newspaper. "Very nice, big fella, that's *so* impressive. Going one on one with a little bitty kid!" Nit flushes, and I pretend to scratch my shoulder.

14

Nit and Nat show up the next day for breakfast, then they just keep showing up. At first they're up early to get to a job, but soon it seems they're just here for the meal. Suddenly, it's as though we've been rendezvousing in the kitchen since the dawn of time, and though I'm glad to be free of those subdued mornings when no one spoke, I can't help wishing Ryan enjoyed this a little less. And I hate seeing those donkeys get a free ride. Still, it's only breakfast. In the evenings, our housemates come and go less predictably, and Ryan and I are often the only ones home. We have dinner by the TV or occasionally out, always where a game's being broadcast, and I allow time for homework and a good night's sleep. Three times I offer the telephone, which he continues to decline, but we no longer struggle over it, and in this way the school week passes. In the wake of our quarrel at Sylvia's, we've fallen into a dutiful, formulaic existence, and I don't blame Ryan if he thinks I'm not fun. Our boxing night notwithstanding, each of us treads lightly, and in the meantime we make compromises. We give conversation, for example, a wide berth.

Laurel decides Nit and Nat are responsible for KP, in return for my cooking, and she also decides they will give Ryan a lunch box. I know this because I go back one rainy morning to find him an umbrella, and as I come through the hall I hear her say, "I just think you boys should do something for *Ran*," in her funny Texas drawl. "Heck, y'all barely speak to him except to make jokes." I peek into the kitchen and see her standing with her hands in the rear pockets of her black jeans, and the two boys nod blankly while Nit lets soapsuds dribble down his bathrobe. Laurel says, "A nice little lunch box, okay? Get one with a thermos so I can give him some soup. I think he'll be pleasantly surprised." She stoops balletically to scratch Ruby's back, and I wish I'd thought of this myself.

They produce the lunch box Friday as we're finishing our eggs. The morning is bright and hot, and half a dozen goldfinches are arabesquing around the thistle feeder. The boys have wrapped their gift in laundered paint rags, with a big, jagged bow made of blue tape, and placed on the breakfast table it makes an unconventional present. Ryan murmurs, "You shouldn't have," which sounds like something he's picked up from the TV, and as the tape breaks he says, "Oh!" and folds down the cloths.

The gift is a silver ingot, with an arched lid and a ridged, black handle. It's a genuine workingman's lunch box, shiny, masculine, and no-nonsense, but so large that it looks like a pirate chest in front of a nine-year-old. Ryan says, "Whoa," and picks it up in both hands, then carefully sets it back down on the table. He flips the snap that holds the lid, and a satisfying click rings from the latch. Inside, the nesting thermos is held by a flange of metal, and the surfaces gleam with the patina of stainless steel. In every respect it's an incredibly cool object, and Ryan says, "Whoa!" again, a little higher, with more emphasis.

Looking up, I catch my reflection in the window above the sink. I'm floored that such triumph should spring from the junky consciousnesses of Nit and Nat, and as I gaze at my dour countenance I realize I was privately prepared to sweep in and save the day. Nit says, "We drove over hell's half acre, man, to get the right one," and I dislike him more than I've ever disliked him before.

Laurel leans over Ryan and brushes a strand of black hair from her face. "Well, isn't that nice," she says quietly. He looks up and meets her gaze, and she runs a hand down his narrow back. "I just hated the idea of your sandwich getting all squashed up before lunchtime." Reaching for the thermos, she adds, "And now you can have soup for lunch. Chicken orzo or black bean?"

One of the boys reaches for Ryan's paper lunch sack, which sits on the counter near Laurel's work area. It's become the first thing she attends to each day. He hands the sack to Ryan, and Ryan draws out a sandwich and places it carefully in the lunch box, then adds a packet of cookies and a bag of carrot strips. He puts the carrots on the sandwich, then moves them so they lie at its side. Laurel fills the thermos with soup and wipes the mouth before tightening the cap; she hands the thermos to Nat, who says, "Glad you like it, man," and presents it to Ryan. He snaps the thermos in place.

I go upstairs. In a bowl on my dresser is a squishy oval change purse with the name of a garage printed on it in white. I drop in the sixty cents for Ryan's milk, and when I come down I find everybody laughing. Ryan flips the lunch box lid absently between his small brown hands, and the inside of the box is as snug as a kit.

I toss the change purse from the doorway. It bounces off the sandwich, and Ryan looks up with a start. I smile falsely and tug the strap of his backpack. "Not," I say. *Let's get you to school.*

15

WE'RE EARLY, but I had to get out of that house. I put her in park and nod officially at Ryan, and as he opens his door he says, "Could you, um, maybe like . . ." He trails off, scratching the lunch box handle with his thumbnail. "Do you think you could pick me up a little — like later?"

I turn down the radio. Ahead of us, a school bus swerves to the curb, and kids pile out, dressed like athletes and rock stars. I think of one of our first afternoons, when I arrived just as they swarmed from the building. A stocky black kid shouted, "Ryan Mohr, your *dad's* here," and Ryan gave the kid a shove before hoisting himself into the cab. Now I wonder if he's gotten shit for traveling with a head case. Children are disloyal, I guess, and you can't take it personally.

Ryan says, "So like five?" and tries to scramble away. I put my hand on his arm. "*What?*" he says.

I draw two circles above my wristwatch to indicate the missing hours. I raise my eyebrows, and I think this is clear. But Ryan only looks at me bluntly. I wet my lips and search for some way to ask what's up. "Day," I say.

He shakes his head. "I don't know what you're talking about." His face reddens, and I know he's bullshitting me. He knows I know, too. He leans over to look at my watch and says, "It's almost eight," and he sounds so impatient that I wave him away. *Go on, then.* For a moment he stares at me, then he presses a dashboard button, and my old station comes on. Neil Young is singing about rust. The door closes quietly, and I lean over the steering wheel and gaze at the oak leaves reflected in my windshield. I don't watch him enter the building.

The school bus that was in front of me is gone, and a little Neon pulls in. I watch a woman lean over for a smooch just as a small, fat girl pops out the other side; then there's a moment of indecision, and the kid presents a kiss in return. I punch the buttons until I relocate Ryan's station, then peel out of the parking lot, and at the gates of the convent I push up the volume. What a day for disturbing the peace! Sister Amity and Robin are out by the Contemplation Garden, contemplating a pair of balled-up shrubs. I get out, slamming the door, and I'm heading for the maintenance shed when Sister Amity calls out.

"Howard! I had no idea you were a sports fan!" What the hell is she talking about? She offers what would be a shameless leer if she were a vaudevillian, not a nun, and I respond with my coolest stare. I think of Ryan letting me circle out the afternoon.

"The fights! The other night, Curtis Hall! I *saw* you there!" She rushes toward me, arms outstretched, and I remember the black-and-white fan club I spotted as Perez entered. "Talk about the last two people you'd expect at a boxing match," she says to Robin.

Robin says, "Really," and I wonder if she means me, too. Robin can't stand Sister Amity, and the look she gives me says *get her the fuck out of here.*

But Sister Amity says, "Stick around, please, Howard. You can help move these lilacs." She fishes in a sleeve for a tissue and dabs some perspiration from her lip, then replaces the tissue with a ladylike smile. It's hot in the sun.

Robin's been hosing two holes in the ground, in preparation for the bushes. Now she drops the hose and exhales heavily, making a little *pfft* sound with her lips. "I need a break first," she announces. She goes to her van and gets a pack of cigarettes, lights one, and smokes it sitting on the bumper. At last she says, "So what *were* you doing at the fights?" I guess she thinks this ought to be good.

Sister Amity says, "One of Sister Hillary's Boys Club students won a trophy."

"Sister Hillary teaches boxing?"

"Not boxing. *Dance.*" She turns to include me, and since I don't know Sister Hillary, I picture a black-clad Sister Amity haranguing a ballerina squad in a room full of mirrors. "So this young man, Nelson Perez, took a course in movement, and two years later he's in the Golden Gloves! Oh, it was very exciting, wasn't it, Howard? Up against a great big fellow who came right out swinging, but in the end they did decide for Nelson."

I avoid reading, so I never checked the sports pages for the results of that match, and this is my first news of Nagy's defeat. I think of the two boys, salty and bleeding under the lights, and I remember the crowd's roars as Perez entered the arena. How I'd wished that crowd disappointed! I wonder how Nagy's feeling this week and whether he can bring himself to climb from his bed, and suddenly I'm picturing the hospital where I woke up. I look at Robin, hunched over her smoke, and I doubt she's even paying attention. She puckers her lips and blows a ribbon of gray, and I look out past the convent to where the ha-ha rises into thin, cloudless air. I can hear the surf noise of passing cars.

Sister Amity is saying, "All the champions will have their own float, then they go off to the nationals in Kansas City." She peers at Robin's holes in the ground, where the water has mostly been absorbed by the earth, then reaches up to finger a lilac leaf. The bush has a waist where its branches have been cinched with twine, and above Sister Amity's head, thin sprays of buds wave like so many lavender gloves. "Sister Hillary is beside herself at a protégé's making such a success. I think she's more thrilled than if it had been one of her *girls*. And to tell the truth, we all of us want to see Nelson again. Well, any time there's a parade I go along. And the majorettes, and the school bands . . ." She pauses, blotting her face again, and says, "But of course, it's a big day for you, too, isn't it, Howard? Won't you be marching with your unit?"

I look at her. I've been only half listening, and it takes a moment to realize what she's talking about. I think of the guys who show up on Memorial Day: fat-bellied patriots with their fists and their slogans, their untrimmed, greasy beards and stickered wheelchairs shaming the spectators, soaking the brightness from every sunshiny spring day. Why, most don't even wear uniforms! My mouth goes dry — I'm not part of that, no matter what happened to me. I glance at Sister Amity's innocent little black-framed face, so square and assertive, and as I touch my scar with my fingertips her eyes brighten, as if I might tell her what my life is like. But I'm speechless.

It's not that her assumption is so terrible, though anyone who knows me knows I go my own way. And it's not that she acts like she's talking to a child. It's *all* the things that have gone down, everything that didn't happen to me that I always thought would. It's being an exemplar of the admirably rebuilt life, the days spent zigging a holy lawn mower around paradise, the nights with strangers in my home. It's having a child on furlough from another family, from *Sylvia's* family; it's wanting to do the best I can. Pretending I don't still suffer from nightmares that set me bellowing in my sleep, while Laurel and the others pretend they don't hear. It's that maybe I wasn't so much to begin with, but everything that was worth parading has been gone for so long I barely remember it. It's wondering by what queer twist I survived, and why I was given sixteen days and a lifetime of bleak endurance. It's the futility, always, of being understood.

"Howard," Robin says sharply. "Give me a hand here, would you?" I turn, wiping my cheek with my wrist, and see that she's leaped at the wrapped ball of a lilac tree, her cigarette still clenched tightly in her lips. I stoop to get a grip on the ball and gesture for her to keep an eye on the branches, and as I do so she mutters through the smoke: "Don't mind her, Howard. Not one more thought." And then, perhaps as much to herself as to me, she adds, "These people just have no fucking life."

16

WHEN I'M ALONE, I attack the underbrush. There's no other way to put it. I have a small, sharp pruning saw for the low branches of the pines and a Weedwacker for the tall grass, and in no time at all my T-shirt is soaked with sweat and pine needles are shimmying inside my overalls. I came through this area earlier in the week with a Bush Hog, so the assertive scrub has already been tamed, but I search for anything unruly to subdue. Around each trunk, clumps of grass stand in spring luxuriance; I go at the grass as if it's done me personal wrong, and in the process send bunnies scurrying and small snakes slithering to find holes in the earth.

Around eleven I realize I've put a crack in the Weedwacker. I set the machine on the ground, and I'm inordinately sorry for having treated it so roughly. A cloud of gnatlike insects pulses about me, inflecting the humidity with the grit of their dry, weightless bodies. For thirty seconds I bat furiously at the bugs. Then I spit out a gob of dusty carapaces and scrub my hands up and down my face: the stubbled jawline and scratchy cheeks, the salt-drenched neck and damp hair, on the shaggy side. Finally, my broad forehead, with its flat dent and semirigid puff of scar.

Some small rodent clatters through the undergrowth, crackling leaves and snapping twigs, and when the sound stops I hear the

babble of the stream. I stroll to where the water slips under an arch
in the stone wall, and on impulse I take a seat on the bank, roll up
my pant legs and strip off my shoes and socks. And my feet are old.
I'm only middle-aged and in not bad shape, but my unshod feet look
sad and fleshy in the dappled shade, with clusters of broken capil-
laries and thick, yellowed nails. There's the small cut I got running
across the lawns in the dark and a hunk of callus where a baby toe
has been forced inward, and I think back to my elementary school
days and the sight of my father's feet, which even in my early memories look like this. They were the first thing about him to evoke
my revulsion. But these are just *my* feet, and I'm alone — here and
everywhere — with no one ever to find them repulsive, so I brush
away a bit of sock fluff and plunge them into the cold, clear water.
Looking upstream, I notice a gray minnow battling the eddies to
nibble at a waterweed. The minnow releases itself into the current,
glancing incuriously at my bare feet as it sweeps past. I sit motionless until my distress is diminished.

Returning to Ryan's school at the end of the day, I think of my
panic the night I couldn't locate him, and when I pull in and find
the playground empty and the glass entryway dark, my throat goes
dry. But then I spot him, way off to the side. He's sitting on the curb
with his chin in his hands, and as I turn the truck in that direction
I'm overwhelmed with relief. He climbs aboard in his shuffling
manner, murmuring, "Hi, Howie," so quietly that I barely hear it,
and suddenly I wonder if he thought I wouldn't show up. I stick out
my hand, and he pulls it to his chest in one of those up-close buddy
hugs the young black guys favor. And though it's awkward bumping
torsos in the close quarters of the cab, the affection's unprecedented.
I rub my cheek on his Indians cap and wonder if we're even now: if
his bullshitting me this morning and my shaking him the day we
dropped by Sylvia's are both now water over the dam. As Laurel said,
things happen sometimes.

I suppose Ryan got a detention he was afraid to discuss, or perhaps he's on some goofy committee or club. Sylvia once nagged me

into staying after school to make tissue-paper carnations for the homecoming ball, and I was so embarrassed I told my dad I'd been kept late for cursing. I can picture Ryan doing exactly the same thing. Whatever he's got going, he's feeling remorseful, though he doesn't explain himself. We go home and cook a couple steaks and eat them with fried potatoes and a nice big salad, and for a few hours I'm content.

Around ten-thirty, we're watching an *X-Files* rerun. It's later than Ryan typically hits the sack, but it's Friday, and when the show comes on I think *oh, hell.* A week ago at this time I was touring the back yards.

Now I'm sprawled at the end of the couch, my feet on a hassock, a bowl of microwave popcorn in my lap. Ryan's not saying anything, but I know he's awake because he helps himself to popcorn, and when an onscreen figure suddenly bursts into flames he jumps. After a while he slides his legs onto the couch and shifts his weight, and then he's leaning against me, his body warm and sticky in the heat. I hear Laurel step to the parlor archway, but when she says, "Boys, can I have a word with y'all?" it takes me a moment to realize she means us. In this house, the boys are Nit and Nat.

But Ryan's as alert as a beagle. "We're in the middle of a show!"

Laurel cranes her neck at the TV. "When it's over, then." She looks firmly at me before disappearing through the archway.

Ryan says, "Sheesh!" and takes another fistful of popcorn, but when *The X-Files* ends we dutifully turn off the set. We find Laurel at the table with bills spread all around.

"Howard," she says, laying a hand on a stack of papers. "Here's the gas and electric, also a water assessment from the city. They're all paid out of your account, so don't forget to file the statements away." She picks up an invoice addressed to one of her cafés, squints at it, and reaches for a pen. I rub my chin and wait. Ruby wanders in, panting, and laps at Ryan's bare leg, and as he squats to scratch her fat fist of a head I see a bright scrape running down his forearm. There's a second abrasion on his calf, and though neither injury looks very deep, they stand out pinkly on Ryan's brown skin. I wonder how he got hurt.

Ryan runs his nails down Ruby's back and wrinkles his nose. "This dog stinks," he says.

"Summertime, honey. Gets awful hot for her." Laurel turns another paper. "Did you guys know we have shortcake? Season's first strawberries." I go to the fridge and get out the berries and a bowl of freshly whipped cream, and I gesture with the whipped cream in Laurel's direction. "No thanks, How." I cut two squares of shortcake and place them in bowls, then spoon on the strawberries and cream, and only after Ryan and I are seated at the table does Laurel set down her pen. "So we had a very interesting phone call today," she says. "Lucky I just happened to be — Howard, do you *ever* check that answering machine?" I shrug cheerfully, and she says, "Well, never mind that now. Anyway, it was Ryan's mama calling, and we had a nice chat. She said things are going along well for her at that place, but she also said no one's been responding to her calls." She looks questioningly at Ryan, whose only answer is to dig in his bowl. "Ryan, sweetie? Your mama would very much like to see you."

Ryan shoots me a guarded look. At last he says, "So?"

Laurel purses her lips. "Don't you miss her?" Ryan puts a huge spoonful of whipped cream in his mouth, and as we watch him swallow, she taps the pen against her ear. I know she doesn't consider herself good at this, and she must wish I could jump in and take over. "Been kind of a while, babe. She said *she* misses *you*."

Ryan sighs. I peer at the little downturned face, inexpressive as ever, and remember the impasse of his nerve-racking first days. I reach over to pat his shoulder, and when he slumps away I feel a pang of pure empathy. I've sat through some well-meant interrogations myself.

Laurel rubs her palms together. She's wearing a slim little cherry-pink tank top, and she's pinned her hair up so her long neck looks graceful. For a moment she watches me, biting her lip as she collects her thoughts. Then she says, "Here's what it is. That center where his mom's at is doing some kind of family participation day. Where people who have loved ones there get to come on in and take part in the activities? She said there's an orientation and after that just their regular schedule, but the guests and everybody are included, with the idea of bringing them up to speed on the patient's — what's it called? — her *program*. So it's somewhat more special than your usual visiting hours type thing." She pronounces it *thang* and bites her lip again, then nods at my half-eaten short-cake. "That good?" I pass her the bowl. "Anyway, a week from Wednesday from like nine a.m. to three-thirty. I guess if you wanted to stay on and hang out or whatever . . ."

Ryan's got the spoon in his mouth, but he talks through it. "I have school."

"You could miss a day, sweetie. 'Specially if it's to see your mom." She smiles encouragingly, but casts a glance at the papers, and I realize she's eager to get back to her accounts. "See now, if you'd been speaking to your mom regularly, you'd know all this already." Ryan takes the spoon from his mouth and starts mashing his shortcake.

Laurel says quietly, "I think it's a big part of her cure." Then the three of us sit quietly as Ryan turns his dessert to mush. It strikes me that since Laurel and Sylvia haven't met, today might well have been their first real conversation. How jubilant Sylvia must have been to discover such efficient aid!

I think, as I so often have, of that morning of Sylvia's departure. Telling Ryan to quit busting her chops; minutes later saying, "Let's just *go*." I wonder how she's doing — I *do!* — but I also know her knack for getting her own way. Suddenly it's a choice between two people's desires, and without really meaning to speak, I say, "Not." It would be different if Ryan were longing to see his mother, but at the moment his preferences carry some weight.

The others look up. I say "Not," again, and then, "Not go." It's never been my position that he should continue to ignore his mother, but suddenly this is what I'm saying. I think of Sylvia claiming *I got* her into this, and I think of that surprise hug today in the truck. I consider the disaster of our visit to Sylvia's house, and I think he'll really hate me if I drag him to her as a hostage. So I say, "Not," a fourth time, and the word comes out easily. I fold my arms across my chest.

Laurel turns deliberately to Ryan. "Well, Ry," she says, and her tone is clipped, "Howard's your guardian here, and you'll do what he says. But *I* think you might take some time to reconsider. I bet you'd learn a lot just seeing what your ma's been doing."

"I don't *want* to," he says. With the battle won, he suddenly turns brattish, and as he sets his bowl down the spoon clatters inside. I keep my arms folded and maintain my expression, but I can't help being surprised by the sway I hold. When was the last time my word meant anything? Have I been hasty?

Laurel has another bite of my shortcake and picks up her pen. She's still not looking at me. "Way past bedtime, *mi compadre*," she says tiredly. Then, as we're shuffling from the room, she adds, "Anyway, I know *Howard* plans to participate in this thing with your mom, whether you go ahead and accompany him or not."

Ryan stops in his tracks, but only briefly. Then he takes the stairs two at a time. And Laurel's great — I'll be the first to acknowledge that — but she's another one who doesn't care to have her will undermined. When I turn to look, she's gone back to her accounts.

17

LATER, I'm on the square second-floor landing that connects our three rooms. Against one wall stands my mother's old sewing table, where a small lamp casts enough glow for finding the bathroom at night. Years ago, my mom spread a white lace cloth on the tabletop and plugged in the lamp, and except for dusting and laundry, nothing's been touched since. But though I'm looking at the cloth and lamp, I'm thinking of Ryan. I'm trying to remember what life is like at nine years old, and whether kids in my day were as inscrutable as this one now. Compared to Ryan's, my own childhood seems a crowded, busy affair, not *important* or even consistently joyful, but bustling with neighbors and relatives and other kids, with projects and passions that carried me from day to day. I wonder if his life is like that when he's at home. It strikes me I've seldom seen playmates around the putty-colored house, and I remember what his childhood comprises that mine did not. The life with no father; Sylvia's habit. I wonder if my first eighteen years were truly the full existence I like to remember, or if they only seem so by comparison with today.

I hear Ruby climbing the stairs, then she lies down on the worn rug. Her legs stick out like stretcher handles in front and back. I think of what happened to me, and I think childhood ought to be a person's happiest days. There's no guarantee life gets better as it goes along.

Ryan's door suddenly opens, and Laurel backs out, stealthily closing it behind her. She turns, notices me, and says, "Oh!" I don't move. Laurel says, "I just go in and check him at night, make sure he's covered up." I nod, and she puts her hands on her hips. I think *here it comes:* my tongue-lashing for letting him skip Sylvia's visitation. But Laurel is silent. In the semidarkness, her pink top appears orange, and all her weight is on one black-jeaned hip. She looks like a long-in-the-saddle Texas gal, which is part of what she is, of course. I could take three steps and shut myself in my own room, but I wait.

Laurel says, "Well, I don't know." She raises a black sneaker to scratch her calf, then looks up and gives an exaggerated shrug. I shrug back, and she chuckles. "You could have the whole world talking like you, Howard," she says. "Only" — she squints contemplatively at Ruby — "only you could smile just a bit more, you know? Sometimes I wonder if your gruff looks frighten him . . . Mind my saying that?" I shrug again, and she nods. "Oh, and did you want to go in? No reason you can't visit him, too."

Ryan's on his back on the futon, a light cotton blanket pulled over his belly. He's still in the white T-shirt he had on earlier, with a spot of crud, probably whipped cream, on the front. His face is turned away.

Laurel says, "Go on," and I step in and squat down. One of his sneakers is lying at my feet, and I pick it up, then reach for the other and place them together by the futon. As my eyes grow accustomed to the darkness, I can see other clothes lying around in heaps, along with Ryan's pack and a couple of schoolbooks. There's some white fluff in the corner, and I realize I should come in tomorrow and vacuum the remains of that Energizer Bunny. The strip of wallpaper has been put back in its place. It looks like somebody's Scotch-taped it to the wall.

Ryan's blue Indians cap is beside the pillow, as if it's the last thing he took off. I touch his shoulder as gently as I can, and once again I see the long scrape on his forearm. I wish I'd remembered some ointment before he went to bed. I wonder what on earth I can offer to make these his good days, and I wonder if it's gruffness and turmoil I project, or survival. I pat Ryan's shoulder again just as Laurel says, "You can kiss him, you know." His cheek's soft against my lips.

I hear Laurel shift her weight, and we leave the room. The door clicks just as quietly as it did before; then she smiles. "I'm glad he's here," she says. "You're a kind man, Howard."

Ruby heaves to her feet and plants her butt on the carpet, her eyes round and lidless in her flat little face. "Well, good night," Laurel says. "Sweet dreams. See you in the morning." I nod and put my hands under my overall bib, and I'm turning toward my own room when she goes on tiptoe. I ball my fists against my stomach, and her kiss is so quick on my cheek that I barely feel it. But it's been so long since I was kissed at all.

18

SATURDAY AT BREAKFAST I notice Ryan needs a haircut. He has the kind of hair that loses its tight curl as it grows longer, and it's begun to look weedy. I think it's possible he'll decide to see Sylvia with me after all, and he should look his best, so once the cartoons have ended, I wave him to the truck. I could use a trim myself.

The barbershop is in a little strip mall, between a cleaner's and a pet supply store. Four boys are milling around in front, dressed in yellow jerseys with swoops of script across the chest. I hesitate as we approach — gangs of kids always notice my scar — then one boy announces, "Radnor Tag Day." Radnor's the local elementary school, but I haven't a clue what the heck the kid means, and Ryan eyes him with suspicion. After a moment the boy adds dubiously, "Care to make a donation?" He holds out a coffee can with a slit cut from the lid.

I reach for my wad of bills and peel off a one, and as I poke it through the slit, the boy hands me a small, square card. "'Thank you for supporting Radnor Little League,'" Ryan reads aloud. "'Have a great day!'" The other boys step forward now, each self-consciously fiddling with his own slitted coffee can, and I notice that on a sleeve of each yellow shirt is a striped emblem like the one on the door of Li'l Tony's Barbershop. Suddenly they seem like decent kids, perhaps even the sons of the Irish and Scandinavian boys who were my own Radnor classmates, and they're about Ryan's age. I nod and pass out three more bucks. Ryan murmurs, "You don't have to give them *all* something," but he follows behind and collects three more cards.

Inside the barbershop, Li'l Tony says, "Tank you, my friend! You supporting my boys!" He's got an Italian accent that's a bit overdone, and I doubt he even knows my name, but he makes an effort. Slapping the chair with a towel, he says, "So. How you like today?" then goes ahead and trims me to the gray-brown fuzz I get every time. It looks fine. Ordinarily, I get a shave with my haircut, just to prolong the interaction, but today I don't want to keep Ryan waiting. When Tony lathers up his brush, I wave him off.

I stand up. Behind me, Ryan's sneaking looks at a *Playboy* in the magazine rack, but he snaps to as I turn around. I nod toward the chair, and he gives a startled look and mouths the word *no*. I go over and lift off his Indians cap, then take a lock of his hair in my fingers. Li'l Tony says, "Come on, young man. I make a look nice." I chuck Ryan on the shoulder.

Ryan whispers, "I can't get my hair cut here. I gotta go to a black place." I give him a moment's appraisal. Because of Sylvia, I've always considered Ryan a kind of disguised Caucasian, but he says, "Andee Barber School, Howie," and we turn to go. The baseball boys perk up as we exit the shop, but Ryan brandishes the fan of cards. "We paid already," he says with a touch of menace. They back off.

He guides me to a mostly black neighborhood not far from Sylvia's development, where the Andee Barber School sits in another small strip of shops. Ryan holds the door, then comes in right on my heels, and I catch him swaggering like a junior gangsta.

This place is busier than Li'l Tony's. Hip-hop music is playing nice and loud, and five middle-aged black men in white coats are cutting hair. One of them nods at Ryan, who nods back vacantly, bouncing his head to the beat. In fact, he's a bit transformed by the environment. He's a black kid now, with a more urban-style cool than he's exhibited around the house, and any similarity to the four pasty Little Leaguers has vanished. The shop's other customers are sharp-looking guys in their teens and twenties, and it's touching to see Ryan work at fitting himself in. When his turn comes, he steps forward with that same tough-boy shamble, and I give him an amused glance. He climbs into the chair without acknowledging my look.

I rub a palm over my fresh-clipped head and sit back to watch the proceedings. I'm the only white guy here, but I don't care; if I learned anything from the army, it's that race is the least of my worries. Ryan continues to bop in the chair, and the barber says, "Keep still, my man, or I'm a cut you," though a minute later he leans around and smiles at Ryan. I can't hear what Ryan says in return.

The barber's a tall, dark man of about my age, with a way of ignoring the movements of his own ring-covered fingers. The other barbers are also in their forties and fifties, and I wonder if this is really any kind of a school. For a moment, I wonder if it's one of the spots Sylvia copped — hair places are famously good for drugs — but the truth is I can't tell. The young guys and the old guys sustain a banter that's hard to follow over the pulsing music, and every few minutes someone runs through the door, but the furtive urgency I recall from my own purchasing days is hard to detect. Still, I watch Ryan's guy carefully. He's been grinning since we arrived, and I wonder if he's lit.

And then I'm ashamed of myself. Even if the place isn't a barber school, I think, that doesn't mean it's a drug place; and even if it's a drug place, there's no reason it's not a barbershop, too. I look at Ryan's barber again, and he catches my eye. "How you doin', brother? Here for a cut?" Big, big smile.

Ryan says, "He got his hair cut already. At another place."

The man nods. "I can tell. But you c'mon to me next time, my friend. I set you up good." At this he cracks a laugh, and I think he's got to be talking hair; anything else is simply too broad. He catches the eye of the next barber over, and the two go gleefully limp; for a second I'm on edge. Then Ryan's barber steps out and slaps my palm. "You a good guy," he says. "Y'all don't think we do white people hair here, but we do." He grins at me some more, and I nod back merrily. No one seems to notice I can't speak. I'm just a white guy, not a mute, and he's only cutting the boy's hair.

Ryan gets his hair cropped close, instead of the fade he had before. At first I think he's emulating my own short cut; then I realize all the young dudes have the same preppy look. The barber lifts the smock with a flourish, and I make Ryan pause before donning the old Indians cap. He'll be a good-looking fellow someday, I think, and I wonder, as I've wondered before, who his father was. Always that pang of jealousy. Ryan whispers, "It's seven dollars," and I hand the man a pair of fives. The barber grins some more and shakes my hand, and I speculate on the tip Sylvia gives.

On the way home, we pass a summer market set up in a parking lot, with booths of fresh produce and baked goods and flats of seedlings laid out on trestle tables. I don't want to prolong this to the point that we resent each other, but maybe we're not there yet, so I pull over. Ryan's slipped from the street pose of the barbershop back into the neutral persona he employs with me, and when he covertly inspects a jar with a piece of honeycomb inside, I buy it.

When I was small and we'd just moved into our house, my dad built two white planters for the front porch railing, and each year he and I would fill them with flowers and dangling ivy. I don't know if Ryan's too macho for flowers, but when I stroll toward the plants he follows along, and together we gaze over the grids of greenery. There are the usual suspects: six-packs of impatiens and petunias and pansies, and I think of a song a neighbor girl made up in grammar school: *Pansy and Petunia are very much in love / They sit together every day just like two little doves.* I suppose that girl has long since married, divorced, and grown embittered, but I wonder what happened to those two old wooden planters. Certainly no one put out floral displays once I came home injured, but when I think of the nice job Robin does at the convent, it seems a few blooms might spruce up my home. I reach for a six-pack of white impatiens, then set it back. I should have done this while my mother was alive.

Ryan is standing by a flat of petunias, squeezing a fleshy trumpet between finger and thumb. As I move toward him, a lady says, "Don't do that, young man. They bruise easily," and he steps back and looks at her darkly. The woman turns to me. "Yes, sir."

I put my hand on Ryan's shoulder so she knows we're together, then pick up the petunia he's bruised. I gesture at him with it, and he shrugs sullenly, then abruptly mumbles, "Nice." I hold up four fingers, and the plant lady reaches for four six-packs. "Purple," Ryan says loudly.

"All mixed colors, sonny," the lady says. "You wouldn't want just purple; it'd be too dark." I hold up my hand again — *we'll have what he wants* — then the three of us peer over the plants and choose an assortment that's mostly purple. In the end, Ryan tries to sneak the one he's damaged back onto the trestle table, but I take it anyway, tapping the Indians cap to make my point. In my world we welcome handicapped plants.

It's not easy locating Dad's two planters, and I'm surprised Ryan tags along, instead of peeling off to watch TV. After all, I can't even say what we're looking for. We find the planters in a storage cubby behind the cupola, and he says, "Oh-h-h," as if all has been made clear.

"Nh-h-h," I echo.

One planter's rotted through, but the other is serviceable. We carry it downstairs and find its old place on the railing, and it upsets the house's symmetry. The annual lady's right about dark blossoms, too, but I let it go because Ryan's suddenly on the case. "I know how to do this," he announces as I cut open a bag of soil; then he all but elbows me aside. I've bought a bunch of geraniums and some morning glories, too, and as I place the pots of geraniums on the stairs, I get thinking about my mom.

We moved to this place the summer before first grade. My folks were working people who took a chance on the neighborhood, and they fell in love with this house and with fixing it up. They saw it as a place where I might raise a family, too. Both my parents were old-school homebodies who enjoyed the sanding and caulking and painting and refinishing, and by the time I left for boot camp the place was a showcase — at least, it seemed that way to us. Then I came home, and all was different. First, my mother let things go, while my father sustained the maintenance and care. Then my dad hit the sauce, and Mom kept the place up. But no matter who led the charge, joy was gone from the upkeep. The changing of storm windows and the mending of porch steps were carried out with the same dutifulness as my own unending courses of speech therapy, and my parents must have many times asked themselves *what on earth is the use?* I think of my father's bottles, stowed under the seat of his car or in the tack room, by the privy. That was how I knew he'd given up. I think of a warm night when I was so wrecked I lay on this very lawn, tearing at my thighs and inventing vulgar poems to ward off the explosions above me; I couldn't speak a word of poetry, of course, but I bellowed and screeched at the top of my lungs, and when my mother came out in her nightgown and begged me to stop, I wasn't even sure it was she, not some figment. Even when she took hold of my hands, I swung out, thinking — or maybe that's another occasion. This happened more than I like to admit.

Even after I got my shit together, after Dad was gone and only Mom and I remained in this place, the sense of mulish duty was hard to shake. I saw reclaiming the house as a sign of my new life, and I mended and plastered and caulked until my hands bled. But I could go no further: no flowers, no bright colors or wallpaper. I looked around me and thought *what the fuck is the use?* And I think that now, staring at the tray of morning glories in the bed of the truck. What's the sense of a display now, after sitting so long unadorned? Do I think things can change? My mother rarely mentioned flowers, and I don't know that she wished for morning glories. But it's a lost opportunity.

I lean on the truck, wondering how the brightness fled from the day. I can't explain why my dark moods descend. The boys screech up in their white van, music blasting, and slog past me with barely a word; but a few minutes later a third-floor window opens, and Nit's head pops out. "Hey, Howard, man. Harrison's taking for-fuckin'-ever in the shower. Lemme wash up in your guys' bath-room?" I stare at the gravel and think *what's the use?* I make him ask twice before I look up.

Then there's the sound of honking, and Laurel's leaning from her Beetle. "I barely knew the place," she shouts. "You busy guys." Ryan runs out, calling that purple was his idea, and Laurel smiles appraisingly as she climbs from the car. I head toward them, arms folded, and she puts a hand on my forearm. "Why the glum look?"

Inside the house, the phone rings, and Laurel's fingers tense on my skin. Only one person calls here. Laurel says, "Ryan —" but he turns with a wild look, and she breaks off abruptly. She leans on my shoulder an instant, and I hear her murmuring, "Let it go . . ." Then she picks up a grocery bag. "Shortcake, shortcake!" she says. "I got more strawberries." And I feel less of a freak.

Around dusk, I return to the driveway. Alongside the stable lies a narrow flower bed edged in paving stones, and I kneel down and tear out a jungle of crabgrass, then space out the tiny morning glory shoots. Tomorrow, I think, I'll rig up a trellis of strings. Maybe Ryan will help — or I can do it alone. We needn't do everything together, I guess, but it is good to have something to tend to. Step-ping back, I picture vines covering the clapboards, green heart-shaped leaves and bright blue morning glory circles, stretching and twining and growing lusher every day. Then I remember the flower that interested the lieutenant.

19

N EXT TIME I TAKE Ryan to school he says, "See you at
five," as he jumps from the truck. He knows I'm not
expecting this and beats a hasty retreat. And there's a way to handle
it, I'm sure. I'm not so incapacitated I can't demand an explanation,
but at the moment our easy weekend still lingers in the air, so I
watch him go.

On a shelf in my bedroom closet is a portable speech device
Laurel gave me the first Christmas she was here, which I put away
before New Year's and haven't looked at since. A picture of that little
machine comes to me as I'm Weedwacking the Contemplation
Garden, and I wonder how a gray box does something so manifestly
beyond me: link an arsenal of immobilized words to its hard, flat,
digital voice. At the time she gave it to me, Laurel was heading off
to Texas for whatever goofy combination of Christmas and Tet her
family celebrates, and Nit and Nat were not yet with us; our house-
mate then was a fiftyish divorced guy who kept to himself. So it was
just Laurel and me a few days before Christmas, and she looked
excited as she handed me the red-wrapped box. But when I lifted
the packing material, all I saw was the consumer version of my
gadget-happy pathologist's office — and I froze at the familiar
tyranny. It was too lavish a gift, anyway, for two people who barely
knew each other, and in the years since, we've kept things simple.

The gizmo wasn't mentioned again. I told myself I was a man of action, not words, and I'd never say more than I could communicate easily; as I remember this, I get too close to a hosta and snip off a spray of leaves. I stoop to hide the broken stems and think of what I *would* say to Ryan if I only could. Jokes and wisecracks and stories of my life at his age and even advice, even tales of combat. I'd gain his goodwill before I made him account for his after-school hours. The same with the phone calls.

Perhaps goodwill is what's in the balance. In the morning, when he takes off so quickly, I tell myself I've got all day to make myself a bad cop, but when five comes I have no game plan. Then something shifts, and the opportunity's lost. We're into the long, lovely evenings of June, and as I wash up the supper dishes, Ryan asks if we have a Frisbee. We go out back, and Ruby charges between us on her stubby black legs. We play in the yard until it's too late to see, and the next morning the pickup time has entered our regimen. Ryan says, "Five o'clock, yo," and gives me a rare hug, and nine hours later he's got a bruise on his shin. When I point to it, he says he fell off the carousel. Why can't I tell him I don't believe him?

Deep down, I'm an optimist. It's my most depressing characteristic. As a teenager, I knew half a dozen guys who beat the draft by claiming to be crazy or homosexual or by heading north, over the border. The brother of one of Sylvia's friends chopped a toe off with a cleaver; I remember him at the senior prom, surrounded by girls and leaning on a carved cane. And though I'd have had difficulty with that cleaver, the other options didn't bother me much, even the gay one, if it came to that. I had Sylvia, so what did I care? But I never believed that what happened would happen, so I let fate take its course. I didn't think the government would call me up, and then they did; I didn't think I'd get sent overseas, but I was. I trusted — crazily, *maddeningly*, despite all warnings, as if picturing safety were any kind of defense — that the large leaves and bright, small flowers of that jungle landscape would shelter me as thoroughly as the dry, limp foliage of my stateside boot camp. They did not. And I sure as hell didn't plan on getting injured . . .

I thought I'd be lucky, because at eighteen my life had been good. Why shouldn't that continue? I thought Sylvia would wait for me; I thought the doctors would make me new. I thought time would pass and I'd adapt; I waited and waited for everything to be all right. And now I look at Ryan, nine years old and coming home scraped up from some activity I know nothing about, and I believe I should dig into this because even optimists stop trusting at some point. Then another day passes, and at five o'clock he's right where he said he'd be, and he seems fine. By then it's *my* time, and I don't want to spoil it. I'm thinking chicken and mashed potatoes and the long hours before dark, and Ruby's waiting for us in the house with purple flowers. Maybe Laurel's there, too, so I opt not to jostle fate. The separate pieces of my existence have been out of joint for a very long time. I want things to be nice.

In a few surprising ways, they are. Nit and Nat are into their second week of mooching breakfast, and I'm adjusting to that. I had to point out that plates have backs as well as fronts, but after this the dishwashing improved, and I like having the paper read aloud each morning. I haven't had that since my mom was alive. The morning hubbub reminds me of the best aspects of the army, so I resurrect a few tricks I learned in basic: it's a hot griddle that sears your pancakes, and a dribble of water will keep fried eggs soft. I notice that Ryan loves Canadian bacon, and Laurel and Nit always gobble up any fruit. Nat eats anything placed in front of him, but he eats a lot; he and I are the big guys here. Remembering the days when I'd scarf two Twinkies on the ride to the convent, I'm amazed at my sudden domesticity. So the boys are coarse and loud and dopey, and each day brings something that gets under my skin. Once breakfast is over, I'm glad they're gone, but their participation has a unifying effect: Laurel no longer stands by the stove to eat, but comes to the table, and Ryan's put himself in charge of the coffeemaker. Nat once said this was the best part of his day.

Another week passes, remarkable for its harmony and for the ease with which we put difficult thoughts aside. Even Laurel seems distracted by the boys' commotion; she lets up on the phone stuff and only once mentions Sylvia's family day. As for me, I'm made weightless by June and Frisbee, by Saturday-night bowling and my mom's coffee cake recipe and the kids' Sunday matinee at the theater I went to when *I* was a child. By morning glories and teaching Ruby to sit and by the fact that Nit and Nat's hooey now bugs me but briefly; by the incomparable strangeness of feeling tired at bedtime. I'm so swept away, in fact, that I almost — unaccountably — lose track of what I'd ordinarily consider paramount: in a few days, I'll see Sylvia again.

20

SYLVIA WAS ONE OF THOSE GIRLS who hung around the art room. Neither of us was a star in high school, but Sylvia found a clique to join among the girls — and a few boys — who stayed after school to make silk-screen prints and fiddle with clay. Because she and I were always together, I was part of that group, too.

Remembering those days, I see a small, neat blonde with small, neat messes down her work apron. Her face was oval, and she had fine bones and thin, precise fingers, which I thought were exquisite. All her life she'd been growing her hair, and by the time I met her she could sit on it if she arched her neck. In the art room, she'd gather the mass of it into a knot, and as the hours passed, strands would slip out and spread in wisps over her shoulders. It may not have been the prettiest hair — it was very fine — but Sylvia got plenty of attention for it, and of course I adored it. Her hair was like a piece of fabulous jewelry she wore every day, just for me.

I never did much art myself. Often I'd read while the radio played and the room bustled around me, but there were hours I sat at those big, wooden tables doing no more than cracking jokes. Sometimes Sylvia would draw me into what she was doing; I remember a clay sculpture I made of a man under a palm tree. There were potato-print Christmas cards and a few other projects, too, and no matter what drawing or little object I created, Sylvia gave it serious appraisal, as she did with her own work. For this she reserved a particular expression: narrowed eyes, hard-set mouth. She'd step back to a certain distance and beetle her pale brows, and if it was her work she was considering, she might lean in for a disapproving tweak. I suppose even then I knew this was baloney, but it seemed like the way an artist behaved, and I guess it helped her feel artistic. We were kids, and we took ourselves seriously! Sylvia was hypercritical of her own accomplishments but always very gentle with anything I made.

So that was our life. I enjoyed chemistry and English and got mostly B's, and though Syl wouldn't show me her report card, I suspected she got B's and C's in everything but art. My hair grew long enough to touch my shoulders, and I broke my arm playing freshman football — but that was long before I met Sylvia. For three years I played clarinet in the marching band; one semester I took an acting class. We weren't wild, but we weren't prudes. I smoked pot when it was available at parties, and Sylvia, who was two years younger, sneaked the occasional beer. What else? I was kind of a chunky kid, and the first time we had sex I was afraid she'd be repelled by my thick trunk and hairy legs, and I wished I could keep my clothes on, just stick my penis out my fly. But Sylvia was already removing her clothes. She pulled her sweater over her head and brushed a piece of red cotton yarn from one breast, and I wanted to lose my soul in her loveliness. I couldn't do that with my school clothes on, so I undressed, too, as fast as I could.

I was such a horny teenager I'd have liked sex under any circumstances, but I really do believe ours was special. We'd spent a long time doing no more than making out — on the couch of a house where Sylvia babysat or in my father's Dodge when I took her home or, occasionally, thrillingly, in the art room during basketball games — and I'd discovered a formula for overcoming my modesty. I'd start out tentatively, with the lightest of kisses, then after a while I'd gasp for breath. I'd grip Sylvia tighter and rub her arm — or her tummy or her breast, when she'd let me — and utter a few moans, just to see how that felt. Kissing, touching, gasping, moaning: I'd escalate the elements until it seemed I was practically overcome by passion, and then I *would* be overcome by my passion, and I'd no longer have to think about what I was doing. My skin would tingle, and my head would swim; my mouth would paint her throat with kisses. The world would narrow to the simplest of prospects, and I'd thrill, in my light-headedness, to the bitter, talcumy scent of an ear. With breaths and nibbles I'd take a turn at her neck, the back flesh of an upper arm, or the taut wedge of belly where she'd allowed her shirt to ride up just a little. Her skin would pebble to goose bumps, and I'd be utterly delighted with what I'd accomplished. Then I'd go back for more.

Sylvia rarely moaned. She was far too self-conscious a girl for that. Nevertheless, I believed I could sense her, too, growing aroused by my technique, so when it came to sex I tried the same thing. Once our clothes were off, I'd start with a little kissing and caressing, and I was always astonished at how small her body was, compared to mine. When I was ready to get inside her I'd continue my gentleness, propping myself on my elbows to stroke her face and touch her with my lips, and when I got to that point where I'd be overwhelmed by her beauty I'd let my weight down so our bodies merged and my newly solid and hairy adolescence dissolved in the sweet, small miracle of her. At the end, I'd heave and thrash and kiss her neck, and even the taste of that thin, thin hair in my mouth seemed to certify love. We only had intercourse eight or ten times, anyway, before I went off; I waited almost *two years* before Sylvia was ready! Then thank God for prostitutes — not over there, but here at home, after my return — or I'd never have made it through my twenties. After the war, Sylvia and I had sex only once. There was no longer any question of our being together, but it was one of those things that occasionally happens, or possibly Sylvia felt obliged. By then I had to be quite high even to contemplate an erection, and Sylvia had shed a few of her inhibitions. What resulted was quick and harsh and very, very different from anything we'd shared before. I never had the stomach to try it again.

What with basic training, my short tour, and the time in hospitals, she was in art college before I got back on my feet. By then she'd had other boyfriends, and she'd cut her hair. In the years I was gone she'd become a painter, and for a long time I told myself *this* was what separated us, far more than my injury. I longed for the equilibrium of those days in the art room, when we were simply two high schoolers who met by glorious, unimaginable chance. But Sylvia had other allegiances, and it was hard, with my difficulties, for me to keep up. Even that day when she showed me the potato-head self-portraits, I could taste her dust.

I don't know why Sylvia never found success as an artist. Maybe the answer's as simple as not enough talent. Maybe she should have gone to New York, or maybe she did too much coke or not enough. For about ten years she had a studio downtown, where the dark canvases she cranked out were less interesting to me than the sentimental drawings she'd done in high school. But this was a period when we saw less of each other, and she didn't discuss her aspirations with me. By the time we connected again, she'd given up the painting studio and found a temp job typing for an ad agency. Ryan was still in the future, and I think Sylvia was at the end of some romance. "Howie, are you there?" she asked thinly of my answering machine. "I was thinking I'd really, really love to get high." She knew I'd have something because in those days I always did. So maybe she's right, as she suggested the day she left: she wouldn't be detoxing if it weren't for me, though she did ask. Or maybe it's because her painting career didn't go as she wished. I'm not one to make much of thwarted dreams, but I know there's *something* I'd have become if I hadn't been hurt. An architect or a jet pilot or an accountant; a married guy with beloved kids. All these destinies didn't happen to me, so maybe Sylvia's didn't happen to her, either.

It's a bright, moody morning when I arrive at the rehab center. I've already done my best with Ryan and failed. At the grammar school I laid a hand on his shoulder, very man to man, and cocked my head at the passing road. *Not too late, buddy! Let's visit your mom.* But Ryan only looked at his lap. "What?" he mumbled. "I think we have like a big quiz today." We sat quietly a moment, Ryan fiddling with his lunch box handle, and at last I set my hand on his. "You said I didn't have to," he murmured resentfully. "You *said*," he repeated, and he looked so cornered that at last I shrugged. It wasn't my intention to go back on my word. I tried to appear heedless as I squeezed his hand to wish him a good day, but I knew I wasn't wearing my amiable face. Ryan climbed down as if he wasn't sure what he was doing himself, and I thought he might ask me to tell her hello, but he didn't. I watched him walk to the building, not the playground, then I drove off.

The place is not what I'm expecting. Years ago, after a summer of hallucinogens, I watched a television feature about a facility near Minneapolis. I remember a spot that was a bit like Sister Amity's convent, with acres of open land and places to walk among a network of brown buildings. The show was filmed in winter, and the icy lake to which the camera periodically returned made the scenes of people confronting their problems seem all the more cozy. This is the world I've been picturing for Sylvia, more spa than penitentiary. Instead, her place is a freestanding brick structure in a developed area on the south side. The building looks like it might house a large dental complex or veterinary clinic, and it sits on a double lot off a major avenue, with tall trees and clapboard bungalows on either side. I'm early. As I wait to go in, I think how much more comfortable I'd feel with Ryan to buffer me.

A heavyset woman enters the building, accompanied by a girl about Ryan's age. A few minutes later a man in a suit arrives, and I get out of the truck and follow him to the glass doors. Inside is a table with name tags spread across it, and a woman says, "May I help you?" I look down at the grid of names until I recognize my own, and when I pick up my tag the woman's eyes flicker over my scar. "Ah, Mr. Kapostash. Sylvia's told us all about you. And you've brought her little boy with you?" As she peers around for Ryan, I step off.

A big, pale, hulking guy arrives with a little wife and a baby, then there's a regular stream: singles and couples, not many kids. I'm wondering where Sylvia is when the suited man asks for someone named Mary Ellen, and the woman says some of the clients haven't arrived yet. But where the hell are they? Don't they live at the facility?

I spot Sylvia before she sees me. She's coming up the walk with a young Hispanic-looking guy, and as they walk along, she fishes in an enormous woven shoulder bag. The Hispanic guy's smoking, and they pause at the bottom of the steps for him to finish his cigarette. Sylvia finds a piece of gum in her bag and pops it in her mouth.

I step out and raise my hand. Sylvia's face is blank for a nanosecond, then a big smile. "You're here! But I should know you're always early, Howie." She drags me toward her friend, saying, "Carlos, Howie, Howie, Carlos." She's very animated, though I'm not sure she looks any healthier.

Carlos shifts his cigarette and shakes my hand. "Good to meet you, man," he says. He's young and good-looking, maybe mid twenties. With renunciation beginning so early, how do young people sow their wild oats?

All around us, people are exchanging hugs and hellos. Sylvia looks at me expectantly. I point to the ground, then put my hands together under my cheek: I'm asking where she and Carlos are arriving from. She stares a moment, then gives a nod. She's always been good at this. "We don't sleep here," she says. "Except for like Betty Ford, detox is an outpatient thing these days, because of insurance. Lucky for me, though, Caroline played the single-mom card and got me in a halfway house, which is supposed to be for hard cases. Like Carlos." She puts an arm around him, and he grins. "There's a break later. I'll take you guys over. So where's my li'l fella, anyway? Raiding the coffee room?"

I shake my head. This is the moment I'm dreading, but Ryan's not here, and that's all there is to say. Sylvia stares at me, her eyes welling, but I'm not convinced she didn't see this coming. I look past her, down the tree-lined street to the busy avenue, and wait for the traffic signal to change to green.

Sylvia says, "Didn't he even . . . ," and lets out a heave. "You were supposed to make him come." At this, Carlos puts an arm around her, but she shrugs him off, and I'm glad she does because I'm sick of him already. He pats her arm before moving away, and Sylvia catches me watching this exchange. "So what the fuck brings *you* here, Howie?" she says.

I start to slide my hands under my overall bib, then realize I'm dressed up today: knit slacks and a short-sleeved madras sport shirt. I put my hands in my pockets and glower at the distant traffic light, and Sylvia says unconvincingly, "I didn't mean that." She pokes in the big bag for a Kleenex and blows her nose, then I follow her inside.

There's a welcome from the shrink who runs the place, but I can't pay attention. Beside me, Sylvia sits like a stone, and when we're separated into client and family groups, she stalks off without looking back. Carlos goes out shoving and goofing around with the big pale guy I noticed earlier, and I realize that two thirds of the clients are men my age and younger. Compared to the rest of us, they seem to be having fun.

The family group watches a slide show about the facility, then a staff member named Paula tells us that children of addicts come in several basic types. The first type, she says, is called the "family hero," and as she describes the hero's characteristics I think of Ryan in the putty-colored house, keeping a watchful eye on his mother. I think of him making coffee at my place and watering the new flowers, and I realize he's been a pretty good guest. Maybe "hero" is a fair term. Then Paula moves on to other categories — there's one who acts babyish and one who's sneaky and misbehaves — and each time she introduces a type I think that's him, too. So I don't know.

When the clients return, we form a circle, and Paula makes us introduce ourselves. The suited guy's wife, Mary Ellen, is a flat-faced older woman who announces grimly that she's an alcoholic, but everyone else is in for drugs. A few say they're one-thing-or-another survivors, and after their introductions they seem more like addicts than clients. It's a sorry lot.

When my turn comes, Sylvia jumps in. "Hi, I'm Syl," she says, "and I have a problem with cocaine abuse. This is my friend Howard, who's looking after my nine-year-old son, Ryan, until I'm able to be a better mom." She sniffs loudly.

I raise a paw, and three dozen faces stare at my scar. Paula says, "Welcome, Howard. We're happy you could join us." They all know. She nods at a dark-haired muscleman who looks like Carlos's brother. "Go ahead, Raymond."

The next activity is one the clients all know. "Think of it like a game," Paula tells us. "Did anybody play Twister when you were kids?" She says we'll be creating a kind of living sculpture that will depict one addict's relationship to his addiction and also to other factors in his life. She selects John, the pale guy, because he's almost completed his program. John lumbers to the center and starts talking, and I tune him out. I don't give a shit about his poor, sad trip. I look at Sylvia and wonder if she's changed in three weeks, but I really can't tell. The little herpes blister I noticed that first morning has bloomed and died, leaving a rose-colored silhouette, and her hair looks clean, but her eyes are puffy. She could use some sun. Paula says, "John, try not to intellectualize so much. Remember the exercise."

I touch Sylvia's forearm. Her skin is covered with thousands of pale freckles that lie in patches on her arms, legs, and shoulders, as if placed there with an atomizer. I touch her arm with my knuckles, just to say I'm here, no matter what, and maybe to reassure myself that she's here, too. But Sylvia only gives me a tight glance and looks pointedly at John, still standing dumbly in the center of the ring. He's scratching his head.

Paula says, "Go ahead. Choose someone to represent your addiction."

John says, "I know, I know." He turns once, assessing the stock of pathetic-looking wives and visitors, plus all his new buddies who are in his same boat. He turns once more and points at me.

I don't know what to do. I heard Paula say I was to portray his addiction, but I can't imagine how I would do such a thing, and I'm not prepared to get up and act. I start to stand, then sit down with a smile, and I hope it seems I've been paying attention. I'm afraid John's chosen me because of my scar, but maybe it's just that we're the biggest guys here. I turn to Sylvia, who stares back as if I'm a bug. "Go ahead," she says.

I get up, and John says, "Just like lean on me, man." He's uncomfortable, too. I put one hand on his biceps and the other on his shoulder, and I tilt forward, shifting my weight. John murmurs, "Okay, so, um . . . What else now?"

Paula says, "Is that how it feels, John? Is that how your dependency *really* feels?" On the other side of the circle, I see John's wife cradling their little baby, and I'm glad the kid won't remember this foolishness. I'm glad Ryan's not here, too. Paula says, "Tell Howard how it should feel."

John blushes. "That's good," he mumbles, "but maybe it — could be more like a weight. Like kind of weighing me down?" I wonder if he's prepared for this brand of closeness, because I'm certainly not, but I press harder on the soft, slack flesh of his shoulder. "Like really bear down," he says.

So I do. I don't share John's quarrel with recreational drugs, but I know what it means to carry a burden, so I lean my chest against my hands and put all I have into crushing his big frame. And to my astonishment, he goes right over. He topples to the floor, and I fall on top of him, knocking my face on his chin.

In an instant the addicts are on their feet. I'm a little stunned, and before I've even gathered my wits, Carlos is pulling me from John's chest. John says, "Sorry, man. Guess I wasn't prepared for that," and offers his hand. I take it, but I let the others help him to his feet. I'm feeling shaky. I turn aside and touch my cheekbone where I bumped it, and Paula tells us that though this wasn't the intended result, it's an analog for all the pressure we take on when we let an addiction rule our life.

We do the preposterous exercise again, and this time we don't fall down. John braces himself against my weight, and I try to look like I'm leaning more than I am. He chooses a busty redhead to portray family responsibilities, though his real wife's on the scrawny side, and the musclebound Raymond as the demands of his job. The alcoholic Mary Ellen is in here somewhere, and a few others, but I don't care how. I've got a sudden dull headache, and my cheek hurts where I bumped it, so I stand like a packhorse until the living sculpture's complete.

Paula asks the spectators to talk about what they observe. The observations are as fatuous as can be — the suit points out that Raymond and I are working in opposition — then we break up, stretching and shaking out our hands. John says, "Thanks again, man," and I gesture that it was nothing, but he looks sharp and adds, "You okay?" John's wife gets up and re-creates the sculpture from *her* point of view, but she selects different actors, and this time, fortunately, I'm not asked to participate.

At lunchtime, we head for a little lounge where box lunches are stacked beside a coffeemaker. Sylvia's mood has deteriorated, and she barely looks at me as we take our boxes to a back yard fenced off from the neighbors. Evidently, the addicts love to smoke, because there are sand-filled tubs beside the doorway and big ceramic ashtrays on each of the six picnic tables. All are filled with butts. I look out over the dappled lawn to where Carlos and Raymond are sitting under a big tree, and I expect Sylvia will want to join them, but she takes a seat at the first table, settling herself neatly, with her elbows tucked in. For a moment I remember how she was at sixteen, and I'd like to tell her her hair looks nice. But when I move the big ashtray she gives me a cross look. "I may need that," she says. I want to tell her to go take a flying fuck.

I eat in silence, barely glancing at her. Sylvia takes a bite of her sandwich and puts it down in disgust, then commences a lot of sighing and heaving to drive home her displeasure. I see Raymond return to the coffee room for a couple of Cokes, and as I watch him and Carlos chatting I realize that for some people today's a reunion. Sure, there's stuff to be worked out, but this isn't the day they'll decide whether they love each other. My head throbs, and I wish we were like that. I wish I could tell Sylvia that Ryan's just fine, and what a time we had at the fights! That he planted flowers and that I'll bring him soon for a visit, by hook or by crook. But today wasn't the day — she must understand that. I think how disappointed she must be not to see him, and I'm looking for a route out of our standoff when she waves dismissively at her lunch. "You want any of this?" she says, in a tone that implies only a real garbagehound could eat such crap, and again I feel like telling her to fuck off. I take her pretzels and turn away, and she says, "You've got something on your cheek." I ignore her, and perhaps she wishes I'd fuck off, too. We'd be stuck like this forever if John and his family did not suddenly appear at our table.

"So how's it going, guys?" John says. He squints crazily at me, and I realize I've got the sun at my back. "Having a good time?" *Oh, yeah.* As he digs into his sandwich, he adds, "Interesting place, isn't it?"

There are people who can only deal with a nonspeaker by asking questions. I get it: silence *isn't* golden, and for some people any dialogue's better than none. But the upshot is that John edits out everything interesting he might tell me, and I'm left responding to a bunch of yes-or-no's. So I agree that the clients are a pretty good crowd, and also that Paula really knows her stuff, and when he asks if I've ever been to a place like this before, I shake my head no. At this John tells me it's his third facility, but he feels three's a charm. This program is one he can really get his head around.

John's wife has a look of weary complacency and a smattering of acne across her chin. She's placed their baby in a basketlike carry thing, and as I watch her poke the child's pacifier into his soft little mouth I guess she's not a bad egg. John says, "So what line of work you in, Howard?" then instantly checks his blunder. And though I could answer by pointing at the big lawn and making a mowing gesture, he won't let me. "I'm a project manager over at GE," he blurts out, reddening. "Environmental management, pollutants. It's not as bad as it sounds." I nod, and Sylvia shoots us a look of disgust.

John's wife picks up the ball. "I understand you're looking after Sylvia's little boy." Nod. "How old?" I hold up nine fingers, and she squints in the sunshine. "You must be a wonderful friend," she says.

I shake my head. That has nothing to do with it. I pat my chest to show it's love more than charity, and I hope Sylvia sees this. Instead, she explodes. "Oh, what the hell?" she says shrilly. "What the *fuck* is the point?" John's wife stares at Sylvia, but I know this is just beginning. "You can't even tell me how my own *son* is!" she goes on. "You can't describe anything about what he's been doing or how his schoolwork's going, if he misses me, or — You *won't* learn to write or make even the slightest concession to what it's like to *communicate* with you, and you come out here with the idea that everyone is just gonna jump through hoops so *you* won't feel left out!" She glares at me, her lips pale. I get up.

"I mean, is it worth it, Howie? Is it *fun?*" She grimaces, baring her lower teeth. "Do you en*joy* making us talk to you in baby talk and play these stupid . . . these stupid guessing games? Do you think this is the way we ordinarily talk? We're not idiots here, Howie. Sure, we have problems, but at least we're capable of some intelligent give-and-ta—"

"Hey, I don't mind." John throws up his hands.

Sylvia glares at him. "Well, I do, John. The one thing I wanted from today was to see my little boy, and instead I've got *this* one just occupying space. The two of you trading *inanities* and —" She goes on, but I stop listening. I could kill her. My head's hot, and I'm churning with bile. I could fly across the table and break her into fragments with my bare hands and never look back. I feel like Nagy the bear. I lean down and take a swing at the box lunch, and it all flies off the table. My Coke spills across the concrete, and one of the sandwich papers is picked up by a breeze. Everyone's looking at us.

I step back into the sunlight, and John says, "Wait a minute." Sylvia's telling me what a sponge I am and how she's through feeling pity. I can't be bothered with this big pale fuck, but he says, "*Wait* a minute," and takes hold of my shirt. "You've got a real shiner coming. Did I do that?" His voice is helpless and dumb, and

I touch the spot where our faces collided. My cheekbone's sore, but that's nothing. *Nothing!* "You better put ice on that," John says.

I can barely move. I stand stock still, but I'm trembling, and whether people are staring or not, I feel a roaring descend. Across the lawn, the white sandwich wrapper blows into my field of vision and then out, and I think this day — this *month!* — has been disastrous. Even Sylvia's abrupt silence is no compensation. When she looks up in astonishment and murmurs, "Oh, Howie. Are you hurt?" I am *out* of there.

21

I STOP AT A 7-ELEVEN for a bag of ice, holding my head down so the cashier won't notice my eye. I keep a stash of rags behind the seat of my truck, but none of them is very clean, so I take off my madras shirt and make an ice pack, then I drive to a shaded corner of the parking lot and lie down in the bed of the truck with the ice on my face. Above me, the leaves of a maple branch look painted onto the blue sky. I doze off, and when I look again, the leaves have begun to sway slightly, as though a film is running in very slow motion, and the sky has turned the color of tin. Most of the ice in my little pack has melted, and I can feel trickles of wetness across my cheek and on my T-shirt. But for the moment I seem to have misplaced my headache, so I don't move. As a few little pebbles of rain tap the chassis, I indulge the fantasy that I can lie here forever, and the water will fill the bed of the truck. The rainwater will rise until it covers me, and still I'll lie here, my eyes closed. In the sky above my box, wind and darkness will lash out at daylight, but I'll ignore everything that goes on in the world. And maybe lightning will strike the maple tree, and . . .

I can't, of course. I have to pick up Ryan at five.

The rain passes over, only dampening my clothes. A little jigsaw of blue appears and gobbles up the metal clouds while I watch, and the maple leaves shake in a single spasm and then are still. I sit up and wring out my sport shirt, then look at my watch. I've an hour and a half before I'm due to pick up Ryan, and I have nothing whatsoever to fill the time. I stare at my hands for a while, trying not to think of Sylvia, then it occurs to me I can go over early and find out what Ryan's up to.

The elementary school looks abandoned, except for two girls playing cat's cradle on the sidewalk. I go inside and make a quick circuit of the shadowed halls, half expecting to see Ryan sitting out a detention. A custodian with a broom nods at me, then a woman's voice calls sharply, "Can I help you, sir?" and I skedaddle. I don't want her thinking I'm a pervert, and I've seen enough to know he's not here.

Outside, the cat's cradle girls are gone, and I stand by the truck, wondering where a nine-year-old goes on the sly. After a few minutes a boy appears, climbing a dirt mound across the oval parking lot. When he sees me he drops a cigarette in the dirt and hurries off.

I walk over and climb the mound. Behind it, a path leads under a festoon of grape vines, then through a small woods. Up ahead, I can hear high-pitched voices and the sound of a lawn mower starting and stopping. The path comes out behind a half-finished residential development, and though I don't leave the cover of the trees for the moment, I can see what's happening. Fifteen or twenty boys have made a civilization of the dusty clearing. For a moment I think of a song I once knew, about bears who set up a picnic in the woods, and then I remember the camp above the half-burned valley, where I spent sixteen days.

It's not a lawn mower the boys have, but a go-cart. They've commandeered an area adjacent to the construction and created a little driving course. The track starts on a flat, in the open area by the trees, and winds toward the nearest unfinished house before disappearing behind a gravel pile. It reappears on the far side of the clearing, where a half dozen cinder blocks have been set up, slalom-style, to create turns. There's a gully with four planks laid across it as a bridge, then a spot where a kid in a green shirt is holding something in his palm. Most of the boys look about twelve, and Ryan ought to be easy to spot, but I don't see him. In the center of the clearing, a few boys are dragging a piece of plywood toward a small mound of dirt, and nearby, a whole cluster of kids stands gathered around the go-cart. There's just too much bustle for me to pick out my guy.

I hear a pop as the motor starts, then it coughs and cuts off. The boys put their heads together. The motor starts and stops again. I watch them tinkering — it sounds like the plugs — and I'm tempted to go over and take a look, but the engine suddenly revs up with a blast. In a wave, the boys draw back, and the cart leaps onto the course with Ryan at the wheel. The vehicle's retreating from me, but I recognize his brown neck and close-cropped dark hair above the seat back. In his wake, a screen of dust.

Ryan's cautious at first, but he's a good little driver. I look over the milling crowd and guess the kid in green is holding a stopwatch, and though I'm not crazy about competitive times, so far I'm not worried. But when the cart moves behind the gravel pile, it doesn't reappear on the far side, as I expect. I hear the motor grinding, and it hits me that the cart's climbing the back of the pile. I cast an eye toward the plywood the boys were arranging. It's a jump, set to catch the momentum as the cart hurtles down the hill.

The landscape shifts. Everything's wrong, I can see now. The jump is too close to the gravel descent, and the angle's dangerously steep. Why, the plywood's not even square! One edge cuts in so raggedly that I doubt it will accommodate the cart's wide axles, and the boys have braced it with a flat stone in an attempt at a springboard. I glance at the packed ground where the cart will land, and my blood rises in a kind of floating nausea. Then the go-cart appears at the crest of the gravel pile, and the boys toss up a cheer.

I charge forward, out of the concealment of the trees. Ryan's not wearing a helmet, and the little jump is built for disaster. I picture the long scabs he had on his arm and leg, and all I can think of is

Rimet in the orange air. The years I paid for walking with the LT! I make a beeline for the gravel hill, and as the boys scatter I knock someone in the dirt. The cart speeds down the pile, and I see the kid's shock as I spread my arms; is this when I realize it's not even Ryan? Everyone's yelling, and I am, too — I'm bellowing out "Ha-oo!" with no sense of what I mean. Just as he's about to hit me, the kid turns on a dime, and the cart kicks up a cloud of dust. It narrowly misses a boy who's appeared out of nowhere, then spins once and goes up on two wheels, toppling over with a dull clunk.

I rush to see that the driver's okay. In fact, he's already climbing from his seat, coughing slightly as he moistens his lips. He looks nothing like Ryan. I bend down to offer a hand, and he stares as if I'm a monster in the yellow haze. I remember I have a black eye now, to go with my scar.

"Howie! What are you doing!" In an instant, Ryan's on me like a monkey, scrabbling at my shoulders and my T-shirt; as I stand up, he starts to fall. I catch him by one wrist and set him on his feet, and he flings himself at me, shouting, hitting my stomach with his fists, though he's so wild the blows barely connect. I put my hands up to ward him off, and at the same time I want to pull him to me. His face is red, and suddenly, after all these weeks, he might actually cry. Stepping back, he glares at me with bared teeth and takes a swing that doesn't come close. "What are you *do*ing here?" he cries shrilly, then turns and dashes toward the woods.

The other boys kick the dirt; despite my appearance, I'm still some kind of authority figure. I reach down and set the little cart on its four wheels, then I kick the plywood jump off its bearings. I give the whole crew a disgusted look. Ryan's Indians cap lies in the dirt at Greenshirt's feet; I pick it up and shake it at him, then turn and follow Ryan into the woods.

I find him on a log with his arms crossed, staring at his feet, and again I'm struck by his not having run far. I sit down and pat his knee, and he jerks his leg away, his heel catching my shin. Down the path, the go-cart coughs and starts up again.

I don't think Ryan meant to kick me, but I lift my leg and tap his shin in return. He moves his leg away. I lean down to look at his face, and I can see tear lines, like the tracks of snails, marking his dirty cheeks. I dust off his cap and place it on his head, then I run my hand over his narrow shoulder blades. He lets me do this, so I rub his neck, and when I rest my hand on the log behind him he's almost cradled in my arm. "What are you doing here?" he mumbles.

I scratch my forehead. What am I doing here? I've got no answer. What was I doing at Sylvia's dry-out place this morning, and what am I doing anywhere at all? I can't think when I spent a more complicated day, yet now, surprisingly, I don't feel so bad. I'm almost cheerful. For one thing, I'm giddy with relief at finding Ryan okay, at learning his truancies are no more than this. I think of what might have been going down, and my thoughts flood with sins I've not wanted to consider — petty theft, weird sex, *drugs* — then I put them from my mind. It seems remarkable that if I could speak I'd tell him he's too young to be taking a go-cart through a homemade obstacle course, while all the time thinking it's not such a big deal.

Ryan picks the bark from a section of log. I lean over to watch, and he tears off a strip and flicks it to the ground. Underneath, the wood is pitted with dark, tiny holes. A spider stretches its legs before moving out of view, and two gray, segmented creatures wander in circles, then move toward Ryan. He inches closer to me.

I watch him tear off three more inches of bark, and my heart goes out. I want so much for him, and I want his attention and admiration for myself. I want things to be easy and natural, and in the movie version of this scene I'd chuck him under the chin. Instead, I nudge him 'til he's leaning against me, and he permits this with a little resistance. I exhale loudly, and he says, "What'd she do, hit you in the face?"

It takes me a moment; then I laugh. Ryan gives me half a smile, as though I'm crazy but more or less interesting, and I shake my head to tell him *no*, his mother didn't hit me. I'll never manage the word *accident*, but I give it a shot and come up with "Hipshuh!" He looks uncomprehending.

There's a rustle on the path, and we look up. Three boys have stumbled upon us, and when the first stops abruptly they bump into each other like stooges. They eye us warily, and Ryan says, "You can walk here. We're not gonna hurt you." Once they're gone, we get up to leave, too. We walk silently to the parking lot, and I'm thinking I could make an interesting tale of my adventure at the rehab clinic if I could only tell it. But I can't, so we climb in the truck, and I'm turning the key when I have to say something. After the fiasco with Sylvia and the worries over Ryan's whereabouts, some stock should be taken. I can't just move on in silence.

I turn toward Ryan and point to the scar on my forehead. I run my finger along it, ducking my head so he can see how fat and spongy it is. If he wants to, he can touch it. He looks, but keeps his hands to himself. "You got that in a war, right?"

I nod, though in my sixteen days I saw precious little of battle. But what's important is I bumped my head and got injured, so I tap his chest, then throw my hands up and make the sound of an explosion. For a moment I'm floating, and I think of the palm trees and the passing rocks, of the bright blue sky filtered in orange dust. I knock my skull on the window panel behind my head, and it makes such a thud that Ryan and I both jump. I could be dead now — easily! — but I'm not; I'm only injured. My head's cracked open, and my fingers trace the blood rushing down my face. With my palm, I hold my brains in my skull. My eyes close very slowly, and when I come to, I clap my hand over my mouth. *That's how it happened, my friend.*

Ryan blinks at me. This is the most complicated thing I've tried to tell him, and I hope it transmits. It strikes me he may think it's cool to be a soldier, and though I'd love him to admire my guts and glory, that's not the point now. I gesture at the wooded path and move my hands like I'm driving the go-cart. I'm driving along when I fly out of control, then I'm crashing, I'm in the hands of fate! I wave my fists and hit the window again, then the blood, the skull, the hand holding brains. I raise my eyebrows: *wanna end up like me?*

I think Ryan gets it, or some of it, anyway. I shake my finger at him and pat my chest, then I put my hands on his head. How precious it is! Maybe this is too much, because he pulls away. He takes the four Radnor Tag Day cards from the dashboard and mashes their edges together, his brown knuckles whitening. "You worry too much," he says. "I know what I'm doing."

I consider this. Probably it's true. Perhaps he's old enough or skillful enough to fool with a go-cart, but he's dealing with me now, and I'm squeamish about injuries. I'm wondering how to convey this when Ryan blurts, "My mom would let me."

To show what I think of this suggestion, I say, "Pffft!"

The go-cart boys are reappearing over the mound of dirt, and I raise my hand to indicate how big they are. Why, the bastard in green will be shaving soon! He sighs, and I cross my arms and shake my head *no*. He's not to go there, and that's final.

Ryan says, "You think I'm a baby." I shake my head again. I don't, but I'm making decisions. He bends one card in half and stands it on the dashboard like an upturned V. "What am I supposed to do for fun?" he says. But hell: there are millions of ways to have fun. Once school gets out I'll take him swimming; I pantomime this. I look at the little bent card on the dashboard again and swing a bat. Or maybe he and I could take tennis lessons. As a teenager, I wasn't half bad. What else?

"I wanna go to Aqua Splash Down." It's a water park in the farmland. I've never been there, but the commercials feature bare, young flesh. "They have a pool with a simulated wave machine and a really big slide," Ryan says. I nod. We can do that. He gives a satisfied look, then asks, "Do you think Laurel would want to come along?" I'm not sure, but I nod again. In this way we have a conversation.

22

THEY'RE ALL HOME when we pull into the drive, drinking beer on the back stoop and playing a damn word game. As I turn off the engine I hear one of the boys say, "It was the best of times, but all unhappy families are unhappy in their own way." This is the last thing I need.

Ryan climbs from the truck and runs toward the stoop. He frisks across the green yard like a puppy, and Laurel calls out, "Hello there, happiness." But I take my time. The day's finally gotten to me, I guess; my head hurts, and I'm feeling my black eye. I'd sneak to my room, but they've already spotted me. Laurel gasps as I approach.

"So that's what she meant. Howard, are you all right?" I nod, flapping my damp shirt. "Do you need an ice pack?"

Nit says, "Hey, Howard, you run into a door?" *Yeah, moron, that's what I did.* Nat cuffs his head, and maybe Nit realizes this is his dumbest remark yet, because he adds, "How 'bout a beer?" and disappears into the house.

Laurel brushes a strand of hair from her eyes. "You okay?" she murmurs, and touches my arm. I nod. "She called — his mom. Left a message sometime this afternoon, I guess. She sounded pretty upset." She puts a hand to my forehead, then touches the skin beneath my eye, and I pull back. "Ooh . . . Well, that'll wait. Drink your beer first."

I sit on the step, and Nit brings a bottle of beer. Ryan's teasing Ruby with a stick, and Ruby's growling and wagging her fat finger of a tail. A breeze passes down all the back yards, touching each neighbor's trees in turn, and when it reaches us I see my catalpa shimmer. I watch Ryan and Ruby skittering around, then Ryan runs toward the little stable building. He scoops up an old catalpa pod and flings it over the stable roof, then circles the yard and makes another toss, then another and another. He has boundless energy.

Nit says, "Frankly, Ishmael, I don't give a damn," but no one answers. Let them have their silly game. I lean my head against the railing and close my eyes, and I might even doze off. I breathe deeply, as though I'm already asleep, and the last thing I hear is Laurel murmuring in low tones.

By the time I listen to Sylvia's message, the sun is setting, and the aimless sky is a hearty blue. I heave myself up and go inside, and the little alcove where my answering machine sits is in shadow. I hit an overhead light, and the stairwell pops in, hard and bright. A red number on the machine tells me there's one saved message, and the first thing I hear is Sylvia sniffling.

"Hi, Howie, are you there? If you are, please pick up. It's Syl." She sniffs again, then says, "Howie, I swear to God I didn't know you'd been hurt. If I had, I . . . This whole thing is really incredibly difficult for me, and I know you only came down to give me moral support, but I was just so — *crest*fallen — at not seeing Ryan there, not seeing my sweet baby boy that I — just, I . . . I'm going to have to be here a little longer than I originally thought, and I feel really —" She breaks off and blows her nose, and I picture the neat way she does it, folding the Kleenex in half, then folding it again and again. Then she collects herself, taking a deep breath and swallowing loudly, and I suppose she knows I'm imagining her doing this. "You've always been there for me, Howie. You always have, and you know I love you for that, because frankly, no one in my whole life has been nearly as — has been as supportive or consistent. But I don't think even you or anyone else realizes what I'm going through, and just how hard it is. The shock of suddenly having your *whole life* taken away. All your support! To lose your home, your child, your job. To be stripped, *stripped* of everything that makes you feel like . . ."

Sylvia goes on, telling me all the things I can't possibly know. I'm feeling drained now, and I'd forget the world, but Sylvia keeps speaking: high, rambling, full of sniffles. A door slams, and I hope it's not Ryan, but of course it is. He comes in carrying the dog, but when he hears his mother's voice he sets Ruby down, then stands in front of me, leaning on my stomach. I put my hands on his shoulders. At least Sylvia's stopped talking about how rough it is for her; now she's asking me to give Ryan a kiss. Ryan tilts his head back and looks up at me, and I look down and raise my eyebrows. I can feel the soft bristle of his hair through my shirt. His mother says, "Don't forget, now, Howie, that I love him very, very much, that he's my precious boy, and that I'm doing all this just so the two of us can have a better —" Then I reach out and turn off the tape.

II

23

I WAKE UP EARLY and do something I almost never do: stay in bed for a while. These days I'm busy the moment my eyes are open, but today I just sit up and look at the half-lit world. Outside, dawn has broken, and the crown of the catalpa is a grayish softness. On the next street over, rooflines are emerging. The house behind us has a turret room just like ours, and as I blink out at the morning its metal weather vane flashes like a struck match.

I look around my room. It's a nice room, with two tall west-facing windows, and it's been mine since the day the folks and I moved in, though it no longer seems like any boy ever lived here. Gone are the psychedelic posters I put up in high school, gone are the yearbooks and Rat Fink statuettes, the troll-doll bong, the concert memorabilia and other teen doodads. Gone is the glass terrarium where Dakota, a rose-patterned corn snake, lived from my tenth birthday until sometime in my twenties; gone is the autographed photo of the Milwaukee Braves. But not everything has been tossed out. My old clarinet is somewhere in the attic, I know, along with two or three military souvenirs I don't ever want to see again and a carton of report cards and school photos and childhood drawings, all carefully boxed up by my mom. She packed away stuff from her own childhood and my dad's, too, and as I sit watching the catalpa molt slowly to green, I wonder whom she thought I'd be leaving our possessions *to*.

We got this place for a song, and though for years restoration was my folks' main preoccupation, I was permitted to do what I wanted with this room. My father's mother gave me a great big oak dresser that had belonged to her uncle, and over the years I gradually ruined it by covering it with STP stickers and Day-Glo peace symbols; then I started to strip off the dark finish and never completed the job. When I first came home and was convalescing, I'd sit in my chair and gaze at the half-naked side of that dresser and vow that once I was recovered I'd knock out the refinishing job. That would be the beginning of my brand-new life. These are the vows you make when you're incapacitated, no matter how sentimental they seem later. Now I recall how I threw all that old stuff away. I balled up the posters and drove the half-stripped dresser to a construction site, where I heaved it into a Dumpster with all my might. It was Mom and me then, and after my dad's death I'd withdrawn from the low life and started at the convent. I threw out almost everything I owned and painted this room white.

I hear a door creak, and Laurel pads to the bathroom, followed by the click-click-click of Ruby's nails. I close my eyes — ten more minutes — and when I open them again, the day has arrived at a full-tilt summer greenness, and the sky is blue. Across the room, there's now a shorter chest I picked up at a furniture-in-the-raw place, with a couple of photos on it. The largest is my parents' wedding picture, and beside it stands a snapshot of Sylvia, taken my senior year. Someone — a girl I've cut from the frame — has her arm over Sylvia's shoulder, and Syl is turning as I snap the shot. She's smiling with her mouth open, showing her tongue. Sylvia always said the photo didn't look like her, and though I carried her yearbook photo into the jungle, I prefer this one for the warm trust of her expression and for something familiar, a look at once distant and contented, that exists now only in photos.

I look at the other picture, the wedding shot. For years, people told me I resembled my dad, despite my mother's bulkier build, and this picture shows him at the age I was when I came home injured. He's all dressed up in a tuxedo, not at all how I remember him at the end: knotted and gnarled with an old man's irritations, drunkenly carping about the *system* and the *government*, by which he meant what happened to me. In the photo he looks as he must have felt on that long-ago day, as if he was accomplishing something. I wonder briefly what a wedding day would be like.

I get out of bed. Yesterday in the parking lot I had an idea, and suddenly I want to put these photos behind me. I'll move ahead. The floor is smooth and cool to my bare feet, and when I toss my T-shirt at the laundry hamper, it drops in neatly. Laurel's in the hallway, dressed in a white kimono, a pale pink towel cocooning her hair. "Morning, Howard," she murmurs, and I give her a smile. In the bathroom I see my eye has grown yellower and greener overnight.

24

Downstairs, life is good. Laurel has the door open, and the birds are making a racket in the yard. Puff, the neighbors' old cat, has wandered over to stare at Ruby through the screen door, and between the dog, the cat, and the birds it seems we've got the Peaceable Kingdom happening here.

Laurel's making borscht. She grins, brandishing her beet-stained hands, and on impulse I catch her wrists and press her palms to my face. "Howard, no! Oh, now look at you! That'll look just like a strawberry mark!" She wets a paper towel and dabs the pink from my cheeks, and as she does so she adds, "Eye looks a bit darker today. How's it feel?" In her Texas accent, *Hah's it fee-ul.*

Nat comes in and turns on the radio, and though this shatters the serenity, I roll with the punches. The song that's on is "Bad to the Bone," and Nat's strumming air guitar when Ryan comes in doing exactly the same thing: same sucked-in abdomen, same low-down, punchy look. Nat makes a little leap, and the two face off in the small space of the kitchen, hunched and glowering like bad things on a stage. Laurel says, "Crazy guys."

When the song ends, Nat swats the old Indians cap with his fingertips. "Come on now, buddy," he says. "Help me set the table. You need to pitch in around here." He peers at my batter and the lightly steaming waffle iron, then puts a hand on my shoulder. "Howard, ya grizzly bear. You hold us together, you know that?" He freezes, as though he doesn't know where to go from there, and I drop a spoon in the batter. "Let's see that shiner." I turn and permit him to squint at my face, and he says, "Still hurt some?" I shrug. *Not bad.* "Well, you look pretty tough. Just say you fucked the other guy up worse."

Laurel says, *"Harrison!"* but whether she's scolding him for his language or the idea of me speaking, I'm not sure.

Nat says, "Am I right, Ry-Ry?"

"Fucked him up *lots* worse," he says. Laurel glares at all of us.

Nat says, "Well, you're the still water that runs deep, Howard, and you deserve a medal." Then Nit comes in, wearing a T-shirt and boxers, and Nat steps off quickly, slapping my ass.

At the convent, Robin and Sister Amity ask about my eye, but it's a lot to explain. I spend the morning alone on the John Deere, and I don't see a soul until I go to the kitchen for my lunch. Sister Margaret turns from the stove and lets out a gasp, then brings me a piece of steak for my face, which is something I thought they did only in movies. I lie there thinking of Nagy the bear, and it's good to be treated for an ordinary injury instead of my usual extraordinary one.

At two-thirty I drive to Ryan's school. The yellow buses park around me, and when the bell sounds, I take the folded Radnor Little League tag from the dashboard and stow it in my overalls. Ryan glances toward the go-cart track as his class streams from the building, but he ambles over and climbs in the truck. "How's the eye?" he asks. I nod. He turns on the radio and sings while I drive, and when we pass a yard where three dogs are frolicking and biting each other's necks, it seems everything in the universe holds its own unique interest. Ryan says, "School gets out next week," and I grin at him. I recall Sylvia saying she's staying in rehab longer than expected, and I think *summer!* When did I stop assuming she'd be home any day?

Ryan sits up when I turn into the Radnor neighborhood. When

I was a boy, Radnor was the newer enclave of square, sturdy homes that bordered our Victorian section, but it's been years since I visited, and everything's different. Saplings planted in my youth now buckle the sidewalks, and the once-new houses have been renovated or refurbished or have simply grown old. I used to pal around with a boy named Timmy who lived right next to the elementary school, and one Halloween we made robot costumes from appliance boxes. That was when robots still looked like boxes, and it was my last childhood Halloween. Timmy and I stayed friends through junior high; then we went off to rival high schools, and I met Sylvia. By the time he was drafted we'd stopped running into each other, but once I knew I was headed there, too, I was sure I'd encounter him sooner or later. Of course, I got injured instead. Still, as Ryan and I draw closer to Radnor Elementary I wonder what became of old Timmy, and I think I ought to stop in — not today, but sometime — because you can't go through life with no associates.

Then we turn the corner, and Timmy's house is gone. My old school has gotten so huge that it's gobbled up everything in its realm, and where his small home once stood there's now a windowless block. Big modern classroom wings spread out left and right, but the pedimented entrance I knew is still tucked at the center, like a little old lady flanked by linebackers.

The mahogany doors of my childhood are padlocked, and a nearby entrance leads us to a dim atrium. I'm a little disoriented until I see something I know. Tucked in a corner is an ancient display unit, its glass shelves lined with taxidermed songbirds carefully posed on genuine twig perches. The birds are old now, their hand-inked identification tags faded and yellow, and their dust-covered plumage looks decidedly moth-eaten, but for a moment I remember a long-ago school assembly at which a white-haired ornithologist offered her life's work to the generations of the future. Then Ryan says, "Gross," and we proceed.

Two women are in the school office, a skinny one behind a desk and a fat one standing by a file cabinet. I take the square Radnor

Little League tag from my overalls and unfold it on the counter, and suddenly it's easy to get out one of my cards, too, stating I'm of normal intelligence. The fat lady reads both cards, then glances at my face. She checks out my scar, blushes, and looks away, turns back with an "Oh," and looks away again. I wait. I lay my hands flat on the counter, and when she looks a third time I raise my eyebrows. She says, "Let me see," then turns to her skinny colleague. "Callie, who do they talk to about the Little League?"

Ryan's been standing by a long bulletin board, pulling staples from the cork and dropping them on the floor, but at this he turns and looks at me, his mouth open. And I get the same charge I got taking him to the boxing match. I'm onto something, so I nod. *Good idea, huh?* He says nothing, but comes and stands at my side, resting his forearms on the countertop. The women tête-à-tête at the desk, and at last Callie stands and approaches. "I believe those teams are pretty well filled. Registration was back in March," she says.

My heart sinks. Ryan's body stiffens at my side, and I can't look down. Instead, I run my fingers over my close-cropped hair, and at the touch of my hand I remember that along with my scar I've got the black eye, too. I don't know why this is worse than ordinary disappointments, but as the day's good spirits crash away Sylvia's berations flood over me, and I know she's right. I *haven't* tried hard enough to be independent, and if I'd worked more at speech and writing I might not be standing here like a goon. I think of Caroline — how right *she* was in wanting Ryan elsewhere! What's the point of dragging him from the sociable go-cart scene if all I can offer are missed opportunities?

I draw my brows together and scowl at the wall. I could easily begin flailing, and I'd end by demolishing everything in sight, from the file cabinets to the glass case of little birds to the fat and thin women themselves. I'd reduce the whole universe to rubble and bone. There's a stereotype here — the flipped-out vet — and I don't know why I've resisted it so long. A frustrated, fucked-up, scarred-up crazy man is dying in this office; why pretend that's not so? I reach out to scoop up the two little cards, and my hand hits the counter with such a thud that we all jump.

Ryan glances at me, then says, "That's cool." His voice is deliberate and uninflected, and I wonder if he's come to his mom's aid this same way. "Sorry for taking up your-all's time." He rubs a shoulder into my gut. "Come on, man."

Callie bites her lip. "There is one possibility . . ." She turns to the fat lady. "June, what was that —"

"Naw," says Ryan. "We probably have a conflict with scheduling, anyway. Thanks for your —" He gives my overall bib a tug. "Come *on*." The two women look severely at him.

"Just a moment, young man." They turn to me. "There's some folks starting up another team," says Callie. "Do you know Mister Luster Kleen?" She's enunciating carefully, and I could scream with annoyance. "We're not supposed to promote it because they're not yet *in* the league, but you might call over there and inquire. Mister Luster Kleen. I believe it's on Healy Boulevard. It's a" — she mimes a vacuum cleaner — "a carpet cleaning service, but he's putting a lot of effort into starting a kids' team. Good luck to you."

The other woman, June, has written something on a quarter-sheet of scrap paper. "You can get the number from directory information," she says, though as I reach for the paper she reddens again. "Or your phone book, or . . ." She looks helpless for a moment, then says, "Would you like me to place the call?" I'm still roiled, and who knows what my face looks like. "Why don't I do that."

Ryan whispers, "Hey," and tugs at my bib. "Lookit, I gotta tell you something. I ain't got a glove." I put a hand on his shoulder. *A little air.* I focus on June, punching the phone buttons with a pencil eraser.

"Yes, hello," she says. "I'm interested in baseball for youngsters? Was there a team forming? The *Snakes?* I've got a gentleman here, came in with his son . . ." She glances doubtfully at us, and I squeeze Ryan's shoulder. June says, "What's your age, young man?"

"Nine and a half."

"He's nine years old." She talks some more, then says, "Why don't I put the young man on, let him give you his data. No, no, the boy. He can speak for himself, I think that's —" She beckons to Ryan, then gives me a giant smile. "You're all set." Behind her, Callie's grinning, too, and I guess they think they've done their good deed.

I use the drive home to gather my thoughts. The disintegration of my good spirits has rattled me, and as always when I lose my cool, the line between hope and hopelessness has become pretty arbitrary. Somewhere, in the middle of my head, lies a decorated theater scrim, complete with corny sun and unconvincing sky, and on it is scribbled my standing figure. And for a moment a second me — truer, *uglier,* threatening but seductive — crept forward from behind that veil. It's a little like being high, when the temptations of control and out-of-control, of good news, bad news, rage, and retreat would leave me feeling profoundly unmoored. Perhaps Ryan could nudge me back with some interest in this baseball team, but he doesn't mention it. Instead, he asks if that was my old school, and I nod. Then he asks if they have a swimming pool inside. I'm not feeling communicative, so we listen to the radio until we're almost home. Then Ryan tells me he has a report due on Jimmy Carter. "Our class did all the presidents," he announces suddenly. "It took like the whole year. Ms. Monetti divided them between everybody in the class, and I got to do Thomas Jefferson, Rutherford B. Hayes, Theodore Roosevelt, and Jimmy Carter. Carter's all I have left before school gets out for summer. Then I'm done, man. *Hasta la vista,* grade four! Are you coming to our end-of-the-year concert? Then you could see me be all four of my presidents."

A concert? This is the first I've heard, but it does the trick. I give him a smile as I hop from the cab. *You bet your life I'm coming!*

25

THE PERFORMANCE IS MONDAY at noon, so I spend the morning weeding. Then I put my tools away. I change out of my overalls in the garden shed, and on my way to my truck I stop by the kitchen so Sister Margaret won't make me lunch. "Why, Howard," she says, "you're all spiffed up." Alain, the nun's bus driver, asks in his French accent if I'm seeing a woo-man, and I'm glad my black eye has begun to fade. It's now just an ochre shadow over my cheekbone.

The elementary school parking lot is nearly full, and parents are drifting toward the entrance. I park my truck on the periphery and get out, and then, to my astonishment, Nit and Nat's old clunker of a van comes careening out of nowhere. Nit pulls up beside me, and Nat leans across him to slap my palm. "Heyyy!" he shouts over the blaring radio. "The troops are marshaling! Von Ryan's Express, bay-bee!" They clamber out, still in their paint-splattered white pants and tractor caps, but maybe it doesn't matter what they have on. The guy ahead of us has a yellow hard hat under one arm and a video camera under the other.

We go into a big gym with a curtained stage and rows of folding chairs, and ten minutes later the thing begins. I'm surprised it's not all somehow very high-tech, but except for the whirring of a hundred video cameras, this is just like the school programs we had in my day. The principal offers a greeting, and the choir troops out and sings a welcome song. And suddenly there's our guy, halfway up the risers! I didn't know he sang in the choir, but when the group performs a medley from *The Lion King*, I realize he's been humming these tunes for weeks.

A couple of kids have solos, and a bespectacled boy toots on a clarinet. Ryan doesn't do anything standoutish, but he remains tall in his spot, looking surprisingly darling in the short blue surplice the choir members wear. He's easy to pick out because there aren't many brown faces on the risers, and he opens his mouth very wide as he sings. Then his class performs a presidential pageant, each child appearing and speaking a few lines. Ryan comes out third, as Jefferson, with a white cotton periwig flat on his head. I wonder if he's self-conscious, playing a slave owner — or maybe he's just a natural performer — because he adopts the little gangsta swagger he used at the Andee Barber School. He looks hilarious, shambling along in the flat wig and long, teal basketball shorts, and when he reappears as Rutherford B. Hayes, the boys let fly with a clamor of whistles. For a moment, Ryan stares out at the audience. Then he grins and waves a big yellow cardboard circle which represents — as he announces when the cheers die down — the gold standard. After this, every kid gets his share of applause, and when our boy comes out again as Roosevelt and finally as Carter, holding a cutout peanut, we take the roof off. There's a band performance and presentations from other classes, and I recognize Fartin' Martin when he talks about penguins, which he pronounces *ping-wins*. But I don't give a rat's ass about any kid but ours, and I don't pay much attention.

The program's almost over when I spot Laurel slipping down a side aisle. "Lunch deliveries," she hisses. "I miss much?" In fact, she's missed practically everything Ryan did, but at least she sees him in the finale, when the choir sings "In the Summertime," which was popular in my army days. The tune has a trudging jauntiness even the sweet, high voices of children can't perk up, and for a moment I'm reminded of the mixed excitement and limited prospects of a weekend pass. Then the event's over.

We shuffle with the other parents to the lobby. Ryan's at the end of a hallway, tugging at some girl's choir thingie, and she's squealing, "Cut it *out!*" as she lets the robe bell out and brush his hands. Laurel nudges me with her elbow.

Then Nit's charging down the hall, arms pumping. He goes down on his knees and slides into Ryan, grabbing him from behind, and Ryan topples against his chest. "Got you now, rascal varmint!" he cries, and wraps his arms around Ryan's thin body.

The girl says, "So there!" and turns on her heel. Ryan gives Nit a push, but Nit's so dumb he doesn't realize he's out of line. He rubs Ryan's fuzzy head, free, for once, of the old Indians cap, and Ryan extricates himself and stomps down the hall. Then Laurel gives a long, low whistle, and he turns and spots us, the three presentables.

"You made it!"

Laurel says, "Wouldn't miss it for the world." He gives her a hug and shakes hands with Nat and me. His bare legs hang out from beneath the short robe, and if I could, I'd say he looks like a flasher. Laurel says, "You were sure great!"

Ryan nods contemplatively. "Wanna meet my teacher?"

We follow him to a classroom filled with pint-sized desks and construction-paper projects. Other families are hanging around, but only Ryan has an entourage of four. "So this is the cheering section," the teacher says as he drags us forward. "We give detentions for that kind of rowdiness." She smiles dryly but makes no mention of our standing in for Sylvia. Of course she must know the score. "Logan Monetti, fourth grade," she says, and shakes hands all around.

I'd pictured a spinster with a pencil in her bun, and perhaps I'd be more comfortable with someone like that. But Ms. Monetti's pretty, with a wild mass of thick, chestnut hair, and I suddenly remember Ryan's calling her a fox. It takes only an instant for Nit and Nat to shift into dude mode, and Ms. Monetti laughs gaily at a riff about gym class. Then Nat mentions the summertime song, and she rolls her eyes. "*Bob*, our new music guy. Bit of a dink." She gives him a sly look and shifts her weight, and the conversation moves to topics other than school.

I wander out to the corridor. I was here last week, when I came looking for Ryan, but the place is different with people around. Now kids bustle about, dragging parents from room to room, carrying shoe-box dioramas to the parking lot. Two moms are packing up choir robes, and I realize that for them, today is simply the stuff of life. They'll have other assemblies, plenty of chances for volunteering, perhaps even more children. But for me this day is unlikely to repeat. At some point, Ryan will go back to Sylvia, and if I come here again, I'll be a hanger-on. I feel a spasm of irritation at Laurel and the housemates — after all, *I'm* the child's guardian — but attention from the mop-headed Ms. Monetti is not what I crave. What I'm feeling is more like panic at how soon this will end, before Ryan has even sung a solo. Only last week I rejoiced at the thought of moving through summer together; now it's shocking to learn what's gone in an hour. By the time school starts again, Ryan will be home for good, and I'll have resumed a life so bland I barely remember how I spent my days. No doubt I'll continue that life until my time runs out. I feel so rushed.

I go looking for a drinking fountain and come across three boys roughhousing outside the john. One of them is Fartin' Martin. The other two have him backed in a corner, and they're poking him with wooden drumsticks and saying "*Ping*-wins, *ping*-wins" in squeaky voices, just like his. I put a heavy hand on one boy's shoulder, and he looks up in astonishment. I point to my scar and make one of my sounds, and the boy jumps back.

The other kid doesn't realize the law has arrived. I snatch his drumsticks, and the first boy says, "Hey!" Then no one moves. Fartin' Martin looks like he wonders where I come from when I do these things, but I've *never* liked bullying, and my gloomy feelings give me something to fight about. I reach for Fartin' Martin, who shrinks back, hugging his chest — but all I want is to get him out of the corner. Then Ryan's tripping on my heels.

Ryan still has on his choir surplice, but he's added the inevitable

Indians cap. He looks at the kid on my right and says, "Get out of here, boner face," then gives him a shove. The boy skitters toward the lavatory and hits the swinging door with a clunk. He's an ugly child, with wet lips and short, dark hair and a built-in mean look, and I doubt Ryan would be taking him on if I weren't standing here. But I *am* here, and with this we win the fight. The kid by the door pushes into the bathroom as the other steps toward the corridor, then they turn like chuckleheads and bump into each other, back up, and slink away. I smack one on the butt with his drumsticks as they pass, and when they're halfway down the corridor, Ryan yells, "*Yeah! We the enforcer, boy!*" Fartin' Martin raises a hand for a high five, and Ryan slaps it lackadaisically. I wonder if Fartin' Martin will high-five me, but he looks around furtively, then he's gone, too.

Ryan grins. "That was fun." He seems to think we're Batman and Robin. Well, we are. I nod, tapping the bill of his cap, and he says, "How'd you like my teacher?" I nod again, though I have mixed feelings about hip young things.

Ryan nods, too. "She's pretty." He sounds satisfied. "So what do you wanna do now?"

I shrug. I hadn't thought about it. I'd expected him to return to class once the concert ended, but it's clear there'll be no more teaching today. The hallways are emptying out, and buses are picking up kids who didn't leave with their folks. Ryan says, "So, ya wanna split? I mean, I'm done."

We turn again down the cool, dark hallway, but at the door to the classroom we falter. The other families have gone, and our group and Ryan's teacher are the only ones left. Laurel's folded herself into a little green chair and the boys are on desks, but the teacher leans against the windowsill, one hand buried in her clump of chestnut hair. For an instant her eyes flick to the doorway, but she offers no acknowledgment. In her cool gaze there's only a look of appraisal. And though she still smiles that sly smile, suddenly it's impossible for me to enter that room. The four attractive young people, bound by their ordinary educations and easy, inconsequential body language, form a band that's impervious to invasion. I don't even try. Ryan murmurs, "You could like show me where you work," and moves from the door.

At this, I feel like racing him to the truck. I want to vamoose before he rejoins that other society, to participate in the gossip and the cracking of jokes. In the parking lot, Ryan pauses by Nit and Nat's white van. "Hey, look," he says, and prints WASH ME on the side panel with his finger. He's still wearing the pale blue robe, though he was certainly expected to turn it in, and I reach for the fabric and rub it with my fingers. He says doubtfully, "Think I could keep it?" *Why the hell not?* I stole the ugly kid's drumsticks. I open the door of my truck, and Ryan rolls down the window. As we leave the elementary school behind us, he's experimenting with the wind billowing at his sleeve.

26

IN THE GARDEN SHED, I change back into my work clothes, making a small square pile of my better shoes, my shirt, and my slacks. When I'm down to my socks and undershorts I catch Ryan eyeing me covertly. It strikes me that a grown-up body's probably an interesting phenomenon to a boy, so I stand there a minute, turning the T-shirt inside out. I don't meet his gaze, but I let him look. It's been a long time since anyone looked closely at me.

At last, I arch my back and pound my chest, Tarzan style, and give a Tarzan yell. It's not so different from my other sounds, but it's loud and echoey in the little wood shed. Ryan says, "You're crazy," and I wink at him as I pull on my overalls. When I'm all covered up, I give the nape of his neck a rub, then tug at the blue choir gown, and he says, "Oh, yeah," and pulls it over his head. I fold it and add it to my stack of clothes. We open the two shed doors, and sunshine streams over the shovels and cultivators and bags of grass seed, the garden stakes and the spare hose coiled on the wall and the little red push jobbie and the big green-and-yellow John Deere mower.

The John Deere's a pretty thing. Nothing but the best for these nuns. Up top there's only the single seat, but it's built wide for all size asses, so I climb on and give Ryan my hand. He settles between my thighs with his hands on the wheel. I reach down to turn the key, and he gives the horn a couple of beeps. He looks up and grins toothily.

A lawn mower's a slow ride, but he seems to like it. His back rumbles as he leans against me, and I realize he's making motor sounds to accompany the tractor noise. He's like a little kid. We chug past the Contemplation Garden and pick up the Long Field, then stop at a stand of immature firs. Some of the trees have gone brown on top, so I stop the mower and grab a pair of loppers from under the seat. I top one tree, then scoop up the clipped bough and examine it for signs of a borer. I show Ryan the brown hole. I cut a little more from the tree, going down to the green, and this time it looks like we got the bastard. I point — *see? No hole* — and Ryan nods. At the next tree I hand him the loppers and lift him high so he can reach, and moving from tree to tree, we clip off the brown. He scampers around, checking that the stems are clean of bores, and when we get back on the mower I let him steer.

An hour passes. Alain arrives and discharges a covey of nuns, and a little while later a FedEx truck arrives. Ryan and I share a bottle of water from the toolbox, then finish the open land and turn to a grove of birches. The trees here are tight together, and after he takes one a little close, I resume steering. I've just about decided to call it a day when we emerge from the grove, and there's the ha-ha.

I hadn't planned on taking him over the ha-ha. Threading the mower among the birches, I was wondering what was on TV and thinking of what I'd make for supper. But when the green slope rises like a wave before us, with four little pearly clouds above, I desperately want to give him the full ride. I want him to feel how we seem to lift, while the cars pass earthbound down below, and I put an arm tight around his tummy.

We trundle forward, Ryan making his putt-putt noises, and when we get to the berm, the mower tips. A moment later, the trench falls open at our side. Ryan lets out a cry and reaches for the wheel, but I pull his hands away. *It's okay, it's okay!* He struggles, and I hold him tighter; if you fall down to where the blades are, that's some *real* danger, but up here with me he'll be perfectly fine. And I want him to feel the fun, so I let out a whoop. This is better than any go-cart; it's euphoria, it's weightlessness, and if Ryan relaxed, he'd feel it, too. *Look up at the sky*, I want to say! *This is wild!* But he's clutching at me, grabbing my shirt, and now there's a sting as he rips out some chest hairs. I've got my arm around him, and I give him a nuzzle to say *easy*, but he grips an overall strap, then he's kicking, thrashing in all directions as I steer. We pass the high point, and I turn down. *Shh! It's over now!* I expect him to calm down, but he knocks my leg aside in his struggle. "How*ie!*" he shrieks, and breaks my hold. Then he steps back and falls from the mower.

It's the incline that saves him. In slipping from the vehicle, he tumbles away, out of the path of the blades. And of course, I cut the motor immediately. I leap down to where he's landed and place a trembling hand on the mound of his small chest, and though he's had the wind knocked out of him, I think he's okay. I still think that little journey is the best I can show him, but my heart pounds as he gasps for breath. Then Sister Amity's barreling across the lawn, her skirt held high. She bellows my name and charges toward me, and I get up, still light-headed. I spread my hands to explain no one's injured, but as soon as she gets to me she slaps me hard across the face. She utters a choked, throaty noise, like crushed gravel.

Sister Amity's strong, and the slap hurts. I step back and see her bared teeth and the blur of sweat on her lip. For a moment she can't speak, and she glances at Ryan, now watching with a stunned expression, but she glares at me. "What on — Howard!" she gasps. I bet she'd love to hit me some more. But Ryan's fine! It was all just a bit of fun, and I'm shrugging my shoulders when she explodes. "With a *child!* Who could be *hurt!* And we've been through this over and over, Howard! Our grounds are not your . . . *Not* your playground. You *work* here, you understand? You work for *me*. And you'll do as you're told, or you'll — Irregardless of *what* happened to you overseas, Howard, nothing excuses such plain stupidit— stupid, *foolish* behavior, which I've told you again and again and . . ."

She breaks off, tears glittering on her short lashes, and grips the hems of her sleeves in her fingertips. Again I have the sense she'd do better with her fists, but she goes on more primly. "As your supervisor I'm telling you *I* make the rules here. You can't seem to credit that." She quivers defiantly and turns to Ryan. "Little boy, are you hurt?"

Ryan shakes his head. He sits up, eyeing her warily, as if no one ever told him there were nuns here; and maybe no one did. I put a hand on his shoulder and speak as carefully as I can. "Hai-*wen*," I tell Sister Amity. "Hai, Hai. Hai-Wen." It's as close as I've gotten to saying his name. Then I lose that, too.

Sister Amity ignores me. "That was a *very* irresponsible thing for Mr. Kapostash to do," she announces. "He ought to be ashamed of himself. Where are your parents?" Ryan shrugs, and Sister Amity stares beadily at him. She wipes her face with her sleeve, then smiles unconvincingly. "Would you like me to contact your mother and dad?"

Ryan mumbles something, but I turn away. I'm feeling much less frisky, and I stare at the green ha-ha, where the four pearl clouds have now dispersed. Sister Amity says, "Hmm?" and when I turn back, Ryan's put on his skeptical face.

At last he looks at his shoes. "I liked it," he says, speaking barely above a whisper. Sister Amity leans closer, and he raises his voice. "That was fun!" he announces defiantly. Without a glance at me, he throws back his head and cries, "It was *bad*! We went *right* to the edge! It was *cool*! Ha! Ha! Ha!" He takes off the Indians cap and tosses it in the air, and it lands behind us.

Sister Amity says, "Howard, who is this child?" She seems to expect an answer, so I pat my heart. She gives an irritated look. "Put the mower away, please." I climb aboard, but as Ryan steps forward, Sister Amity grabs his arm. "I don't want you on that machine." Ryan's eyes bug out, but Sister Amity says, "Howard, we'll meet you there," and I can only drive off. I put the mower away, then close the big doors and stand by the shed. I'm holding the stack of our clothing in my hands, and I can see the two figures crossing the mown field. Sister Amity tromps along in her customary athletic fashion, but when she offers a hand, Ryan pretends not to notice. A moment later the hand is withdrawn.

When they're not far away, I step forward to meet them. She's right, of course. He's a little child and could so easily get hurt. I drop to my knees and put out my arms, and the square pile of clothing topples to the grass. Ryan continues toward me, step by step, but when he reaches me, he doesn't hug me. He slaps my palm, then pulls the choir robe on over his head. I gather my own clothes, and we head back to the truck, three individuals spaced out in a small line.

"Howard —" Sister Amity lowers her voice. "Howard, Ryan and I have had a little discussion. I think it's fine what you're doing. Very kind and very —" She breaks off meaningfully. "Nevertheless, I'm truly provoked by what occurred here today, and you put *all* of us — why, what kind of lawsuit would this institution face if someone should get hurt? So I need to reach a decision, and I think you, too, should consider the example you set. Especially for a child." She shoots me a hard look, but now I've had it. She's got some nerve, treating me like a schoolboy.

It *is* fine what I'm doing — it's fine and admirable and more generous than anything I've attempted before — and the wiry bitch slapped me! I give a *pfft* of contempt at her lack of contrition and remember how much fun we were having. How Ryan helped with the borers and steered the mower, how he *asked* to come and see where I work. Why, without Sister Amity's interference, we'd have put this behind us already!

"Come and see me once you've given it some thought," Sister Amity says. "I think at least a week. I'm sorry to say it, Howard, but if you can't grant me my authority, then perhaps this isn't the convent for you. You may simply need to find another place to work. But let's communicate once we've both cooled down, and we'll decide if, and under what circumstances, you may return."

This I don't dignify with acknowledgment. I step off, putting Ryan between us, and the three of us march in silence to the truck. Sister Amity opens the passenger door and gives Ryan one of her awful grins, and he picks up the ugly kid's drumsticks and beats furiously on the dashboard. She and I exchange last glares before I pull out.

27

BEYOND THE CONVENT GROUNDS, traffic is slow, as if every car and truck's united in a private underwater ballet. I've no patience for this, and I join in like an interloper, switching lanes, tapping the horn. If I could shout curses I'd do that. Jerking my way through the clogged intersections, I replay my grievances. Getting slapped; getting slapped in front of Ryan; having my livelihood toyed with and my fitness questioned and a simple tumble blown out of proportion. I think it will be a cold day in hell before I return for Sister Amity's verdict, and I give the finger to a teenager in an Audi. Then there's a crack as Ryan snaps one of Little Uglyfuck's drumsticks. He mumbles, "Sorry."

I stop at a red light. Ryan's picking splinters from the pleats of the choir robe, but he looks up, and I do my best: a miserable smile. He stares back noncommittally. Now that it's just us, his team spirit's evaporated, and as I recognize that old defensiveness I'm filled with remorse. Bloodshed, broken bones, a mangled hand, a severed foot: these are the disasters I haven't wanted to consider. If I could get out of this traffic I'd pull to the curb and apologize for having frightened him, and I'd tell him I'm sorry things turned out as they did. I wish he'd enjoyed it. We seem now to have reached the limit of what I can communicate with nods and gestures, and to explain myself, I'd need to discuss that day in the jungle. How it had been wet, but the sky was for once blue. The patches of sunlight on the path where we walked seemed just like the light in the woodlands of my childhood, and for the first time I recognized the planet as my own. Then the LT saw something blooming and stepped to his right. To communicate *anything* to Ryan I'd have to explain how I long for those last minutes when life was good. Sometimes I imagine I was thinking of Sylvia — how she'd have loved the flowers and the foliage and the light — and sometimes I think I only *think* I was thinking of her, that this is a detail I've added in the years since. It doesn't matter. What I'd say to Ryan is that life exists in moments of floating, of rising high to find joy and glory, not living earthbound. He sees me mowing lawns and frying eggs and shuttling my truck around, but there's more I know, and I'd tell all if I only could. I'd tell him that behind the brittle scenery of everyday life lie other existences in which our outward lives are strangely secondary. Maybe I could explain why his mother likes drugs. And the ha-ha is my discovery, a modest gateway to something bright. It's a compression of that day in the jungle, and of my whole eighteen years of freedom before, into one or two moments of breathless grace.

I turn down my street, and the leaves make camouflage patterns on the vehicle. I'd like to slip in and take to my bed, but Nit and Nat are standing in our driveway. One of them aims a squirt of liquid at the barbecue grill, and when flames leap up they jump back in terror. Dummies. As we crunch over the gravel they flash sparkling grins, and Nat calls, "Heyyy! The guest of honor at last. Where you been, man?" At the entrance to the old stable building stands a wooden table with a platter of chicken, a glass pitcher of barbecue sauce, and a house-painting brush for applying the sauce. They've assembled a dinner to celebrate the end of school, and Nit lifts a frothy drink in salute.

The screen door slams, and Ryan edges behind the boys. "What's Ms. Monetti doing here?" I look, and the pretty elementary school teacher is crossing the lawn. She's changed from the dress she had on in school to nice jeans, a cream-colored top, and sandals — a little yuppieish for Nit and Nat, but what do I know? We watch her set a salad bowl on the picnic table, then she waves gaily. I glance at Nat, who has the sense to blush.

"She wasn't doing anything. Year's ending for her, too," he says, then claps me on the shoulder. "Howard, my man, let me get you a piña colada." He picks up a pair of cooking tongs and gives Ryan's nose a pinch —"Wonk, wonk!"— then hands Nit the tongs. "Watch the grill, okay, Stevie? Don't squirt no more of that shit on it, neither." We watch him saunter to the picnic table and say something to Ryan's teacher, then they go into the house together. Nit shrugs at Ryan.

I stare at the graying coals until the screen door opens again and Ruby bursts out, followed by Ms. Monetti with a tall glass and a short one on a tray. She offers me the tall glass, garnished with a hunk of pineapple and a cherry on a toothpick. I'm not feeling sociable, but I take a sip.

"Call me Logan," Ms. Monetti says with a dimpled smile. "You're sweet to include me." If she remembers the look we exchanged at the school, she's putting it behind us. She stoops and offers Ryan the half-sized cocktail, and he stares skeptically, as if it's a pop quiz. "Go on. I left the rum out of yours, silly guy. Nice choir getup." She rubs his ear with her thumb, then glances at me, and I nod at my glass. "My specialty," she says. "Just about the one thing I make. Don't I envy your household, though, with all these cooks." You should come for breakfast sometime, I think.

Nat reappears and fusses noisily with the grill. Ms. Monetti saunters back to the kitchen. I don't offer to pitch in. I take my piña colada and drift around the back yard, looking at the catalpa bark and the caulk on the stable windows as if I've never seen them before. For once, I've no complaint with the housemates, and even Ms. Monetti's presence is nothing to be disturbed about. But the afternoon's shaken me more than I suspected. I find a stick and pick a mud wasp's nest from a window frame, and when Nat starts singing in the driveway my problems seem mine in isolation. My lack of speech can render me not merely unheard, but unseen also, and as Laurel ribs Nat about his un-Texas barbecue sauce, as Nat sings and Ms. Monetti passes around drinks, as Nit asks Ryan if he paid for that blue robe, I feel how fluidly life continues without me. During dinner, I stew about Sister Amity, but the talk is of their world, beyond my reach. Ms. Monetti announces that for her everything's different this time of year, then she adds confidentially, "I take off my spectacles and let my hair *way*, way down." Perhaps this is more revealing than she intended, because she changes the subject. "So, Ryan, any summer plans?"

Ryan's far away, at the end of the table. He hasn't spoken, and I don't think he's looked at me since we returned from the convent, though I've watched him lick the butter from his asparagus and slip the spears down under his seat. Now, though, he looks up sharply, as if he's in class. He thinks a moment, then says again that he wants to go to Aqua Splash Down. He looks around hopefully to see who takes the hint. Laurel says, "And you're doin' baseball, too, aren't ya, hon?" He nods. "Little League?"

"Sort of."

Nat drops a chicken bone onto his plate. "Oh, buddy," he says. "You gonna have some fun. Gonna have a ball, man. You know who used to be a *big* baseball jock? High school, Little League, all 'at shit. Who you think?"

Nit says, "Here it comes, gang." Ryan shakes his head.

"Guess," says Nat in the avid-salesman manner he employs with Ryan. He raises an eyebrow, then taps his chest with a finger. "Swear to God, dude. Best pitch: my slider. Not-too-shabby fastball, neither. Only problem, my fielding sucked." He darts a grin at Ms. Monetti and adds, "Comparatively. But look: I could show you the whole damn catalogue, you know that? You and me put our heads together, boy, I make you a power player. An MVP. One southpaw to another, hey." He raises his left hand, still holding a fork, and nods broadly. I'm surprised he's noticed that Ryan's left-handed.

Ryan stares back, shrugging. He takes an enormous bite from

his drumstick, and we watch him chew. Then Laurel says, "You know, Ry, you don't hafta do this." He goes on eating. "There's absolutely no law says you have to like sports . . ."

Ryan looks up. He's got barbecue sauce on his mouth, and he looks like an outraged clown. "Of *course* I like sports," he says. "I *like* sports." He gives an exasperated look. "I just can't —"

Then, like a rush of birds, the flutter of commentary descends. Nat says, "Or like *I* pitch to *you*, if you want. Might turn out you're a slugger, not a pitcher," while Ms. Monetti says it's not always the star players that have the most fun. Nat says, "You never know, you know?"

Laurel says, "Is it *base*ball, sweetie? Do you think you're not good enough?" and Nat says they'll start with easy ones, really soft breaking balls. Nit announces that he never really dug team sports, not even basketball, which might be the only cool one if you think about it, though also hockey blah, blah, blah. Ms. Monetti says she's the world's biggest klutz.

Ryan looks from one to the other, then down at his plate. He's still got the drumstick with its bitten-out cavity, and he flings it down and scrambles from his seat. Laurel says, "*Ran?*"

Blue robe flapping, Ryan darts to the stable, where my morning glories have slowly been climbing the wall. He takes a shoot in his fist, and a spray of dirt rises against the clapboards. He uproots another, then another and another, clawing and tearing at my trellis of strings. We're on our feet now, picnic benches toppling behind us, and Nit calls out, "Whoa!" Ryan looks up savagely. He kicks at the plantings, then gives a last flail and takes off running. Ruby bobs after, like a balloon tied to his ankle.

The barbecue grill's still smoking at the entrance to the stable. Laurel gasps as Ryan charges toward it, but he executes a sudden zig, and if Ruby weren't on him he'd be just fine. As it is, she gets hold of the robe, and Ryan falls against the table the boys used as a cooking station. Tumbling headlong, he comes down on an ankle and skids forward on his elbows and knees. "Ow!" he says plaintively; then he cries out, "Ruby!" and raises his fist. The little dog sits back, wagging her stump of tail. Ryan glares furiously and gives the table a shove. It topples away from him, the glass pitcher sliding away, and strikes the grill, which hovers on two legs. Ryan puts his hands to his head, but the grill goes down with a rattle of coals. A spray of sparks, like the bright, sudden fan of a peacock, flares at the stable door.

Laurel is there first. Ryan's crying now and clutching his ankle, and when he catches his breath he gives a shriek of frustration. Laurel bends over him, and I hear her say, "Ruby, *back!*" then, "Jesus! Someone grab the damn dog! Broken glass here!" I crouch down next to them, and she says, "Honey, tell me. Where-all does it hurt?"

Ryan points at his foot, then his bloodied elbow and knee. He flicks some gravel from the knee and wrings his hands. His face is a small fountain of spit, tears, and snot, and I think of when he first came and I *expected* crying, and of how I finally stopped expecting. Ms. Monetti says, "Maybe we should ice the ankle," and Laurel nods absently. I know she doubts this is about bruises and scrapes.

"Shh, shh," says Laurel, and rocks Ryan against her chest. "S'okay . . ." She hands me the Indians cap. Ryan remains still, but when I wipe some red barbecue sauce from his shin he lets out a wail. At last, though, he starts to subside, and Laurel says, "Howard, can you get him in the house?"

I slip an arm beneath him, but as I do so he suddenly comes to life. "Nnn-*ngg!*" he says, and shoves me square in the chest. I fall back on my palms and let out a grunt, and Laurel stares in astonishment.

And now Nat's here. He straddles my legs to hitch Ryan by the armpits, and Laurel stands, too. "The child's upset," she says. "Little guy's borne up well these weeks, considering. Good he gets some of this out." She reaches down to squeeze my shoulder, then follows the others to the house.

I stay where I am, in the middle of the driveway. I've got a headache, and all I can think of is that shove in the chest. I try to remember if Ryan's ankle looked swollen, and I guess Laurel and the others are doing what's necessary. I suppose, too, they're hearing what happened at the convent. I wish I could dissolve right into the ground.

"Hey! Kapostash!" I look up. My neighbor's on his back stoop, smoking a cigarette. I think his wife makes him smoke outside since the baby's come, but we don't talk much. "What are you doing?" he asks.

I shrug. I'm not doing anything. *I'm sitting on my ass in my drive-way wishing everything were less fucked-up.* I'm staring into space.

"Why the hell don't you put that out?" says my neighbor. He's in a starched business shirt with the sleeves rolled, and there's nothing neighborly in the look he gives me. I look behind me and see the briquettes smoking in a heap. Some of the coals have tumbled toward the stable, and the few morning glories Ryan left standing are wilting in the smoke. "You could burn down the whole street," the neighbor says. I doubt it, but it's not a bad notion.

But duty calls. I start to rise and gasp as I lean on something sharp. A curved triangle of glass protrudes like a sail from my palm, and when I pluck it out a red line wells up. With my free hand, I right the wooden table and set the piece of glass on it; then, wrapping a dish towel around my cut, I squat and gather the pieces of the pitcher. I don't want Ruby or Ryan getting hurt. My neighbor yells, "What the hell are you doing?" and I don't look up. Let everything burn, I think, right to the ground. *Whoosh!*

There was a time, of course, I knew everybody on this block. I took the neighbors with easy sociability, and after I was wounded they showed me respect. Now, though, those families have mostly moved on, and my current neighbors I leave to themselves. So I place my collection of glass shards on the table, then kick gently at the pile of ashes. As red coals roll away from my boot, my neighbor asks, "What are you *doing?*" A screen door creaks, and his chubby wife joins him, carrying their bald-headed daughter. I hear her whispering and saying his name, *Dwayne.* "Honey, I don't give a damn," Dwayne says. "I'm not gonna let him burn the place down." I start toward the side of my house, where the garden hose hangs on a rack, and I'm moving slowly just to bust his balls. "Hey, I got a family to protect, man," the guy calls out. "Two minutes, I'm calling the fire department. Where you going now?" I turn on the water.

I hear Laurel say, "Howard?" and when I return with the hose she's standing at our screen door. "Everything okay?"

"Ms. Kim," our neighbor calls. "You oughta keep a closer eye on your boyfriend. He's starting a fire." Laurel steps outside and stares at him without a word, and the neighbor holds a whispered conference with his wife. "Or whatever your name is. Sorry. But I mean it. That's a dangerous situation."

Laurel says, "Keep your shirt on." Then, to the wife, "How's little Samantha doing?" The wife picks up the infant's hand and waves it, and Laurel steps toward me. "Ryan's fine," she says. "Just being a baby, which I must say is okay by me. He likes the attention, so Logan's told him to stay off the ankle. I wonder how long *that* will last." I aim a squirt at the stable wall, and wilted leaves break from the morning glory stem. Laurel says, "And you won't believe what all his hoo-ha was about. Seems he *lost* his old baseball mitt, and his mom won't buy a new one 'til he learns the value of personal possessions. So he was afraid he'd get ridiculed. But it makes you wonder how some people think!" She shakes her head, and I stare at her, dumbfounded. *Is that all?*

I squirt the coals, and a cloud of ash billows up. Laurel and I cough. Dwayne shouts, "About time!"

"Hey!" cries Laurel. "It's out now. Just relax." She coughs again, and under her breath she says, "Asshole."

"What?" He stubs his cigarette in an ashtray. "Guy's sitting on his duff, I don't know how long. If that thing goes up —" He nods at my stable building. "It's summertime. I'm in a wooden house here."

Laurel says, "Soak the *en*tire driveway, Howard. Just to make sure."

"What's it take to get through to him, anyway?"

Laurel says, "*Hey!*" again. The wife is pulling the guy by the sleeve. "Jean, your husband's out of line. You know that, don't you?" She pauses a moment, then adds, "This man fought for his country." And with that I turn the hose on them. The spray doesn't reach their stoop, but it's enough to send them scurrying inside, and Laurel's laughing and tugging me by the waist. "Ho*ward!*"

So Ryan didn't tell them about our convent ride. Instead, he ragged on Sylvia for not replacing a baseball glove. It's funny, I think, how things even out. Some glitch in the cosmic machinery scooped up whatever injury he might have suffered at the convent and redeposited it in my yard. There's never any escape. But if an ugly cut is the sentence for my foolishness, it's a price I'll pay.

We're heading inside when Laurel says, "He said one strange thing, though, Howard . . . Did you fight with that nun?" I gesture dismissively, and when she spots the bloody dishcloth the subject is dropped. "Howard, you might need stitches! Come on. Let me take you quick quick in my car."

But I don't want stitches. Darkness is falling, and already the family's reassembling. On the picnic table lie half-empty platters, and Ms. Monetti is gathering glasses. Nit and Nat emerge from the kitchen with Ryan in a fireman's carry, and I settle the Indians cap on his head. "Hi, Howie," he whispers. We're embarrassed, both of us. In the bathroom is a first-aid kit, and as Laurel digs through it I again decline a trip to the ER. There's a lemon cake waiting downstairs on the counter, and I've a sudden feeling that if I step away for even a moment, nothing will be here when I return.

28

SYLVIA'S PARENTS HAD SOME WEDDING out of town and took Caroline with them. Sylvia begged off, saying she had a paper to write; I told my folks I'd be catching a Bulls game and staying the night in Chicago. So Sylvia and I had a day and a half at her house, and we cooked and had sex and called each other "dear" in solemn jest. Sylvia really did have a paper due, and she made me stay quiet so she could work all afternoon. I lay on the floor near the little pink desk where she tapped away at a manual typewriter, and whenever the bell rang, I licked her toes; then we pulled each other to the bedroom. All afternoon it snowed, but the house was so cozy that I prowled naked around the upstairs, even entering the master bedroom to gaze lustily in the full-length mirror. The weekend was filled with liberties I'd never take in my own home. I wanted to do it with Sylvia right there, by the mirror, and I called to her, and by the time she appeared I had another hard-on. But Sylvia came bundled in her thick white terry-cloth robe, modest even with me. "Howie!" she said, "come *out* of there! Put something on!" She opened the robe and wrapped it clumsily around me for the walk to her own room, as if holding me against her tempting legs were somehow less indecent than letting me flop around in the open. I knew we'd have other chances at that mirror, so I let her shuttle me off.

Sunday I awoke overjoyed. The snow had continued all night, and the falling snowflakes lent an extra blueness to the walls of Sylvia's bedroom, which were blue already. Sylvia had not permitted me to shovel her parents' drive for fear a neighbor would see, so we'd stayed in, with no one but ourselves as witnesses, and I woke still flush from our long day together. In the afternoon there'd been sex, and sex again in the evening, after which we'd raided the freezer for her mom's special hors d'oeuvres. Then I chopped while Sylvia cooked, and we ate in the dining room, with candles. We washed both plates and all the pots and put everything away to leave no evidence, and when we finally turned in, I curled bigly around her in her girl's-size bed. I reached for her breast, but Sylvia murmured, "Shh, Howie. Go to sleep. Tomorrow!" and I did as she asked. Then it was morning, and I was staggered by my good fortune. Here I was, with still hours to go! For once, I awoke not caring what the day would bring — how long Sylvia would let me stay, or when her parents would return; whether there would be more sex, more romantic meals, more capering like newlyweds. I had my own homework to complete, too, and the timing of my return through the snowstorm to consider, and it was my tendency to worry about such smallish concerns. But for once I was able to put them aside. It was as if I were watching myself from a nearby distance and feeling that all was luck and possibility — though in fact, I was never again blessed by a whole night with Sylvia, or anyone else. That was the only time.

I don't know why I wake thinking of that morning. I'm alone in bed, but there's a lightness to my mood and the same sense of — strange concept for me — luck. Even when I remember I'm angry with Sylvia, I flex my legs and feel great. I'm *free*, I think. I've even overslept. As for Sister Amity, I push her aside. Instead, I contemplate the strange household that held a barbecue, and I wonder why I should go where I'm not appreciated. The convent shackled me, I see now, and Sister Amity can take her week to consider. Render judgment? She can have all fucking year, then kneel and *beg* me to climb back on that mower. Perhaps I'll be unemployed for a while and spend time with Ryan. I can be irresponsible, go through my savings. What the hell am I saving for? Again, I feel I'm watching from the outside, and I see myself stretch as I rise from my bed. It's an uplifting sight. The unemployed man takes a long, long shower, shampooing the smokiness from his sparse cap of hair. He shaves carefully, standing naked at the washbasin, and adjusts the razor to the growth of his whiskers. A red-winged blackbird calls to him through the window, and he realizes his bandage has come loose in the shower. Peeling the sodden pad from his hand, he drops it in the wastebasket, then carefully replaces it using his teeth. He goes down late to the kitchen.

The others are all there, and someone's made breakfast. A honeydew I bought has been cut into sections. Toast and juice are on the table. Laurel casts an eye at my gym shorts and asks if I'm playing hooky today, but Nat shouts, "Yo, big man! We saved you some coffee!" I slip past Laurel and sit beside Ryan.

The boys wipe their faces as they stand from the table. "How's the bum ankle today, Ry-guy?" Nit snickers. "Might be you oughta lie on the couch and eat bonbons, take all the weight off." Then they're banging a ladder up the cellar stairs, arguing about drop cloths, revving the motor on the old white van, and I feel less cocky about my sabbatical. Despite Nit and Nat's doofusness, there's a work ethic to this household, and when I notice the unwashed breakfast dishes, I wonder if they're onto me.

Laurel's packing up, too, pouring green soup and red soup into plastic tubs for the cafés. She says, "No work, Howard?" and though I don't want to get into it, I hold up ten fingers. Laurel says, "Ten?"

I'm damned if I'll return to that convent, but I'll break the news gradually. I've been Steady Eddie as long as Laurel's known me, and I'm the same guy now. I give the waggle that means *maybe*, and Laurel says, "Ten, sort of . . . The thing is, Howard —"

Ryan looks up from the funnies. "The nun made him go away for like a week or so," he announces.

"Oh." Laurel blinks. "Did something happen?"

"Not!" I say. *Not at all!* I give a thumbs-up. *All is fine!*

Laurel says, "The thing is, Howard, your disability payments alone —" But at this I pull her to the hallway. I hate that word, and I don't want him hearing it! My hand shakes as I repeat my message, and though Laurel looks doubtful, she says, "Well, Howard, a little vacation never hurt anyone. I can't remember the last time you weren't on call. Maybe it's a chance for some time with the boy, now he's out of school." *My thoughts exactly!*

When Laurel's ready, I carry her tubs to the driveway. It's amazing how much soup she gets in that little Beetle. "But if you needed something, you'd let me know, right? Because budgetwise, we cut it pretty close." Biting her lip, she tugs a thread from my sleeve, and for a moment her hand remains on my biceps. "I don't know, maybe Stevie and Harrison need a helper for a bit." I pat the air. *That won't be necessary!* "Or maybe I could hire you to make deliveries, if — but damn!" She blushes. "I'd have to write out a list."

29

How do we spend the free time? First we go shopping. I drive Ryan to a mall in the suburbs, where there's a sports emporium I've heard advertised on the radio. But very large stores rattle me, and as we wander past walls of tennis rackets and through a glitzy surfboard boutique and even a dive shop, I want to cry *what the hell is a dive shop doing in the Midwest?*

Ryan tags along without inquiry. He's so quiet that despite our moment last night I still wonder where I stand, and I worry that when we find what we're looking for, he'll pull some kid stunt and refuse my gift. Then we locate the baseball section, in the basement, and he troops right to the rack of gloves. A good-looking black man in a fitted shirt and violet tie squats comfortably beside him. "Interested in getting a glove?" Ryan nods solemnly.

I reach down and tap Ryan's left wrist, and he says, "I'm left-handed. Lefties have to wear a right-hand glove."

The salesman says that's absolutely correct and points to a section where the gloves are all marked with *L*'s. He gives me a tidy, professional nod, and if he has any ideas about a white guy shopping with a black child, he doesn't let on. Lowering his voice, he says, "Did you have a price range in mind, sir?"

I didn't. Dozens of gloves hang before me, and it takes me a minute just to decipher the price tags. They're priced higher than I'd have guessed any baseball glove could cost, and this week's paycheck will be my last. But I didn't wake up happy just to worry about money. I shake my head, punching my palm with my fist, and the salesman gets that look that says he's onto my deal. "I'm gonna play shortstop," announces Ryan.

The man chooses a glove from the rack. "Try this. Good, solid infielder's glove." He takes a ball from behind a counter and gives a toss, and Ryan snags the ball out of the air. "Nice," the man says. Ryan chucks the ball back, and the salesman catches it one-handed, and after several more tosses he puts a hand on Ryan's shoulder. "Lemme tell you something about shortstop," he says casually. "*Not* a great position for a lefty, and I bet you already know why. It's the pivot to first — when you turn, you keep your front to the plate, whereas a lefty's gotta turn away. Understand what I'm saying?" He demonstrates gracefully, pantomiming an infield throw, and I'm wondering if I knew this fine point when he suddenly shrugs. "Now *first* is a position where a lefty can make a mark. Plenty of action there, and a big guy like you — what are you, eleven? Twelve? *Nine?* Get outa here." He's a smoothy, but Ryan listens with fierce concentration.

The salesman looks from Ryan to me and says that at this stage a guy should try all positions, not get hung up on one role, and if he's doing Little League, some rotation will be mandatory. He gives the ball another toss — "Pop up here, reach for it, attaboy!" — then suggests Ryan sample more gloves, make an educated selection. "See how the glove hand *stops* the ball and the throwing hand *traps* it?" he asks. He's one of those guys who's always moving while he talks — stretching, gesturing, signaling, demonstrating — and I think if he ever loses his speech he'll be just fine. The two of them chuck the ball back and forth, and I slip on a glove, too, just to see how it feels. Without missing a beat the guy says, "How about you, sir? Will you be coaching the young man yourself?"

In the end, we walk out of that store with two gloves, not one, plus a regulation baseball. When the guy announces the total, I feel like fainting, but I'm clearly committed, so I dig out the credit card I almost never use. And in fact, I like putting this stuff on the card. I make a scribble for my signature, and as I tuck the receipt away, I think it's normal to carry some debt.

As the week progresses I get a few projects knocked out around the house, and we play a lot of backyard catch. One night after Ryan's in bed I sit on the picnic table drinking a beer. The moon is full, and the clapboards look as if they've been rubbed with chalk. I think back to my high school days, when I was just feeling grown-up. How long has it been since I couldn't predict what lay ahead? I climb down from the picnic table and go inside, rinse the empty bottle and drop it in the recycling tub. The next morning I sleep in, skipping breakfast altogether, and on Thursday I take Ryan to Aqua Splash Down.

Miraculously, Laurel joins us. She and I don't socialize much beyond the house, so perhaps this is for Ryan. We get a late start, after her deliveries, and when we arrive at the park, Ryan runs from pool to slide to diving board like someone in a relay. Then we find a shaded spot to eat our lunch. As we wait out the hour before swimming again, the three of us play pickle-in-the-middle under the trees, Laurel talking Texas trash in a black one-piece and wrap-around sunglasses. She's not much for capturing the ball, and once, when she's had a long turn in the middle, she lets out a cowgirl yowl and flings herself at me. I feel the soft skin of her arm on my naked chest, and I backpedal three steps and tumble down, pulling her into the dry, mown grass. The ball plops to earth maybe two feet beyond our reach, and as Laurel crawls toward it her leg slides between my thighs. I give a grunt as I try to turn over; she squeals my name, and soon we're laughing. I feel her fingers in my chest hair. She stretches across me, slippery, Lycra-clad, and one of my legs is between *her* thighs, too. As I feel her wriggle, I pretend to reach for the ball.

Then Ryan's there, holding the ball aloft as he dances around us on his skinny brown legs. "I got it! I got it! And *she's* still in the middle!" Laurel and I sit up, panting, and I use my torn bandage as a reason to avoid eye contact. Getting up, I put my hands on my knees to catch my breath. I stare down at my flat, pale feet, already pinkening from a few hours of sun. I'm noticing a cigarette butt under a dandelion when a patch of shadow crosses my field of vision, then Laurel's little fingers are plucking the cut grass from my back. I can smell her suntan lotion over the scent of my own meaty perspiration, and as her fingers go pick, pick, pick, we don't say a word. Meticulously, she removes each blade, dropping it to the ground between us, and I pant deeply and blink at her satiny, close-shaven legs. It's a long time since I've felt that particular species of vibration, and I could stay like this for the rest of my days.

I volunteer to take her place in the middle. Ryan thinks I'm crazy to do it, but I hand over my glove, and maybe I look hungry, adjusting my shorts. Laurel blushes, but does she think I'm a stone? The day is bright. The cluster of swimming pools, with its boisterous music and shouting families, is across a broad field, so the tree-shaded spot where we've chosen to picnic seems suddenly intimate. Laurel dashes to the blanket and pulls a shirt over her black suit, and we go back to our game without looking at each other. There's nothing between us, but she's pretty cute, crossing the grass with my big glove clamped on her hand.

30

LAUREL SAYS, "LOOKIN' PURTY SHARP THERE, cowboy." Ryan's attired himself as a kind of badass sports hero: dark Cubs T-shirt with the sleeves rolled to the shoulders, sweatpants sawed off to baseball length, puffy sneakers, Indians cap. Laurel nods appraisingly. "Got your mitt?"

"Harrison took it. He's out back."

I step onto the stoop, and Nat's in the yard, tossing the baseball in the air and catching it. He's shirtless, and his ponytail frisks over a circular something-or-other tattooed on his back. Nat's a lefty like Ryan, but I'm afraid he'll stretch the leather with his big grown-up's paw, so I shout, "Na!" and toss him my own right-hander's glove.

"Thanks, Howard. I gotta get my mom to mail me mine." He switches gloves, then throws the ball high, and when it comes down he tries catching it wrong-handed. The ball hits the tip of the glove and bounces toward the stable, and Nat scrambles after it, all tanned legs and bare feet. He looks so playful that it's hard to begrudge him being himself, and for a moment I see the high school hopeful he must have been, privately imagining a big career. Cocky, but not yet such a joke. I wonder what life he expected to have, because when you're young you dream of anything you want, then nothing comes true. Nat's music thing seems stalled now, but there was a time not so long ago when things went his way. He threw sliders; he majored in U.S. history. I doubt he envisioned himself painting houses at thirty. Yet as he bobbles another fly, Nat hasn't a care. It's not a way I can imagine feeling, but for the moment I'm not offended.

Ryan comes and stands beside me, and Nat tosses him his glove. "It's a beauty, Ry-Ry. You want to tie it up at night to keep its shape." He rubs his face with his forearm and says, "Here: show me what you got." Then, as if to remind us he truly *is* a dope, he throws the baseball right at the house, where it could break a window. But Ryan jumps out and catches the ball handily. He flips it back, and I hardly bother scowling at Nat.

Laurel comes out on the stoop, and we watch them play catch. "Been more'n a month, Howard. Any word from his ma?" I shake my head — no date yet — then make a gesture of drawing things out. "Sure nice having him," she says, and leans against me. Our shoulders touch, but she's just being affectionate.

Laurel's her old self today: cheap sneakers, baggy pants. The girl in black Lycra seems like a mirage. I've decided it wasn't really Laurel who got me so hot and bothered at Aqua Splash Down, but the heady mix of bright, common pleasures; if I ever imagined a familyoid excursion, it was as something far beyond my sphere, as remote from me as from Sister Amity. Then the sparkle, the giant slide and the fountains, the soft comfort of a picnic under trees! The big pool with its high-tech surf and Ryan bobbing on the swells. I think even Laurel realized how spectacular this was, because she ran to a concession stand for a disposable camera. The way the sun cavorted among the clouds and the sound of the ball dropping to the dry grass, and someone so relaxed that she let out a war whoop and *threw* herself at me! But no one's more aware than I am of my romantic deficiencies, and I'm grateful that Laurel let our moment pass.

Ms. Monetti's appeared at the edge of the yard, but Nat doesn't see her. He's set my glove aside and is playing bare-handed, clowning around by nearly missing each throw, then snagging the ball at the last possible minute. Backpedaling toward the driveway, he reaches up and tumbles like an otter, then comes up with the ball high over his head. His handsome fool's face is lit by a game-winning grin. Laurel waves her hands and chants, "Harri-*son*, Harri-*son!*" and what the hell: I put my hands together for the guy, too.

When it's time to leave, Laurel gives Ryan a hug. "Okay, m'boy. I sure can't wait to come watch a game." She kisses him on both cheeks and says it's for luck, then shakes her hair from her face. For a moment I think she'll offer me some luck, too, but it doesn't happen.

31

T HE BASEBALL FIELDS are on the south side of town, closer to Sylvia's rehab than to home. Within a large city park lies an oval parking lot shadowed by trees, where two dusty diamonds bleed together at their outfields. Kids of all ages are milling about, and a chubby man in Bermuda shorts is taking an armload of bats from a white station wagon. Ryan climbs from the truck with an air of toughness and makes a circuit of the parking lot, but almost immediately he's back at my side. "There's girls here," he announces skeptically.

I look around. It's true. Not a lot of girls, but several who are unmistakably here to play ball. A tall girl with beaded dreads is fiddling with the clasp on a baseball cap, and over by the third base line a much bigger girl is taking batting practice all alone. We watch her flip a ball in the air and whack a solid liner across the infield, and I give a whistle: *there's* one to beat. A wiry, blue-haired kid scrambles to make the catch, and as he sails it back I pat Ryan's shoulder. He blinks at me, then swaggers off. Girls! He could do worse.

Someone calls, "Howard!" and I turn around. It's Robin the gardener. She grins crazily and gives me an unexpected hug. "Not exactly who I expected to run into today," she says, taking a puff from a cigarette. "So where is he?"

I raise my eyebrows. *Where's who?* Robin says, "I heard from Sister Anthill you're Big Brothering now. Cool, cool, cool, Howard." I wait for a comment on my disgrace at the convent, but Robin only glances around the parking lot. Perhaps Sister Amity kept the bad news to herself. "I can't imagine which one's yours."

I point out Ryan. He's standing by a nylon equipment bag, self-consciously rolling a bat with one foot. He looks as though he's not quite sure he can touch anything, and Robin calls out, "Go ahead! That stuff's to be used." I nod, and he stoops for the bat, then inches toward the big girl batting by third base. And though I'd prefer to watch how he proceeds, Robin drags me away. "Did you meet Ed yet? Come on, I'll introduce you."

Ed Mesk is Mister Luster Kleen. I'd pictured an iron-jawed drill instructor with a chip on his shoulder — the type who has to compensate for a life cleaning carpets — but Ed's the chubby fellow with the shorts and the white wagon. He's short and amiable, with a beaky mouth and round, hairless forearms. "Oh, great," he says as he pumps my hand. "Another dad. Boy, can we use you. Welcome to the Snakes." He hands me a sheet filled with letters and numbers, then glances anxiously at Robin. "Could I ask you not to smoke around the kids?"

Robin rolls her eyes at me. "Hey, Ed," she says, "did you know Howard's differently abled? He doesn't talk much, but don't treat him like an idiot, okay? He could be the smartest one here, you never know." Ed looks helpless, and after a second Robin claps us both on the back. "Hey, you're both good guys." Then she calls out, "*Come on, people, let's play some ball!*"

Ed honks the horn of his station wagon and says, "Sorry, but could I get everyone's attention?" I see Ryan and the big girl walking in tandem across the infield, each acting as if the other's not there, and as the crowd assembles I hover on the periphery. Across the circle, Robin slouches beside a pretty woman in green knee-length pants. She checks her pocket for cigs and yawns like a tiger. The other woman stands very straight, her hands on the shoulders of a narrow-faced boy much smaller than Ryan, and as Robin stoops to whisper in the boy's ear it strikes me they're a family unit. The little boy nods and says something in return, and Robin slaps him on the butt as she straightens up. Next to them stands a woman with two boys, one the blue-haired kid I noticed earlier, and further on, a husky Asian boy is standing alone. The Asian kid's bigger than Ryan, and he's dressed in full catcher's gear; while Ed is speaking he practices brushing the mask up to the crown of his head, then back over his face. All in all, there must be twenty-five kids here, and a handful of adults; but it's the grown-ups, not the children, who remind me of childhood.

My family wasn't big on organized activities for kids, and we were a bit condescending toward families who were. I never did Little League, and I was a Boy Scout only briefly. But the street I live on used to be filled with youngsters who got together without supervision to create races and contests and fights and games. We played kickball and football when the spirit took us, and if we weren't sure about some rule or technique, we made it up. Now, I'm sure Ed Mesk is trying hard to sound legit, but the casual atmosphere conspires against him. Instead of structured athletics, it's as if the children from my old street have come together to invent a game *called* "Little League" — or even "Saturday" or "Good Parenting" or something to be named later. At least, that's my reverie when I notice a small, birdlike woman eyeing me sharply. She's wondering what I'm doing here, I think: memorizing my scar and casting me as some weirdo. I make a mental note to keep Ryan near me, like a membership card.

Ed asks if we'd rather sit on the bleachers, and no one responds. He says we might start today by just loosening up, and that sounds good. "Let's spend the first hour on fundamentals, then toss together a couple of teams and play however many innings," he says. "Okay? The point is to have a real good time." Pointing a finger around the circle, he gives each kid a number, then divides them into groups: "One through seven will work on batting: eight through fifteen, catching and throwing; sixteen and up, fielding. Twenty minutes, then we'll rotate. And I'm still trying to line up a pitching coach, guys, so pitchers sit tight a week, okay?" He claps his hands a little daintily and adds, "Let's have some fun."

Ryan says, "I'm on batting," and gives an air bat a mighty swing. I watch a home run fly off toward outer space, and we high-five. I'd like the bird-woman to catch this. The slugger girl calls for batters, and the kids scurry off importantly, their shadows hustling along beneath them. For a moment, I think of boot camp. I take a seat on a bleacher and watch a little boy, gasping like a four-minute miler, guzzle three cupfuls from a Coleman drink dispenser; then a grand-dad tells him that's enough. Robin's girlfriend appears, carrying shopping bags, and smiles at me without knowing who I am.

"Howard!" Robin slaps my knee with her cap. "What the hell are you doing?" I spread my hands. *I'm not doing anything*. She says, "You can't just sit here. You have to pitch in."

I stand up, but there's nothing to do. The girlfriend's emptied her bags of rice cakes and oranges and is chatting up Gramps; there's a mom reading a magazine and a few parents out with the kids. On the nearer of the two diamonds, Ed Mesk is hitting grounders and pop ups, and young fielders are running the balls down. At the far diamond, Ryan's in line with the batters.

Robin hisses, "You really want to hang with the ladies?" Then suddenly she laughs. She's so dour at the convent that I doubt I've ever heard her laugh, and it's surprisingly goofy: *ha, ha, ha*. The girl-friend turns, and Robin says, "Howard, this is Ann. Her little boy Jamie's around here somewhere. But come on. We need to teach these babies how to throw." From a corner of the outfield, the catching-and-throwing group watches our negotiations.

In general, I'm more able than people expect, but I steer clear of statements beyond *yes* and *no*, and I'm not confident with instruc-tions. But I'll lend moral support, so I grab my glove and head for the outfield. And Robin's got things under control. "Guys, this is Howard. Who's gonna be coaching with me. Now the hard thing about catching's keeping your eye on the ball, okay?" I stifle a smile, and she says, "Well, it's true."

Robin has everybody toss a tennis ball straight up and snag it when it comes down. "*Reach* for the ball, people! Don't wait 'til it bonks you on the head. A little higher now." One delicate blonde girl isn't doing much, and Robin crouches behind her. "Hold your glove *up*, hon, not down, so it's ready." She gives a toss and guides the girl's hand, and I wish I could tell her about *stopping* and *trapping*. Robin says, "Now push yourself, babe. Take a chance on success, 'kay?" A tubby freckle-faced kid loses his ball in the sun, and I chuck it back at him. His eyes flicker over my scar, and I contemplate getting a cap.

When it comes to throwing, though, I see why I'm here. Robin doesn't have Sylvia's classic ball-in-the-dirt throw — she gets some lift. But she stands stiffly and employs only her arm. I think she knows this is no example to set, because she keeps glancing at me, and at last I step up. Waving the kids to follow, I shake out my shoulders. I'm like a mime up here, but at least I'm good at it. I've been a mime for years. I think of that salesman demonstrating the pivot, and I turn sideways and plant my foot. Placing my hands at my sternum, I move slowly through the entire motion, letting my body follow my arm. The kids watch closely. No one's told them why I communicate as I do, so they gape unself-consciously. I do the slo-mo again, and miraculously, they do it with me; then I just *throw* the ball, using the motion I've used since childhood. Ryan's over with the batting group, at the edge of the far infield, and I get him in my sights and send the ball out as far as I can. As it lofts into the sky, the freckled kid goes, "Whoa!"

I've always had a decent arm, but this time even I'm surprised. Could be the loosening up. Certainly there were guys who hurled grenades farther and faster than I ever could, and I bet most of these kids' dads throw as well as I. And it's only a tennis ball, and these are grammar schoolers. Still, the ball lands squarely at Ryan's feet, and he picks it up and sends it back with a grin, getting it just over halfway here. The freckle-faced kid charges off, elbows pumping, and when he heaves it back, I catch it in my glove. I feel a funny little tearing sensation where I cut my hand, but I give a thumbs-up: *darn nice throw, buddy.* After this, we practice throwing until Ed calls for a switch. I haven't even discussed aim.

"I suspected you'd have a knack for this, Howard," Robin says as a new group straggles toward us. "You know, a lot of guys throw just like girls." She goes through the slow-motion movement again, then laughs goofily and asks how to place her fingers on the seams. Damned if I know. But I do think we might train her out of her bad habits, and though I never considered a career in teaching, I bet I'd have been good at it.

Halfway through the morning, we gather again. Ed and the big girl redivide the crew, distributing older and younger kids, boys and girls, athletes and stumblebums. Ryan's chosen opposite the blue-haired boy, and the two knock fists as they step off to their separate groups. Ryan's team heads for the bench, and the big Asian boy steps up to lead off. He taps some imperceptible mud from his sneakers, and Ed Mesk stands behind the plate to call balls and strikes.

The Asian kid's set to go when I realize something. It's an obvious point, and as I walk to first, I'm even chuckling to myself. Two gestures, the spread arms for *safe* and the punch for *out*. How difficult could it be? I take my position and put my hands on my knees, and Ed nods at the big girl to go ahead and pitch. For a mime, umpiring might be the world's easiest job.

32

M Y PLAN WAS to swing by Home Depot, then build a
new porch planter. But by the end of the game I'm too
happily wiped to think about chores. With no midfield umpire, I've
spent six innings running between first and second, and my T-
shirt's soaked with perspiration.

Ryan's winded, too, but mostly he's ravenous. His big moment
was an RBI double, and he really scrambled down the baselines, giving a small superstar performance — head down, phony exertion —
though the throw in was pretty wild. Next time up, he got to first
on a dropped catch, but after that he fanned, spinning around so
hard he nearly toppled over. He stomped off, throwing his batting
helmet at the backstop, and I gave him a look that said *mind your
manners*. But even with the strikeout, he's a lefty who connects, and
this gets him noticed. Coming home after his double, he hit the
plate with both feet, and the husky Asian catcher was there for the
high five; when the game is over they walk off the field together.
The other kid's explaining something to Ryan, and as they pass the
big girl she calls out, "Nice game, guys."

"Juliana Mesk," Robin murmurs in my ear. "I guess she always
dreamed of coaching, and the local Little League was filled up with
dads. So her pops cooked up this thing." She bites down on a carrot

stick, and I realize how hungry I am. Ryan's elbow-deep in a potato chip bag, and two yellow triangles cling to his lips like tiny moths. I brush them off, and he gives me a grin.

The birdish woman hollers for her car pool to hop to it, but I'm now indifferent to her validation. Ed Mesk calls out, "I'll have a game schedule soon, guys, but in the meantime . . ." He hands out dark blue Mister Luster Kleen T-shirts, and with a flurry of skin the kids all change, the tall girl slipping behind a minivan to shimmy into hers. "I'm gonna order Snakes shirts, too," Ed announces. Ann and Robin are unpacking a picnic, and Ann offers Ryan half a PB&J. He takes a huge bite, then gives a look of revulsion. I take a nibble: salt-free peanut butter. I better get him out of here before he eats a tree.

When I first came home injured I did a lot of speech and re-adjustment therapy down here on the south side, and I'm thinking about a little rib place that wasn't too far away. In those days, I wasn't yet driving again, though my license was still valid, and I was much too self-conscious to take a bus. My dad and mom both worked, but Dad arranged for shorter hours on a six-day week, instead of five, to get me to my appointments. Neither of us had yet accommo-dated what had happened, and those were long, sad drives for me and my dad. Sometimes we'd spend the whole time with tears streaming down our cheeks, then turn away to wipe our eyes before I went for my sessions. Dad would wait in the car. When I came out I'd be hungry, and though he was expected at Hanran's Men's Wear in the afternoons, often he'd blow off work for an hour or two, or even the whole day. He and I would go to this little joint and eat ribs and drink beer, and we'd sit at a patio table, saying nothing and watching the cars through a tall, wrought-iron fence. Eventually we began hanging out at this place on a regular basis, and this was the beginning, I think, of several things: my forsaking the therapy industry for self-medication, and Dad losing his job. But by the time that happened, none of us — not even my mom — cared enough about anything to give his firing a thought.

The rib place is still there, to my astonishment. The glass-fronted counter area with one narrow table and the small concrete side patio with six tightly packed picnic tables: all unchanged. A middle-aged woman shows no surprise when I point to the menu items, and I wonder if it's possible she's the same big-Afro'd girl who worked here in the old days. Her hair is straightened now and going gray, and when she brushes an eyelash from her cheek I see she has lightning bolts drawn on each long nail. She asks if we want corn on the cob, and Ryan says, "We want the works!"

The woman cocks her head at the Indians cap. "You into the tribe?" He nods. "That Omar Vizquel is one *sexy* man," she says, then grins and heads for the kitchen. "Be right out."

We choose a table on the patio. Another family's already eating, and a toddler in a fancy dress takes an interest in Ryan. She stares at him until he says, "Boo!" then she laughs raucously and stomps off, slapping her skirt with her palms. The counter lady brings us our lunch on paper plates, and Ryan digs in, getting the first stain on his Mister Luster Kleen shirt. For a few minutes we don't speak, and out on the street the cars keep going by, just as they did years ago. Sometime in my second or third year of recovery I began to drive, and Dad could have returned to his regular work schedule if he'd wanted, but he didn't do that. For years, right until I gave up on therapy, he preferred to ride along with me, never coming in, always sitting in the car. I suppose remembering all this should make me blue, but the fact is I was grateful for my dad's companionship on my terrible appointments, and those slow-paced afternoons are among the happier memories of a dark, dark time. In such small considerations was my sanity forged, and I've always liked the ribs here.

"Hey, Howie," Ryan says, and I turn from the street. "How'd you like my double?" When it happened, early in the game, it didn't seem appropriate to express too much pride, so now I nod wildly. *Best doggone hit ever!* Ryan beams, then says, "We had a good team for not knowing each other before. Here's who I think's the best players, okay? Jeremy, Elizabeth, Shawn, and that kid who — I don't know his name." I nod. I don't know any of the kids' names myself, but I take a bit of my short hair between my fingertips and rub it inquiringly. Ryan goes blank. I look around until I find a bright-blue stripe on a paper cup, and I point at the stripe, then at my hair again, and when he gets it, he grins. "Oh, that's Shawn. He's eleven," he says. "Some guys are multitalented, but I think he really wants to pitch. His hair looks pretty cool on him, but if it was me I don't think I'd do it blue. Yellow, red, maybe, with my coloring. Think I should be a pitcher?"

I've been considering something since Ed Mesk mentioned pitching, but I'm not sure how to put it into words. I try out, "Na," but this just sounds like my old catchall, and no one knows I call those guys Nit and Nat. I say, "Ha—" and then, with an effort, "Haw-suh," but I'm not transmitting. "Haw-suh," I say again, then one more time. It's a hard name to say. Ryan looks patiently at me, but I can't get any clearer, and at last I give up. The day's too nice for such hard work. We're finished eating, and I spread out a paper napkin and draw a diamond on it in barbecue sauce. Ryan adds the little upside-down U of the pitcher's mound. I dig in my pocket and set down coins for each of the players, and this is how we discuss the game. A sparrow arrives and picks at something under the table, and I move a nickel from second to third. The sun shines down. The other family troops out, a thin man with a moustache carrying the toddler, and I pantomime throwing the helmet, then wink to let Ryan know I'm just joshing. He says he wanted to see how it bounced. He crumbles corn bread for the sparrow, and the bird's dazzled by the fluttering crumbs. It smacks its beak and begs for more, and no one's in any hurry to leave. I go inside to buy another beer and a Sprite for Ryan. The radio's playing an Al Green tune that was popular when I was here last.

I'm at the counter when I hear a sudden shriek, and as I turn to look, Sylvia rushes through the restaurant. *Sylvia?* But when I step to the patio, I see it's true. There she is, kneeling in the corn bread crumbs, her arms tight around Ryan's neck. She's laughing and crying and rocking him back and forth on his bench, and Ryan's saying, "Mommy, oh, Mama, I missed you *so* much!"

It's not so surprising that she's here. The dry-out place is only five or six blocks away, and the house where she's living must be close by, too. But at the same time, it's a coincidence, and as I stand in the doorway I know my bad luck has returned. Out on the sidewalk, the flat-faced older woman from family day peers through the wrought-iron fence. She and I nod grimly at each other.

Sylvia's crying. "What are you *doing* here? Oh, let me look at you, my big, tall, handsome boy!" Ryan's telling her he had a big hit and scored a run. Neither listens to the other until at last Sylvia says, "But honey, are you by yourself?"

Ryan puts on an are-you-crazy look and points. "Howie's right there." Sylvia turns, and she's beautiful. Her skin, so sallow a week and a half ago, is a healthier color now, and her thin face is nearly the oval of our teenage years. I catch my breath — irresistible reflex — but after the phone calls and the catastrophe of family day, I don't know what my greeting will be. I stand in the doorway, struggling to remain expressionless.

"Howie!" Sylvia puts her arms around my chest. "Did I run right past you?" I've got the beer and the Sprite, so I can't hug her, and as she lays her head on my shoulder, I hold the cups away from our bodies.

"How's that eye?" she says. "You never answered my . . . Never mind." Furrowing her brow like a school nurse, she peers at me. "Still a little green there under the lid. Ryan, love, did Howie tell you how he hurt his face?" Then, without waiting for an answer, she calls to the woman outside the fence. "Mary Ellen, Mary Ellen, come on *in!* I want you to meet Ryan. And you know Howie — dear, dear friend and my first high school beau. Sit, come on and join us for a moment while we catch up!" The woman comes in reluctantly, saying they shouldn't stay. I think I catch her eyeing my beer, and it strikes me this place may be out-of-bounds. But Sylvia says, "Come *on!* It's Ryan!"

Mary Ellen whispers something I don't catch, and Sylvia murmurs back. "I can't go without you," Mary Ellen says. More whispering, then a glance at me. "Perhaps you gentlemen would come with us."

But Sylvia bridles at this. "Ten minutes. *Ten*, okay? God, I just don't want to take them to that rathole. This is my boy, and I want to be out in the world!" Sighing pointedly, she says, "Howie, do you suppose there's *coffee* here?"

I look at Mary Ellen. "Black," she says. Sylvia?

"Well, sure, why not? Maybe . . . lemonade? Here, let me." She takes a little purse from her big shoulder bag, but I wave her off: *I've got it.* I set my beer on the seat where Mary Ellen won't have to look at it, and Sylvia calls after me, "*Pink* lemonade, if they have it."

The place doesn't serve a lot of coffee, and it's a minute before the counter woman understands what I want. I don't even try *pink*. When I get back to the patio, Mary Ellen's sitting stiffly at the end of the table, and Sylvia has Ryan's baseball glove on. She's holding her hand out as if assessing a manicure. "Howie, this is a beautiful glove. You shouldn't have." I set the lemonade and the coffee on the table and pantomime swinging a bat, and she says, "A *double*. He told me. Funny, I've always found team sports so dull, but — here, Howie, sit by me."

Sylvia's always been able to recast her emotions at will. When we spatted in high school, she made me suffer before abruptly forgiving me, and today she's intent on keeping things friendly. She mentions the disastrous family day only to tell me that Big John, on leaving the facility, sent me his best, and she makes no inquiries about the phone calls. Instead, she's extravagantly affectionate, not just with Ryan, but with me, too, reaching out to stroke his cheek or touch my arm as she speaks. I'd chalk this up to the dry-out program's sensitivity training, but Mary Ellen sits ignored over her Styrofoam cup of coffee.

This I recognize, too. Sylvia's always had an aversion to losers, and with each confidence she draws a tight circle around Ryan and me. Mary Ellen grows drabber by the minute. But I'm just glad the loser's not me, and when a smile gets me nowhere with Mary Ellen, I give up. One thing no one expects from me is small talk.

At last, Mary Ellen announces she can't stay any longer. Sylvia says brightly, "No? Well, I'll be back before too long. Cover for me, can you? I just want to savor these guys a little . . ." Then, with no wasted words, she draws the circle closer. "Ryan, baby, I'm so thrilled Howie's is working out for you. I knew it would. Who else could I trust with — and how about *Laurel!* Who sounds, the little I've talked to her, like a real — a levelheaded *gem.* So that's one resolution for when I get out of this damn program, is to get to know Laurel and some of these other . . . And did you visit Mercy Convent, baby, visit Howie at work? Did you see the Contemplation Garden?" She takes our hands, and it's the moment to tell of my break with Sister Amity; but the moment passes. "Because you lead such a life of mystery, Howie! I just think it's shocking how long since I was invited for a visit, or that I never met Laurel or these marvelous young men." She looks at me squarely, and her brown eyes glitter. "I'm grateful you have good people in your life who care for you, because if anybody deserves a bit of love . . ." And though I'm more familiar than I wish with Sylvia's palaver, I can't resist something bold. I put my arm around her.

I don't squeeze her or pull her against me, but I place my hand at her waist, where I can feel her slim hip bone through the fabric of her skirt. And with this, I'm done for. From worrying that my luck had changed I've gone to sitting in the sunshine with the woman I love. Woman and child! And Sylvia doesn't shift aside or run to the ladies' room or employ any of a million crude tactics for escape. She simply allows me to hold her while she talks to Ryan, waving a persistent yellow jacket from her lemonade, asking about homework and weekends and baseball, shooting me a wry, almost seductive glance at the mention of Ms. Monetti.

The yellow jacket lands on the rim of my cup, and I let it stay. *Drink your fill, brother! These are good times!* I'm aware now not just of Sylvia's perfect hip, but of her soft shoulder brushing my chest each time she leans forward, and of the sweet, clean fragrance of her hair. I'm aware of my own developing hard-on, too. When the yellow jacket's gone I sip my beer, drowsily celebrating the sunshine and the buzz, and drifting from memories of getting drunk here all that time ago to thoughts of high school, when I kept my arm around Sylvia for two solid years, to a gauzy fantasy of being here right now — today! — as a family unhampered by injury or sadness, a threesome just out in the daylight for lunch. In the dream I'm dreaming it's not that I *can't* speak, but that I'm the dad, and I'm silent the way we dads are, drinking my beer as I smell Sylvia's hair and keeping the secret of my dick plump and tingly under the table. I keep it secret for later, when it will be us two.

When Sylvia says it's time to leave, I have to remain a moment, rearranging myself on my bench, and I picture the convent building and my old speech therapist and my idiot neighbor Dwayne in quick succession, just to calm myself down. Then we pile into the truck to take Sylvia to her residence. She sits in the middle, between Ryan and me, and it happens again. I don't know what's gotten into me — I'm *never* horny — but today I'm crazed, and my erection's so undeflectable that I'm afraid I'll catch it in the steering wheel as I drive.

Sylvia directs me to a square, three-story house a few blocks from her facility. It's not a bad house, only shabby, clad in brown asbestos shingles with false white plastic shutters. A huge pot for cigarette butts like those in the garden of the dry-out place sits on the porch, and even if I didn't know this place had no permanent residents, I'd guess it anyway from the forlorn atmosphere. And Sylvia suddenly seems forlorn herself. "Look, guys," she says, "that was just so nice sitting in the — do you mind if I don't bring you in this time? It's dreary, and it would break the spell." A man with a shaved head and wire glasses gazes at us from the porch, and she adds, "Oh, Christ, there's the law. Probably wouldn't let you in now, anyway." For a moment it seems she may start to cry; then she straightens her shoulders and turns to Ryan. "Well, my big darlin'

Snake, this sure was a wonderful surprise! Mama loves you, remember that always. If we can, maybe we'll do the same thing next we— well, let's see." Ryan throws his arms around her, and she holds him tight. "I'll call you, baby."

She asks me for a moment, and I get out of the truck. My deflated boner's no longer a threat. We walk a few steps across the grass, and Sylvia kisses my cheek, but as the bald guy jumps off the porch she mutters, "Yes! *Yes*, I have people who care about me, you jailhouse bastard. I went off on a Saturday for a little *time*. So fucking what? Curtailed privileges? Jeez!" Her eyes water, and she says, "Look, Howie, this is going to be an altercation, and I really don't want him to see it, okay? So take off quick and we'll talk soon. Thanks, hurry, love you." Then she pushes me away.

33

THE RADIO PLAYS ONE SONG, then another, and I wonder if Ryan's second-guessing the joyful reunion with Sylvia. But he only says, "Okay, here's the players who are pretty bad," and I have to smile. I suppose the inconsistent heart is childhood's great liberty, and if Ryan let the phone ring for weeks out of sheer sullenness and anger, yet still feels swept away by his mother in person — well, is my own response to Sylvia so different? Now he says, "Howie! Think we should go get my bat?"

We drive down their street, and Fartin' Martin's in his yard. Does this kid never go inside? With him is a girl who looks just like him, and both kids are wearing swimsuits. The sister has an inflatable sea-horse ring clasped around her waist. "Hi, Ryan," she says with singsongy flirtatiousness, and the two jailed Rottweilers take up the cry. A dad appears, smoking a pipe, and the girl shouts, "*We're* going to Magalloway Pool."

Fartin' Martin pads toward us. He's got a pale, round tummy, and his flat nipples are terra-cotta colored. The boys put their heads together a moment, then Ryan looks up. "Can I go swimming?" he asks. The dad and sister amble over, and the dad gives a satisfied puff to his pipe and says he's Martin Reed, senior. Ryan says, "This is Howie." We shake hands, and it's a done deal. I'll wait here.

Ryan runs up the three front steps of his house. He crouches defensively by the flowerpot, as if the Reeds could never imagine where to look for the house key; then the screen door slams raspily. A moment later it slams again, and he comes out in orange surfer trunks and hops bandy-legged down the steps. He gives Far-Mar a shove, and it seems going home is exactly this simple. Halfway to the Reeds' car he shouts, "Five-ish, Howie?" I give him a wave.

When they're gone, I scout out the bat in a corner of the garage. I find a Wiffle bat and ball, too, and I put all three in the bed of my truck. I get Sylvia's mail from the box and shuffle through advertising flyers as I stroll up the walk. I'm thinking about nothing. Then suddenly I'm in her house, and the screen door wheezes behind me. I can smell the faint, airless scent of Sylvia's housekeeping supplies, and I remember she loves to clean when she's on a binge. I think of her bingeing and cleaning and bingeing and bingeing until she was too strung out to clean anymore, and I think of Caroline carting her away. But for some thin dust, the place is impeccable.

I stand there a moment, clutching the mail. The house has no vestibule, so the instant I enter I'm right where she lives. All around me, on bookshelves and low tables, are the interesting small objects Sylvia loves to collect. An antique brass bird with a spring-catch beak for needles; a toy car that went through a fire. Glass paperweights and souvenir statuettes and antique teacups on wooden stands, dried flowers and shells and odd-shaped thingums Ryan created in art class. There are photographs, too, murky in the dim light, but I know them by heart. Photos of Ryan at every age, in all possible moods, and photos of Caroline, of Bindi, of college friends, of Sylvia's folks with Syl and Caroline after the baby was born. I'm here, too — once — in a shot I'm ambivalent about: Sylvia and me at a summertime picnic, snapped by my dad soon after I came home. When he gave it to her, she said I looked brooding.

All these photos and keepsakes are so familiar that I rarely give them a thought when I come in. In my mind, I walk through the door and this is *my* house, and I call out, "Honey, I'm home!"— a phrase so familiar it's become a joke. Sylvia doesn't answer, but I hear her chuckle. She's in the kitchen making sandwiches. There's a knife-tap on the mayonnaise jar and the movement of a shadow on wallpaper. I take a breath.

The house smells fresh. It's summer, and we keep our windows open. I don't smoke a pipe. I've brought our boy back from baseball practice, and I can't wait to tell my wife how he hustled when he hit that double. "You should have seen it," I'll say, and give her a soft peck. "Beat the throw by a mile!" Then Sylvia will say she'll catch a game soon, and that's enough to look forward to, because really it's father-son time, this Saturday morning sports thing, and that's how we like it. In the winter, ice hockey. My kid's fearless on the ice.

Sylvia and me: not the sad, gray Sylvia of "Let's just *go*," but the pink-cheeked, upbeat Sylvia of today, though with longer hair, if I have my choice. And no history of drugs, no long disappointment. No dead-ended art career, no bitter edge, either. No flat-faced under-dogs or circles of exclusion, no single-motherhood or numbing sec-retarial work, no scarring young grief . . . *no* teenage grief! And of course, I'm different, too. Alone in our kitchen, we two will chat about the game and what she did while we were gone and how well Ryan's doing in school. I'll brace a hand against the cupboard above her head and watch her lay out the bread for sandwiches, then add some of the roasted peppers I like so much. Slowly I'll lean against her, touching her back with my chest and feeling her hips soft against mine. Sylvia will rub demurely against me; then she'll cut each sand-wich with a carving knife and ask if I'd like to eat outside.

I would, but can we hold off, please? Our boy's off with his friends, and we have no housemates, so our privacy's our own. Hungry as I am, I pull her toward me, and she knows what's coming. I plant a kiss on her neck and rub her abdomen, and she turns to face me, run-ning her fingers through the short curls at my neck. My skin peb-bles until I'm nearly blind with . . . *Oh!* But I don't want this to go too quickly, so I hold her still and close for a moment. She's mine, and I'm so gentle. She is mine.

Sylvia's wearing a yellow cotton dress with big white buttons up the front. I'm sliding a hand between the buttons when one pops off and hits me in the chest, then clatters away. I could tear this whole dress off, *pop, pop, pop!* — but I kiss her cheek, her neck, her ear, and ease her onto the clean kitchen floor. It's any room in the house for us: the floor, the table, in front of a mirror, wherever the mood strikes. My wife's crazy about me. This is our home.

Sylvia's eyes are closed, her lips parted. I kiss her as I set her down, then undo my belt and the hitch of my Bermuda shorts. She raises her head and finds my mouth, and though I've been holding back, I kiss her harder now, and her lips give against mine. I tug at the buttons of the yellow dress and spread the fabric, then pull back to look at the thin waist, the small, round breasts. A pair of panties with a pattern of flowers and a bra that clips in front, which I undo. My shorts have slipped to the crook of my knees, and I kick them away, toward the doorway and the whole empty house, and Sylvia pulls me over her, grappling at my boxers and my ass and hiking my shirt up under my arms. Her fingers tear through the hair on my sternum; I press my face between her breasts. I'm absorbed by the feel of her skin — soft, powdery, so lightly textured. For a moment that's *all* there is: let me be consumed! A stand of soft, mysteriously filmy blonde female hairs gathers in a line due south of her navel, and I give these hairs a lap with my tongue. Sylvia tugs at the panties, and when she lifts a knee I rub my cheek on her thigh, then I'm where we both want me, my face in her curly pubic hair. I'm on the linoleum, my hands clenched tight between my legs. Hump and *grind!* There's a peak where her labia separate that's like a swirl of taffy; I go for it with my tongue, and Sylvia gives a high gasp of joy. I'm done fooling around now, I'm impassioned, I get serious! I stick my tongue out just as far as I can, and I'm pushing, *pushing* with my feet and humping my own hands on the kitchen floor and *gasp*ing and heaving and grunting, *shouting* for joy and using my tongue, my lower lip, my stubbly chin, *whatever,* on the soft, sweet bald spot at the very zenith of her pussy. This is something we were both too shy to try those few times before I went to war, but now — *now!* — we do it all the time. Sylvia's hands are lost in space for a while, but when I feel her fingers in my hair I crawl up her body and put my mouth to her ear. "I *love* you," I say, my strong hands working between our legs. I kiss her breathlessly and settle my weight so she can feel me. I stifle a laugh. "I *love* you," I say again; I *say* I love her! And Sylvia gasps, sucking in her breath, and tells me she loves me, too.

Which is not, of course, what really happens. Instead, I walk in a kind of daze through the spotless house, down the short bedroom hallway to where Sylvia's room is in front and Ryan's in back. A drawer is open in Ryan's room, and the clothes he had on this morning are heaped by the door. Otherwise, everything's in place.

Sylvia's bedroom is white, with tiny tea roses on the wallpaper. I lie down on the bed and undo my fly, then I go whole hog and shrug my pants to my shins. I hike my T-shirt to my armpits, and I can feel her quilted bedspread under my ass.

It doesn't take long. I'm good at this, believe me, though I do it more now from habit than desire. I close my eyes and stick out my tongue, I place my free hand way down under my balls, and I think again of the big-buttoned yellow dress I've invented, and of Sylvia's soft, fragrant, enveloping skin. The way she'll gasp and shout out loud — and suddenly I'm finished. I come silently, despite the empty rooms, but I come a lot. One small, wet dollop hits me on the chin, and I'm weightless for a few dizzy instants.

I lie on her bed, catching my breath. My stomach's a stew of semen and body hair, and in a sort of caress I gather the wet with my palm, then pull my T-shirt down to blot. I don't want anything dribbling on the bedspread. With my free hand, I reach down awkwardly and pull an edge of the fabric over me so I'm in a kind of dark pod, scented with Sylvia's laundry detergent. It's the type of place I could stay forever, but almost before the gunk has crusted I jump up, thinking of Ryan's return. He's not due for hours, but I can't take any chances, and I want to get Sylvia's lawn mowed for her, too.

34

I T TAKES ME AN HOUR to decipher Ryan's practice schedule, and even then I'm not sure I've got it right. Ed Mesk has abbreviated the days of the week and reduced the dates to digit-slash-digit, and once night has fallen I sit on my bed and puzzle over his broad, loopy handwriting. All the housemates are out, and Ryan sleeps silently in the next room. He was really tuckered. Now the big leaves on the catalpa slap together in a sudden gust, and a minute later it starts to rain. I go down to the driveway and roll up the windows on the truck, and the smell of the rain is so sweet and strong that I stroll to the porch and settle in the old rattan glider to watch the cloudburst. The rain pounds the porch roof and splatters hard on the asphalt road, then suddenly desists.

I'm accustomed to sitting alone at my house and waiting for the hours to tick by, but lately — even without a job — I've been too busy to sit around. Maybe that's for the best, because I don't know how I'll cope when this ends. It's fine to take an evening when the boy's asleep and watch the puddles dry up in the street, but I wouldn't want a steady diet of it; so I wonder what my options will be, and I think of Sylvia. Remembering my ripe behavior at her house this afternoon, I'm pretty embarrassed, but the memory of the barbe-cue joint makes me feel good. I think of sitting with my arm around her — first time in decades — and how she turned with tears in her eyes when the bald guy leaped from the shabby rehab-house porch. How she praised the baseball glove and said getting to know my life was her new resolution. What she said at the end.

Across the street, a car turns into a driveway. A man and a woman get out, and as she sidesteps a puddle he offers his arm. They enter the house, and a little later the door opens again, showing a stair hall that's the mirror image of mine. A teenage girl steps onto the porch and stands in the light of the doorway, chatting with the woman. The man appears, and he and the girl move down the steps toward the car. As he helps her around the puddle, I realize he's taking the babysitter home, and suddenly I can't help wondering what we looked like at that barbecue restaurant. Sylvia's the second of my two great burdens, but isn't it possible we looked like a family? Even considering Ryan's race? But there's a limit to how far I should go in this direction, so it's good my thoughts are interrupted. Laurel's little Beetle comes shushing down the wet road.

I go upstairs and get the practice schedule, and I meet Laurel in the kitchen. She's all dressed up: tailored slacks, a bit of blush on her cheeks. "Oh, Howard, what a night," she says, and kicks off a pair of black, pointy shoes. "You know, I just do not do enough cultural stuff!" I don't know what she's talking about, but I open two beers, and Laurel presses the cold bottle to her face. Evidently a client gave away tickets to the ballet, and just for a moment I wonder if she went alone. And Laurel studied ballet for most of her childhood, so she knows just how difficult the steps can be. One particular dancer did something magnificent, and there was an excerpt from *Swan Lake* and a modern piece with bare-chested men. The response was thunderous . . .

I stifle a yawn, and Laurel says, "Sorry, I'm rambling. But if you'd seen this girl, how *young* she seemed! They talk about ballerinas floating, but *really* —" I might be more interested if she acted it out.

At last she says dryly, "Thank you, thank you. You've been a wonderful audience," and glances at the paper I'm holding. "What you got there?" I lay the schedule on the table. Laurel says, "Hmm. Okay, this is . . . 'Practice sched—' Oh, my gosh, Howard, I forgot all — how *was* it?" I nod, and she says, "That's ter*rif*ic." I feel better now, and I want to tell her I got involved, too, so I indicate a bunch of kids and point to my chest. She doesn't get it. I gesture the kids again — I'm patting many small heads — then make a throwing movement. "Okay," says Laurel. "He got to pitch?" I shake my head and try once more: kids, me, throw. I leave Ryan out of it. But still Laurel knits her brow. It's not like her to struggle so with making me out, but it's not like me to have so much to say. And now I think I started with the wrong topic, but before I describe Ryan's hit, she yawns. "I'm really sorry, Howard. Maybe I'm tired or my mind's elsewhere. I'm just not — but I can help with *this*." She picks up the paper and confirms what I already suspect: "Looks like he's got long practices Saturday mornings and shorter ones, five forty-five to seven, two evenings a week. And this here's the locations: ball field Saturdays, then Healy Boulevard during the — what's Healy Boulevard?" It's the Mister Luster Kleen shop, but Laurel doesn't expect an answer. Tapping the paper thoughtfully, she says, "You know, there's no *games* listed. You got any other papers?" I shake my head. *Forget it, forget it.* I'm tired, too.

We blink at each other. Ordinarily we do better than this. Laurel bites her lip and says, "Well, Howard, I'm sure glad we both had successful days," and bends acrobatically to pick up her shoes. Suddenly, whatever flurry of connection we ignited at the water park has gotten short-circuited, and as I head upstairs I think how much easier it was to discuss baseball with Sylvia. And I completely forgot to tell Laurel about Sylvia.

35

THE WEEK PASSES, and we fall into the routine: practices twice weekly before supper, then Saturday mornings at the paired ball fields in the park. I'm back to my old habit of breakfast for the household, but I no longer wake up wondering what to serve. Instead, I think about my day with Ryan, and it's amazing how easily we fill the hours. One day we rent in-line skates and troll through the big city park, Ryan zipping ahead like a bug. Another day we drive north and rent a canoe. I'm spending a lot of money, but I want no regrets. Sometimes Ryan and I play catch in the back yard, but mostly I leave baseball to the Snakes. I'm more content than I'd have imagined with Mister Luster Kleen's baseball, but I'm not one of those sports-crazy adults who ruin kids' lives.

We receive a shaky phone message from Sylvia. "Hi, Ryan and Howard. Me, guys, Thursday night. So it looks like they're not going to let me out again Saturday like we'd hoped, damnation. Nobody really liked me hanging out at that place last week, even if beer is *so* not my problem. I swear, the turnkeys I live with are worse than the hotshots at the center! And it also had to do with" — she lowers her voice — "goddamn Mary *Ell*en being along. Be careful who you hang with, that's what I say." She sighs dramatically. "But also about learning to accept limits, resist impulse, change my pattern of thinking so that I look at the bigger picture, which I'm . . . I see the point, but I — And who on earth seriously understands how to change? But I'm here, so I'm working pretty hard to absorb those good lessons, et cetera. And I'll miss you fellas, and wasn't it amazing running into each other? Almost more fun than if we'd planned it in advance. So hit a big home run for Mama, baby, and remember every single thing so you can tell me. Much, much love . . ."

Ryan and I hear this message when we get in from practice. It's unlike me to monitor the answering machine so diligently, but Sylvia's been on my mind, and at the sound of her voice I'm back in her kitchen, in her arms on her floor. Still, I wince a little as I listen. Doesn't she think about what she's saying? The voice on the recording comes not from the vivacious Sylvia of last weekend but from some whiny stranger, powerless and conflicted. When she mentions Mary Ellen I smile weakly at Ryan, as if it's a joke, but when she launches into jargon I give up pretending. As the message finishes, Ryan takes up the dog-eared envelope with her phone number on it. "What would I say?" he murmurs, picking the flap with his thumb. I believe there's plenty he might say, and I know words will come once he hears Sylvia's voice. He could start by telling her how much we miss her, and he needn't respond to her sad meanderings. But he looks so awkward that when he says, "Can I do it tomorrow?" I let him off the hook. Even this is progress.

The machine clicks and starts again: a second call. I hear a throat being cleared, then "Howard Kapostash, this is Sister Amity Bridge, calling from Mercy Convent." The voice is raspy. "I thought you'd come by and speak with me this week, and I'm a little surprised that that hasn't come to pass. I also want to make sure there's been no misunderstanding, Howard. I hope you know that what I said last week was not categorical. Perhaps we both had some thinking to do. But I hope you'll come see me at your earliest convenience. As I'm sure you can imagine, the grass is *quite* long. You know where to find me; I'll be around tomorrow. I'd like

to get on this, Howard, and I look forward to speaking with you."
She puts the receiver down with a clunk.

Ryan's leaning in the parlor archway. He meets my gaze and
looks quickly away, and I feel my face redden. I can recognize a
poor impulse at fifty paces, but his shifty glance embarrasses me, and
I'll never forget how he witnessed my humiliation. I don't want him
thinking I'm beholden to anyone, so I give the answering machine
the finger and delete Sister Amity's message.

36

I'M STANDING BEHIND the Mister Luster Kleen shop, watching batting practice. I'm still the sultan of throw, and on Saturday I umpired as the kids played six innings against each other. But on the evenings we meet here there's less to occupy me, so I have the opportunity to assess the world.

Healy Boulevard is a commercial strip, and Mister Luster Kleen stands in a small plaza in an endless sequence of shopping plazas. A service road, where our vehicles are parked, runs behind the strip, and across the service road a vacant lot's been cleared for the kids. The lot's too narrow for a regulation diamond and outfield, but home plate and a single base path for sprinting, plus a low pitcher's mound, have been laid out on the bias. Most of the kids don't hit deep, anyway. Tonight, several Snakes are taking turns on the mound, while the others rotate fielding and catching duties. The birdlike woman who once gave me the evil eye — I've dubbed her the kid wrangler for the carload she chauffeurs to every practice — has proposed that each turn at the plate last until the child connects, and between a certain wildness from the pitchers, a burgeoning heat wave, and the flapping of the young batters, things are moving slowly. Juliana Mesk, in bright green madras shorts, stands in the batting area advising on form, but as a wafer-thin boy named Rajiv takes his fifteenth or twentieth swing, I can see her getting fidgety. "Remember what I told you, Raj: line your knuckles up. Attaboy." With a Sharpie pen, she draws a line across both sets of Rajiv's knuckles. "Just line 'em right up when you grip the bat."

Juliana and her father have done a nice job creating this little field. The coarse, chest-high yellow grass has been carefully mowed, and a softer, lawn-style grass fills the gaps. Behind the plate, a tower of hay bales serves as a backstop. And there must have been a ton of rubbish to remove. Looking at the neatly pruned perimeter, where the grass of adjacent lots stands like a wall, I wonder why Mister Luster Kleen's neighbors haven't volunteered their back lots, too, so a full ball field could be established behind the plaza. But this is one of those complicated questions I'm unable to ask, so unless someone volunteers an explanation, I'll never know. Liability, perhaps. A car pulls in behind me, and the mother of Ryan's blue-haired friend Shawn waves a paperback in my direction. "Think the heat's getting worse, Howard?" I point to the mound, where her boy's now pitching, and she comes and stands beside me, fanning herself with the book.

Ten days in, and I'm absurdly happy. I doubt I've felt so involved since the army, but there's nothing about this that's much like the army. Perhaps it's that I jumped in that first morning — throwing, umping — or that with no job to go to, baseball's our big event. Either way, the easygoing, fluid atmosphere reminds me of life before I was injured.

Shawn's mother laughs suddenly, nodding at a short-haired dog who lies panting in the outfield. "Who brought the extra fielder?" she says. I point out the kid who owns the dog, and as I do so I wonder if she's realized I don't speak. She strikes me as pretty spacey, her nose usually stuck in a book, and the team's broad cast of characters makes it easy for me to pass. "He's paying a hell of a lot more attention than most of the kids. I don't suppose he can throw," Shawn's mom says dryly, and I picture Sylvia getting to know these people, chuckling along with me and responding for both of us. In school, before the bitterness set in, she was pretty well-liked.

Rajiv finally pops one up. He throws the bat, sending Juliana and the young catcher jumping, and scampers toward the single base. In what I figure for the middle infield, the freckle-faced kid gets under it, but throws wild. Two kids part the yellow sheaves to hunt for the ball.

This is the type of thing that gets on Ryan's nerves, and under different circumstances we'd be listening to some mouthing off. But it's his turn to bat, and he moves to the plate, pausing like a big leaguer to lean the bat handle against his crotch. Ed takes a blue handkerchief from a pocket and mops the back of his neck, then flips Shawn a spare ball. "Batter up!"

Ryan hits the first pitch high, and we watch it sailing into the blue. It descends toward the center of the lot, where a couple of kids would have a chance at catching it if they weren't locked in some kind of wrestling match. The ball plops behind them, but only the dog seems to notice, adjusting its pointed ears before lowering its chin with a yawn. The woman I call the kid wrangler hollers that it was a nice hit, but Ryan doesn't sprint to first. Whatever pleasure he derives from a big smack is undone by the fielding, and he slams the bat to the ground and yells, "Catch the goddamn ball, ya asswipes!"

Everything stops. I sigh and stroll toward the plate, and Ryan cries, "They just stood there, bro!" I know they did, and it's hot, and I suppose he's frustrated at getting one swing after Rajiv's long turn at the plate. He's his mom's kid underneath it all, with her tart tongue, and sometimes he reminds me what she's really like. But Ed's a stickler for sportsmanlike behavior, so I pantomime disapproval, and when Ryan stomps to the sidelines I walk over and hand him his glove. *Catch some goddamn balls yourself*, I want to say. But he only says loudly, "This is supposed to be *practice*, not goof-off. We gotta win games."

More than anything in the world, I hate being a spectacle. I point again to the outfield and think how I'd handle this if I could say what I'm thinking. Oh, I'd be eloquent! I'd tell him we have standards for considerate discourse, and that after a nice hit the name-calling lowered him. I'd teach him about teamwork. Elizabeth, the tall black girl, sidles up to me and announces sanctimoniously, "Those two *are* A-wipes, Mr. K," and I want to tell her to mind her own business.

Then, abruptly, the spectacle dissolves. The next batter bops out a laconic liner, and one of the asswipes flops forward to stop it. It's clear from the laughs that greet this performance that the kid's been called to order. Juliana yells, "Pitching change, guys! Who else wanted to pitch? Come on now, almost quitting time. Let's *move!* Let's change catchers, too, okay? So Jeremy gets a chance to hit." She gives the stocky Asian catcher a clap on the shoulder and waves at Ryan. "Put your money where your mouth is, guy."

Ryan's approach is more fervent than mine. It took him no time at all to align himself with a posse of older, more competitive players — Shawn, Jeremy, one or two others — and though he can be playful at home, he's a terrier here in Luster Kleen Land. When other kids use the bats for sword fighting or lawn bowling, it's usually Ryan who suddenly *needs* one for batting practice, and when some kid goes dreamy and loses track of the play, it's always Ryan hollering to look smart. If he were my teammate I'd want him to calm the fuck down, but though the kids sometimes snarl back, they fall into line.

And yet, impatient as he can be with individual teammates, he's lost no faith in the broader enterprise. We still have no scheduled games and no real pitching coach, but he's never doubted that these will come, and he seems not to realize it's his cadre of überjockboys who are out of step with Snake inclusiveness. This amazes me. I expect him, at his spikiest, to throw the Snakes over, say he wants a team that kicks butt, and drag me off to sweatier pastures. But three times a week he's raring to go, and we're always the first to arrive.

Ann's Jamie is up to bat. He swings and swings, and as the time passes for practice to end, a few kids drift from the field and climb into waiting cars. The new pitcher's a long-faced, inscrutable boy with the team's best arm. He seems in no hurry to call it quits, and Ryan, catching, is in his element. He lunges dramatically as each pitch comes in and tries to get a patter going. "Yo, Ibrahim, Ibrahim. Show the fans how you nick the corner, Ib." But Jamie at the plate has begun to look trapped, and it seems we'll have to pull him or be here all night.

At last, I crouch behind him. His head's no higher than my earlobe, and I imagine saying to him *keep it flat, now! Don't be afraid to turn toward the ball, and if it feels right, stick your butt out.* I guide him through a few practice swings, but all I'm really murmuring is "Mbah . . . Mbah . . ."

Maybe Ibrahim can read my mind, or maybe he's just a very nice boy. He waits 'til we're ready, then lobs in an easy one. Jamie flinches, but I don't let him pull back, and we manage enough tap that the ball jumps forward eight feet from the plate. In an instant, Jamie's slipped from my grasp and is hightailing it toward base, and Ryan's saying, "Hit the whole *ball* for him, why don't you, Howie."

We're stowing the equipment in the back of the shop when Robin stops me in the roadway. "Howard, if it weren't so hot I'd give you a hug. I think you just salvaged a boy's fragile masculinity." She laughs her goofy laugh, then adds, "Speaking of fragile, what's the deal between you and Sister A?" With a stern face, she says, "The grass is *very* long." I'm not sure who she's calling fragile, but I won't get into convent stuff, so I just shrug. Someone yells that we're all going to Burger King, and I cock my head toward the vehicles. "Damn, wouldn't I like that," Robin says with a sigh. "But Ann would surely shred me alive if I fed him fast food. We live vicariously, ha, ha, ha, 'cept for these." She flicks an ash from her cigarette.

Ryan runs over to ask if we can go to Burger King, too. Sure! No food nuts in our household. Robin says, "Hey, Ryan, nice going with the bat. Think you could teach Jamie a thing or two?" He nods, though I'm not sure Jamie quite appears on his radar. She grins at him, then says, "Seriously, though, Howard —" But I especially don't want to discuss this in Ryan's presence, so with a hand on his shoulder, I steer him away. "Look, I don't know what exactly went down with you two," Robin says. "And Lord knows I'm no fan of Sister Shmamity. But you oughta look out for number one, How! It's not a bad gig, right?" It could be I pull away more abruptly than I intend, but it's my view I *am* looking out for number one.

37

R YAN PILES INTO A BOOTH with five other boys, and Ed waves me to one with Shawn's mom and the kid wrangler. "What the hell happened to the girls?" Shawn's mom asks sleepily, and Ed points out Juliana and Elizabeth sitting in a corner with a couple of pigtailed moppets. Elizabeth's declared the corner a no-boy zone, he says. Shawn's mom murmurs, "Look at them. So pretty and neat, even after playing sports! I wonder what it would be like to have girls for a week. Or for a *day*." We watch Elizabeth break up her fish sandwich and eat it in dainty bites, and the kid wrangler says girls are no picnic either.

I've never figured out which child the kid wrangler belongs to. She's always got a bunch piling out of her Caravan, and she's full of suggestions for the kids as well as for Ed and Juliana. Things grind to a halt whenever she's involved, and she kept that eagle eye on me early on. So I'm not a fan, but I nod amiably as I dig into my burger.

"Well, Ed sure knows what girls are like," she says now. "How long have you been a single parent?" Ed says his wife died when Juliana was seven, but they were separated at the time. The kid wrangler says she's also going it solo. "*Not easy,*" she announces. Turning abruptly to Shawn's mom, she says, "Now, Eleanor, your husband travels?" Shawn's mom looks briefly amused and says her husband's a pilot and the boys don't see enough of him, and the kid wrangler says she's comfortable with her divorce, but she's certainly not *dead*. There are times when a little romance, or even the *notion* of romance, just to see what came of it . . . Or even companionship. "I mean, who wouldn't?" She smiles lavishly at Ed, who nods a little blankly, and I sip my milkshake and think of high school. I didn't worry much about dates because Sylvia and I held steady from junior year on, but there were girls who flirted with me from time to time, and sometimes they got me into trouble with Syl.

"You've done an amazing job with Juliana," the kid wrangler tells Ed. "Ooh, isn't it chilly in here!" She wiggles her shoulders, and though I don't find her alluring, her short focus nettles me. I like Ed Mesk, and if he's susceptible to this nonsense I wish him the best. And I can't say by what shift I suddenly consider myself a player, but I'm here. I'm more virile than Ed, even with my scar, and I, too, am raising a child alone, at least for the moment. And no one has to know I'm unemployed. A cloud descends, and to keep it at bay I turn to the clowning boys at the next table.

The chubby freckled kid has on a Burger King paper crown. He's announced he wants to be called Sammy Sosa, and after chanting, "*Sam*my, *Sam*my," for a minute or so, the other boys choose alter egos, too. Ryan says he's Ken Griffey Jr. Shawn says, "Hey, hey, I'm Roger Clemens. I'm the rocket, man. Ninety-seven miles per owah! Pshhhhh*ooo!*"

Ryan says Clemens is a pussy. Some kind of rivalry's developed between Shawn and him. Looking shrewdly across the table, he adds, "Anyway, if you seriously wanna learn how to pitch, you gotta come to my house, dude. There's this guy there, he's like a friend of Howie's? And he — and also of mine, too. He was practically a pro, like he — Okay: *dy*namite slider, not-too-shabby fastball . . ."

Sammy Sosa says, "Oh, right, and he'd be friends with *you*."

"He is, man. He lives in our house. He's like old now, but I play ball with him."

Shawn says, "He's teaching you to throw sliders?"

"Yeah, man. No sweat. I mean, it's not like I have it *down*. But he showed me the grips." Jamming a French fry in his maw, he chews absently, a cool customer. "He was some all-star or something. I forget."

The boys blink at him in silence. At last Shawn says, "Sounds awesome. So when?"

"What?"

"When you wanna invite me over?"

Ryan tucks in his chin. "I'll have to get back to you on that," he says. "I mean, the guy has a *job*. But maybe some Saturday —" Then the lightbulb goes on. "Oh my God! Howie!" He flies from the booth and grabs my forearm. "Howie! How 'bout Harrison?" The adults are watching now — even the kid wrangler's on hiatus — and Ryan says, "Ed, Ed! Ed! There's a guy in our house who was like an all-star or something, and he's a lefty, like me. I bet he'd be a pitching coach. He already said he'd be happy to teach me." He turns for high fives all around.

Shawn says, "Mom! That would be so *cool!*" Ed says it would really help. I nod to suggest I'll do what I can, though I wish we'd nailed Nat down beforehand.

Ryan says, "Hey, wait," and I can see him thinking. "Wait, wait. You said that, about Harrison, didn't you? Before Mom came. At the rib place; *now* I get it." He looks quizzical. "I gotta listen better." I wipe a smear of milkshake from his eyebrow — how does he do it? — and he shouts, "Hey, Juliana!" When they tell him it's the no-boys corner, he says, "No, I really, *really* got something to say."

The kids, Juliana included, retire to the play area, and the adults stand by Ed's station wagon, shooting the shit. It's hot, and we're all grubby, and the Burger King parking lot is as unappealing as a place can be, but no one's in any rush to depart. The kid wrangler says Ed and Juliana should come for a meal sometime; she makes a mean chicken and biscuits, and Ed mumbles, "Sure," and "Thanks." I've let my attention wander, but Shawn's mom, Eleanor, catches my eye with a look. Ed says, "So Howard. Think your, um, pitching buddy might come through?" *I sure hope so, Ed.*

Ryan's still milking the Harrison connection when they troop back from the play area. "We're not related, but he like lives with us," he tells Ibrahim. "There's five of us in like a nontraditional household." I wonder where he got that phrase, and when the kid wrangler stares at me I really don't care. Let her imagine I live in a group home, a gay bar, a commune, a shoe. The scarred man has no need for the grass widow's blandishments. I live with Sylvia, in a Silly Putty house.

"Technically, though, I live with my mom," Ryan goes on. "But I'ma do the same thing when I grow up, just a big house with all my friends, and if you ever want somebody to play with or eat breakfast with, they're right there! That's how I know Harrison will want to coach pitching. It's like a brotherhood, man." Sammy Sosa says he's going to do the same thing when *he* grows up, and how about if they lived in the same big house, just the Snakes. And I never thought of myself as living with my friends, but there you go.

38

RYAN'S SHOWN LITTLE INCLINATION to pitch, but he's certainly keen on getting Nat to coach. "You, me, Harrison, man. We three are gonna be the *heart* of the Snakes." But when we arrive home the house is empty, as it so often is, and after a little television he drifts off, and then I do, too. I wake in darkness in the middle of the night, and it's a minute before I can fix my coordinates; then the draperies of the parlor fall into place, and the roughness against my cheek becomes the nubby couch fabric, and the soft lump that figured so heavily in my dreaming merely a pillow I've doubled up under my crotch. The big chair where Ryan had been is empty, and the television's off. Upstairs, he snores lightly on the futon, curled against a pillow of his own.

Laurel's door is closed, my own open doorway a swatch of dark. I should get to bed. I go into the bathroom and brush my teeth, then lean on the sink, staring at myself in the mirror. Laying a hand over my scar, I consider my gray eyes, my even, rather supple mouth. My face would be more lined, I think, if I'd spent years *using* my mouth, and I pantomime talking, just to see what I'd look like. With my hand still covering my brow, I watch my jaw move, my tongue flash, my lip catch the overhead light; then I raise my eyebrows to make some imagined point. I smile wryly and go serious:

I'm a teacher, an actor, a motivational speaker. Maybe I'm persuasive. I'm not — *I wouldn't have been* — bad-looking, I think, with my kind mouth and strong features. Just a nice-looking, middle-aged man with gray eyes, clear skin, and thinning hair. Sexy, maybe. Maybe even a catch. Then I move my hand, and my scar appears like a splatter of grease.

I go downstairs and slip out the front door. I'm not going anywhere, just getting some air. The warm night smells familiar but indefinable: pollen, I guess. Not a car rolls down the street. I don't linger on my porch but set out purposefully, though I'm not sure what I want. I can't think when I've felt so restless. Along my street, one house after another is shut down for the night, showing only the occasional blue of a television or the pale glow of a night-light. Up ahead, where the wide avenue crosses my street, a motorcycle passes, the sound inflating to fill the intersection, then collapsing and moving off.

At the crossroads, I turn south. In eleventh grade I learned to drive and fell in love, and I've been turning south at this corner ever since — it's this way to the convent and Sylvia's and the ball fields and anywhere else I might want to go. But in all those years I never came on foot. Now the road is a file of streetlamps whose peach-colored realms I enter and depart one by one, crossing residential streets very much like mine and wide boulevards where cars wait at traffic lights. As the bluestone sidewalks of my own neighborhood give way to concrete, I feel not like myself but like some stranger I'm merely watching to see what he'll do; I'm the walking man or the lonely man or the hopeful man or the man who just wants another chance, the man who, in all of these guises, keeps on going, lamp by lamp. After a while the road splits, two lanes curving off to the right, and it's necessary to cross one fork to follow the other. I'm in the middle of the roadway when I pull my shirt off over my head and stretch out my arms, letting the warm air wash around my elbows and armpits. A traffic signal changes from yellow to red, but there's no one around, and I'd like to strip off *all* my clothes, kick my work boots in the gutter, leave my jeans in a V on the sidewalk and my boxers figure-eighted under a bush. But of course, I only hang the shirt from my neck, as we used occasionally to do on commando. Entering a fancy residential area where each long driveway is guarded by a lamppost, I take my shirt from my neck and hurl it into the branches of a tree, where it hangs in effigy.

I come to the large traffic circle which was the turnoff in my teen years for visiting Sylvia. In the center of the circle sits a small white monument or temple, the sight of which meant I was almost there. How broadly I'd spin through the big curve, one hand on the wheel, then descend from this wealthy plateau to the more modest blue house where she was waiting! Now Sylvia lives farther away, and this is my halfway point, but I pause for a moment, and as I step toward the little edifice, my longing deepens. Round, with white columns and a domed cap, the temple is like something in Washington, DC, though I've never observed it very closely before.

The traffic island's planted symmetrically, with radiating fans of red and white annuals. As I watch, one of the beds shimmers suddenly, like water, then resolves into a figure — a genie — that stands stiffly and moves toward the temple steps. The genie is taller than I am, with a messy beard and long hair thinning atop a seed-shaped head, and even in darkness his shirt and trousers appear filthy. It's that ragged man I've spotted occasionally at curbside. I freeze, and for a moment I'm once again watching myself. I'm high above the traffic circle, and there's my figure and his, as if we're trapped in a kaleidoscope of impatiens. We face off across the patterns of the flower beds, then he says, "Bro," and I swoop down into my skin. He offers a hand, and as I step closer to slap his fingertips I enter a pungent cloud of body odor, the smell of the street, and some metallic scent I can't quite identify. I'd back away, out of the cloud, but he gets me in a kind of secret handclasp, thumb to thumb. Slowly he looks me over, nodding sagely at my scar and my bare chest. "Yeah, I know, man," he murmurs. "Timothy knows." I extract my hand, and he says, "Timothy," again, louder. I can't give my own name.

Timothy's eyes are large and protuberant, with whites that swell around his tacklike pupils. He holds my gaze belligerently, moving his lips as if reminding himself of how much he knows, and I step away, wiping my hand on my pants. A moment later he calls out, "Fuckin' *vet*, man!" and when I look again he's at the edge of the flower bed, staring dully at me as he fiddles with his fly. He takes his dick out and sprays one arc, then another, over the sheet of white flowers, never shifting his hard, white eyes from mine. "Fuckin' vet."

I turn hastily, then think I'd better not look away from this guy, and I turn once more and start to back toward the roadway. Timothy glares at me as his stream ends; then he drops his dick, as if forgetting it's there. The whites flash off as he closes his eyes, and he spits deliberately, the way some guys do after urinating. The spit dribbles from his chin to his dirty shirt, but he doesn't open his eyes. "C'mere, c'mere," he hisses, grappling at his trousers. They slip away from him and fall to his knees. I'm at the curb when he stumbles backward and goes down suddenly, and his head makes a terrible clunk on the concrete.

I stop short. Already Timothy's attempting to stand, and it doesn't look like he even lost consciousness. But I had a head injury myself, and I'm a vet, too. For a moment, struggling to organize his pants, he's like a roped calf, and I tell myself he'll be up in a moment. Then I'll take off. But he only makes it to his hands and knees before toppling hard and full on his face, and at this I rush over and clutch his arm.

I help him shuffle to the steps of the little temple and get him leaning against a column. There's blood on his head, but when I reach up, he flinches and looks dangerous. I'm not eager to touch him any more than necessary, so I hold up my palms — *okay, okay!* — and I'm backing away when I think something should be done about his poor, bare ass. Averting my face from the terrible smell of him, I gingerly raise his pants and hitch the fastener at his scrawny abdomen. I won't touch his dick, though, and when tugging the fabric doesn't jiggle it inside, I leave it snagged on the zipper. It's like an animal in a snare, but I doubt Timothy gives a shit. He's still clutching the column when the metallic smell hits me. It's the slag of a strung-out body processing pharmaceuticals. I've met guys like this before.

Timothy says, "I fought in a war." He looks hazily at me, and I wonder if this is my old friend Timmy, who lived next door to Radnor and preceded me to the jungle. Many years ago, Timmy was a long-haired teenager with slit eyes and a pointed jaw. He ran with a rougher, more delinquent crowd than Sylvia and I, but whenever we ran into him he was surprisingly affectionate. Now I gaze at this bearded wreck of a guy and wonder if there's anything I recognize, and the eyeballs flash and he says, "Gimme a dollar." Baring his teeth, he says, "I *killed* people, motherfucker," and I think *then you've got me beat, thank God*. If this poor guy is Timmy, he doesn't recognize me, either.

Timothy pokes my dollar in his fly, then draws it out, looks at it, and pokes it in a hip pocket. "I do. I fuckin' kill people," he says. He puts his dick away and starts to zip up, but topples facedown on the marble floor. This is clearly my cue to take off, but Timothy says defiantly, "*Asian* people," and suddenly I'm afraid to move. I inch down opposite him, my bare back against a pillar, and Timothy turns his face in my direction. "Asians," he says, his cheek flattened by the marble floor. "Never killed no American dudes. That I know of. Saw a guy run down by a tank once, ran some gook down with a tank myself once, too. Didn't I? Naw, that wasn't me. But this one guy, motherfuckin' nine-life bastard, couldn't kill 'im. Couldn't kill 'im with a, with a, with a — with a *knife!* Got a motherfuckin' bouncin' betty, got lots of sharp sticks, got all the firepower you could — got North *America*, man, North fuckin' America, *tanks* and shit, *na*palm, though I rather use my damn *fists* myself, and you put your napalm up against some cocksucker who builds fuckin' burrows, you go in with your *own* sharp sticks, say, 'Take this, take *this* sharp stick, little slant-eyed shitboy, take it right up your narrow fuckin' *ass*.' But this one guy, this one guy, this one guy, this one guy, this one mother*fuck*in' nine-life guy . . ." He goes on, dribbling saliva on the marble, maybe remembering my presence, maybe not.

Timothy's story doesn't make any sense, and his voice gets flatter and flatter, then trails off completely. I stay where I am, feeling suddenly too tired for the long walk home. Every so often a car rounds the circle, its headlights illuminating the columns one by one, and after a while a girl appears, walking slowly on the far side of the roadway. When I look again there are two girls, one dark and one blonde, and when the blonde girl leans on a lamppost and lights a cigarette she looks like something from a vision. I wonder if they're streetwalkers. It's not the neighborhood for it, but I'm out of touch. And the blonde one's pretty, with her hair cut tight to her skull. The girls stay a long time, languidly chatting, and I wonder if they see me here, by the pile of rags that is Timothy. I wonder if I, too, am a vision, and I imagine how I must look from afar: a small figure, haggard and sleepless, propped by a pillar. The hair on my bare chest is thick but graying as I grow older and more naked; the fat scar on my forehead never changes. I could be turned to stone here and remain sheltered by this little structure, and Timothy and I would become a monument. A monument to what?

The next thing I know, the girls are gone and the sky is yellow in the east. Timothy hasn't budged except to wet himself, creating a paisley of urine that catches a column top in its reflection. Stepping around it, I think the water looks unpleasantly dark. I take another buck from my pocket and flick it at Timothy, trying to aim it so it lands near his face, but the bill flutters lazily to the edge of the puddle, and I get the hell out of there. On the far side of the circle a landscaper's truck is parked, and two men are unloading a John Deere. They stare at me as I hurry into the early morning traffic, and I wonder if waking Timothy is their regular ritual. I might come back someday and inquire about work, I think, then shudder the idea away. How would I explain myself if I were recognized?

39

I SLIP IN THE FRONT DOOR, shower and shave upstairs, and join Laurel in the kitchen. Shifting a saucepan on the stove, she says, "Did you get up early, Howard?" I think of my open bedroom door. So I nod as I get to work on our eggs. Let her think I've taken up jogging.

Nit and Nat are up early, too. I hear them in the driveway, loading scaffolding on their van, and when breakfast is ready, I wave at them from the stoop. Nat comes in and says they've got a hell of a drive, and do I mind if they take an egg sandwich to go? "Thanks a lot, Howard; no disrespect. I don't know why Stevie accepts these jobs out in the boonies." To Ryan he says, "Not now, bub, ya mind? Tonight or later, okay? Hey, Laurel, are you leaving too? Want me to move the VW?" From the driveway comes the toot of a horn, then Laurel bustles out also, and everyone heads to the salt mines.

"Howie!" cries Ryan, in a voice of anguish. "I couldn't talk to Harrison!" I'm so sleepy that it takes a minute, but I rub his shoulder sympathetically. *We'll catch him tonight.* I yawn through my fog, and I'm very glad not to be working myself. When the dishes are done, I wander out to the catalpa and lie down in the grass for a nap.

I wake to hear Ryan whispering, "Ruby, shut *up!*" Peeking through my lashes, I see him stretched on his back, like me, with an arm over his eyes, just like me, too. Ruby wheezes as she nuzzles his neck, and he bats her away. An anxious yip, then another. Ryan says, "Shhh," but doesn't open his eyes.

I make one of my customary noises — a yawn in this context — and stretch so my arm falls heavily across his body. Ryan doesn't move. I roll over and snore cartoonishly, whistling on the exhale, and ruffle my fingers against the underside of his forearm. He endures this for a moment, then cries, "Howie! You're not asleep!" He pushes my arm away. "Wake up!"

I sit up and look at him, stretched out like a hayseed. Ruby's barking now and tugging his T-shirt, and in an instant I'm a canine, too. I'm up on my knees, and though I can't match Ruby's yap, I do what I can to growl. Ryan says, "Uh-oh. Looks like I'm surrounded by bears." He makes some kind of kung-fu movement, then, with an "Arggh!" claps his hands to my head. I bellow back, wrapping my arms around him, and roll onto my back so he straddles my chest. He's laughing now, in the giddy, over-the-top way of very small kids, and as I laugh back at him my stomach jiggles, tossing him like a rag doll on a mechanical bull. "We're — We're — We're —" he calls out, then collapses in hilarity, leaving the thought unfinished. What has become of the Snakes' ruthless competitor?

At last, I roll him onto his back. The laughing jag's died down, but he's trying to sustain it. He pants some, then breaks into giggles. His T-shirt's hiked up his chest, and on impulse I put my head down and kiss his brown belly. I say, "Grrr . . ."

I feel a hand on my forehead. The touch is light; he's fingering my scar. My flesh is damp and sticky in the heat, and my sparse hair's plastered to my skin, but I close my eyes and offer him my face, and he carefully follows the fretwork of small lines. He moves toward the puffy central zone, where I have less sensation, and I feel him probing as if he might find fluid or pus or tapioca under the skin. But it's only skin. At last he sighs and takes his hand away, and I roll over on my back beside him. I look up at the broken pattern of leaves on the blue sky and wonder if this is something he's thought about for a while. I figure people either have an abiding curiosity about my scar or it grosses them out.

Ryan stretches, letting his arm fall across me this time. "Hey, man," he says, and I can tell from his voice that he's a tough guy again. "We got anything doing today?"

40

W E PACK A LUNCH and head for a small local pool, where I make myself useful checking out women's figures. Toward afternoon's end the weather changes, and we return home under a livid sky that I hope will mark an end to the heat. Ryan scampers right inside, but I stay in the yard for a while, smelling the electric air and tending to my replanted morning glory seedlings. I'm aware of him lurking at the screen door, but only later do I realize he was waiting for me.

Coming in, I almost stumble over him. I scratch his brown neck and offer him an apple from a bowl on the counter. He shakes his head. I take one myself and head for the parlor, and I'm reaching for the remote when I hear him dialing the phone. He dials carefully — must be his first time with a rotary — then says, "Ms. Mohr, please," in a cool, rather secretarial tone. There's a long pause while Sylvia is fetched, then the smallest, most kidlike voice imaginable says, "Mom?"

I ease onto the arm of the couch and go on crunching at my apple. For a while Ryan doesn't say much, and I imagine Sylvia blathering at full throttle. "Good," he says finally. "Uh-huh, swimming and stuff." A moment later he says, "Different positions. Last time I caught for a while . . . No, like *being* the catcher, silly," and gives me a look that comes straight from his mother: eyes rolling at the idiocy. "Yeah, but — Oh, but wait, one thing, one thing! Howie and I are going to get Harrison to teach pitching. He's an amazing pitcher." Then, "*Har*rison. Who *lives* here," and that look again. "Nah, Howie's here most of the time now . . . Me and him, mostly . . . While the others are at *work*." He watches me finish my apple, then says, "Hey, did you know he eats the whole entire apple, even the core?" I know Sylvia knows this about me, and I try to imagine her telling him that she knows. I've never been inside that place she's staying, but what I see is a drab room with cheap, scuffed furniture. There's a beam of light, and Sylvia's in a yellow dress. She smiles at the memory.

Ryan says, "Me too, yeah. A lot, a lot." Then, to my astonishment, he adds, "Howie wants to talk to you."

I take the receiver, and Sylvia says, "Hello, dear." She's a little crisp today, less effervescent, and if I could speak, I'd counter with charm. Instead, I bark a syllable. "Well, what a relief to finally hear from him," Sylvia says, "I tell you. I wonder if I'll ever really know what *that* was about . . ." She pauses a moment so I can contemplate this, then executes one of her lightning shifts. "But he sounds *great*, Howie. You've all done a marvelous job, and I'm . . . You know, my biggest worry through all this was for Ryan at his age, and I think we've, *every*body's truly managed to minimize — or at least make certain things — as painless as possible. Will you thank the others for me?"

I say, "Putt." I'm the one to thank. Holding the phone to my ear, I rub my chest and imagine her in yellow, in a swimsuit, stretched out by the pool. I want to say *it's all been a pleasure*, and I wish I could tell her how delightful it was running into her, how wonderful she looked, and what a surprise. It made my day. If her child weren't standing next to me, I might even describe my reverie in her empty house. I'd tell her we could have that, we could start right away. But I can only say, "Putt," again, and I turn as I say it so Ryan won't see me feeling so naked.

Sylvia says, "I'm really thinking about the future, Howie. Just really reevaluating how I've been living. I've been speaking with Caroline, too, and of course she — well, it's too soon to say anything definite, but I've made wonderful friendships here, one in particular. I think it's important for Ryan to be —" In the background there's a thunderclap, and Sylvia gasps. "Did you hear that, Howie? *Right* overhead. I wonder if we — look, it sounds like it could be quite a storm, and we should get off the phone. But I — Oh, *God*, I wasn't going to say anything, and I probab — but I must tell someone! I'm nearing the end of my time here, thank heaven, thank *heaven*. I'm so incredibly ready, and we're thinking as soon as Saturday, not this one but next. That would be eight weeks, can you be*lieve* it? So it's what I'm visualizing, but —" She pauses to breathe. "Without expectations, with patience and serenity. *God*, I can't wait to get back to my life!"

I tell Sylvia, "Mmm," but I sound like a bug. Nothing is less suited to my abilities than a telephone. If I could place myself before her I'd let her know that I, too, am thinking of the future. I'm longing to look after her.

Sylvia says, "I don't have to tell you I didn't mention my release to him. Ostensibly it's the client's, or at least a mutual, decision, but there's all sorts of pressure before we — These people *never*, ever tip their hand. So I can't be definite, which is maddening, crazy, crazy maddening. But in the meantime, don't take any long vacations." She laughs shortly as thunder booms again overhead, and when I pass the phone back to Ryan I'm reeling with unsaid thoughts.

I make spaghetti for supper, which he loves, and we eat in the kitchen with the windows and doors open. Regarding the call to his mother, I limit my commentary to a pat on the back. I'm suppressing plenty already, from a panicky yearning for Sylvia to come home to the fear I'm not ready: that more could be in place first, that the trio of Ryan and me and her is not inevitable, that in ten days he'll simply leave. Around the house the world darkens and pales as the thunder passes with nary a drop.

In the stable are the boards I bought to build a new porch planter, and it's a relief, after the tumult of that phone call, to turn to something material. A transparent moon rises over the catalpa, and as I step out the back door, Puff the cat saunters by for a scratch. By the time Ryan joins me I've got the five pieces cut, and while I rummage in a cupboard for clamps, he arranges a rectangle on the concrete. I show him how to apply the glue and set the clamps so the corners stay perpendicular. Then I let him tap the nails in himself.

Through it all, he's waiting for Harrison. Each time a car passes he looks toward the street, and when at last the battered van pulls into the driveway he throws down the hammer. But it's only Nit, flying solo. Ryan says, "Where's Harrison?"

Nit looks at him a moment, then says, "Well, hello to you, too, man. How the hell should I know?" *Because you guys are joined at the hip*, I think — though in the short time Logan Monetti's been on the scene Nat's been around less. Nit digs a bag of Doritos out of the van and offers it to Ryan, then kicks the gravel. "Listen, Howard. Think I could stash my crap in the garage, just for the night? My back's killing me, and those cellar stairs . . ." This one's always got some kind of hard luck, but it's no skin off my ass, so he and Ryan stack the drop cloths in the stable, and I follow behind with two five-gallon drums of paint. Hell, the man's got back troubles. Nit says, "Thanks, amigos. Fucking Harrison was supposed to help me with this junk. But." It gets dark, and we go in and turn on the TV, and I bet those Doritos were Nit's only supper, so I snap my fingers and gesture that there's food on the stove. Ten minutes later I wander in for a beer, and he's eating the cold sauce right from the pan. Poor hapless individual! I rattle the spaghetti box at him and set a pot to boil.

Laurel bustles in, smelling like a brewery. She's in a Vietnamese language group that meets at a tavern, and she always comes home cheerful from their meetings. Sniffing the pan, she says, "Mmm-*ma*ma. Anything but soup," and when Nit tells her I made the sauce, she picks a fleck of plaster from his hair. "*Duh*, Steve. I didn't think *you* cooked." I add pasta to the water so there'll be plenty for both, and when I look again, Laurel's pouring kibble for Ruby, and Nit's staring at her ass. I let him know I caught him looking, but I'm feeling companionable, and Laurel does have a cute ass. When she straightens up, I gesture *little guy, phone*. She says, "No way, José! Talk about the unlikeliest thang."

"Is Harrison here?"

We all turn, and Ryan's in the doorway, looking serious and sleepy. Laurel says, "Darlin', are you still up?" and as I gather him in my arms, he accepts the fiction that he's a rather small boy. "I heard you called your mom," she says, and he yawns, letting his eyelids flutter. "Okay, hon-bun. Nighty-night."

Nit's slumped against the countertop. He smiles foolishly and says, "So long, man," dipping his face to Ryan's eye level. I give him a moment to register how lucky we are, and at last Nit plants a hurried kiss on Ryan's cheek. He stands up, pulling the hair from his face, and when I turn to go he slaps my butt, the sheepish nitwit.

I'm halfway upstairs when Ryan decides to wake up. He raises his head and says, "My note!" then repeats himself as I turn back downstairs. "*Mynotemynote!*" On the coffee table by the TV is a sheet of blue-lined notebook paper with a message:

DEAR HARRISEN,
   WILL YOU PLEASE COACH PITCHING FOR THE SNAKES BASEBALL TEAM?
               LOVE, YOUR FRIEND, RYAN MOHR

In the kitchen, Laurel's straining the pasta. Nit does a double take and says, "Morning already?" I bend to let Ryan place his note on the table, setting the sugar bowl on it as a paperweight. "Good *luck*," says Nit. We troop upstairs again, and I straighten the sheets on the futon. When I'm finished, he's got a shoe off. I slip off the other, and I'm helping him with his shorts when he calls for his cap. But when I come back with it he's fast asleep.

I don't exactly wait up for Harrison, but I don't go to bed, either. I'm thinking of Sylvia on the telephone, and more than ever I want the happiness to cohere. I won't *permit* Harrison to slough off Ryan's request. In the meantime, I'm in the cellar, contemplating that Gothic window frame the nuns gave me long ago. I move some milk crates, and the frame makes a scraping noise as I pull it from the wall. The middle arch stands more than seven feet tall, and the side wings could catch foul tips. With some netting attached, it would make a nifty backstop.

I'm sponging the wooden mullions when a car door slams. Ms. Monetti's green Saturn is parked at the curb, and as she and Harrison pass my window she says, "I mean it. Just a nightcap." I creep to the top of the stairs.

The screen door opens. Ms. Monetti's giggling, and I remember that she lets her hair way, way down in summer. Harrison says, "Wanna tuck me in? I could tuck you in, too." A body leans on the cellar door, just inches from where I stand.

Harrison says something I can't hear, and Ms. Monetti replies, "Because. It's not ethical. I have a student here." Harrison says Ryan's not her student anymore. "That's not the point."

"Just stay in my room, Logan. No one even has to know. I'll bring you breakfast." There's a longish pause, and I imagine them kissing. "Howard's waffles," he says. "I'll keep you in my pumpkin shell. Come *on* . . ."

I hold my breath, wishing I'd gone to bed. I never imagined him not coming home alone, but I'm stuck now, and as the kissing continues I despair at how easy romance is for some people, how hard for me. I ease my butt down onto a step, and my shirt snags a nail and tears with a deafening zip. Harrison and Ms. Monetti hear nothing.

Ms. Monetti says this is ridiculous; she has to go home. She sounds like a grammar school teacher. Harrison says, "Shh, shh,

shh, o*kay!* But how about a little schnapps? Or crème de menthe?"
At last, they step the few feet to the kitchen. Glasses tinkle.

Ms. Monetti says, "Okay, look. As just about the perfect example why I can't stay here." She's spotted Ryan's note; I put my ear
to the wall.

Harrison says, "Huh. That's Saturday mornings. Man, you
should see him. How keyed up he gets."

"Maybe some other weekend."

"Well, we try not to work Saturdays. But like . . ." He breaks off.

There's a silence, then Ms. Monetti says, "Aren't we going to
Chicago?"

"Oh, sure. But I don't know if — I might even have offered.
Lemme think a minute."

"Babe, look. Not to sound like a bitch, but some people really
can't say no to children. It's not a job."

"Would ya hang on?"

Harrison sighs and clicks his tongue; Ms. Monetti says, "I
should go."

"No, come on. Come on, now, Logan. I mean, I know it's not a
job, but like for you, you get your fill, I guess, for a whole year. And
it's not that I can't say no to Ryan, but maybe, like if it was like only
the morning? I did that shit myself as a kid. I — What's a couple
hours?"

"Oh." A glass clicks to the table "If it's what *you* want. I mean, I
thought we had plans. Can I be disappointed?"

"No, sure," says Harrison. "We do. We totally *have* plans, and
I'm not trying to disappoint you. But I mean like . . ." His voice
warms. "What's my incentive?"

This is the last I hear. A silence follows, and I lean my head on
the wall and smell the dampness in the plaster and the dust motes
seeping down from the cupola. Last night's ramble has suddenly
caught up with me, and my next thought is that I've missed Ms. Monetti's departure. I seem to have been dreaming that it's not Harrison but that fucked-up Timothy who has something to teach Ryan,

and with a jerk I catch myself from tumbling downstairs. I listen a minute, then open the door.

The hinges creak, and Ms. Monetti screams. I step from the dark staircase and blink at the kitchen, and they're in the corner between the sink and the stove. Ms. Monetti's chestnut hair is fluffed out around her, and though she stops screaming when she recognizes me, she goes on cowering against Harrison. Sliding a hand in the pocket of his tented-up shorts, Harrison says, "Howard. Jesus Christ," and I don't know if I should cross the kitchen or back out through the dining room and take the long way upstairs. "What are you doing?"

I brush off a cobweb. I'd say I dozed off washing the Gothic window, but it's a moot point. Then Laurel's standing opposite, her white kimono bright as a plinth. "Guys?" she says sleepily, and smiles at Ms. Monetti. "Hi there, Logan." *Hah* there.

Harrison looks from Laurel to me. "What is this?" he says. "A posse? Sheesh." He glances at Ryan's note, and I think he's trying not to laugh in our faces. "Fine, you two. I'll do it. You don't have to gang up on me."

Laurel says, "I don't know what you mean. I'm not ganging up. I heard a cry." A *crah*. She glances at Ms. Monetti, now fussing with her blouse, though as far as I can see she's all buttoned up. Ms. Monetti shoots me an aggrieved look.

Laurel yawns, gathering her kimono at the throat. "Come on, Howard," she says. "Good night, y'all." Mission accomplished, I tag along. Laurel calls out, "That's real sweet of you, Harrison. He'll be pleased," but at the top of the stairs she starts to snicker. "What'd you *do?*" she whispers. "Walk right in on them? Oh, my lord!" She picks up Ruby, who's sitting expectantly on the carpet. "That poor girl must think she's in a zoo."

I give old Ruby a scritch of the ears. Downstairs, a latch clicks, then a motor starts up, and in the kitchen the water runs briefly. Laurel asks, "What *were* you doing?" I shrug. *Checking my Gothic window.*

Harrison takes the steps two at a time. He sees us standing between our rooms and rubs his goatee. "Mom? Dad? It's time for you guys to let go a little. I know that's gonna be hard for you, but us fledglings gotta leave the nest, okay?"

"Gawd. We are just so ashamed of ourselves," Laurel says. "Aren't we, Howard?"

41

I LIE ON THE SHEETS and stare at the ceiling. Despite the slumberers in the rooms around me, the house feels like an engine that's continued idling after the ignition's been cut, and despite my exhaustion and the sleeplessness of the last twenty-four hours, I'm vibrating, too. In rapid succession I see disordered pictures from the recent past: Laurel bursting into the kitchen in high spirits; Ms. Monetti, with her hair and buttons. Pretty young mamas at the pool, Sylvia in yellow, Laurel with her cheeks flushed after the ballet, kicking off her shoes. Sylvia promising visits, saying I'm a mystery man, praising the baseball glove. Sylvia in yellow, under a light. The blonde girl by the streetlight and Shawn's mom and Sylvia talking and Ms. Monetti clutching at Harrison in the corner of the kitchen. Harrison clutching Ms. Monetti, too. Nit, as he checks out Laurel's behind. Then me, having a small second supper of spaghetti and trading nothings with the people who live here. Ryan living with his friends. The man in the house opposite, taking the babysitter home, and everything around me that's so much like a dream. Sylvia in manicure posture, the big brown baseball glove on display. That girl by the traffic circle and the light on the pool, Sylvia on her way home, Sylvia telling me she's coming soon, Sylvia in good health in the crook of my arm, filled with excitement and the same potential for disaster as always, but the same promise, too. And it's not Ryan this time who's got me so riled; in fact, he's barely present in my thoughts. Instead, it's something bigger, more worldly, that's out there waiting. Something other people take as a matter of course, and I might, too. The way I felt in that putty-colored box, gazing at tea roses in the bedroom wallpaper and tearing dream buttons from a dream yellow dress; the feel of the bedspread just before I came. The soft quilting against my ass, the mirror in her parents' house, the floor of the kitchen, and me and Sylvia doing things we never tried as teenagers, things I've never experienced, even with prostitutes, everything I've yearned to do and be and have . . .

I twist in my sheets and can't even dream of sleep, so I get up and pull on shorts and a shirt. Easing the truck into gear, I don't know what I seek, whether it's the girl under the streetlight or another of Timothy's demonstrations of abasement or just a reminder of the streets of my old love; but as I picture the descent to that blue house where Sylvia was always waiting, I'm reminded of the John Deere putt-putt-putting toward the ha-ha and the soaring bodilessness all those years ago. This night is younger than when I came here on foot, and driving down the boulevard I have the company of other cars. I turn toward the traffic circle and watch myself round it slowly several times, but I spot neither Timothy nor the girl. Turning south, I wend my way through several neighborhoods until I come to the asbestos house where Sylvia's staying. And when the lights are off in those cheaply shuttered windows I don't sit watching for very long, but drive home and fall into dreamless sleep.

42

How quickly it's become familiar: the dusty ball fields, the old bleachers under the oaks, the faces of Jeremy, Sammy Sosa, Elizabeth. I spot Ed Mesk humping a load of bats, but I don't rush to pitch in. Right now I'm avoiding Ed.

Harrison didn't appear for breakfast, and when Ryan went to wake him, his room was empty. I can't tell how Ryan's taking this; he pulled his blank act over breakfast, though now he's dashing across the green, waving his glove and calling out, "Throw it here, man!" But watching him tear away from me, I've a blind, sudden fury at Harrison. Since Sylvia's announcement, I've been on edge, wrestling with what I may have always suspected: that when this short dream ends it could go quickly, the whole contraption collapsing at once.

Ed catches my eye, and I busy myself with snacks. The day after Ryan left his note, I cornered Harrison and showed him the Snakes' practice schedule. I ran my finger down the line of dates and pointed to Ed's phone number at the top, but he only glanced at the paper. "How about if I just show up Saturday? Like kept it loose," he said; then he yawned, stretched way back, and let out a roar. "Aaa*aaah!* Sorry, Howard. No, I just mean, say I call this stranger and tell him I'm like all *coming in*, say I'm Ryan and Howard's big pitching machine? Isn't that awful rude and pushy?" But I didn't think so. The kids need a pitching coach, so who would resent us for bringing one in? I pointed to Ed's number again, jabbing it with my finger — *do as I say!* — but Harrison went off singing, "Here I come to save the day!" and that's the last I saw of him.

"Howard." Robin squeezes my arm. "We should talk." I glare darkly from my reverie. "Far be it from me to carry messages for nuns, but this feud with Sister Amity —" I push past her, nearly knocking down little Jamie. When Juliana calls for order, I position myself on the far side of the circle.

Juliana announces they've lined up a real game for Saturday, a week off. A bona fide Little League team, she says. "But in the evening, okay? 'Cause all the certified umpires had day bookings. Real umps! Isn't that exciting?" Ed says we'll have team shirts by then, and he shows us a drawing of a big-fanged rattler forming the *S* in *Snakes.* Glancing across the circle, I get a thorny look from Robin, and I'm conspicuous, maybe, in my failure to cheer the drawing. Then, without a word about pitching, we retreat to small groups.

Six impossibly small children gaze at an array of paper bull's-eyes Ryan and I drew yesterday at home. Dutifully I point my finger at my eye, then tap a red center spot. *Look at your target!* But I forget to tell them to line up and take turns, and my *go* signal brings such mayhem that I have to duck to avoid a beaning. One sneaky-looking kid positions himself a foot from a target, catching the ball each time it rebounds. "Bamp . . . bamp . . . bamp," he chants mechanically. I shoot him a baleful look and move him to a competitive distance.

We're starting over when the green Saturn swings under the oaks. I recognize Ms. Monetti's lush brown hair, but when the passenger door opens she just stares straight ahead. Harrison climbs out of the car, holding a cup of take-out coffee; he's electric in a yellow T-shirt and baggy, loud-patterned pants. He slams the door, and when the Saturn rolls off he gives the bumper a kick with one big-sneakered foot, then shakes his hand vigorously, as if he's scalded himself.

The old granddad's on the bleachers, and Harrison strolls toward him, sipping through a hole in the lid. From his lazy gait you'd never guess he's so tardy. Gramps points at Ed Mesk, now helping a tall kid locate a batting stance. Harrison runs a hand through his damp hair.

I watch Harrison introduce himself to Ed, and I see Ed think a moment, then pump his hand. Ed beckons to Juliana, then offers Harrison his black leather glove. Ryan's shouting, "Howie! Howie!" as he runs in from the farther field, and he points at Harrison with a toothy grin. I grin back. My little ones are clustered in idleness, but I pat the bamp kid on the shoulder. *This won't take a minute.*

Ryan charges the infield, screeching to a halt near Harrison and the others. He kicks the dirt and glares at the mound, and at first they don't see him. Then Harrison shouts, "Heyyy, buddy!" in a voice that carries across the grass. He grabs the old Indians cap and swats Ryan on the butt with it, and Ryan does a jig in the infield. Ed Mesk is explaining something, but Harrison's stopped listening. He squints out at the broad field, and when he locates me he spreads his arms. And yes, it's a beautiful day! I give two thumbs up, and he makes the pistol-shooting gesture that's part of his Joe Cool repertoire. "Awright, *Howard!*" he calls out, and I return to my dwarf hurlers a different man.

When it's time to play a few innings, Harrison prowls the baselines, slapping his gaudy pants with Ed Mesk's glove. Five kids rotate pitching duties for his benefit, and Harrison stops the game several times to go to the mound. This makes the innings interminable, but no one minds. Now Ibrahim faces the batter, and he looks like a pitching threat, long-limbed and sallow, with a wad of gum that distends his cheek. He kicks high and fires, and the batter swings to no avail. Jeremy chucks the ball back. But with Ibrahim's next pitch, the batter manages an infield hit, and Harrison walks to the mound and squats. I watch him draw an index finger down Ibrahim's chest, and the boy nods seriously. The shortstop and second baseman start horsing around with the runner on second, and in the outfield Jamie and some other pipsqueak kick at a Big Mac carton, soccer-style. A plane with a white trail divides the sky. Then Harrison squares his shoulders, and Ibrahim does the same. "Play ball!" shouts Harrison, brushing the hair from his eyes.

"Wild, isn't it?" he says when the game's over. "You figure out shit you weren't sure you knew." I nod, remembering how I broke down the throwing motion. "You know, I was so crazy about my coach when I was this age? Thought every one of my teachers was a geek, but *Coach*, boy . . . Guy could have been an embezzler, a drunk, a junkie, a complete, unmitigated jerk, but he was the man." He shakes his head dubiously, biting a rogue moustache hair, but in confirmation, Ibrahim approaches and offers a shy handshake. "No problem, dude. You guys *rule*."

We stroll toward the white station wagon, and Harrison hands Ed his glove. By next week he'll have his own, he says. "Oh, sure," says Ed. "I mean, gosh. Thank *you* for pitching in, ha-ha. No pun intended!" From the far side of the wagon the kid wrangler giggles seismically and looks Harrison up and down.

Harrison says, "You maybe noticed I've got no ride. Mind, Howard?" Of course not. I look toward the bleachers, where Robin and Ann are unwrapping their sandwiches, and I know I've a penance to serve with Robin. Then Ryan appears and slaps our palms.

"Aw*right!*" he says. "Hey, Harrison, you coming with us? Me and Howard go to this one place for lunch. One time my mom was even there." Harrison says he could eat a horse, and I leave Robin and the nuns' mission for some other day.

At the barbecue place, the counter woman says, "Little tribe fan. I know you." Ryan asks if she's seen his mom, and she says, "I don't think I know the lady." Well, who does? Then Harrison offers to pay, and I squint at him.

"I mean, I had a shitload of fun, okay? And you always do break-fast." He reaches down and takes Ryan by the waist. "Course I wouldn't of *been* there with*out* that com*pell*ing ap*peal* from my *li'l buddy!*" So this is what it's like hanging out with Harrison. Or maybe this is what it's like hanging out in general. How would I know? It's all new ground.

43

I'M DRIVING, and Harrison's on the passenger side. Ryan's squeezed between us with a pint of Bing cherries in his lap, and we're spitting the pits out the open windows. Harrison and I are drinking Mexican beer. The radio's tuned to some station I never knew existed — Harrison's choice, like the cherries and the beer — and a woman is singing an old cowboy song. I hear pops and wobbles of the tinny old technology, and I wonder how long ago the song was sung.

The singer comes to the end of a verse, and Harrison conducts with his bottle as he sings the chorus: "*I want to be a cowboy's sweetheart!*" He claps Ryan on the knee and says, "Come on there, buddy!" but Ryan says it's a girl's song. Harrison says, "Kind of an idea is that? Music's music, man." A dribble of cherry juice runs down his chin. Next time through, I hum along nasally, keeping time on the wheel, and Harrison says, "See, man? Howard's singing, and no one's butcher than him." At last, Ryan bellows out the ending. "Atta*boy!*"

By the time I turn into my driveway, all three of us are going to town. I ease to a stop, and Harrison says, "Don't cut it 'til the end, okay?" I put her in park and turn the volume way, way up, and Laurel comes out the front door and stands watching from behind the petunias. When Harrison and Ryan wave, she puts up a hand, then walks down the front steps with the three of us serenading her. At the very last note, Ryan sprawls, arms spread, across my lap.

"Hi, there, kiddo," Laurel says. She smiles absently, and he sits back in his seat. "Didja have fun?"

Ryan says, "Uh-huh." He holds out the little basket of cherries, and she shakes her head, then takes one anyway. I shut off the motor.

Laurel says, "Harrison, I've been trying to reach you."

"I was at baseball with these guys."

"I think you should — Listen . . ." She takes his arm as he climbs from the truck, and they move away, Harrison smiling quizzically. Ryan goes in the house and hollers for Ruby, but I pause on the porch. The night before last, we set up our new planter, and I stop to check how the seedlings are doing.

Laurel has her hands in her back pockets. She stares at the driveway, and Harrison does the same. In his hand, the half-finished bottle of beer. His face is ashen now, and he watches her foot trace an arc in the gravel. I snip off a few drooping blooms and poke the soil, but when Laurel looks up at me I go inside the house.

I wait for her in the kitchen. Ryan's in the parlor, watching a baseball broadcast. I hear Harrison climb the stairs to the third floor, then Laurel comes in and checks a pot on the stove. "Lordy," she says, and digs around with a wooden spoon. "Y'all eat?" I nod. She puts the lid on the pot and takes an open Pepsi from the fridge. "I tried to reach him all morning at Logan's," she says. "When I finally got through she said they'd unplugged the phone. Well, his dad's had a stroke."

I wince. My mom had a series of increasingly bad strokes in her seventies, and at the end she could no longer speak. I wonder how old Harrison's father is; I imagine him about sixty. Laurel says, "It's bad, I guess. The mom finally called your line midmorning, said she'd been calling both Harrison's numbers, leaving messages. By the time she got me, she was a train wreck, let me tell you." She crosses her arms, then nods at the upstairs. "He's gotta fly home ASAP. Heck, they don't even know if the dad'll still be there. Are you sure you don't want soup?"

I smile, patting my stomach, then run a hand over my skull. Laurel peers out the screen door. "There's that cat, under the bird feeders. Yo, Puff! Go on home!" I pour myself a glass of water and drink it down, and as I'm heading upstairs I hear her speaking to Ryan. "What on earth are you doing watching television on such a fine day?"

An open suitcase lies on Harrison's unmade bed, a couple of T-shirts and a stick of roll-on deodorant inside. Bureau drawers are open, and the floor's covered with wrinkled clothes, but the boys' rooms are always disaster areas. Harrison stands by the bed, picking at the drawstring of his colorful pants. "Think I should put on jeans?" he asks. I nod, and he fiddles a minute, then says, "Oh, this knot!" and pulls. Something tears, and the pants fall to his ankles, revealing red plaid boxer shorts. He says, "What the hell else?" and plops down hard on the bed. "I do not fucking know."

I haven't set foot in this room since the day I helped them carry in their stuff, so I wait in the doorway. Harrison stares at the floor, his elbows on his knees, and whistles a bar of the cowboy song. Then he turns and sees me still leaning against the jamb. "Sorry," he says. I shrug. He looks away again, and I cross to a pink laundry basket where the clothes look clean. I dig out a pair of black jeans and shake out the wrinkles, then hand them over. "Thanks, Howard," he says bleakly. "Let's see. Socks, shoes, razor, contact lens shit, clothes for like what, a week? How'm I supposed to know when I'm even coming back?"

I try never to think about when my dad died. He was outside one snowy morning, brushing off his windshield, and his heart went, just like that. My mom was at work already, and I'd spent the night in the parking lot of a downtown tavern, passed out in my car. I never knew whether to call it luck that I didn't freeze. When I finally dragged my ass home I found Dad by the walk, in his long gray coat and a hat with fur earflaps, spread out just like a snow angel. A dusting of white had fallen on his face, but just a dusting: I don't think he'd been there long. I hauled him inside and dialed 911, and when the operator asked for our address I yelled "Na!" at the mouthpiece until she disconnected me. Somehow she managed to send the paramedics. By the time they showed up, I had Dad piled with blankets and coats and a pair of cushions from the couch to warm him up. I was pounding his chest and blowing down his throat and wailing and wailing at the top of my lungs, but the guys said they doubted he'd had a chance. They said it was the type of coronary that's over in an instant.

We held the service at a local church none of us had been to in years. Some neighbors came, and a few of my dad's colleagues from Hanran's Men's Wear, though he'd been let go from that job a few years before. I can't remember if Sylvia was there or not. My mother had a book group she'd joined early in her marriage, and those ladies were a great help to her. That was good, because I was no help at all.

I would have liked to deliver a eulogy for my dad. I would have loved to tell anyone who could hear me that my dad got a rougher deal in life than he deserved, but he remained a sweet guy in spite of everything. Instead, I did mushrooms before the funeral, and as I sat in my room, swallowing the dusty things, I knew I was an awful — a truly *terrible* — person. I went through the ceremony and the burial and the reception with my jaw clenched and my back-bone stiff, worrying I'd get giggly at inappropriate moments, but I didn't come close. And if I had? In those days, not much was expected of me.

Harrison says, "Fuck!" and I look up. I've been folding his laundry as I stand here, and I'm holding a pair of lime socks I've made into a ball. "I've got to plan for like" — his mouth goes weak — "some kind of funeral shit?"

I don't move, but I hope Harrison has one opportunity that I never had. More than a eulogy, I'd have liked the chance to tell Dad good-bye, and this I *know* I could have managed. I think of my father, gone as soon as his fur hat hit the snow, then of Harrison's dad, now hovering in a pit between life and death. I don't remember that pit, but I did time there myself, when everyone assumed I'd go any day. No one but a few soldiers visited my bedside, because I was green and not well known, and my important people — my mom, dad, Sylvia — were in the States, awaiting word. So I think there's no time to waste in these situations. You plan for both the best and the worst.

Harrison has a camel-hair sports jacket in his closet, but when he shrugs into it the armpits bunch and the sleeves telescope above his wrists. I riffle the hangers and find a green tweed jacket and plenty of khaki pants, but not even a pair of flannels. This is no wardrobe for a grown-up.

I own two suits, though it's been years since I wore them. My mother and I used to go out to nice dinners once in a while, and she liked me in a blue suit with pale gray pinstripes. And when her doctors told me she was dying, I bought a nice gray suit for the funeral. I made Sylvia go with me to pick it out, and it may be the last favor I ever asked of her. Ryan was just a little guy then, not even walking, and we went to Hanran's because I thought my dad's cronies would be there, but I'd forgotten how time flies. Sylvia let Ryan crawl around beneath the racks of jackets, and while the tailor chalked my inseam, a young salesman squatted at Ryan's side. "Won't be too long before we're picking out a suit for you, too. Right, junior? Just like Daddy's." I remember Sylvia rolling her eyes.

I go downstairs and look at my suits. The gray one's newer, but the blue pinstripe is from a time when I was slimmer, and I think it will fit better. I carry it upstairs, still in its clear drapery from the cleaner's, and find Harrison at the nightstand, listening to his mother's messages. She does indeed sound just like a train wreck. When I hold up my suit jacket he says, "Where'd that come from?" then turns and slides into it, both arms at once.

I'm surprised at how well it looks. I've always been barrel-chested, and I'd expected the fabric to flap in front, but Harrison's broad shoulders pick up the difference. I motion for him to turn, and when he says, "How's it look?" I tug the lapels. I feel like a haberdasher.

I gesture for him to take off the jeans. He does so obediently. Sliding the blue pants off the hanger, I hold them out, but instead of taking them, he steps in like a boy. I hook the front, and he says, "Not bad, hey," and reaches for his own clothes. But he's holding the waistline with his stomach, and when I make him stand straight, the trousers drop an inch. Harrison says, "It'll be fine, Howard. Hopefully I won't even need —" But this should be perfect! I run to my mom's sewing table for a safety pin, and at the back of the trousers I create a pleat, pinning it as my dad would. *Get a nice white shirt*, I think, *a good tie; comb the hair*; and I'm enjoying this until I realize I'm alone. Harrison's lip looks as though someone's hit him. His eyes well, and when he blinks at the floor I freeze. Hesitantly, I touch his arm.

Even in the service, I was not one of those physically affectionate guys, but I pat Harrison's shoulder and wonder what I'd want in his place. Then I can only put my arms around him. He drops his head, and my suit crumples between us; his goatee tickles my neck. I think how angry I was with him earlier, but when he showed up at baseball I thought things were improving. Now he sniffs loudly, and his shoulders collapse; he gives a heartbreaking sigh. Awkwardly, I rub a hand over my blue suit jacket and think how odd it is to feel sorry for Harrison. I may even miss him.

Behind me, Ryan says, "Harrison?" and I jump. Where did he come from? But Harrison's still leaning on me, and his knees don't seem secure, so I hold him up a little longer. "Excuse me, Harrison?"

We step apart. Harrison's eyes are red, and he runs a hand under his nose. "Yeah, man." He pats the blue suit jacket to smooth out the wrinkles.

"Laurel asked me to — Are you okay?"

Harrison says, "Sure." He takes off the jacket, and I fold it into the open suitcase. "She tell you about my dad?" Ryan nods. "Well, I'm feeling kinda upset. You know."

Ryan nods again. "She said to tell you she made a plane reservation." He casts an eye around Harrison's messy room, at the suitcase and at Harrison himself, now stepping out of my blue trousers. "At five."

Harrison glances at a plastic alarm clock on the dresser. "Well, that means get my sorry ass in gear. Right, guys?" He raises an arm to sniff an armpit and says, "Whoa! Sports, man. Make you stink. Hey, Ryan, how about giving me a hand while I grab a shower? Scrounge up seven pairs of socks, seven T-shirts, et cetera, et cetera? Can you do that, bub?" He gives the Indians cap a tug and disappears toward the bathroom. He seems completely recovered.

In the end, I'm the one who counts out Harrison's underwear, giving him four plain T-shirts and three with band logos. I look over his white dress shirts, but they're in lousy condition, so I go down and get one of my own, tucking it deep in the suitcase, where he'll find it if he needs the suit. I hope it fits. In the closet, there's a wire hanger with neckties slung on the crossbar, and I let Ryan choose three bright ties, then I add the most somber one and fold all the ties together. When I look up, Ryan's by the window, watching a squirrel skitter over the maple tree. I go and place my hands on his shoulders, and the squirrel stares with unblinking eyes. I wonder if it really sees our two faces, watching from behind the glass, or if it only senses our presence in ways that are unimaginable to us. What ideas does a squirrel have? We watch him wring his front paws like a little worrier, then something moves in another part of the tree. It's only wind, shifting clusters of leaves. The squirrel takes a few short steps and gives us a glance, and Ryan says, "Hi, cutie." I kneel down and put my arms around him. Everything is so fragile.

Harrison returns, water beads glistening on his shoulders. "All packed. Thanks, guys!" He pokes a finger at the detritus cluttering his bedside table and whistles a snatch of the cowboy tune, and it's a minute before I realize he's shaved off his facial hair.

Laurel meets us at the foot of the stairs. "I'm bummed not to see old Stevie before I go," says Harrison. "Tell the sumbitch to give me a call, right? And Ry, tell those pitchers I'll be back before they know it." He gives a weak smile. "Hit a bunch out of the park so they miss me. Make 'em work, right?" When he turns to me, I put out my hand, but he pulls me into one of those A-shaped hugs that are the purview of men; only our shoulders touch. "I'll be fine," he says heartily, though I haven't said anything.

I'm really getting low on cash, but I need diversion, so I take Ryan to the movies and to a Tex-Mex restaurant near the house. When we get home he runs to get ready for bed. Laurel and Nit are in the kitchen, but after two margaritas I'm ready to turn in, myself, and I'm heading for the stairs when I see my answering machine with its red light blinking. I stare at it a moment, then on impulse close the kitchen door. Neither Laurel nor Nit looks up. I hit the button on the machine, and when I hear Sylvia's voice I lower the volume. "Hi, boys," she says gaily. "Guess what? Mama's getting sprung! Can you believe it?" I look around to make sure no one's listening, then turn the volume down even more. Sylvia says, "I have to be very, very, *very* good. But I can't wait to *see* you, my guy! It was so wonderful getting your call, and I really . . . Things are gonna be better now, baby, a lot, lot better. And it *was* a good idea coming here. Is Caroline *ever* wrong? And when I see you I'll be making lots of amends for the way I've, um, disrupted our lives. Okay, my Ry?" She seems to drift a moment, then says, "But anyway. Howie. They're having another of those family seminars Wednesday, and the staff here thinks it would really help if Ryan participated. You remember how Big John had his wife and daughter? I guess *he's* had a rocky time since getting out, one reason I want to be vigilant about . . . But Howie, I do have one — And it's, uh . . . It's not that —" She pauses again, then says, "But look. I was hoping, I'd really appreciate it if you could get him to that thing on Wednesday, and I think I'd be more comfortable, frankly, if it was just Ryan and me, if you didn't accompany him in for the program. We need to — I just want things to be as *clean* and straight*for*ward as — Remember last time? It got so complicated. So maybe you

could wait at that little patio place, or — or go back to work or anywhere, or — well, I'm sure you have places to be, and you know it's
not personal. It's . . ." She exhales loudly. "Thank you. And I *need*
to thank you, Howie, for so much, when I see you. So that family
thing's Wednesday, same place, same time. About nine in the morning, okay?" She blows a line of smacking *x*'s before hanging up, and
I can't delete her quickly enough.

I stand in the stairwell, barely able to breathe. I'm nowhere near
sober, and I could sit on the porch for a year or two, thinking about
nothing. Then Ryan calls out, dispelling Sylvia's voice. "Howie?"
he says. "Are you gonna say good night?"

44

I HEAR A DOOR CREAK, then Ryan's bare feet descend the stairs. I open my eyes and see daylight, and I imagine him getting the pitcher of grape juice from the fridge. Grape juice was the first food he asked me to buy, and when I see him later he'll have a cordovan moustache. The screen door slams, and I picture him on the stoop, holding the glass of juice like a highball. The little man surveys his domain.

I'm glad I got him at this age. If I imagine him in ten years' time, or fifteen, all I can think of is what happened to me and Sylvia. Maybe it's not possible to grow up unscathed, but I hope Ryan never has to wake up and ask what came over him. Remembering how my folks' bedroom light would flicker on, then off, when I'd pull in in the wee hours, I wonder what I've already wondered so often: was it purely my injury that made those dark nights happen, or would I have ended up guilty and ashamed no matter what?

I was out rambling again last night. I woke up after two and parked for an hour by the asbestos house, and though I did no more than sit in my truck, I'm feeling soiled and exhausted. Grabbing my robe, I head to the bathroom, and in the shower I try to shake this depression. I imagine the toast I'll deliver at Ryan's wedding: raised glass, hand on my heart. Whatever needs to be said I can say with gestures, as I should have realized when my father died. Standing under the water, I force myself to think optimistically, and by the time I step out I'm feeling a little better. I'd like to get busy before my sanguine mood slips away, but downstairs, life moves at an agonizing pace. Laurel opens the door for Ruby and sniffs the air thoughtfully. "Gray day, birds like it," she drawls. "Any word from Harrison?" Tightening the belt of her white kimono, she announces she forgot to eat supper last night and wonders about the prospects for a little French toast. I realize I've cut the pineapple into five sections, not four.

When breakfast is over I pull Nit to the cellar and show him my Gothic window frame. I want to try out that home backstop, so I gesture at the window, then at the stairs. I'm sure Nit's going to start in on his back, but all he says is "Think I could get dressed first?" Of course. I'm no tyrant.

Nit's stronger than he acts, but we're both puffing when we get the thing outside. Ryan mans the doors and skitters around excitedly, and once we clear the stoop, he takes a corner. We lug the frame toward the stable and open the two side sections, then brace it with flat stones and fireplace logs to make it secure. Nit says, "Fuck, Howard, the hell you gonna do with it?" When I don't answer, he wanders off.

Ryan and I go out and purchase plastic netting and staples for the staple gun. By the time we get home, the sun's making marble patches in the cloud banks, and Nit's sprawled on the stoop with a magazine. I climb a ladder and start with the central arch, stretching and stapling the netting in place, shearing the excess with a matte knife. I get a rhythm going, and even when the sun slithers away and a few soft drops fall, I stay where I am until the job's complete. By now, Ryan's drifted inside, but I imagine him at a window, so I get his bat from the stable and back up to the yard's edge. The shower's picked up suddenly, but I toss the ball and connect with a metallic pop, much sweeter than that day at Sylvia's. I picture an infielder missing the catch, and as the bat slips from my fingers I take off running. It's just me here, in my very own yard, but I'm pumping and pumping with all I've got, and as I round the picnic table I see the center fielder skidding in the outfield. He digs in and falls, rolling once, then he's up. He's up, he's got the ball, he's throwing, and I *know* the motherfucker's got a damn good arm, so I pour on the steam. My only chance at second is a headfirst slide, so I dive, arms out, and my chest hits with a surprising smack. Could be my chin hits the ground, too, but I can't be sure. Maybe I black out. I slide on the wet grass, right over second base, then I collide with the new backstop, and the gauze rips from that old cut on my palm. But I've made it! I've beat the throw, and perhaps someone scored or something, though I'm heaving rather hard now and can't quite focus. In the air, tiny lights are sparkling. The rain increases, and I roll over, panting.

"Howard! Howard!" Laurel's calling from the back door, and I raise a hand to let her know I'm okay. "Come on in here." I get to my knees, then stand a little dizzily, turning away so she won't see if I retch. *"Howard!"* High in the plastic netting is a dent where the ball hit, and I wonder how long the material will hold up. But a backstop's really for *behind* the batter, not for batting *into*, and when we donate it to Mister Luster Kleen we'll use it right.

"You ninny," says Laurel, holding the door open. "It's pouring out there. For heaven's sake, there's a time for baseball and a time for . . . other stuff. Wipe your feet." I'm muddy from my chin to my knees.

In the kitchen, they're making cookies. The windows are steamy, the air smells wonderful, and the counter's spread with tubs of colored sugar and sparkles. Ryan's not at the window but at the table; he looks at me cheerfully and starts decorating a sailboat. I blink at him, then tromp to the bathroom. Outside, the sky's grown dark, and from the window I see a branch of bright green leaves sail from the maple tree. As the raindrops make drumrolls on the window-panes, I rinse my cut and wonder what our squirrel is doing. I go back to the bedroom and watch leaves collecting in the netting, and I wish I'd sprung for fishing net, of genuine rope. It never does to economize.

One of the backstop's side wings begins to shift. The log that was holding it has blown aside, or perhaps I knocked it when I slid. It flaps like the shutter on a haunted house, and I watch as it tears an arc in the lawn. Then there's a gust, and the whole thing tilts forward, testing the wind resistance. Down it goes, making a filigree on the green grass.

My melancholy floods back, and I think of Sylvia's disinvitation to family day. I've just spent hours on a project that went nowhere, and I don't know whether I made bad decisions or the whole idea was cracked to begin with. In a moment of stark clarity I realize it's anyone's guess whether I give that toast at Ryan's wedding — or even attend. A newspaper blows across the yard, the pages following each other like a flock of lambs. I watch them tangle in the torn-up netting. But already the rain's lessening, and a curve of light appears on the stable roof. I touch my chin and decide I did indeed bump it sliding, and it's okay, I guess, that Laurel was curt with me. I am a ninny.

45

WEDNESDAY MORNING I get Ryan up early. All week I've wondered how to prep him for today's event — and for his mother's return. But I shy from addressing Sylvia's terrible message, so at last the day arrives unexplained. Trustingly he puts on his button-down shirt, which I've washed and ironed and laid out with a clean pair of pants, and at breakfast he uses a napkin to keep off the alluvia. Since Harrison's departure, a vague unease has overtaken the household, making the mornings quieter than they'd been, but today Ryan seems to be toeing some additional line: sitting up straight, finishing his eggs and toast, holding himself in readiness for what the costume might demand. Perhaps he reads the anticipation in my own demeanor, or perhaps he's noticed I'm also in nice clothes, on the chance I'm invited in, after all.

A pot of pink geraniums provides a summery garishness, but the brick facade of the rehab place is otherwise austere. A few people are gathered at the entrance, waiting for the thing to begin, and when I peer through the glass doors I see the woman at the folding table spread with name tags, just as before. But we don't go in to find out whose names are on those tags, and as I turn from the glass I take Ryan's hand. I look around for someone I recognize, but perhaps most of the previous visit's clients have departed. At last, I spot a dark-haired man coming up the walk. The man moves with the exaggerated swagger that suggests too much gym time, and though I can't place him exactly, he looks familiar. I give a nod, and the man nods back shortly, as if he's not sure about me either.

Other people are gathering now, some heading right inside, others joining us expectantly on the lawn. The faces are new, but the familiar types are all represented: hopeful wives and tired husbands and tired, hopeful parents and bored, anxious little children waiting for it to end. Then Ryan says, "There she is!" and lets go of my hand. He runs to Sylvia, and they clamber all over each other.

Sylvia's laughing: all flushed cheeks and shining teeth. She murmurs, "Hello, Howie," and leans toward me, but turns abruptly to sing out, "Hi, Raymond!" She sounds like Fartin' Martin's little sister, and I recognize the muscleman as Carlos's brother. Carlos has materialized, too, still with his cigarette and sleepy grin, and Sylvia says, "Okay. Ryan, honey? This is Carlos, who's one of my new friends, and this is his brother Raymond, who's a visitor, just like you. Guys, here's my darling Ryan, and you both know Howie from before." The two men shake Ryan's hand, then mine, and Sylvia says, "Wow! When worlds collide, right? I bet some people were wondering if this *Ryan* even existed at all." She takes the Indians cap from his head and places it on her own, then says the keepers here disbelieve everything she says anyway, but la-la-la. She's mugging for the two brothers, and I've seen her play for attention in just this way a million times, but I chuckle along with everyone else. Sylvia's a cute bad girl. She looks great.

Ryan stretches for his cap, and Sylvia hands it over with one more smacking kiss. "Well!" she says. "I guess we better move our fannies into that auditorium before we're marked absent!" Carlos and Raymond turn toward the entry, and as Ryan drifts after them I shift my weight like a man who could just as easily stay as go. But Sylvia sets her hands on my shoulders. "*Thank* you, Howie. We'll see you later. I can't tell you how much I appre— and you must, at this point, be *incredibly* grateful for a few hours on your own, my

Lord!" I raise a finger — *not grateful at all!* — but she breezes on. "Anyway, I guess we'll be done by half past three, and you can swing by then, though don't worry if you're not right on the button. I can certainly accommodate him for longer if —"

I pull back, remembering my black eye and how the lunch papers blew over the grass. That feeling from a month ago wells right up: I want to get the hell out of here. Sylvia's now offering the pecky kiss she aborted earlier, but I push her away; she says, "Ow," very quietly, but without further spin. She knows who's accommodating.

Ryan says, "Come on, you guys. They're all going in." He's standing on the steps with his hands on his hips, and clients and family members are stepping around him. Sylvia mouths *thank you* at me, and for an instant I wish I'd wrung her neck. Then she turns to Ryan, who asks, "Isn't Howie coming?" Sylvia says I've got things to do, and isn't it nice to be their old twosome for a couple of hours, but I'm hurrying to my truck and can't gauge his reaction.

For a while I just drive. I go two or three blocks until I see something familiar, then I turn away and go two or three more. I want to get lost, but I've lived in this city my entire life. Down every street is someplace I recognize or someplace that looks like someplace I recognize, and again and again I keep turning away. I turn from an enormous bread factory my second- or third-grade class visited on a field trip, then I turn from an empty lot that once was a car wash. I rode through the scrubbers many times with my mom. I turn from the familiar sight of a church spire in the distance and from a low, bright 7-Eleven store — not the 7-Eleven where I nearly threw up on a hooker, but close enough — then I turn from the boulevard where the Andee Barber School is located a few blocks down. I turn from a brick house where Mom once admired a clematis, and suddenly Hanran's Men's Wear is straight ahead, and I turn away. By midmorning I've zigzagged myself out of the city, and the fields of corn and flax and wheat all look like each other and all look familiar. When I come to a little nothing of a town, it seems like a town I've driven through before. I take a left, pretending I don't know which way the lake lies, which way the river; but the sun in the east gives my direction away. I pretend I don't remember any teenage picnics, or one later outing with an infant Ryan, in country like this, and that I don't see how many bright fields where we lay kissing and daydreaming are now twenty-year-old residential developments.

I'm on a small road now, where dry, bleached-looking blossoms and skinny trees line the shoulders. The macadam shimmers in the heat, and I pass under an interstate to see a worn billboard nestling in the undergrowth, the faded image of a cartoon bird on its surface. Suddenly I recall a day not at all like this one, when I did not want to be here but drove out with my parents. The leaves were greener than they are today, the sun was not baking down, and the folks had requested a single afternoon, just the three of us, no one else. It must have been early summer, maybe a week before I reported to boot camp, and I was grumpy in agreeing because I'd been spending every moment with Sylvia. But even in those days I was generally compliant.

We drove to a state park that was famous for its buzzards. My father always wanted to see the buzzards, and we'd come out other years but never during the migration period when the birds are easy to spot, so we'd never seen them. We didn't see them that day, either, but it didn't matter. My mom had packed a lunch, and as we spread an old rose picnic blanket on the bank of the reservoir my father said, "Helen, honey, give him a deviled egg to make him stop sulking." I did love her deviled eggs. After lunch, my mom and I walked to a boathouse where there were rowboats for rent. We rented one for a few hours and I rowed her across the water.

I remember I had on a loud-patterned, clingy knit shirt with a long, pointed collar, and my hair was to my shoulders then, like every other high school boy. When I began to perspire, the shirt grew uncomfortable, and I took it off. Immediately, I felt self-conscious. My mother had seen my body before, of course, but always in the context of some activity like swimming. Now she sat just a few feet away, with nothing to look at but my pale, imperfectly developed chest, its small containment of hair at the center and a few zits in awkward spots. How juvenile I must have looked to her then, how unsuited to soldiering! But she only murmured, "Howie, you've gotten so strong!" and gazed off toward the shoreline until my father came into view. She had a knack for that, for being intimate and complimentary without causing me embarrassment, and she could remark on my physicality in a way my father, for all his years in haberdashery, never could. I remember the same quality years later, when there were only two of us, and she'd tell me I looked handsome in my pinstriped suit.

I took my father out rowing next, and he asked if I was frightened. I said I wasn't. My dad said it was all right to be scared; he'd been scared himself when he went off to the service, even though he remained stationed in England and managed to escape D-day. He looked down at the oarlocks and said there were times he wished he'd gotten himself out of the whole damn experience, and I knew he was giving me permission to find a way out myself — go to Canada or Sweden or declare myself bonkers — but was too shy to say it. Maybe in later years my dad looked back on that conversation and regretted speaking so elliptically. Maybe he wished he'd urged me to flee. But I knew what he was getting at and didn't need clarification. As I turned the boat toward shore, he took the Masonic ring from his finger and said he'd like me to have it, and I've worn it since.

It must have been one of those long, long days of June, because we stayed for hours. My father waded around at the reservoir's edge, and about thirty yards down he discovered a spring that ran out of the hillside. When I strolled over to see what he was doing, I found him building a dam across the stream, and I pitched in, helping him wedge a slab of bluestone into an outgrowth of roots. By the time my mother wandered over, my jeans were wet right up to the waist, and Dad had pondweed on his cheek. Behind the dam a pool was forming, and Mom kicked off her sneakers and knelt in the water to shovel clay and silt at the dam's leaky interstices. Slowly the pines at the distant shore merged into silhouettes, and the sunlight flashing on the water turned gold. Perhaps a buzzard even flew overhead.

We didn't speak much as we worked. My father was generally disinclined toward idle chat, and we had other means of communicating. We stayed well into dusk, pointing and lifting and working as a troika, and saying no more about the war or my impending departure. And as I sit now in the hot cab of the truck, gazing across the wildflowers at the faded sign, I want to return to the rowboat and the buzzards and the dam, but I don't want to return alone. So I back the truck up, turning away one more time, and head back to the city.

46

I T'S NOT LONG BEFORE I'm cutting through the subdivision, then the long stone wall is on my left. Alain is just pulling the yellow school bus through the gates; he taps his horn as he passes my truck, as if we saw each other only yesterday.

Inside the grounds, all is still. The big convent building stands like a high bluff beside the turnaround, and the bright red rhododendrons have given way to hydrangeas. In the parking area, a few vehicles stand empty, Robin's green van among them, but Robin herself is not around. I turn off the engine and look out toward the Contemplation Garden, tapping my fingers on the steering wheel. Then the silence gets to me, and I sit still. It seems eons since I was last here, the years of lawn service and my idiotic rides over the ha-ha blending as foggily in my head as that day of dam-building with my folks. In fact, it's a mere three weeks.

I consider strolling toward the little sitting area where I found refuge the day Ryan and I quarreled. Beyond is the shed that was my professional domain. But though I've the same rights as any tourist to wander this acreage, I stay where I am. The truth is I have only a partial notion of what I'm doing, and I'm waiting for something to spur me to action. If Robin should appear, for example, I'd hasten to compensate for my grumpy mood Saturday. And if Sister Amity happened to join us, we'd take it from there.

A few days ago I stopped at a cash machine with Ryan. I know the drill of those stations by heart, of course, and when no cash appeared I simply repeated the sequence. When the machine balked a second time, I began to suspect something, and I leaned over the screen, struggling to make out the pixelated words. Then Ryan said, "You're out of money, Howie," and gave me such a shocked look that I felt shamed to the core. Early on, the folks set up a money market account to be used in case of emergency or incapacity, and with a great deal of help from Ryan, I put some twenties in my pocket. But I long ago vowed to leave that money alone, and I've never before dipped there, so I was shaken. The next day, Laurel reminded me about the taxes.

So there may be something I need to do. But it seems like a long time since Sister Amity telephoned me, and I dislike supplication. I gaze at the nodding hydrangeas and wonder how Sylvia and Ryan are doing, and I wonder if Sylvia built a living sculpture. Would that sculpture include me? I picture Ryan learning about the family hero and all the other types of kids, and I wonder if he's wondering, as I did, which category he falls into. I want more than anything to avoid succumbing to the old life I had *before*, but it's clear things would be different if the convent were just a job. If I got up in the morning and my life was full, it wouldn't matter that my work was routine and my supervisor maddening. I'd complete my duties, then return to where I really lived. With this in mind, I look around for Sister Amity.

Then something does happen: I hear a sound, no louder at first than the buzz of a fly. But I know it instantly. I tended that motor for years. The noise grows fuller, and the stately green chariot moves out of the long north expanse. A fat slob in a tractor cap is perched on its high seat. In an instant I realize I've made the kind of blunder brain-damaged people make, misjudging how mercilessly life moves on. I watch the John Deere putt toward the ha-ha, then carefully turn, holding to level ground. No doubt the guy returns with the push mower, as Sister Amity's always wanted.

In a flood, my reasons for coming here are gone. I picture Sister Amity's canny expression when the grass gets *very* long, and I feel her slap on my cheek. Squealing through the turnaround, I glance in the rearview mirror and see a black-clad figure stepping from the Contemplation Garden. She starts to wave, and I step on the gas. Behind her, the ha-ha arches its false back against the sky, a lie of the landscape.

The next few hours I drive around. To punish myself for having no money I don't eat lunch, but I probably waste the cost of a sandwich on gas. And of course, I'm parked opposite the dry-out joint long before three. By now I'm calm enough to put on a jaunty front, and I lean on the truck with my hands in my pockets. A group emerges, and several families say goodbyes on the lawn before I finally spot my two, Sylvia still chattering at the Carlos brothers, Ryan brooding oddly at her side. He eyes me furtively as they approach but gives no response to my wave. I step forward, and he screams, "Howie!"

I jump back, and there's the sound of a horn and a rush of wind on my face. An orange plumbing van slams on its brakes, and from inside the van comes a clatter of shifting cargo. The driver leans over and screams, "Almost lost it that time, shit-for-brains." Where on earth did the vehicle come from?

The van peels off, leaving the street empty. I look both ways to be sure, then look again, and at last I cross. I put my arm around Ryan as the musclebound brother says he's a hero. Sylvia says, "I completely missed that."

"Howie," she says, once the Carloses are gone. "You never told me you lost your job. What will you *do?*"

I should have expected this, but I'm caught off guard, and there's a blank moment while I marshal my reserves. Then I shrug. *I'll get by.* And Sylvia picks up my cue. "Of course, Howie, there must be eight million things you can do besides mow lawns, and you'll find something. A man of your — You know, I'm exactly the same way. I figure I can *type* anywhere, for God's sake, and of all things *work* ought to be the least of our worries." I wonder in what respect she's looping us together; then she murmurs, "Of course, you must have a lot of equity in that house," and I guess she's just talking. To shift things away from my financial affairs, I wave toward my truck. Maybe we can get a bite before I drop her off.

Sylvia says, "Oh, you know, Howie, I can't leave yet. Of course they want us to do this whole big postmortem, and because I'm — oh, but I'm actually getting out Saturday! Can you believe it? I really am!" She pauses to hug herself, rocking with glee, then adds, "And I heard about the big ball game, so I'm going to push them to finish the paperwork, et cetera, just so I can be there. Maybe you'd even like to — well, I thought we might go together, if you were able. If you picked me up?"

I grin at her, and I can't stop nodding. Sylvia's all business now, arranging for me to come at five. Then she says, "Now, Howie, can I give you a little kiss, or are you going to pull away like you did this morning?" When I put my arms around her she says, "Whoa, tiger!"

On the way home, Ryan says, "Howie?" He hasn't shed the brooding aspect he brought from the dry-out place, and he's been quiet for blocks, despite his mom's happy news. I pat his thigh, and he says, "I'm sorry I told her about your job. I forgot that was classified."

I reach over and drag him toward me, stiff and wiry at first, but softening, as always, when I hold him to my chest. I want to laugh, because of course it doesn't matter now. Things are fine, and Sylvia's right that I can find *any* job, doing any number of things. On Saturday she'll sit with me in the bleachers, and we'll watch him together, just like . . . I'll fill that putty-colored house with flowers for the homecoming.

Ryan settles against me, and after a while, he says, "Howie?" I rub his head. "You think my mom might get married again?" *Not the question I'm expecting, bub, but I sure as hell hope so.*

47

THURSDAY, BASEBALL AS ALWAYS, in the narrow lot behind Mister Luster Kleen. Ed and Juliana inquire after Harrison's dad, but they're too polite to worry openly about pitching. Still, everyone has Saturday's game on the mind, and I see Ibrahim turn at every approach of a car. He's waiting, I imagine, for that green Saturn. At Burger King, the kid wrangler's less successful than usual at steering us toward lonely hearts.

It's still light when we get home, and we find Laurel in the kitchen, smoking a cigarette. Her eyes are red, and she's been crying, and I think she knows Ryan will be leaving us soon. When I stare at her, she stubs out the cigarette. "I'm sorry, Howard. You know I don't smoke. Did y'all eat supper already, or you want some soup?" Ryan runs and puts his arms around her waist, and she rubs his shoulder. "Thanks, darlin'. Silly gal me." *He'll still be around*, I want to say.

Laurel brushes her hair from her eyes. "I suppose it's — I was awful young when I lost my own daddy," she says, and I realize Harrison's father has passed away. I put my hands in my pockets and sigh.

Laurel waits until Nit comes home to telephone Harrison, and I sit in the kitchen and listen as they each take the phone. At the end, Laurel says, "Well, dear, we send you our love. Howard, too, who's right here with me." When she gets off the phone she says, "Did you loan him a shirt?"

It's only five days since I helped Harrison pack, and I'm still surprised at how he collapsed. His knees buckled; his head fell to my shoulder. Now I wonder if he's as helpless with his family, or if he's strong and stalwart, or the jokey jock I used to call Nat. But nobody says. There's no "Well, he's holding up, under the circumstances" or "Dude's falling apart, man" from Laurel or Nit, and as I drift toward the television, it strikes me I don't even know if Harrison was with his dad at the end. I don't know if his dad went peacefully, and I don't know about brothers and sisters. Maybe Harrison's alone with his mom now, as I was with mine; for me, that was an important period. The others know more than I do, I suppose, but they forget to tell me, and it shouldn't matter: I hardly know Harrison. But I wish I'd taken the receiver and made some sad sound, just to tell him I'm thinking of him, and I decide that for the sake of the Snakes I'll find out when he's expected home. I head out to the picnic table, where Laurel and Nit sit sipping beers, but when I start to communicate Laurel says, "I got a big sympathy card I thought we could all sign."

Laurel's card has lilacs on the front. She reads a sweet message she's added, then Ryan writes his full name in careful script, and I make a crooked *H*. Ryan announces he's drawn a picture to send with the card, but when he brings it to the kitchen we can only stare mutely. I think we'd expected something domestic and wholesome — breakfast or pitching or a portrait of the house — but instead he's drawn a mournful casket with five figures standing around. There's me, in my overalls and pink scar, and Laurel, with black hair and embarrassingly tilted eyes. The elongated hexagon at the center looks more like a motorboat than a coffin, and Nit's the first to crack a smile. "Whoa, man. Pretty grievous." Ryan ogles him dubiously.

Laurel says, "Isn't that thoughtful," and gives Nit a tiny scowl. But once Ryan's asleep she says, "I guess I should send it, right? I mean, he did it special, and what if he asks Harrison?" She stares at the grim picture a moment, then says, "Nice likeness of you, Howard. I'd just hate to see it misconstrued." Getting out a one-liter soup container, she fills it with the cookies she and Ryan made Sunday, then packs the drawing and card in a large envelope. "Well," she says, wrapping the package in brown paper, "I feel better already. In fact, I'm gonna go right down to the FedEx bin and send these on their way." She picks up the cigarette pack she left on the counter and says, "*Oh!* I am *not* starting that again!" and drops the cigarettes in the garbage. To avoid listening to Nit slurp his crab bisque, I head out to the porch.

I watch Laurel's taillights disappear down the road, and I watch her headlights return. Then the parlor light clicks off. I hear her open the screen door, and when she says, "You all right, Howard?" I put up a hand. "I guess Stevie's gone up already," Laurel says. She steps outside and stretches, filling her lungs, then suddenly runs a hand through my hair. "'S early, but I'm off to bed, too. You lock up, okay?" I don't budge, and the screen door closes.

I don't have anything against Laurel, but sometimes I've just had enough of voices. Now peepers pulse from every direction, and I think I hear an owl, too, a rare sound in the city. But the owl I think I hear is drowned out by a cry next door. A light goes on; then the door opens, and Puff the cat dashes out, followed by Dwayne in a bathrobe, carrying baby Samantha. It's Samantha who's squalling, in impossibly long wails that rise through the night air. Jean, the wife, leans out to caution Dwayne about disturbing the neighbors, and Dwayne says, "Honey, fuck the neighbors! I can't pace that hallway another night. I'm gonna give this kid some breathing room." He carries the baby down the steps.

They pass slowly in front of my house, Dwayne rocking at each step. I don't think he sees me, tucked in my own shadows, and I don't do anything to reveal my presence. Samantha goes on screaming, but after a minute I don't mind the sound. It's not late yet — not even eleven — and most of the houses on the street are still lit. I've been known to think *fuck the neighbors* myself. And something in the sheer fullness of Samantha's voice makes me feel cheerful. Listening to her wails, I realize that this is not *true* sorrow or grief or any kind of trouble one must take seriously, but simple feeling, unprocessed by words. There's almost a melody.

The noise recedes as Dwayne and Samantha continue up the block. Bracing a foot on the porch railing, I rock the glider and think about the weeks to come. Sylvia will need support as she gets back on her feet, I think, and I make a vow to do all I can. I'll be extra vigilant, extra present, bringing muffins in the morning and flowers at night, and on days she's subject to temptation I'll be ready with outings. And who wouldn't appreciate the homey baseball scene? We'll resume our picnicking habit, too. We'll find fields which have not yet become parking lots. We'll go to the buzzard place and create a dam, we'll have picnics at home. Making myself indispensable to Sylvia will keep Ryan from slipping away, at the same time reminding her why she loved me at all. Hell, we might even have another child. Why not? We're not young, but it's not out of the question. This is a big house, as Sylvia herself suggested. A darling baby girl, to go with our strong boy; a girl to grow up playing dollies with Samantha — or beating the crap out of her if she likes.

I smile at the world beyond the porch and realize the wailing's stopped. Dwayne and Samantha are returning down the far side of the street now, and the little melody I heard is only Dwayne singing a lullaby. For a moment, I feel a burst of warmth for the poor, bathrobed schmuck, walking his sleeping bundle to bed.

I give Dwayne a nod as I back the truck out of my driveway; he glares back as if I've threatened his kid. Then Jean beckons them to the light. I turn and drive the half block to the boulevard, and it's earlier than my other wanderings, so the route is bustling. I park a few doors from the asbestos-shingled group home, where lights still glow in the upper windows, and though I don't know which light is Sylvia's, I feel like a troubadour as I cross the lawn. On the top floor a man paces the gold square of his window, appearing and disappearing like a pendulum; below him, a thin woman drags on a cigarette. One room on the second floor is lit by a red bulb, another by a flickering blue TV. For a moment I gaze at the grid of white-shuttered windows, wondering which one is hers. In high school, I never woke Sylvia by tossing pebbles at her window, but I always liked the idea, and we did our share of sneaking around.

I hear laughter, and a familiar voice says, "Stop it! Shh!" I follow the sound, and Sylvia says, "We're not supposed to get involved for a —" She breaks off. Rounding the corner of the house, I see her on the porch, her little butt against the balustrade. She's dressed in the merest nothing of a shift that hangs like a flag down her slim, arched back, and a bit of moonlight falls on her bare shoulders. Her arms, straight and slender pylons, support her. I picture her turning to lean toward me like Rapunzel, but I don't want to startle her, so I approach slowly, from behind a pine, remembering the times we met in secret. Then two big hands, square as work gloves, take hold of those hips, and in a swanlike explosion, Sylvia embraces a dark head at her shoulder. The glovelike hands don't caress her waist the way mine would, but hold her stiffly, like an urn.

Sylvia purrs, "Stop it! Seriously, Raymond. If someone caught us —" She lowers her voice suddenly, and I hear no more until she chuckles, pushing playfully at his chest. "I'm going in now." I see that dark head bob forward again, and Sylvia's hand catches the moonlight as she touches his cheek. I turn and run headlong into the dark, spreading branches of the pine.

Raymond's crossing the street as I unlock my truck. He's dressed in a red polo shirt that hugs his absurd muscles, and I remember that orange plumbing van and feel an impulse to lay him flat. Climbing into some low-slung gold Nissan, he seems not to notice me screeching toward him, headlights off. I pass so close that if he stuck his head out the window he'd be history. Then I peel out.

Inside the cab, I'm beating my fists on the steering wheel. I'm crying out "Braaaah!" and "Phnnnng!" and raging at Sylvia, at that musclebound shit in his cheeseball Nissan, at Caroline for setting so much in motion, at the arched branches of the trees and the low lights of the plazas and everything else in the whole indifferent world. I run three stop signs and don't care who sees me, though it's later now, and the traffic's lightened. There's a close call with some kid with a Domino's Pizza sign on his jalopy, and after that I ease up. I stop at red lights but go on bashing the wheel.

I come to the traffic circle and steer around it. Rounding the little temple, I think I see something, and instead of turning toward home I stay on for the full tour. Then I spot him, dressed in a greasy coat like an old-fashioned duster and shuffling slowly from the granite steps. Along the walk the white impatiens shine weirdly in the moonlight, as they always have.

I pull to the inside lane so fast that my wheel jumps the curb. Timothy looks up as I climb from the cab, and who knows if he recognizes me? Who knows *what* he sees? He's muttering something and reaching to scratch himself, and then I'm on him, bending low to hit with a shoulder, as we were taught in football, then turning to jab my elbow at his chin. I get a faceful of that chemical scent — metal, filth, urine, war. It's as if I've plumped a particularly nasty pillow. He falls into a shape of impatiens, and I go right after him. Suddenly, I don't mind the stench, and I set my bulk on his thin, stinking chest. His filthy beard brushes my skull, and I give a growl. I'm Howard the bear! A knee to his rib cage, blows to the face — openhanded at first, then punches, with my clenched fist — and I wish I had a tire iron or andiron or a sharpened stick of any size. Something cracks, and there's wetness. Timothy's face is a slippery, sticky mess. Some of the wetness is undoubtedly blood, but some must be saliva, both his and mine, because I'm coughing and drooling and frothing, literally, at the mouth.

I could stay here all night. I could go on thrashing this guy long, long after I've finished him off, but suddenly Timothy lets out a terrible, plaintive shriek, and at the sound of such noise I come back to the world. I jump up, like the ruffian I am, and dash off, and from one of the surrounding houses a voice cries, "What the hell's going on?" I'm clambering into my truck when I step on the gas, spinning a little topsoil before making a U-turn. I drive a quarter-circuit in the wrong direction, narrowly missing another pizza vehicle, then veer back to the boulevard and home.

48

I CAN'T GET OUT OF BED in the morning. When a knock comes on the bedroom door I'm certain the police have arrived, but it's only Laurel, wondering what's up. I turn away, gesturing that I'm not well, and she touches my forehead and says I seem feverish. Then I spend two hours running to the bathroom with loose bowels. I hear Laurel and Nit take off for work, and Ryan putters about downstairs, channel surfing, making himself lunch, talking to Ruby. He doesn't come check on me, and for this I'm grateful; I can face no one. For hours I lie in bed, my mind shifting from despair over Sylvia to despair over what I've done. I rage at the whole sequence of events that brought me to this spot, and my thoughts lead me back to Timothy. Midway through the afternoon I pull on my overalls, all set to check on him at that traffic circle. But I think of the maintenance men I once saw unloading gardening equipment, and I realize someone must have found him by now. And it's impossible for me to slip off without Ryan, and if Timothy's dead, my appearance will raise suspicions, and I can't be sure the sight of what I left behind won't prompt me to turn myself in, from sheer remorse. With this, I lie down and bury my head in the bedclothes. At last, Laurel comes home and brings me some consommé, and I'm puking it all into the toilet when she calls up to say she and Nit are taking Ryan to play minigolf. Then a terrible, restless, dream-filled night, cold sweats in the wee hours and a dog that barks relentlessly several streets over, until finally I dream that it's a man barking, not a dog, a ragged, musclebound figure who stands in the jungle and bays at nothing. Then the barking stops.

Saturday, though, I get up and make breakfast as usual. I listen to the radio news for word of Timothy, and though there's nothing on the broadcast, I'm paralyzed by nerves. Only a fluttery, jittery feeling at the back of my stomach connects each moment to the next. It's baseball Saturday, though, with Ryan's game this evening, so I'm presenting my game face. The one thing I can't accommodate is Sylvia's homecoming, but I press forward, like a beast of burden, and manage, for the most part, to put her from my mind. I think it helps, too, that Ryan has his own preoccupations. The minute we pull in he runs to tell Ed about Harrison's dad, and Ed takes his cap off and places it at his heart. "Well, Howard," he says, "can't argue with death."

The day is gusty. Veils of dirt dance through the infield, and when Gramps shows up with doughnuts, the little wax-paper squares blow all over. During practice, several kids get grit in their eyes, and at last we move to the farther, more sheltered diamond to knock out a few innings. But the wind just expresses everyone's edginess as the game looms.

We stop playing early, and Ed has Juliana announce the starting lineup. "This is hard, people. Every one of you's worthy of starting." She unfolds a piece of notebook paper and reads, "Starting pitcher: Ibrahim Williams." Across the circle, Ibrahim looks cowed, but Shawn stomps away from the group. His mother grabs him, and when Juliana reads, "First baseman: Shawn Indig," a moment later, he's not much mollified. In the end, Ryan's not chosen to start, but he bears it like a champ, merely slumping a little at my side. I touch his shoulder, and he moves gently under my hand. With all the eleven- and twelve-year-olds here, I knew a spot for a nine-year-old was iffy, but we had our hopes, so I stroke his soft neck with my thumb and feel the weight of his disappointment. I watch Jeremy, in his catcher's gear, sidle toward Ibrahim, and the two of them discuss signs as, beside us, the old guy tells his grand-daughter she'll have other opportunities. I'd like to believe that applies to us, too, but who knows where Ryan and I will be when the Snakes play again?

Juliana's looking pale. It's clear she didn't expect so much anguish, and between the wind and the dust, the dividing of the children into A lists and B lists, and my own depression, there's a palpable sorrow under the trees. And Juliana's just a girl herself. "The thing is," she calls out, "hopefully you'll *all* get a chance at starting. We'll have more games. And it's really important to have a full bench tonight, both for like team spirit and if we wanted to put in a pinch hitter, pinch runner, or whatever, okay? Also, don't overload on heavy food or junk food before coming to play, even if you're not starting. Some carbs in the afternoon if you want, but like . . ." She goes on, with more announcements, speaking faster and faster until she runs out of steam. "Okay, I guess that's it. So, um, Dad?"

Ed raises his hands. "Hey, who's got the best team?" *Snakes!* "Who's got the best team?" *Snakes! Snakes! Snakes!* I'm like a sleep-walker, but I pump my fists, and once we're revved up, Ed hands out the new baseball shirts. They're beautiful: midnight blue with the white rattler *S.* The team name swooshes across the buttons, and "Mister Luster Kleen" is printed discreetly on one sleeve. "Wear 'em proud tonight, okay?"

Ed's ordered adult shirts, too, though he asks for a donation to cover expenses, and as I hand over my money I realize I'm short again. "Take one for Harrison, too," Ed says with a wink. "My little insurance policy. Tell him he can pay me after he gets back." In his excitement, Ed's forgotten I can't tell Harrison anything, but I take the shirt and toss it in the truck.

"Looks like a Snake, dressed like a Snake, must be a Snake!" Robin squeezes my arm. She's already customized her own blue shirt by rolling the sleeves, and she steps back to consider mine. "You know, that looks damn hot on you, Howard." She undoes my top button, then tugs at my T-shirt so it stretches at the throat. "Oughta show a little chest hair, though," she says. "As long as you got it. Let the consumer check out the merchandise, ha, ha. Come on now: smile!" For a moment, the two of us watch the kids tidy up the diamonds, and I stand as still as a post, wondering if I deserve any kindness at all. Over by the bleachers, Ryan's with a group of also-rans he's never deigned to acknowledge. He's peeling an orange, and when Ann's little Jamie says he guesses the two of them will be warming the bench, Ryan hands him an orange section. Then he and I take off.

We don't go to the barbecue place because I can't risk an encounter with Sylvia. Instead, I drive west, into the countryside, and as we leave the city limits behind, I think I could keep going. I've no illusion of escaping forever, but we might have a week of touring Old Faithful and the Grand Canyon and everywhere else I've always wanted to see, and we'd spend our nights sleeping under the stars. Then, of course, we'd be spotted, a scarred white guy and black child, and Ryan would be taken away and returned to his mother, while I'd go to jail for kidnapping and what I did to Timothy. I don't do it, but it's not such a bad deal.

Ryan says, "Howie, are we gonna get lunch?" and he sounds so tentative that I feel like a monster. I turn on the radio, still tuned to Harrison's funny station, and when we pass a roadside store I pull in. At the back of the store is a deli counter where a fat man is carving a big country ham, and the whole place smells richly of smokehouse and cloves. I give the man a sign for two sandwiches, then remember I'm short of cash and correct that to one. I don't care if I eat lunch. I'm happy to find something special for him, and I grab a couple bottles of ginger ale and two beautiful, large peaches, and a box of Cracker Jack for later on, and the teenager at the cash register is pretty peachy herself, telling Ryan it's the first time they've had two snakes come for takeout. The money in my wallet covers our lunch, with a dollar back. Ryan says, "Hey, Howie, you didn't get —" then breaks off, and I tug the beloved Indians cap over his face. "You can have half of mine," he says.

There's a picnic table outside the store, and the wind's died down. The sun's out. I make Ryan remove his team shirt before unwrapping the sandwich, and then, for solidarity, I take mine off, too. Side by side, we sit in our T-shirts, looking at a yellow field that rises like a ha-ha at the center of the view. The air's tinged pleasantly with cow manure, and Ryan's lunch smells good, but though I nibble at a few bits of meat that fall on the paper, I decline his offer of half the sandwich. Truly, I need nothing.

Then back in the truck and down the road to the buzzards' park. The entrance, with its Davy Crockettish gateposts, brings back that day I spent with my folks, but inside, suddenly, nothing's familiar. Too many roads branch off from the main one, and the rustic signs, flashing from the underbrush, are hard for me to read. I drive around searching for the boathouse or a glimpse of the reservoir, but the place is a maze of dry, midsummer green. Then Ryan murmurs, "Buzzard's View Trail," and when I look at him he adds, "It was like a sign back there." I back up and park.

I'm not sure my folks and I ever hiked this trail, and the route's longer than I expect. We're panting as we near the top, and Ryan's torn through the Cracker Jack. But we step out onto a bare, shallow dome of rock, as smooth as a scar on the mountain's crown, and the blue sky arches above us. An older couple is just leaving as we arrive. They smile at Ryan and speak to each other in some foreign tongue, and after that we're by ourselves. We look around in all directions before settling at a scary ledge, where grids of farmland and residential areas stretch for miles. Right below us, that metallic reservoir. The buzzards have a fine view.

I pass Ryan his peach, and he devotes himself to peeling the skin. He does this so carefully that at last he's created a golden sphere, and when he holds it up I nod admiringly. The real sun is starting its slow descent, lighting the reservoir until it glistens like foil, and I look for that boathouse, but I still don't find it. I think again of how easy it would be for us to disappear, even briefly. The last place I slept in a tent was overseas, but I imagine remaining here for the sunset, then retiring to a tent by a campfire in the woods. In the morning, I'd crawl from my sleeping bag to drink cowboy coffee while the sun rose over the water, and once sleepyhead emerged I'd fry a panful of eggs and bacon, with sliced bread skewered on sharp sticks for toasting. But this is my dream, not Ryan's, and I know he has other things he wants to be doing. We better get going or we'll be late for that game. So I make a pact: we'll leave as soon as he's finished his peach. Maybe he reads my thoughts, because he eats it in the tiniest bites.

We're back in the residential outskirts when Ryan suddenly says, "Hey, aren't we gonna pick up Mom?" I look across the seat and shake my head, and when he says, "I thought she was coming to watch me play," I don't respond. "Howie!" he says. "She's waiting for you to go get her!" But at this I just look out the windshield, and no matter how many times he asks, I keep on driving. I can't do everything, but I'm doing the very best I can, and some things just go unexplained.

49

THE DIAMOND WHERE the game will be played is tucked behind a new high school even glitzier than Radnor. Ryan's been silent since I stonewalled him on his mother, but as we pull in he murmurs, "Yo, it's my high school." We're in Sylvia's district now, where in four short years he'll be a freshman.

Robin pulls in beside me, calling out, "Welcome to Yankee Stadium" as she and Jamie and Ann pile from the green van. And, yes: we've arrived at some kind of baseball Shangri-la. The field is fancier than a minor-league park, with a real grandstand cheerfully roofed by a metal awning, and a bull pen area behind green outfield fencing. Looking up at the racks of stadium lights, I wonder what it would be like to watch Ryan play a night game, and I think of those few football scrimmages before I broke my arm. I remember how excited I felt tying on my shoulder pads, with all the other guys getting ready, too.

I grin at Ryan. He's not looking at me, but he gives little Jamie a high five and says, "Know what, man? My mom might be here." Looking around, I see that Jeremy and Ibrahim are already in the bull pen, and Elizabeth's in the outfield, playing catch with her dad. She waves, and we wave back, though Ryan tells Jamie, "They had to get a girl in the lineup, *so* . . ." Then both boys race to the dugout, which really is dug out of the ground. The Mesks and some other Snakes are already gathered there, and Ryan grabs a ball and flings it high, then steps back and catches it beautifully.

The other team is in red. The Snakes' uniforms consist of only the blue shirts, but the opponents are in red baseball pants with dark red stirrups, red shirts with white lettering, and bright-red caps. Most of them seem to have red baseball shoes as well. On our team, only Jeremy wears baseball shoes, and I never considered them for a child Ryan's age, but now I wonder if the red team's got cleats. I tell myself the opponents only look forbidding because there's a bunch of them, all identical and clustered like bees; then a very large bee emerges from the dugout and gazes at the diamond with his hands on his hips. He, too, is red from head to toe. I watch him a moment before recognizing the handsome salesman who sold us our gloves, and he looks so at ease, addressing his crimson charges, that I recall how he talked through the pivot with Ryan. I can't help wondering, a little disloyally, if Ed and Juliana have his baseball smarts. Then Robin's beside me. "Twins. How original," she says, deciphering the lettering on the red shirtfronts. "Are *all* the players boys?"

Juliana says, "Hey, let's use the infield while we've got it. Do some drills, okay?" The kids who will play third, second, and short go out and chuck the ball around, but Shawn hasn't arrived yet, so first is empty. "Who'll fill in?" says Juliana. "Maybe Ryan?" Ryan lets out a whoop and barrels off, calling for the ball, and when Shawn still isn't here at game time, he stays in without question.

I'm beside myself. Parents aren't permitted to remain in the dugout, so I take a seat in the stands, with first base right in front of me. I watch Ryan stand ready, one sneakered foot just holding the bag, and I could yelp for joy and do the bump and buy cups of beer for the crowd, if beer were available. Suddenly I realize how parents become idiots: for the present, my woes with Timothy and Sylvia are forgotten, and I want to call out Ryan's name, blow kisses, and make boisterous jokes 'til he turns around. With just a nudge I could get very weepy. A Twin walks toward the plate wearing a hard, red batting helmet, and I see spectators gathering behind the other dugout. One lady's in a wheelchair, and three barechested boys are waving shirts. There are parents of Snakes here, too, of course, and I know each of them holds some very deep something for one or two of the players. But it's inconceivable anyone feels what I'm feeling. This moment is mine, and the blue sky casts a golden light.

Then real life returns. Ibrahim, on the mound, squints at Jeremy. Ryan holds up his glove, and Juliana waves encouragement at our fielders. The umpire calls, "Play ball!" and Ibrahim goes into his long, cool motion. The batter swings, getting a tiny piece, and the ball pops back at Jeremy, who seems to grab it purely on instinct, then jumps up with a silly grin. A fluke, but our kids have their first out. The ump gestures neatly, and some people in the stands mark homemade scorecards. The Snakes fans cheer. The next Twin gets to first on a short drive, and the one after that lands a pretty bunt. The fourth Twin in the lineup is a fat kid they call Monster; across the diamond, the crowd chants the word. Monster takes a strike and two balls, then hits a high fly that Elizabeth catches. But the runners advance to second and third, with two outs. A wiry, big-headed black kid's up next.

The play happens almost before anyone's ready. Ibrahim kicks and throws, and the big-headed kid hits a drive between first and second. The ball bounces when it hits the dirt, and Ryan has to dive — but he *does* dive and snags it handily, using the superstar belly flop he's practiced in my back yard. He's up in a heroic instant, with runners heading toward first, third, and home, and then he freezes. He seems uncertain where to throw, though he's close enough to first that he could run to the bag. And though in my gut I know the pitcher should be covering first, when I see Ryan hesitate, I'm not sure myself. Of course, I'm the guy who can't call out instructions. Ibrahim hasn't budged from the mound, but he's shouting to Ryan to throw the ball home, while Juliana points to first and yells, "Over here!" In the instant it takes Ryan to realize the play *is* at first, the play ends. Big-head crosses the bag just as Ryan steps toward him, and the runner from third is safe at the plate. The red fans cheer.

Someone on our team yells, "God, Mohr!" at Ryan, who looks down and kicks the dust. I wipe my brow, and Ann reaches over to pat my hand. I think blame should fall on Ibrahim as well as Ryan, but that's not how things go, and of course, everyone's forgotten he made a great catch. Ed Mesk calls out that we're still a team, fellas, and there's an out yet to make, but the next Twin batter hits a blooper, which Elizabeth drops. One more run scores. Then Ibrahim gets a strikeout to retire the side.

Ryan comes in looking as sad as can be. He seems awfully young suddenly, and Ibrahim and Jeremy and the others seem huge. They might sprout beards before the sixth inning. Elizabeth tells Ryan it's not really his fault, but who wants consolation from the *other* person who fucked up? Passing Ed and Jeremy in the on-deck circle, he hesitantly says, "Go get 'em, man."

I lean from the stands, and he shuffles toward me, blinking. Ann hands him a Dixie cup. Ryan turns to watch the Twins' pitcher tossing practice throws, and I rub his back as he sips some Gatorade. Then I turn him by the shoulders and pantomime batting: he'll earn back that run and more when it's his turn to hit. Ryan nods and moves toward the dugout, then stops in his tracks. "*Oh*, boy," he says suddenly.

Shawn is here. I don't know when he arrived, but he's standing with his mother, who's talking to Juliana while the little brother slaps a glove against a bench. I slide off the bleacher and step toward them as Eleanor says, "Of *course* it wasn't intentional. If you had any idea how we hustled to get here —"

Juliana says, "Well, I can't put him in now."

"I don't see why not. You had an unforeseen circumstance, so you used a temporary replacement."

"Yeah, but like . . ." Juliana looks doubtful, and though she's only a teenager, I move to where she can see me watching her. "I mean, the rules," she says.

Ryan's beside me, looking ashen. He seems to want to say something, though he's not sure what, and I wouldn't mind saying something myself. Then Shawn sighs audibly. "He already screwed up once," he says.

"Shawn!" Eleanor shifts a book she's holding and gives a tug at Shawn's blue hair. Her face reddens as she catches sight of me. "Juliana, honey, you know the game much better than I, but with all these players? Aren't there such things as substitutions? To benefit the team as a whole?" Juliana's silent, and I cross my arms and make myself fierce. Sure, the kid ran into trouble, but no one's pulling him before he can hit. I glare at Eleanor, who turns to the son bopping the glove on the bench. "Clark! Would you *stop* that?"

Shawn says, "Come on, Ryan. Give it up. You weren't even supposed to *be* in the lineup."

Ryan juts his jaw. "Oh, yeah?"

"And I'm like twice as good as you. You already cost us a run!" He looks at Ryan a moment, and his eyes narrow. "Oh, what are you gonna do now, you gonna cry? Little baby gonna cry?" And with this, Ryan's at him. He leaps forward and pushes Shawn in the chest, and Shawn nearly falls on his butt. He takes a wide swing that misses Ryan's ear. Ryan squares like a boxer.

"Come on, shithead," Ryan mutters, and I grab his waist. Everybody's yelling now — Juliana, the other Snakes, Shawn's mom, even the kid brother. Ryan settles down when I get my hands on him, but no one's got control of Shawn. He does what he may think looks like a kung-fu kick but is really a sucker move, catching Ryan on the knee, and rather than see my guy take a beating, I let Ryan wriggle away. He jumps at Shawn and knocks him to the ground — "Mother*fuck*er!" he shouts — and it looks like he lands at least one decent punch.

The boys tumble across the concrete, spilling Dixie cups and sending everyone scrambling, and behind me I hear one of the Twin fielders shouting that there's a fight. Ed appears, crying out, "What in tarnation?" and drags Shawn by the armpits, but Ryan follows them, swinging wildly. Ed hollers, "Howard, get ahold of your boy!" and this time when I tackle him he doesn't come easily.

"Damn bastard!" he shouts. "It's not fair!" I get my arms around him and try to say *shh*, but I can only whistle through my tongue. "Howie! It's not *fair!*" he cries. His face is red now and completely contorted, and he says, "Let me *go*," but I pull him to me. He jerks back, and I wipe a gob of snot from his chin; in his thrashing, he hauls off and hits me in the face. This first blow may be unintentional, but the next certainly isn't. It catches me below the ear. Suddenly he's a wild thing, and he lands several hard ones before I clamp down his wrists. Even then, I can't calm or cradle him as I'd like, because he's struggling so, and nothing's any damn fair.

Shawn, though, has shut the fuck up, and Ed's released him. He stands now with the group of Snakes, and as they watch Ryan pummel me they all seem like strangers. Shawn's mother begins explaining the complicated reason they were late in arriving, and Ed says, "Eleanor, please!" and squats by my side. "Ryan. Hey, come on now, son." His voice is sterner than I've heard it before, then it softens as he murmurs, "Shhh . . ." Patting Ryan on the back, he says, "Ryan. Hey, Ryan. No one's gonna —"

Ryan cries, "*Stop* it!" and Ed moves his hand. He catches my eye, but I don't know what he sees. Ryan stands stiffly between my knees. "Go away," he says. I let go of his arms.

Ed says, "Ryan, no one's taking you off the field. You're our first baseman, and the Snakes are behind you. But you gotta try to pull it together 'cause we can't be holding up the game like this. Come on, now, guy. Suck it up." For a moment, no one moves, though Ryan's chin trembles. Eyes welling, he glares fiercely at me; then he scowls at the ground.

Ed glances at Shawn, who's been watching self-righteously. His mother's beside him. The bony kid wrangler has materialized too and placed a hand on Eleanor's shoulder. Ed says, "Shame on both you fellows, making us a laughingstock. You'll get no more warnings. Now, Shawn, I'm not about to replace a player half an inning in. You ought to know that." Both Shawn and his mother start to speak, but Ed raises a hand. "Ryan, you're —" He pauses a moment, but Ryan doesn't move. "You're up sixth, and I think you need to get a hit. Everybody else, I want to hear —"

"We're gonna lose!" Shawn says. "How come only *I* get punished?"

A voice calls, "Shut up, Indig." I look up, and it's Jeremy, still cradling his bat. Another kid says we should get on with the game.

"I want dedicated cheering," Ed says. "For everybody on the team. Let's play ball."

This would seem to be it. Ed and I stand, and though the moment's uncomfortable, I think we're all glad to return to the game. But Ryan erupts again, as though a switch has been flipped. "I don't *want* to play in your butthead game!" he cries, his arms windmilling. Then his shoulders slump, and he seems suddenly done in. I reach for him, but he says, "Howie!" and puts his fists to his head, and all I manage is a syllable. "Unn-*nnnh!*" he cries. "This is so *stupid!* It doesn't matter, anyway. Who even watches?" Kicking the dugout bench, he says, "Take your stupid, stupid, fartball first base if you have to have it so bad. I'm done here!" and shoves through the crowd, pushing even Juliana away. He takes the steps to the playing field in a single leap and runs headlong for the exit just as the big red-clad glove salesman trots out to investigate the delay. Ryan passes him, then I do, too. I can't tell if he recognizes us.

I find Ryan sprawled forlornly on the hood of the truck, as if he's taking a catnap. He doesn't move when I come up behind him, and I feel so battered and blameful and thoroughly beyond hope that I don't even pat his back. I just stretch out on the hood beside him. For several minutes we remain like that, side by side, and I drift into a reverie of someone showing me a flower, bending the stem so I can see it clearly. I gaze at the blossom's delicate white center, and nothing happens. There's no explosion, no orange air.

A bit of dew falls against a stamen, and flecks of pollen, like tiny, tiny rust spots, appear on the petals. I say it's so beautiful I wish I could take it home. Then Ryan says, "Howie?" and I open my eyes. "I guess it's good my mom didn't come after all," he says; but if Sylvia had been here things would have gone differently. I sigh and turn around, taking a seat on the bumper with my head in my hands. Ryan does the same. After a while he says, "Please don't cry," and I lay my hand on his knee; there's a pause before he puts his hand in mine. A shout comes from inside the ballpark, and I pat his knee and jerk my head at the entrance. I think it might help to go in and cheer. But Ryan says, "Can't we just go home?" in such a small, reedy voice that I have no heart to force him to do anything. Out on the road, it's barely dusk, but when I pass a vehicle with its headlights on I turn mine on, too.

50

THE INSTANT WE TURN onto my street, I spot the gold
Nissan in front of my house. I should have anticipated
this. On the porch stands Raymond, arms folded over his padded
chest, and the sight of him standing sentinel turns my heart to lead.
Raymond stares hard as I turn the truck into my driveway, then
turns and heads into the house. My house!

I put the truck in park and turn off the motor. For a moment I
don't move. It strikes me that even with the best of projections, this
is the end of something, and these the final moments of the existence
we've been leading. Already, my dream life with Sylvia has become a
chimera, patently unrealistic and foreign to the world I inhabit, the
self I am. I can feel myself packing it up for storage, just as I did several decades ago. But what I can't stow so easily away is the prospect
of waking tomorrow with no Ryan in the house, and as I listen to
the peepers pulse out their strange, orderly rhythm, I don't know
what I'll do. I don't remember how I lived before.

I tell myself to pull it together — to suck it up, as Ed said.
Catching Ryan's profile in the twilight, I suppose something might
be made of this moment, and I think again of that rowboat ride
with my dad on the reservoir. My father wasn't big on ceremonial
remarks, and now, as I consider our dwindling minutes together, all

I want to say is that the incident at first was as much Ibrahim's fuckup as his, and no one expects him to be the perfect infielder. As for the other stuff — how happy I've been and how thoroughly I love him; how he's given me something I'd never, *ever* have known — all this I hope he understands already, or will figure out for himself as he grows older. I'm glad, too, that we hiked down from the buzzards' roost, instead of disappearing into the wild as I'd contemplated, because he got to play after all, and I'm still proud of that catch.

A shadow appears at the corner of the stable. Ryan and I sit up, and I believe for a moment we both think it's a raccoon. But it strolls up the Volkswagen's roof with a gait that's too sultry for a raccoon, and Ryan whispers, "Puff."

I say, "Mmm."

The cat shows us his glowing eyes, and Ryan says, "Howie, are we going inside?" *You bet we are, buddy, because I sure don't want them coming out after us.* I reach over to tousle his head and let my hand linger on the soft, tight curls. It must be past time for another haircut. With a shock, I realize he's not wearing the old Indians cap, and I look over the seat and on both sides of the floor, but I don't find it. He must have lost it in the scuffle.

We go in through the back. The kitchen lights are on, and when the screen door wheezes we hear Sylvia call, "Is that my guy? Is that my Ryan honey?" Ryan stops so abruptly that I almost fall over him, then he flies from me, taking off through the dining room as she appears at the hall door. "Where is he?" she barks.

"Mom!" he shouts, coming up so fast behind her that she barely can turn. He throws his arms around her neck as if expecting to be picked up, and he's laughing and hugging her, Ruby's barking, and Nit and Laurel are in the doorway.

"Oh, I missed you, babybaby, but here you are! Here you are, and gosh, you feel big!" At this, Ryan leans all his weight on his mother. They topple against the refrigerator and collapse in happy chaos. "Ouf!" says Sylvia, straightening her legs out across the floor. "Isn't this a welcome!" She looks up, her cheeks wet.

Laurel turns and speaks into the darkened hallway. "Raymond. Better call off that . . . Just say things are fine now, not to bother coming, okay? Phone's right there." She plucks a tissue from a box on the counter and blows her nose, then sets the box on the floor beside Sylvia. But Sylvia's stopped crying now. She's laughing as Ryan covers her with kisses. Smiling up from their spot on the floor, Sylvia catches Laurel's eye, and I think a look passes between them, though it's the first time they've met. As for me, I've not budged from the doorway. The raucous display strikes me as embarrassing, and my allies have defected. I feel profoundly irrelevant.

Laurel says, "Howard, didn't you know about this?" I shrug. "Well, was there a mix-up? They've been here for hours, even got a little worried." So that's how she and Sylvia became buddies. And though I customarily resent suggestions that I confuse things, this time I nod. *Yeah, a mix-up. And the hell with it.* Sylvia snorts derisively, and Ruby yaps at her. Laurel says, "Ruby, *enough!* Howard, would you mind?"

I carry Ruby out to the stoop, where she woofs tentatively in Puff's direction. Behind me, I hear Sylvia admiring the blue Snakes jersey, and when she says, "Did your team win, darlin'?" I wish there were a hundred little dogs I could carry out one by one, just to busy myself until this is over. "There'll be other chances," she says.

I follow Ruby around the corner of the house, nudging her occasionally to keep her from the flower beds. Across the street, small figures leap behind a second-story window shade — it must be bath time for the children — and I stop to watch. I'm in no hurry to go back in. A police cruiser approaches from the boulevard, moving slowly under the trees, and pulls up behind the Nissan. Two patrolmen get out and, to my astonishment, move toward my house.

I'm not at ease with cops. Even more than with the rest of the world, I feel the burden of explaining myself. But I step from the shadows and place myself in the officers' path, and one of them says, "We're responding to a call. This your house, sir?"

I nod, holding my hands up to say *all's well*. I wave the cops to the patrol car, but they ignore me. The taller one is pale and skinny and about my age; his partner's shorter and younger, with a pumped-up torso that fairly bursts his blue uniform. These young peacocks and their muscles! "Looking for a Serena Mo-her," the younger one says, as behind me a window in Dwayne's house slides open. The cop checks a spiral notebook and corrects himself: "Sorry: *Sylvia*. She here?"

I reach for my wallet, and though I'm only getting my little cards, the policemen stiffen. I hand them each a card, and they look at me as if this is more reason to be wary. The older one says, "Is Ms. Moore on the premises, sir? Do you understand what I'm saying?" But it's right there: *I am of normal intelligence!*

I can feel Dwayne staring at us, so I pick up Ruby and lead the officers to the door. Inside, the hallway's dark, but the kitchen, ahead of us, is brightly lit. Nit and Raymond step aside to let us pass, and when Laurel sees me with the cops, she steps forward. "Oh, hi," she says. *Hah.* "I'm so sorry to make y'all come on out here. We got a little worried when Ryan didn't come home, but he's back now, as you can see. Turns out Howard just took him to a baseball game."

"Sylvia Moore?"

"Sorry, no. Laurel Cao. I live here." Laurel shakes both officers' hands, then gestures at Sylvia, who seems to think it's adorable to remain floorbound. "This is Sylvia, right here. And I guess you met Howard." I've moved to the far end of the counter, away from the two cops, but I raise a hand. "And, of course, Ryan." Who stares up, openmouthed.

The young cop nods and folds up his notebook. He's probably eager to get back to the gym. The older guy looks at Sylvia. "You the one that filed the complaint?" She nods. "And it's all good now?"

"Well, I have my *child* back."

The cop chews on this a minute, then says, "Wanna tell me why you were concerned?"

Sylvia takes a breath. "Officers, I've been away, I confess. I had a problem, I received treatment, which I'd rather not . . ." She nods at Ryan. "And I'm really incredibly grateful to everyone here for all they've . . . But if one thing's sustained me — and the last weeks at a place like that are in some ways the *most* frustrating, because you know just how close you are, with so, so much at stake. So if one thing sustained me, especially this incredibly grueling and difficult final week, it was the thought of returning to some kind of . . . well, peace and *nor*malcy. Of going *out* on my very first day back and" — she pauses, taking a long, hideously hammy moment to wipe away tears — "of watching my little boy play *base*ball!"

The officers look bewildered, and Laurel jumps in again. "We had a little bit of mixed signals, with Sylvia anticipating that Howard would pick her up, and Howard believing —" She stops to take Ruby from me, and the look she gives me says I'll get mine later. "But everyone's home now, so things are fine. Course I know you always gotta check." She sets Ruby on the floor. "My dad was a police officer in Texas," she adds, though as far as I know, this isn't true.

The cop looks at Sylvia. "That right, ma'am? You knew your son was with Mr." — he squints at my card — "Kaps—"

Sylvia says, "Kapostash."

"And there was a misunderstanding about Mr. Kapostash's exact whereabouts, and the boy's, during this period?" The cop glances at me, and I nod. I even smile.

For a few seconds I expect Sylvia to play along, letting this ride as a simple misunderstanding. It's her chance to make a graceful exit: to stand up, offer thanks all around, and slither out on Hercules's arm. But she looks at me derisively. "Oh, cut it out, Howie! We had a plan! We had an absolute *plan* to — even Ryan knows you were supposed to come by and — my God, why else would I call the police?" A pair of creases forms between her brows, and though she's filled out during her sojourn away, her face as she glares at me is crystal sharp. Turning to Ryan, she says, "Wasn't he supposed to pick me up, baby? *Wasn't* that what we expected to happen?"

Ryan's still plopped on the floor, but now he freezes. "Ryan, honey," she prompts sharply, and at last he mumbles that he doesn't know.

Sylvia's mouth turns down, but she gives Ryan an affectionate squeeze. Then Raymond puts his two cents in. "Officers," he says, "you gotta understand. This woman's child was missing. Who knows where we would've had to go looking?" He squints at me. "You got some nerve, you know that?"

Sylvia sighs philosophically. "You know, I had less than twelve hours to put things together," she says. "And I was in no condition. I had to choose someone to trust with my most precious care and responsibility, which is my child. And *nothing* is more —"

The younger cop's drumming his fingers with impatience. He coughs suddenly, and Ruby barks, and he squats down to offer her his fingertips. The older officer asks if there are charges to file.

Sylvia appears to think, then says, "No, not really." But one of her poorer instincts is the tendency to press any advantage, and she adds, "But I was just so frightened, you can't imagine. To think that after all this work on myself — and it's real *work* — I'd come out and not be able to see my boy, that he could be just anywhere in the whole wide . . ." She squints resentfully at me, as though it's not familiar Howie standing here, but some stranger who presents a threat. "Because the worst thing, which I don't think anyone quite realizes about a place like that, is the *lone*liness, despite being always surrounded by people. You miss your loved ones and you feel all at sea in just every way, and there's no one to offer comfort in any way. So loneliness, *lone*liness is really the big —"

"Bahshht!" I cry, and everybody jumps. Loneliness? She's got her muscle-hunk boy toy waiting right here! I point to the street and the gold car and the *what*ever, and though Laurel tries to take my hand, I shout "Bahshht!" again, and "Kargh!" and several other words of my own devising. I took the kid hiking, I want to say, and to his baseball game. Then I brought him home! That's all there was to it, and I'd like to state also that it's because she's *not* lonely that I left Sylvia hanging. But the cops are telling me to calm down, sir, and Sylvia's cringing as if I might do her harm. Suddenly, this is intolerable. Everything's intolerable, from "babybaby" and her other twee endearments to the chirpy way she said there'd be more baseball chances. The fact that she's had only "Where is he?" to say to me is intolerable, too, as are the simpering alliance with Laurel and using rehab as a dating service and reporting me — this especially! — to the police. The terrible, flirtatious way she invited herself to the baseball game is intolerable, and when I think how I hugged her that day I swing out, and the coffeemaker flies off the counter. This brings Sylvia to her feet, first asking if Ryan's been cut by the flying glass — it was nowhere near them — then shouting that she's got a right to her life, and I'm no judge. She parked Ryan here out of the goodness of her heart, she cries as the two cops advance on me. Despite a host of other options, she practically *loaned* me her *child* because she thought he would be *good* for me, because she thought spending time with him would enrich my *life!* She took pity on me for having no prospects, for living always in the past, with no kids, no loved ones of my own, and she thought taking responsibility for another human being — having for once someone besides *myself* to care for — might do me some good. Is this how I repay her?

It's how I repay her. I'm on the ground now, I'm fucking roaring. I'm pounding my palms on the linoleum. As the short cop throws himself at me, I kick back and topple a chair, hitting my head on the floor. Laurel screams, "Is he having a fit?" but this is no fit, it's an act of *intention*, and to show I mean it I bang my head on the floor again, and vibrations ring through my ruined skull. Now Ruby's yipping and my name's being called. The cop gets his legs around me so he's straddling my back like some kind of foreign wrestler, but he's not nearly strong enough — *no one's* strong enough — to make me subside. No sir, this is not a fit, but it's nothing like Ryan's paltry tantrum at the ballpark, and I don't care what happens to me. I could rip out my hair, twist off my cranium. There's a hand or an arm or a stick at my throat, and I press my fists to my forehead and they grab my wrists. I aim to finish everything the war started, if the miserable, cracked globe of my head would just split . . .

Way off, beyond my bellowing, is a small voice that's Ryan, telling me to stop. Then a small hand on my ear, and a voice shouts to back off, son. I grit my teeth and hear Sylvia announcing she's leaving, this is ridiculous, and I bang my face on the floor again, splattering that same blood-colored mucus that was all over Timothy. Sylvia shouts shrilly that she hopes I'm satisfied with the way I've turned a joyous reunion into a *bloodbath*, and after that I don't think anything at all. As the cops get the cuffs on, maybe I do slide under for a minute, but I go as far as I can until finally I'm tired; and the last thing I register is Laurel screaming, "Oh, please don't hurt him! Please, don't you dare hit him!" By then, they're already dragging me away.

III

51

THE FIRST TIME MY LIFE CHANGED, I didn't realize it for a very long time. When the dust-off choppers airlifted us out I was unconscious, but I imagine them rising through the cover of the trees, then slipping along the edge of that former plantation, now the partially burned valley I'd glimpsed from the lookout tower. Upon my arrival at the field hospital I was placed in an induced coma to reduce blood flow and the swelling that's a major cause of brain-tissue injury, and I went right into surgery to have a shunt implanted. Occasionally, in the years since, I've believed I remember my surgeries, and I have clear recollections of having my brain tinkered with. I picture the astonishing showbiz brightness of the operating tent where army doctors leaned over me in their caps, and I see gloved hands reaching in and out of my head, the fingertips shiny and a little greasy; I see all the metal instruments, too, their sheen dulled by my blood. Also the suturing thread, which, no matter how fine, seems terribly fibrous and absorbent when I think of it looping around inside me, and the various hairy, naked forearms that crossed and flexed above my face. But of course, it's impossible that I recall anything, even from later operations. And it's especially implausible that I should remember that first surgery, because I was not only comatose, but practically dead. The fact that it was more than six hours before I was operated on reduced my chances to less than fifteen percent, and people who don't know better have said my survival alone is a kind of miracle.

I remained comatose for forty-six days after my injury. During this time the shunt, which had served to drain hydrocephalous fluid from my cranium, was removed, and a breathing apparatus was installed, then also removed once I returned to breathing on my own. Sometime during those six weeks I experienced a heart incident, and a stint was placed in my chest to keep a vessel clear; I suppose it's still there. And early on, while both of us remained quartered at the aid station, Rimet paid me a visit. I imagine him sitting by my bed in his fatigues and his sling, and because I've never known where exactly he got burned, I picture him not puckered or blackened by scars, but as untouched as that first morning we met in the chow line. Rimet had an angular face that went all crooked whenever he smiled, and I see him squinting as he cradled his arm. I wonder what he saw. Just a guy with a head bandage and the sheet pulled tight to his neck, the breathing thing clamped to his nose and mouth, and nothing visible but a chin and two closed eyes: that was me. I suppose Rimet told me jokes — they were his forte — but I hope that as he sat watching the equipment breathe he made some serious remarks, too. Not counting medical professionals, this was the first of the one-sided conversations that would constitute the rest of my life. Then I was shipped off to Japan to continue my recovery, and Rimet went somewhere to continue his. I imagine him in Bangkok, purchasing Thai stick and managing to get laid despite the sling, and I hope he had fun, because later he must have returned to the war. And I don't blame him for disappearing from my life after that. Rimet had three hundred and forty-nine days to go. He had to be friends with the living, and if he survived his year he probably knew plenty of fellows who got injured, some of them guys he liked better than me. So the casualties piled up, and if I remained in Rimet's thoughts at all, it must have been only as the first. I wonder if he even knows I came to.

A few procedures, then, a bedside visit, and a change of venue. This is the record of my activities during that period, and it's not much, especially compared to my eight busy weeks with Ryan. Throughout my comatose period I was carefully monitored, and the fact that I remained alive was considered encouraging. At some point, I suppose they decided I was not going to die, but no one made projections about when or if I would awaken, or what my recovery would be like if I did. Even my parents were told nothing for weeks after a telegram informed them I'd been injured in the head and leg. I was a cipher, and there was no way to read me until I awoke.

I should remember what that was like, that return to consciousness. What was my first thought after sleeping for so long? What was my first sensation? But the process was so gradual that I remember little, and of course, I was full of drugs. At the first signs of consciousness they began diagnostics and therapy, and because other factors were addressed first, it was a while before we recognized the depth of my speaking impairment. One thing I relearned in those early days was how to swallow, and I remember holding a spoonful of applesauce on my tongue while I groped for the appropriate muscles. The nurse would offer a little coaxing until, with excruciating effort, I'd take a giant chance and usually send the applesauce spewing into the room or down my chin. I did this again and again in the months after I came to, though I was desperate to get off the needle and taste real food, and I spat on my therapist so often that she took to wearing a bib. But I always thought swallowing would be a benchmark, and that once I'd mastered it, life's *other* oral function would fall right back in line.

I had a little foot-drag, too, at first, though never much difficulty with hands or arms. My right leg was still functioning slowly when I returned stateside, and there were those who felt I should go to a live-in care facility rather than my parents' house. But I'd been institutionalized for a long time at that point, and my folks were eager to have me home. I think we all believed returning to this place and my old room was the quickest route back to the guy I was, the me who'd been a different and optimistic and talkative person. It was also an affirmation that I had not, in fact, died in a war.

Thus began those daily trips with my dad. For every two hours of speech work, I put in forty minutes of physical therapy on my leg, and I reveled in those forty minutes. The tasks were so manifest! I could *see* the rubber balls I was asked to flex against, as well as the ankle weights and the sets of footprints painted on the floor, and I could adjust my movements to meet these objectives. I made terrific progress and felt myself getting stronger, and I practiced walking as a matter of course. I made progress with speech, too, but nothing ever stuck as it did with my walking. When I practiced my verbal exercises I never lost the sense that I was guessing how to form sounds. I was not good at visualizing the inside of my throat, and I never succeeded in isolating or differentiating the myriad muscles used in speech. There was something more profound, too. Some desert realm had sprung up between my mind and my lips, where ideas — of my mother, for example — inevitably languished in passage, never completing the transformation that brought *mom* into bloom. And though I was supposed to practice at home, I rarely did. Our house had never been a rowdy place, but with my injury it became quieter. My dad, always a taciturn man, now said even less, and Mom was so eager to build my confidence that she couldn't be tough when it came to my language. She led me through each conversation we had, offering word suggestions and anticipating what I wanted to say; and at home I was permitted gestures, which were taboo at the center. (In one particular sphere of my rehabilitation, my mother was the talker and I the listener. When I first came home, my memory was shaky, and Mom made it her project to replenish my past. Every day, she told me stories of our life before, and when Sylvia was around, her help was enlisted, too. My memories did return, though at times I wonder where my own reconstructions end and true recollection begins.) So the months, then the years, passed, and gestures became my dominant mode of discourse. I don't blame anyone for this. I think my mom was spooked by my silence, and I was lazy and impatient. In the years following my injury I suffered from adynamia: I had trouble mustering the procedural capacity even for very simple tasks. Morning ablutions remained insurmountable, and if my dad didn't lead me to the bathroom and guide me through, I could spend an entire morning attempting to shave, while the washbasin overflowed and the razor got mislaid on the toaster and I stood helplessly at the window, my face dabbed with tufts of foam. So I might spend days with my speech therapist, learning about S's, and I'd learn how to imitate the sound she made. Then we'd move on to something else, and the next time I needed them, those S's would be gone, just as if I'd been robbed. I slipped back so thoroughly after each improvement that I think I would have slipped back anyway, no matter how much I'd practiced at home.

After a while, I no longer saw the physical therapist, and as my focus returned I was able to drive again. But Dad still rode across town to my sessions, and we spent more time at the little barbecue joint. By then I was doing high-intensity speech therapy, still trying to build on a few early milestones, and I was also involved in what was called "transitioning class." This consisted only of extreme head cases, the others commuting from nearby group-living facilities, and of the six of us, three were there because of the war, two for car wrecks, and one had had his skull bashed in during a robbery. Between us we had the whole patchwork of symptoms and abilities: sensory loss, cognitive loss, motor control loss, difficulty with social/adaptive behavior, emotional volatility, and plenty more. Physically, another guy and I were the least disabled — I'd done well with my right leg and was pretty much the picture of health, and he was the same — but in the speech department, I was way at the bottom. During our sessions I'd sit quietly, feeling contempt for my comrades' labored drawlings and chagrin at my own silence, and as the months passed I let myself slip from that world.

What finished me off, I suppose, was sheer embarrassment. I've always been mindful of what other people think of me, and I was as uncomfortable with those five guys registering my lack of progress as I was in my parents' world, with its ongoing reassessment by neighbors and shopkeepers. Sometimes at night, after my parents went to bed, I'd imagine a life in which speech was a distasteful activity, like shitting, and I'd get stoned and let myself feel very good; and before long I wanted to feel good in daylight, too. I found a connection for acid and began my practice of picking up hookers, and soon I was missing sessions. I bailed internally before I stopped showing up, and I tripped my brains out during the last of my transitioning classes. What did it matter? I couldn't contribute, anyway. So I sat and giggled, and during speech therapy I didn't try. When I finally abandoned that place, I'd been participating in the help industry for nearly a decade, and I never went back. But a few years ago, to my astonishment, I saw two guys from my old transitioning group. They were at the movies, and I was amazed to see them still hanging out together. I was alone, of course. One of the guys still used a walker, and both had the big, round hips of people who've done a lot of wheelchair time, but I could tell they'd made progress, as I had myself. I was a bit behind them in line, and I thought I might go up and renew our acquaintance, but in the end I didn't. They were busy talking, the taller one clearly still struggling with speech, and I couldn't imagine how, once I'd made myself known to them, I might contribute to their good time.

I think of the acid years as my absent period, during which my rehabilitation was suspended. I had no sense of improving or of trying to improve, but after my father died, when I cleaned up, I learned what had been going on in my absence. Gone were all vestiges of the adynamia, and some processes that had been difficult had grown easier through regeneration. Speech, of course, was not one of those processes. Nevertheless, it was as if a chink of yellow had appeared in the clouds, the chink growing broader and brighter until it commanded the sky. As I began to move forward again, shouldering responsibilities in the household and accepting the convent job, I traced this clearing of the heavens back years, to when I woke from my coma. It was all part of the same unfurling, I felt, and all continuous.

52

THIS TIME, THOUGH, there's nothing gradual about waking to change. Rather, I'm so frightened I can barely sleep. By the time my head is bandaged and I've been processed it's well after midnight, and a large Indian-looking orderly guides me to a small dark room with neither lock nor doorknob on its swinging door. The orderly holds the door open, telling me not to act up — as if, with this terrible headache, I might try something fast. I go in, groping for a light switch, and he announces that the lights are controlled from a central nursing station. He reminds me again that I shouldn't act up and lets the door swing closed.

On the far side of the room is a barred window from which a gray tic-tac-toe of light seeps over a couple of iron beds. But along with the headache, the last few hours have brought waves of double vision, so the gray squares circle nauseatingly as my heart pounds under my hospital gown. At last, I step over and peer through the bars, but I can't tell whether it's a hospital courtyard I'm seeing or an air shaft or city street or bottomless pit. Then something twitches behind me, and I almost scream. I turn and make out a shadow on the bed to my right, under a mound of black blanket. The shadow lies quietly a moment, then suddenly thrashes. It scratches, pummeling itself, and doubles up like a fist. Then it's still again.

I lie down on the other bed, pulling a blanket over my bare legs and keeping my slippers on for a speedy exit. A few feet away, the shadow continues its sporadic clenching, and I stare at the ceiling, my body braced for attack. Hours pass, and the evening's events drift through my consciousness, but in a distant, soothingly pastel realm, and held at bay by my headache plus a general depressed passivity and the sedatives they gave me at intake. I imagine Ryan falling asleep in his own small bed, and I wonder if it seems he never went away. I can see how it would. Then my imagination moves to the adjacent room, where there are small roses in the wallpaper, and the quilted bedspread has been folded over a chair. I wonder if Sylvia allowed herself and Ryan to be dropped off at home, or if she required company to help her recover from her ordeal. The headache worsens.

Slowly I become aware of a low *shish-shish-shish*, as rhythmic and measured as the tick of a clock. The sound surges, then disappears, and I listen to it rise and fall, then rise and fall again and again, and I think that between the shishing and the thrashing in the dark I may truly go mad. It occurs to me that what I'm hearing is the sound of my own blood pulsing into the corners of my head from some tiny leak in a vessel, and I wonder if I've made it worse by lying prone. Keeping an eye on the next bed, I sit up, and the pain bobbles around like a yolk in an eggshell. For a while I can only breathe, elbows on knees, then the shishing starts up again out of the silence. It strikes me that the sound is not inside my head at all, but out in the corridor, and though I don't know if venturing beyond the swinging door is what the big Indian would call acting up, I rise carefully to investigate.

The hallway's almost as dark as the bedroom, with a single row of very dim bulbs — perhaps twenty watts — strung like a spine down the ceiling. The lights are out of reach, but each is surrounded by a yellow protective cage, and the wispy shadows of the cages cross-hatch the walls. At the far end of the corridor is the security barrier I came through with the orderly, but I can see no guards beyond the bars. The only figure is a lone walker dressed in a blue gown just like my own. He moves resolutely toward the barrier, his reinforced-paper slippers creating the sound that drew me from my room.

The shisher disappears around a corner, and I head toward the gate, hoping to score some aspirin. In a far corner, a young black guy reads a book in the square light of a desk lamp. "What you want?" he says.

I point to my head, then mime taking a pill. "Medications at the desk." He cocks his head. "Don't worry. They tell you when you ready." He squints sourly at me, and I wonder how bad my face is. Certainly the hospital gown does nothing for my credibility. The guard says, "Git on, now. I got studyin'."

Halfway down a side corridor is the nursing station. An attractive young woman is looking up when I step to the doorway, and I realize the rasp of my own slippers has announced me. But if she knows me as the new guy she gives no sign. I run through the headache gestures, and she says, "No meds without your doctor's say-so." It's as if we've been through this many times before. "Name?" But of course, they took my clothes, right down to socks and underwear, and in this fucking gown there are no little cards stating I'm of normal intelligence. Suddenly it dawns on me that I'm about to encounter people who have no reason to give me a break, and I back away. The nurse is on her feet in a flash. She grabs the plastic ID bracelet they've attached to my wrist, reads my name, and says, "Oh." I clutch my fingers to indicate pain, but "You'll see someone tomorrow" is all she says, perhaps daring me to contradict her. I step back to the dim web of the hallway.

I hear the *shish* guy again. He turns a corner, rhythmic and inevitable as a robot; then, like a robot, he stops before me. For a moment, there's only the convulsive twitching of his fingers, which battle one another before his sternum; though the light is dim, I think he's made his cuticles bleed. He reaches out, and I spring back, but he's only reaching toward a small table by the office, where a plastic vat the size of a tackle box stands upright. Shakily selecting a cup, the guy holds it under a plastic spigot, and a stream glugs out: milk, juice, poison, I can't tell. But when he offers the cup to me — if I trusted my vision it would be a *pair* of cups proffered by two bloody hands which overlap at the center — I head to my room in terror.

Perhaps I get some sleep before morning dawns at the barred window, but I'm staring at the ceiling when the shadow sits up. My thrasher turns out to be a thin, sad-faced boy of roughly twenty, with a poor excuse for a Vandyke and the tattoo of an apple on the side of his neck. He's pretty shaky and has a hard time focusing, but he's so much more ordinary than last night's shisher guy that I begin to hope it's not all loonies here. The shadow says his name is Ansel and he checked himself in, hoping to make it a few days without heroin. I gesture that I, too, checked myself in, because the Indian — as well as the physician who spoke to me before him and the squirrelly little intake guy before her — said that if the state did it they could keep me for fourteen days of observation. But Ansel only looks at me sideways and doesn't pay a lot of attention. I'm not sure he even registers my lack of speech.

With the dawn, my double vision begins clearing, though my headache persists. I follow Ansel to the can, where there are no doors on the stalls, nor even seats on the toilets, and a handwritten sign I'm unable to read probably explains why the showers are cordoned off. A battered steel mirror bolted above two metal sinks reveals me as a bruised and ugly cuss, with a real goose egg and a new set of black stitches embroidering my scar, but I have to admit I fit right in: my fellow inmates range from unkempt to openly drooling. Those of us who are better off skitter out of the way of the others, and when Shisherguy appears and vibrates toward a urinal, I hope the dampness in my paper slippers is only water, not piss.

A breakfast room is open, and I eat quickly and alone, avoiding eye contact when anyone approaches my table. I'm hoping to slide through under the radar, and the kitchen clatter, from a steamy realm I'm not permitted to enter, reminds me I should be forming a plan for getting out. But there's a guy not too far from me who can't sit still, and at the far side of the room someone's playing a piano while someone else shouts, "Stop the music!" and no matter where I look, white-clad people are scurrying, cleaning up messes, telling someone to remain seated, holding someone else by the hand. It's so demoralizing that I barely make it from moment to moment, and finally I get up and return timidly to the nurse's station. This time, a redheaded nurse shuffles some papers and rewards me with two aspirin, but my own craven gratefulness gives me the jitters, and I go back to my room wondering if yesterday's bashing has made me docile.

The aspirin don't do much, and I spend the day on my bed, even skipping lunch. I guess it's sunny out, because for a while a grid of light from the window moves down the wall, then onto the floor. When I first woke up in Japan, I used to watch the light play across the big ward I shared with nineteen other wounded soldiers. I wasn't able to move at the beginning, so I'd follow the light with my eyes until it drifted out of sight. Now, though, I roll over to watch it creep across the floor.

I tell myself I mustn't get comfortable, that visualizing my real life, in the world beyond, will keep me sane. But the sedatives that made everything pastel have long since worn off, and my outside life is filled with danger zones — Sylvia's betrayal, my crime against Timothy, almost anything to do with Ryan — and the difficulty of skirting those pain areas makes my head throb more. I think of yesterday, at the buzzards' roost, and for a few moments I marvel at how happy we were. I listen to the rustle of the aspens in the breeze, and it strikes me I've always loved sitting high on a perch, with movement in the air and strong sunlight and human life — towns, agriculture — spread out before me. I think again of that burned valley; what was it like when the plantation was in full swing? I remember how I contemplated taking off with Ryan, going camping and driving until we were tracked down and captured, and I'm impressed by how bold I was, how wide my sense of possibility. Then, with a shift of some dark counterweight of the soul, I'm back in the danger zone with Sylvia. No matter how hard I try to go back further, to visit times *before* yesterday — to remember breakfast and backyard catch, petunias, Aqua Splash Down with Laurel, Harrison's radio station, almost anything good — those memories are all part of a frail, distant dream. They don't compete with the gray walls, the chaotic sounds from the hallway, or the sudden entrance of a hyped-up, chattering Ansel. Throwing himself on the floor beside his cot, he tries pulling the mattress over him like a shell. But the mattress is attached to the bed and the bed's attached to the floor, and rather than watch him struggle, I flee the room.

The ward's laid out in a squared-off U. There are doorways leading to terrible common rooms and occasionally a bank of windows, and every window gives onto an air shaft like the one Ansel and I have as a view. The shafts have begun darkening as the sun slopes landward, so I give up on windows and stick to the hallway circuit, U after backward U, again and again. In the Japanese hospital, once I became ambulatory I walked as much as possible to resolve the drop leg as well as a certain exhaustion I felt standing upright. Then, too, there was a circuit I'd walk for as long as I could stand it: hours. I had such ambition! Back then, everyone knew who I was, and most of the nurses remembered me as a coma patient. They'd stop and congratulate me and tell me I was doing well, and I'd signal my thanks. No one doubted I'd get my speech back eventually. Here, though, I'm just a guy doing laps. Other patients pass me without registering anything, and the white-clad staff have crazies to attend to. I pass the milk dispenser for the umpteenth time and reach down to put my hands in my pockets; but the damn robe has no pockets, and suddenly I feel like a panther in a zoo. I head to the bathroom to see if the showers are open, but the barrier's still hung with its unreadable explanation. Still, I don't want to let myself go. I haven't showered since yesterday, and I can smell the sweat of a long summer's hike, plus the ballpark and Ryan's tantrum and last night's exercise in the kitchen and the stale, pungent scent of rage. I peel the robe from my shoulders and set to washing myself, lathering my hand with soap and smearing the froth through the hair on my chest, under my arms, even my crotch. I use wet paper towels to rinse. And I feel better, so I do my neck, which is grimy, and my ears, and then delicately, because the stitches are sore, the skin of my face. I'd like to shave, too, but I make do with lathering and rinsing my stubble. Finally there's just my mouth, and it strikes me that the orderly should have issued me a toothbrush or a bottle of mouthwash or a pack of Dentyne, but what's good for the face should be good for the mouth. So I make some soapsuds, and with my finger I rub my teeth and my gums. It's a little sickening, but I'm on a clean spree. Then I look up and catch sight of the reflection in the metal mirror. Directly behind me is one of the wide-open toilet stalls, with a huge smear of brown on the wall.

I rush to the office and stand before the redheaded nurse. I'm a patient with rights, and I'll see someone in charge! Adopting a stiff pose, I mime a stethoscope. She's unimpressed, but she gets it. "Just residents on weekends," she drawls. I spread my hands: *I'll see a resident.* "Unless you're in crisis, there's not much the residents do, sir. You'll see your treatment manager first thing Monday." She looks me over — paper slippers, blue gown, clean but lousy-looking face — and cracks what may be a joke. "You're not in crisis, are you?" When I maintain my composure she asks a passing doctor to give me a minute.

The resident's a young guy with square fingers and a broad, smooth forehead. He takes me into an examination room and points to a chair, then hitches up a trouser leg and plants a butt cheek on the examination table. He's so comfortable with his own generous condescension that he doesn't realize I've *met* doctors, and I know they're geeks. Still, I feel he can see through my gown. "So what's up?" he says.

I stare at him. I'm here, for starters. Isn't that bad enough? I wave at the terrible robe and slippers, then at the door. Must I lead him to the shit? The doc swallows, tapping a finger on his thigh. "Okay, I'm just the resident, see. So I'm not really familiar with, uh, every case. You want to tell me how you got in here? In your own words."

53

Monday morning I'm at breakfast, recovering from another night of Ansel's turmoil. The showers were open when I arose this morning, but the line was so long that I decided to eat first. Now I'm worried they'll close before I get there, and I'm gulping my French toast. An orderly appears and tells me to follow him, even pronouncing my name correctly.

I stand up. There's a bead of syrup on my gown, and I gesture that I'll clean up quickly. But the guy says, "Nah, just come on along. Unless you have to urinate, they're waiting for you, Mr. Kapostash." He leads me down a hallway and unlocks a brown door, then there's a short corridor with a staircase at the end. As we walk down the corridor, I remember the treatment manager the redheaded nurse promised yesterday, and I worry that with the syrup and two days' growth of beard and my hair tufting over my ears I don't look at all sane. And B.O.! What was I thinking, I who for years have showered first thing every morning? Today of all days, how could I let myself go?

The orderly stops before we get to the staircase, opens a door, and stands back. In a square room, a woman and two men in doctors' coats sit behind a table. The table's spread with patient records, and there's a bentwood chair, like a chair from a waiting room, which is obviously for me. I sit down, tugging my gown over my hairy thighs. Two of the doctors are conferring in low tones, while the third flips through the pages of a chart. With half-glasses and a shock of handsome, steel-colored hair, only this last doctor might be my age. None of them looks up.

At last the gray-haired doctor says, "Well, Mr. Kapostash, you've certainly got influential friends." This is not the remark I'm expecting. I wonder if they've confused me with someone else. "And you've kept out of trouble since — this is your first hospitalization since the seventies, is that right?"

I nod warily to this, and the woman doctor turns to her colleague. "Now, am I right in understanding that he doesn't speak in any way, shape, or form?" She looks at me. "You don't speak?" I shake my head. "And he doesn't write, either?"

"Apparently not. Mr. Kapostash?" I shake my head.

"And he doesn't sign." No, none of the above. But at least we're getting this out of the way.

"And he's here since —" The female doctor glances irritably at me, then turns again to her colleague. "Yet he seems to manage satisfactorily on his own."

"According to the nun." The gray-haired one passes a paper to the woman. Folding his hands before him, he says, "Mr. Kapostash, you *are* gainfully employed."

This is so clearly a statement of fact that I don't know how to respond. I glance at the third doc, who still hasn't looked up. Then I nod again. I'm sure not telling them I'm out of a job.

"And you're comfortable with the work you do? No difficulties there?" I shake my head. "Good. Miss, uh, *Bridge* is it —" I blink, and he leans over to glance at the paper. The woman taps it with a fingernail. "Yes. Sister Amity Bridge. Well, Sister Bridge certainly thinks highly of you." I nod slowly, and he goes on. "The hospital has always had a strong relationship with the convent. I've not met Sister Bridge, but several of the sisters work as support staff in the wards."

"Mr. Kapostash," says the woman. She has auburn hair and a shield-shaped face, and she'd be pretty if she put on a pretty expression. "Can you provide any explanation, by any means at all, for your behavior this past weekend? Do you understand what I'm asking?"

Of course I understand. I'm of normal intelligence. I take a long breath and puff it out sorrowfully, then pat my heart. I put my hands together and give a little bow that means *mea culpa*. I pat my heart again. The doctor looks carefully at me, her lips pursed. "Now the crux of the matter, as I understand it, has to do with the woman who made the original complaint. Ms. Mohr. This is someone you've been involved with?" I nod, waving dismissively: *long, long time ago. It's over.* "In a romantic capacity?" Yes. "The child, however, is not your son."

In a flash, I see where she's going, and I hope the color doesn't drain from my face. I open my hands wide to show how innocent it all was, then stand up and swing a bat and march uphill. I smile broadly, spreading my hands again, and if it's humiliating putting on a dumb show, I'd rather they took me for a clown than a pervert. But the woman interrupts my antics, almost as if I've gotten off point. "And Ms. Mohr found someone else," she says thoughtfully, "and you felt . . ." She blinks inquisitively. Now I notice the silk blouse under her doctor's coat, and a necklace of gold filigree, and I realize that to these doctors we're a tale of tawdriness, not perversion. Sylvia's an unwed mother with guys on the side, and I'm the Quasimodoid chump she strings along. It's insulting, but I hold my tongue.

The older doctor says, "Mr. Kapostash, we are not a law enforcement institution. Ms. Mohr has declined to press charges on behalf of either herself or her son, and the officers at the scene reported that you were not a danger to anyone besides yourself. Under the circumstances, that would be enough to recommend your remaining with us for a course of psychiatric evaluation and treatment, and I'm not sure I don't recommend such a course, if you're so inclined." He pauses, looking straight at me, but doesn't ask if I understand, for which I'm grateful. "Certainly, your VA benefits entitle you to any help we provide.

"On the other hand, you have here a testimonial to your stability and work ethic and the fact that" — he peers at the letter through those little half-glasses — "'despite his disability, Mr. Kapostash does an admirable job of maintaining an independent and autonomous life. He has for many years been a respected member of the secular staff here at Mercy Convent, and his contributions to both our comfort and our well-being are much valued.'" He raises his eyebrows, dropping the paper on the table.

I try to look as if this is my due. The fact that such a document exists is astonishing, of course, and I hope my demonstration with the air bat hasn't compromised my dignity. The doctor continues, "Mr. Kapostash, let me stress again that you should not take the incident of Saturday evening too lightly. Someone with your history needs to be especially attuned to shifts in behavior, emotion, cognitive function, et cetera, all of which can change even this long after an initial injury. And while you can check yourself out, of course, just as you checked yourself in, you should know you remain responsible for your actions. Your personal record and the letter from the sister suggest you do pretty well, and that's commendable, but I urge you to adopt a highly vigilant attitude. I refer to mood swings, inappropriate behavior or ideation, difficulty in coping, breaks in reality perception, and so on. I think you might, before taking your leave, ask yourself if it wouldn't be a good idea to meet with a staff member for one or more sessions, just to iron out this event." He pauses, and I wait a moment to make sure he's finished. But really, who are they kidding? Does anyone really imagine I'll stay voluntarily, what with the shisher and Ansel and all the other fruitcakes for company, the rude student and the nitwit resident and the rest of the keeper staff warning *me* not to act up while someone actually *does* smear shit on the walls? The doctors don't look at all surprised when I shake my head.

"Very well," the steel-headed doctor says, offering his hand so quickly that I wonder if they're glad not to deal with me. I stand up and shake his hand, then the woman's, and at last, the third doctor looks up and shakes my hand, too, murmuring as he does so that I should take care. The old doc nods at the orderly, who's still standing, hands folded, by the door. "John will take you out," he says, and though I do no such thing, I have an urge to raise the horrible blue gown from my backside and moon all three of them as I take my leave. Inappropriate ideation!

We don't return to the ward, so I make no goodbyes. Instead, I'm led down the stairs to a kind of large coat check, and when a Spanish guy asks my name, John answers for me, again pronouncing it perfectly. On the far side of the coat check, an opening like a wide window gives onto a bright waiting room filled with people. When John gives my name a shriek goes up, and Laurel swims out of the brightness like a fish in an aquarium. "Howard?" she screams, and pushes through a set of swing doors. Then she's hugging me: Laurel, who's not girly or squealy in that way at all, hugging me despite my filthy gown, stinking hair, and terrible breath, telling me I look unbelievably awful and asking John if they really have let me go.

54

LAUREL'S LITTLE BEETLE looks like close quarters, and I stand beside it for a moment, plucking at my Snakes baseball shirt and fanning my armpits apologetically. "Oh, Howard, stop it. I've got windows. And a moonroof!" We open the car up entirely, and Laurel says, "Must be great to be free, I can't imagine." The air flaps her black hair across her face.

It's one of those spectacular July mornings, bright and warm, with just a little breeze, and the storefronts and high-rises sparkle as we pass through downtown. I wonder if it was this nice yesterday, when all that filtered into the psycho ward was a patch of sunlight moving down a wall. And then I want to forget I was ever there. Laurel's delighted by the coup she scored in getting me out; she pulls herself up tight to the steering wheel and tells me I had a close call, and I sit barely moving, my arm dangling out the window. "I didn't know what the heck we were gonna do, Howard," she says. "We were sick with worry." She says Robin came by the house yesterday to drop off the Indians cap and Ryan's glove, which we'd left at the stadium. "Good thing she did, too, because that's how I got the idea of contacting your nun. Who's really a peach; wants you to stop by, talk about work. And Robin was splendid, too. How come you and *Ran* never told me about her?"

We enter the residential neighborhoods, and I feel I've been away a long time. Laurel says she's heard nothing from Sylvia, but she knows there weren't charges filed, because she called the precinct. "I suppose she didn't want anyone looking too closely at her own decisions, or maybe she had a change of heart. I don't know." She slumps back in her seat. "House sure was lonely, though. I doubt I've spent a night there, Howard, without you, all these years; isn't that funny? And then Ryan gone, too. Sudden change." Remaining undiscussed is what happened in the kitchen Saturday, and if Laurel's dying to dissect it, I appreciate her tact. Cruising down the boulevard, she says, "Well, the main thing is, I'm glad you're back. I think we all need to return to some kind of normal something and not lose sight of what's been gained. Seems our household barely knew each other eight weeks ago; who'd have thought . . . And your old job might be still available, too, so I'd advise — oh, hell, we'll talk money later!" She reaches over and squeezes my hand, holding it just a moment before fiddling with the gearshift. Then we turn onto our street. "Oh, and Howard, I forgot! There's a surprise waiting for you at home. Well, sort of a — I mean, not Ryan, don't think that. But sort of a surprise."

Our street looks cheerful, in the glittery way of everything that's not a mental hospital, and on the railing of my front porch the paired boxes of petunias catch the sun. Yet suddenly I'm not glad to be home. I don't wish I'd remained where I was, but I look up at my tidy house and dread walking into a certain empty room. I wish I had anywhere else to be. For a moment I stand dumbstruck, then Laurel runs a hand down my spine. The heart-shaped leaves on the morning glory vines flutter, as if in response.

In the back yard, a lawn chair's been dragged into the sunlight, and a long figure sits wrapped in a patterned sheet. When the figure stands, I see it's Harrison, very wan and still strange-looking with no hair on his face. He and I hug awkwardly. "Oh, man, How. I guess you've been through the wringer," he says, and as he shrouds himself once again in his sheet he looks like an Indian chief draped in a blanket. I signal that I'm sorry about his dad, and he says, "Yeah. It sucks." He looks expectantly at me, so I pat my heart. But I've been patting my heart so much lately that I'm really sick of it. If I never touch my heart again, that will be fine.

The kitchen door opens, and Ruby dashes out, making a quick circuit of the yard. I look at my fingernails and wish Harrison would speak, because despite the sunshine and the happy dog and the children's voices in a yard not far away, I'm being drawn toward the tube of my own dark feelings. But Harrison, too, seems to have moved out of reach. His face and body have grown thin in his short absence, and as he draws the sheet around his shoulders his mouth is downturned. I suppose any friendship I thought we had was too brief not to be illusory, and perhaps kids and baseball aren't enough for a connection, anyway; so we sit mutely, two gloomy, depressed men. At last Harrison says, "Well, I guess the little guy got to play a real game after all," and I realize he has no idea what a disaster that was. I nod.

Laurel pushes open the screen door and asks if we want anything. We shake our heads. She strolls down the steps and puts a hand on each of our shoulders and asks Harrison what's with the sheet, and he says he wanted something around him. When she asks if he told me about his time at home, he says the service was nice. "Harrison was with his dad before he died, which was the most important thing," Laurel adds.

Again I remember the complicated, terrible time of my own dad's death, and I reach over and touch Harrison's hand. He squeezes my fingers. Thinking a moment, he says he appreciated the card and the cookies and Ryan's drawing. "Dude, that picture!"

Laurel says, "I think we ought to all do something today, cheer ourselves up. Maybe get out, take like a walk or a hike? *Be* someone, for heaven's sake. Aren't there some kind of little hiking parks off to the west where you can get out and enjoy nature? What's that hawk center?" I look up, amazed, and she says, "But first, I hope you boys are hungry for soup, 'cause I got a mother lode didn't get delivered this morning."

I'm not sure why this hits me so hard. Perhaps it's simply the burden I've become, pulling Laurel from her customers to get me out of stir. Or that the notion of three sorry souls slogging up to the buzzards' roost doesn't strike me as redemptive. But suddenly my eyes well acidly, and I can't sit here any longer. Laurel says, "Howard?" but it's not her fault. I stand up blindly and rush to the house. I can feel my shoulders shaking, and in my mind the crushing and folding of everything I've ever known, until I'm crushed, too. I run up the staircase, and two steps from the top I trip on a step and go down on my palms, but I keep going. It's a long way to my bedroom.

Laurel gives me twenty minutes, then taps on my door. "Howard? Are you okay?" I don't respond. I know I'm being childish, but I don't want to see anyone, and it's not as if I can call out for solitude. A moment later the door creaks. "I guess we're all sad right now," she says. "Maybe we should be sad together, you know?" Still I don't move, but stay curled on my big double bed. I hear Laurel walk into the room, and when I open my eyes she's standing before me. "Why, Howard! You haven't even washed. Don't you want to take a shower?" I look at her balefully. *I can't or I don't.* She sits on the edge of the bed, scooting my feet back with her butt, and puts a hand on my leg. And despite the times I've thought it would be sublime to lie in bed with Laurel patting my thigh, at the moment I abhor her pity. "Come on now," Laurel says. "Get up. Eat something, give yourself a shave. That twenty-five-o'clock shadow is not your style." She gives a rueful smile and adds, "Does your head hurt?"

I should ask to be left alone. I can do that with gestures, but I close my eyes. After a moment Laurel says, "And that *baseball* shirt! Did you know it's got blood on it? Take it off and let me work on the stain." She reaches to unbutton the front of the shirt, and though her touch is gentle, I simply can't bear it. I think if I allow this I'll end up clutching at her more desperately — more hopefully, intimately, needily than I can live down — or I'll bash myself on the floor again, and I'm not sure there's a difference. So I kick my legs and thrash out with one fist, and I come close to striking her. In my embarrassment, I pull a pillow over my head. Laurel says, "God*damn* it," and walks out.

In the evening she sends Nit up. "Hey, uh, Howard, man. Laurel wants to know if you had any supper. Me and Harrison and her were thinking of going for pizza." I hear a board creak as he shifts his weight, then he says, "Yo, Howard?" I roll off the far side of the bed and cover my ears to block his idiot voice, but he's already gone.

I try to be aware of nothing, and to a certain extent, I succeed. It's a hot night, but I remain on the floor, wrapped in my white quilt, and maybe I get feverish. Nestling a little way under my bed, I find a layer of dust that feels soft on my fingertips, and I make friends with the dust. I'm not sure what exactly I'm after, but it has to do with obliteration and lying here always, until I'm nothing but bones inside a quilt on the floorboards, until Laurel and the boys have moved on to other lives and the house and all the memories collapse over my remains. For a while after I was injured I used to lie in bed for hours at a time, and nothing would happen. At extremely long intervals someone might come by to bring me food or change my sheets or shine a tiny flashlight in my face, but there were days when it was *only* food, and I got pretty good at learning how time passed. Now, of course, no nurse will be bringing me food, but I'm older now and require nothing. Only contemplating the empty guest room do I want to tear my ears off.

I wake up to the sounds of morning: Laurel heading to the bathroom, Ruby's nails on the wood floor. I try to picture what Ryan's doing, but I can imagine only what he'd be doing here, in this house. Moment by moment, I remember the sounds of him opening his bedroom door and going downstairs. I picture him pouring his grape juice and conversing with Ruby and doing all the little things that made up his morning, and I picture each moment in detail, just to remember his voice and the shape of his mouth. Laurel comes and knocks on my door, but I'm too deep in imagining to answer any summons. His tongue stuck out when he read the funnies. Laurel says, "Howard, why don't you come on down for breakfast, please? Steve's making pancakes." When she's gone, I pull the quilt over my head and grieve.

Laurel calls up the stairs that they're leaving the batter in the fridge in case I get hungry, and I hear the van, then the Beetle, take off. I clomp stiffly to the landing, wondering if Harrison's gone, too, but the house is empty. The air smells ripe, and I realize it's my own self, still in my sneakers and what I wore to the ball game, but despite my yearning for a shower during the time I was locked up, I'm not yet ready to wash off that last day. Halfway down the stairs I realize my mouth tastes like I've been sucking on a turd, but if I go back up to brush I might never come down.

Nit's pancake batter is too thick. I picture the dense, soggy pads it produced and wonder if anyone misses my cooking. But I'm hungry, so I thin the batter and fry up an enormous batch. I take my plate and a glass of grape juice to the picnic table, sitting with my back to the idiotic backstop. I should start living, I tell myself. It's a decent day. But one bite of sweet, grainy mush and I give the plate to Ruby, who digs right in. Then, though it's broad daylight, I step behind the stable and piss into Dwayne's yard. When Ruby comes sniffing, I carry her inside.

The kitchen's full of dirty dishes. When Ryan was first here, Laurel assigned KP to Harrison and Nit, and they stayed on top of it. But now the table's not wiped and there are splatters of soup and pancake batter on the counters and stovetop. The disarray strikes a chord with me — life doesn't go on — but I put away the milk and wash the frying pan, and I've got the big mixing bowl filled with soapsuds when I decide I just can't. I turn off the water, and for a while I sit with my head on my arm. Time passes; nothing happens.

I get up and pick up the bowl again, but I'm going to drop it, so I return it to the sink. Upstairs, I shut myself in my room. My quilt cocoon is rank with perspiration, but I crawl in like a hermit crab, pulling my torpor over my head. Ruby comes and kisses my face, and though I think crying might help, the most I can manage is to remain as I am, large and dirty and silent and inert. Around my nest, the house stands silent, and the whole city seems vacant, too.

Everything beyond this void is meaningless, anyway. After a while I hear Ruby whimpering and scratching at the door, but that's miles away, and I don't budge. Later she vomits in a corner.

It's late afternoon when a phone rings in the distance. I sit up, forgetting for a moment that I've forsaken the world, and as dust motes shimmer in the heat, I gasp for oxygen. Downstairs, Laurel's familiar greeting fills the hallway, and I vault over the bed and open my door as the beep sounds.

"Howie?" says a familiar voice. I lean over the banister, but he's silent so long I'm afraid he'll be cut off. Then he says, "I got the answering machine," and a voice says to leave a message, dummy. Ryan says, "Okay, it's me calling, Howie, and I'm at, um, Martin's house." He turns away again, asking Fartin' Martin for privacy, and I hear the Rottweilers in the background. "I couldn't call you before," Ryan says, "because first we went down to Chicago to get Bindi, and I don't think Mom really wants me to . . . um, you know, whatever. But like I wanted to know if you were okay. And we didn't really say goodbye because of what happened, and I wanted to tell you also that I'm sorry for being a bad sport at the Snakes game." He lowers his voice. "I'm really ashamed of myself. And I know you can't call me back, but I just wondered how you were doing. I mean, I guess Mom doesn't really want to, um . . . but like maybe . . ." He breaks off, confused by the task of sorting all this out. "Hmm." At last he says, "Thanks for everything, Howie," and the machine clicks off.

I go down the steps and hit the button, just to hear that voice again, and I'm surprised to find a message from Sister Amity, too, saying she hopes I'm out of my pickle, and I should come by the convent as soon as possible. But I'm so impatient I skip to Ryan. Even while his voice is playing, I start looking for my keys, and I'm circling the downstairs when I see his glove and the old Indians cap in the dining room. I suppose they've been there since Robin dropped them off Sunday. I tuck them under my arm, and I'm out the door just as Ryan says, "Thanks for everything," a second time.

55

THE STREET IS ITS customary row of boxes, the Silly Putty one about halfway along. Sylvia's ancient pink Buick is parked in the drive, and I pause a moment before pulling in behind it. I'd hoped, I suppose, to find Ryan outside, perhaps hitting the baseball across the two front yards, but for once not even Fartin' Martin's on his front steps.

I peer through the screen door and see Sylvia with her back to me. She's fiddling with an earring. I tap, and she turns, and I think for a moment she'll scream; but Sylvia never stages a free show without an audience. "Look, I don't know what you're doing here," she says sullenly, "but I'm running to a job interview. Don't even come in." She turns, then looks back and squints through the screen door. "Is that the same shirt?"

I've been through this since the old days, and frankly, I prefer it. I'd much rather Sylvia acted as if Saturday never happened than pick up at the terrible spot we left off. So I let her give my appearance a disdainful once-over, and I stare back through the screen. The house looks as it did the last time I was here, when I lay on her bed. Every photo and object is in place on the shelves. The picture window in the living room gives onto the back yard, where the hedges have filled in since my encounter with the neighbor, and the foliage reflects greenly over the unlit room. Sylvia glances toward the bedroom hallway and calls out, "Ryan, honey!" and at the sound of his footsteps I turn expectantly. Sylvia takes a deep breath and adopts a kind of statuesque pose, one foot before the other, as she smoothes her skirt down. "Do I look all right?"

From the hallway comes Ryan's voice: "Uh-huh." Sylvia frowns, and the voice adds, "Really pretty." Then he appears, so familiar in his long shorts and giant basketball shoes, and at the sight of me he does a genuine double take. "Heyyy!" he says, more like Harrison than himself. He opens the screen door for me, and I'm flooded with joy. Every unhappiness seems inconsequential.

"Howie," says Sylvia as I step into the house, "I cannot have a replay of . . ."

I squat down and open my arms, and Ryan looks uncomfortably from me to his mother. Perhaps he's aware of having summoned me surreptitiously. At last, he offers one of those formulaic hand greetings, and though this is no substitute for affection, I play along. "You got stitches," he announces enviously.

I hand over the glove and cap. "My two precious possessions!" he says. He puts them both on, punching the glove with his fist. "You know what? We should play catch. You bring your glove, Howie?" No, but I'll play bare-handed.

Sylvia lifts the Indians cap from Ryan's head. Here's one thing she'd hoped was out of her life, she remarks dryly. Running her fingers through his hair, she says, "Ryan, love, I want you ready to go, okay? There's no time for baseball, and I can't be late for this thing." She glances briefly in my direction and says, "Howie, thanks. We're thrilled to have the glove returned." I don't move, and she says, "I'll call you sometime."

Ryan says, "Why can't I just stay here? Like if Howie stayed with me, maybe we and Fartin' Martin could —"

"Don't call him that, please." She nudges a rubber flip-flop from under a living room chair. "And put your shoes away. Raymond is coming specifically to take you to the barbershop, and I —"

At this, I step forward. *Let* me *do it!* I'm perfectly able to get the boy a haircut. Look after him, give him dinner . . . I'm in practice, and I'm here. I point to my chest, but Sylvia blinks impatiently. "I really don't have time right now, Howie." Outside, a phone company van is pulling in behind my truck, and she says, "Damnation. Now the circus begins."

We watch Raymond get out of the van. He's wearing a phone company shirt and shorts, and all his equipment hangs redundantly from his belt. After a few seconds' primping in the side mirror, he leans into the van and pulls out a soccer ball, still in its store packaging. He tucks the ball under one arm and strides up the walk, and he's not even inside before he cries, "Hello, beautiful." He gives Sylvia a peck and presents Ryan with the soccer ball, calling him *muchacho*. Then he turns to me. "Harold. Didn't expect to see you here, man. You all recovered from your . . ." *Harold? Bite me.*

Ryan says, "Come *on*, Mom. Please?"

"Ryan, no. Another time, maybe. Ray —" She looks helpless. "I've got this interview."

Raymond holds up his hands. "Okay, okay. Not trying to rock your boat. You go on and go. We're good." He steps to a chair where Bindi is sleeping and says, "Hey there, girl." The motherfucker knows the whole cast and crew.

I catch Ryan's eye and mime the swing of a bat. Snakes on Saturday? I could pick him up. But he glances at his mother, so I touch Sylvia's arm. I make the swing again, and she says, "Howie, dammit!" and though I'm trying to communicate, she turns away. "Ray, help me out a bit," she says. When he looks up, she cocks her head at me.

That does it. Does she think I'm blind? Christ, I'm the *king* of gesture! Turning furiously, I push at the screen door, and my hand goes through the screen. Behind me, Sylvia says, "Oh, very nice!"

I spin around. Raymond's big chest is inches from my own. "The lady wants you outa here," he says. I look beyond him at Ryan, and I think we two should make a plan for baseball. I hope he realizes I didn't mean to damage his mom's screen, and of course I'll repair it. I've done the repairs here for years. Sylvia's checking her lipstick in a wall mirror, but when I catch her eye she looks away. And now Raymond's on automatic: "The lady wants you outa here," he says again. "And brush your teeth! Whew!"

I get the screen door open, and I want to slam it with a bang, but it's got a pneumatic closer and shuts quietly on its own. I climb in my truck and pull up to the Buick, and though I ought to back right into that phone van, I swerve onto the grass. Raymond comes out and holds up a hand, and behind him Sylvia's face appears, then disappears. My wheels make a sputtering *chirr* as they dig up her lawn, and as I back up, two brown stripes unfurl before me, like ribbons. I step hard on the gas.

A horn blares, and I hit the brake. A station wagon approaches, with a woman in dark glasses at the wheel and four kids as passengers. The woman gives me the finger as they pass. I take a breath and look up at the putty-colored house, and Ryan's standing on the stoop beside Raymond. I raise a hand, but neither one moves, and after looking both ways, I back carefully off of Sylvia's lawn. As I head up the street I see Fartin' Fucking Martin back on his front stoop.

56

I DRIVE HOME GRITTING my teeth. The streets seem bright and strangely crowded, and no matter where I turn I can't find an open lane. Several times I hit the horn and try to slip around some Sunday driver, but nothing happens; no one hears me. Even on my own street, I find myself behind Dwayne's maddening wife, poking along in their little family sedan and cooing at baby Samantha in the back seat. I can barely breathe.

Pulling into my driveway, I lurch from the truck and almost throw up. My face is clammy even in the July heat, and when I reach the stoop I grip the railing with a shaking hand. I'm breathless and light-headed, and I could use nothing so much as endless sleep. Looking out at my yard, I find it brutal and jagged, as if the familiar realm of my youth and family life, of whatever recovery I managed since my return home, has turned against me. In this fragile environment all the attributes I take as *me* — my thoughts, my hands and feet, my moral sense — bob against each other like balloons in a cluster. I turn hurriedly toward the house, and even my shadow, cast on the white clapboards, struggles mightily to escape.

The kitchen is still a mess, with crumbs standing out like boulders in the raking light. A white bag of garbage and a blue one of recyclables stand tied by the stove, and as I step in, the recyclables collapse forward, as if fainting. I might anchor myself by tidying up, I think, and I gather some cups; but within minutes I've made things worse. There's jam on a drawer where I reached for a dish towel and dribbles of stickiness across the countertop. Looking down, I see I've dragged the towel in a puddle of pancake batter. A gob splats to the floor, and I hurl the towel at the cellar, then fold into a protective crouch, arms covering my head, as we were taught in basic. The close scent of my body makes a kind of personal atmosphere, pungent as a greenhouse, and I think *this* is what the future holds: a world of me and no one else. But a moment later I force myself to stand, and I step to the doorway. For an instant, the summer evening loses its luridness, and there's the scent of my childhood. I must get myself clean, I think, then tackle this kitchen mess. Pick out some clothes and toss these in the incinerator; clip my nails, shave carefully, trim my nose hairs, move my bowels. Maybe even get a haircut myself. And teeth! I'm not unmindful of Raymond's response to my breath.

I'm in the hallway when I hear voices above. On the landing, Laurel's talking to someone. "I just —" she says. "I'm at the end of my rope. In a matter of days I watch this place going completely to pot, and I can't be the commandant a hundred percent of the time. I mean, take a look at that kitchen! A damn disaster area!"

A male voice says, "Sorry . . ."

"I mean seriously. Do you guys think that because Ryan's gone we no longer maintain a civilized front? Was that some two-month performance in which we all, you know, *pretended* to be a household of manners, pretended to respect each other and pull our own —"

"Hey, I'll do it." The voice is Nit's. "Come on, Laurel. Because Harrison's having like a . . . He's like really on edge right now, kinda difficult. But put me to work. We don't want to make you mad."

"But why should I even have to *say* —" Laurel breaks off suddenly, and from my spot below I think *good for you!* Serves those sloppy boys right. But she says, "Oh, Stevie, it's not really even that. Frankly, nobody expects much from the two of you, and of course

Harrison has his own, you know, burdens. It's more just —" Her voice rises, and as I strain forward I step on a creaky floorboard. I freeze. Laurel says, "Really, it's *him*. I mean, jeez, I got home, and there's this unbelievable stench. His room was just, in the corner there was — I guess Ruby was sick, plus diarrhea and who knows whatall. Which I can't imagine she would have done if she'd had anywhere else to be, so what'd he do, shut her in the room? Or just forget to let her out? I can't even tell, but you know Ruby: house-broken! And the flies, even with the windows open —"

"You want me to go in and pick it up?"

"Oh, please. I did *that*. I mean immediately, and there was no *pick*ing it up, either. No, I mean it's just so lazy and, and *unkind* where an animal's concerned, and dirty, willfully dirty. Weird and out-there, beyond his usual, you know, gruffness. Is this a break-down?" She starts to sniffle.

I'm so shocked I can't move, even when a fly alights on my ear. I remember coming in years ago, all fucked up, and catching my parents having this exact conversation in the same spot, outside their bedroom; I stood where I stand now and listened ashamedly. The fly maneuvers to peer inside my head, and as I wave it away Nit says, "Look, I'll speak to him. I'll tell him don't pull that shit with us, grow up, be a man, et cetera." I redden at the thought of Nit telling me where to get off, and maybe he knows how ridicu-lous he sounds, because he adds, "Or Harrison will. He respects Harrison."

"And where is he now? Gone off, probably in that same filthy shirt, and who knows if he's even safe on the road. The bed's all pulled apart in that room, but it doesn't look like he's been near the bathroom. And yesterday when I went up to talk to him, he was just so awful. I think we —" She sniffs again and says, "Oh, Christ," and then, very quietly, she starts to cry. I put my hand to my face and bite down on my index finger, and Nit offers inarticulate murmurs of comfort. Then Laurel sighs. "It's just stress, really. I know we all miss having the kid around, but I kind of liked how it brought us togeth— You know, I've lived with Howard a long time, and there's more than just neutral feelings. We —" She breaks off again, and my instinct is to run up and put my arms around her, but in my current state I'm no consolation. Perhaps I'll sneak back to the kitchen and beat Nit to cleaning the household mess. Then I'll slip to the bathroom for a shower and shave. And once I've chased all the flies from the house and scrubbed my bedroom floor with Mr. Clean and made nice with Ruby and dressed myself in fresh clothes, I'll be able to face Laurel. Only moments ago I caught a whiff of summer in the evening air; now that same emotion, a little like hope, see-saws in again. I'll get through this with elbow grease, not discussion.

There's a movement above, then Laurel says, "Thanks, I'm okay. The thing is, I pulled some strings to get him released. Because I just thought Saturday was . . . well, an unusual situation, and I know he gets frustrated. I didn't want one slip turned into some big psychiatrical veteran's *thing*, just so a couple meathead policemen could score a few points." She blows her nose. "*Anyway*. So I call the nun, and I said it was pretty much a gross misunderstanding, that it was nowhere near what the report said. Because on a gut level I understood where Howard was coming from, or I thought I did. So I minimized it, okay? I was confident. And the sister vouches for him, but we kind of agree, the two of us, that he should go back to work, both because he should have some stability *and* for the money, because he needs to have income. He's just . . . *going* through his pension, and with taxes and utilities there's not a big cushion. And I assumed that being home in this house, with people who, you know, *know* him and love — or are accustomed to his ways or whatever — was gonna be better than receiving treatment from strangers. But what happens? He comes home, and I've done all this nonsense to get him released. But he's, he's so weird and hostile, like you sometimes hear those cases can get. He's all different and *off*. And the *dirty* thing, and the dog! He should be checking in at the convent, but yesterday he nearly *struck* me because I wanted to get that filthy Snakes shirt — Oh, *look* at these damn flies." She stamps her feet, and several more appear in the stairwell. Laurel says, "The thing is, Stevie, this is all so different from what I expected. Or what I promised that nun. And I think maybe I have a responsibility for not being more truthful. I mean, I don't *think* he's dangerous, but who knows? He's so difficult and strange suddenly. And I wonder — I can't help feeling I did wrong getting him out, so should I attempt to rectify it? Because if this is how he's gonna be, it maybe would have been better for him to stay where he was, just long enough to get some real treatment. Maybe if I spoke up he still could, you know?"

I don't listen to any more. I feel nauseous and shamed, and my body's light and hollow and brittle, like a sculpture made of egg whites. The tethers that anchor me have been suddenly sundered, and this time no hope swings in to uplift. I turn stealthily, like an intruder, and ease my weight off the noisy floorboard. I sneak back through the dirty kitchen to the yard, where the lawn probably could use mowing. Close the door of the truck quietly. Back down the crackling driveway to the street. In the gutters lie plastic bags, McDonald's cups, even broken toys, and I don't breathe 'til I reach the boulevard.

57

I DRIVE TO THE Andee Barber School. Ryan and Raymond are long gone, but the place is still open, lending a fluorescent brightness to the sunset sky. Only two barbers are working at this hour, one of them the tall, many-ringed guy who cut Ryan's hair. A small boy is seated in his chair now, and a large, tired-looking woman leans forward to watch the barber work. I don't want to make my inquiry with a child in the shop, so I turn off my headlights and remain in the truck, rubbing my knuckles over my cheek. I listen to the sawlike sound of my whiskers.

The woman comes out, holding the boy's hand, and the two of them walk off down the sidewalk. I wait until they're out of sight. My mouth is dry, but everything else feels light and counterfeit, and it's easy to float toward the glass front of the barbershop. Inside, a singer from my recovery era croons soulfully at high volume, and there's none of the high-key jangle of my previous visit. For a moment, I wonder if I'm misremembering how it was — if this is not, in fact, a place Sylvia might come to cop. But hair parlors are generally good places to score, and as three faces turn toward me I put my impressions aside.

The tall barber's working on a good-looking, broad-faced kid of about twenty, while his colleague, older and stockier, sweeps up around the chairs. The colleague turns and says, "About closed." I moisten my lips.

The tall guy says, "What you want, bro? A shave?" He shows me his wide smile, eyeing my scruffy appearance. "Haircut, too? Want the works?" I do want the works, but I don't say anything. The guy glances at a wall clock and says, "Aaaight, why not? Take yourself a seat and we'll do you proud. Won't be a minute with my friend here." As the older man starts to protest, he adds, "I got it, Joe. You go 'head home."

I slip onto a vinyl-covered chair, clutching the armrests to hold myself down. But almost immediately I'm on my feet again. The heavy barber watches me suspiciously, but the tall guy says, "You worrying about those stitches you got on there, I know. Sure, they look nasty, but I can be gentle. Let's see your head." I can't tell if he's figured out the deal with me or is just very easygoing, but he beckons with a flashy finger. "Hey, I *know* you," he says amiably. "Where I know you from?"

I stop dead. I don't want anyone connecting me to Ryan. But the conversation I overheard in the hallway was so familiar that I might well be moving backward through life, rather than forward, while Ryan sweeps on ahead, out of my reach. And really, I'm reckless. All that interests me is escape.

I step to the barber chair and mime placing something in my mouth. The three guys stare at me. I do it again, plucking a small square from my palm and placing it on my tongue, and I wonder if acid even comes in blotter form these days. How would I know? But it doesn't have to be blotter, and it doesn't even have to be acid, so I make a gesture I think must be universal: I put my thumb to my nose and sniff.

The kid's the first to respond. He's got a sassy, through-the-teeth *ts-ts-ts* of a cackle, and his smile flashes gold. "Motherfucker wantsa get high!" he exclaims, showing his tongue. "Get out!"

The old guy hollers, "We don't do that here!" and brandishes the broom like a jousting lance. I'm unprepared for being turned down, and until this moment I've thought only of getting wasted. I step back as the jouster comes toward me, and the young dude cackles and grins disrespectfully at my garb. The soul singer rises to crescendo, and I want to say *where, then? If not here, where? For God's sake!*

The tall guy drops his scissors in his breast pocket and turns me by the elbow. "Listen, friend. You in a bad way. You need to go home, get on the straight and narrow, do some thinking. Maybe talk to your — what faith you from, man? Got a pastor?" He looks at me quizzically, but his grip doesn't lessen. I feel like pleading with him, telling him I've tried the straight *and* the narrow and I've given up; I'm pursuing alternatives. I look around, at the young guy smirking and the older man poised to run me off like a dog, and I try to remember how I solved this problem years ago; but in the old days, I had a few dependables who knew what I came for. The barber says, "You go home now. Things look better in the morning," and for a moment, crazily, I think they're shitting me. This is a game they pull before bringing out the Ziploc bags. But the tall guy says, "Find your people, man. Give them the opportunity to show you kindness and love." Then he pushes me out the door.

It's fully dark now, and I sit in the truck wondering what to do. Andee Barber School is the last shop to remain lit, and I watch the young client emerge, rubbing his crown. Then Joe the broomstick-meister goes home. I wonder what I'd do if I were home now, and for an instant it's not Laurel or Ryan or my mom I think of, but those guys from my transitioning group I saw once at the movies. Is this what the barber meant by my people? I wonder if those two live together. Are they still in a group home? I wonder if they see the others and if anyone remembers me, and suddenly my alienation, which has been growing for hours, feels uncannily familiar. It's the feeling of then.

At last, the overhead lights in the barbershop switch out one by one. The nice barber emerges, locking the shop door in several places and rolling a metal shutter down over the glass front. As he strolls along the sidewalk, I get out of the truck, and at the sound he looks at me narrowly. "You still here," he says. "I told you to go home." To avoid frightening him, I place my palms together in a gesture of supplication, though the instant I do this I feel ridiculous. How much easier it would be to say *friend, help a friend find the route to bliss!* But the guy says, "You take that shit downtown, you got no self-control. You don't mind the advice I give you, you can just beat it, hear?" He's at his car now, and he unlocks it slowly, watching me all the while. I step back, swinging my arms in frustration, and I think *what the fuck* and bang a fist on a metal mailbox, and the barber reaches into his car and brings out a tire iron. "I mean it," he says, no longer nice. "You go now, don't come back. Don't make me use this. I can give you some stitches, you'll see that."

I drive downtown to a bar I remember called the Blue and Gold. I never liked this place, but it's a place to score, and I used to know a little fat guy who could set me up. The street alongside is a well-known trolling ground for streetwalkers.

Long ago, when Sylvia and I were in high school, the Blue and Gold was owned by the father of a girl we hung out with, and he went to prison my junior year. I remember Sylvia holding up the front page of the paper, with a photo of our friend's handcuffed dad, and saying she'd literally die of embarrassment. The newspaper called the Blue and Gold a hangout for gangsters and lowlife, and as Sylvia read the article aloud I wondered if Mara visited her dad at work, and I knew such a dive had no place in my existence.

But one night when Ryan was very young, I was in my truck in front of the Blue and Gold, smoking a joint. By that time, of course, I knew the place well. I'd bought acid from the fat guy, and several of the girls on the stroll were acquainted with me. On this particular date, though, my dad had died and I'd made some decisions. I was having a bad night, and as I wrestled with my soul I saw Sylvia standing at the corner of the street. She had on a short, brightly colored skirt and a tight top, which might have looked sweetly daring on any other city block but blended in disconcertingly here.

And she definitely looked altered. A long-haired, pug-faced guy was guiding her along by the small of her back, and Sylvia was laughing showily and stumbling a little in tall, cork-soled shoes. I watched the guy steer her into the Blue and Gold, and I climbed from my truck and followed surreptitiously.

Pugface took a seat on a barstool and spread his thighs, and Sylvia stood close enough that he could have clamped her between his knees. Even in the hubbub and darkness of the bar, I could see how she swayed on those tall shoes of hers, and I watched her drink a couple shots of tequila and look around with glittering eyes. It was more than a year since that night when she'd called late to ask about getting high, and absorbed as I was in my own stuff, I'd put it from my mind. But now the path she was on was as clear as the fact that she'd taken it without me, and as she laughed her cartoon laugh I glowered in my corner, and the ropes of looping jalapeño lights cast her in silhouette. The little fat guy appeared and tried to sell me some mesc, but I brushed him off; then some terrible, cheesy song of the era played on the jukebox. Sylvia raised her slim arms and began unsteadily to dance, and when Pugface put his hands on her thighs, I burst from my corner. Looking back, it's a miracle I didn't sucker punch him, coming up behind his stool, but my thoughts were of Sylvia. I grasped her wrist and pulled her from between his legs, and her eyes spun with a look of revulsion. Then she recognized me and jerked her hand away. Before I could move, Pugface hit me in the sternum. I fell to the floor, and I think he'd have kicked my face in if the fat dealer and some other so-called acquaintances hadn't dragged me to my truck. The next time Sylvia and I saw each other, we didn't mention the incident, but things were out in the open.

The jalapeño lights still hang in the Blue and Gold. In the corner stands the same shabby pool table, and three boys preen as they bend over it. Coming in on my heels are two very young guys and a girl, all giddy and dressed in the spotless collegiate clothes kids wear nowadays. And this is how it is. The fat guy's nowhere to be found, but happy, fresh-faced children abound, everyone in laundered uniforms and tickled to be visiting the famous dive. The girl who just entered bobs her head to some innocuous tune, and I think of Sylvia, sampling the rough side. And though I bet I could turn to these spoiled, brightly clad dudes and score some ecstasy or almost anything else, a cloud descends, and I want no part of them. Hell, with my derelict appearance I'm part of the atmosphere, anyway. I lurch past a plump redhead with a jeweled stud in her clean, clean nose; she falls against an all-American and says, "Excu-uuse me!" Well, fuck them all. Around the corner, a few girls are still working the desultory streets, and though the first few tell me to keep on walking, I find one who's small and thin and missing her front teeth. We get in the truck and she guides me to an alley, and as she sucks my dick, I tell myself to enjoy it, because this is my first sexual contact with another genuine human in what? Five years? Ten?

But when the girl's done I open my wallet, and there's only the dollar I got back after buying Ryan's country ham sandwich a century or two ago. I don't know how I would have managed the acid, but this is worse because the girl has definitely completed her job. Though she doesn't look particularly young, she must be new to the game, or she'd have gotten it in advance.

Shamefacedly I show her the wallet, and when she doesn't budge, I pluck out the singleton and hand it over. I'm ashen with humiliation, and if I felt more alive I could easily start weeping. I take off my father's Masonic ring and hold that out, too, and the girl's face hardens. Keeping her eyes on my scar, she reaches for the door latch and slides out, slippery as an eel. Pausing just long enough to spit a gleaming hocker on the seat beside me, she screams for support troops and disappears. In the rearview mirror I see a dark figure enter the alley behind me. I gun the motor, but the figure hurls something, and the window behind my head shatters with a crash.

Who knows where I go? I make a turn and cross a bridge where I can't imagine there ever was a bridge, and some time later I'm in a city park. A bridle path runs by the road, and as I round a curve, a ghostly rider rises up from a hollow. But it slides off into the darkness, and as I leave it behind I wonder if it was a statue. For some time I seek out the ballparks where the Snakes held baseball practice, but I find only parking places, shadowy figures, couples kissing, and the red lights of vehicles. At last I decide I'm not in that park at all but in a different one, and as if the realization determines my whereabouts, I'm expelled suddenly onto city streets. Small brown bungalows, like workers' housing from an ancient photograph, line the road, and as I turn and turn through the maze of these little homes, I wonder why the city is so unfamiliar. The roads are empty but for me, and the brown houses flutter like cardboard scenery on either side.

The street of houses abruptly comes to an end, and the cross-street curves into a familiar circle. At the center stands the memorial temple, and a gaunt figure wanders the impatiens. I pull to the curb. *Timothy!* I want to cry. *You're all right!* Climbing out, I run toward him with outstretched arms, and I'm babbling as if he's a long-lost comrade; but when he spots me, Timothy turns on his heel. Knees pumping, he makes a circuit of the temple and scampers across the traffic circle, and a red car appears out of nowhere and mows him down.

A thin kid climbs from the driver's side and says, "Fuck." He looks like Ansel. "Fuck, fuck, fuck, fuck, *fuck!*" he says, then turns to a sidekick. "What the fuck are you doing?" The sidekick says he's fucking calling the cops, what the hell does he think? This second boy also looks like Ansel, and there's a third one who's out of the vehicle now, too. All the boys look alike.

When the kid first hit him, Timothy flew up the hood, but he slid off and his body unspooled on the pavement. Now he lies face up, an arm crooked under him, a shoe upturned a few yards away. I kneel down and touch his cheek. One eye is half open. I place my hand on his chest, but my hand is trembling. I learn nothing, so I put my head down and listen. He smells very rank. Behind me, the three Ansels are arguing over a cell phone. One says, "Fuck you, man! No fuckin' way I'm not reporting this."

We had elementary first aid training in basic, and to quell the panic I try to recall what I learned. Basic was so long ago. I listen again to Timothy's chest, and a rhyme comes to my head: *face is pale, raise the tail.* Timothy's face is creepily white. I look for something to prop up his legs and see Ansel number two still fiddling with the cell phone. Number three murmurs, "So maybe we just like drive him to the emergency room, son."

No way! I wave my hands. We're not in the jungle now, and casualties should be moved by medical personnel only. It strikes me that what we *should* do is stabilize the head in case of a spinal cord injury, but a lot's happening, and my heart is set on raising the tail. I stand up; the boys recoil. The driver says, "Fuck, that your buddy, man? Ran right in front of me." I push past him and look in the car for something to raise Timothy's legs, and he says, "The fuck! Get outa there, ya fuckin' bag man!" But the car holds nothing beyond fast-food wrappers and a trace of marijuana smoke.

In his flight from me, Timothy sloughed off his long coat, which lies crumpled in the gutter. The coat is heavy with stuff he's stashed in his pockets, and it smells horribly of rotten meat, but I bunch it into a pad and add the shoe. When I place all this under his feet, the stack slowly collapses. I'm panting heavily and muttering at Timothy, and I take off the blue Snakes shirt and wrap it around the coat and shoe. As the red car's doors slam, I replace my bundle. *Blood: go to his head!*

The air fills with a terrible smell. Timothy's bowels have given way. Two little patches of darkness now glint on the pavement by his torso, and I don't know if they're shit or blood or both together, but I crawl over and take his hand. It's fairly cold. I put my fingers to his neck and wrist, and I don't feel a pulse. I let out a wail and press down hard on his rib cage, and just as I'm thinking one of the Ansels might lend a hand the car backs away. Tearing the buttons from Timothy's shirt, I put my hands on his thin chest, and even in the low light of the streetlamp I notice the V of dirt at his throat. I press down, getting up on my knees, and I'm certain this is how it's done. Press and release, press and release. We're alone now, Timothy and I, in the middle of the road. No cars pass us. I bear down again and again, putting all my weight into it, and I test the wrist another time. Then I put my lips on his. I can feel the tickle of whiskers on my chin, and I pull in my nostrils and exhale hard; I don't want to think about the inside of this mouth. Blow out, then up, and fill my lungs with the gorgeous summer night; then down, holding his mouth open with a hand on the chin. Timothy's lips are crusty, and I come down so hard that our teeth clank and my tongue touches something frightening. But I get in a good breath, and I fill his lungs. *Come on and breathe!* Then up again; then down, up, down. Another lungful, impelling him to fight, to give what he's got, to hang on for love of country. Then back to his bare chest, harder now, working ferociously to get a rhythm! A bone snaps, just like wicker, and he's looking at me with that half-open eye. I wish he'd say something. I press down, all the weight of me, so he'll pump and breathe and stand up and make something of himself, and I'm weeping now, panting and murmuring nonsense, wishing I could speak his name, *Timothy*, *Timothy*. This is where we are when the ambulance shrieks into the traffic circle.

58

I'VE BEEN PAST MY OWN HOUSE four times since eluding the paramedics, slowing to a crawl at every circuit. I've said goodbye to Sylvia's place, too, though it meant taking the long way to avoid that traffic circle. In front of both houses I looked at the darkened windows and tried to empty my mind, and possibly I succeeded. I'm calm, finally. I've stopped wailing, stopped hitting the dashboard with my fists. Now it's three a.m., and the convent gates are closed for the night, but I know a spot where the stone wall's low enough to scramble over. I park my truck on a cul-de-sac, and between two homes I find a wedge of woods too small for a house lot. I slip among the trees and vault the wall, landing with bent knees as we were taught in basic. Straight above me, the sky is black, but a blur of light hangs over the convent building. Clouds pass like tracing paper torn from a pad, and when at last the moon's revealed, it's not quite round. The air whistles at the dent in *my* head, too.

It's a short walk to the garden shed, and I'm in no hurry. I'm on the least important mission there is. Ahead stands the dark bulk of the convent, with lights in every stairwell and lavatory. The other windows are dark; the nuns are asleep. Ryan's asleep, too, I suppose, dreaming of soccer and go-carts, and Sylvia's getting her beauty rest. At my house, the windows were all dark, though two bedrooms remain empty.

I think of that last afternoon, walking the narrow path between palm trees and scrub growth. Rimet was saying something about something back home, and though he was a decent guy, I really wasn't listening. Rimet liked big-time auto racing, which I never got, and he spoke of becoming a criminal lawyer. He said the jungle reminded him of *Hawaii Five-O*. We were pals because we were in the same fix, and the last I remember, he was flying through the air. I suppose now he really might be practicing law, or maybe he became Timothy. Remembering that floating figure, I'm not sure it's one face and not the other I recognize.

On that day we were stoned and reasonably happy, under the circumstances, and I was more interested in what the lieutenant was saying, so I edged forward to respond. And what did I say? This has always bothered me. The LT saw a bloom in a tree and made some remark, but what were *my* last words? I can only guess. I'd been overseas all of sixteen days; I talked like a tourist. The camp and the surrounding paddies still felt very new, I'd only just discovered the burned plantation, and I wondered how far it was to the sea. I remember urging myself to take what happened as a chance for adventure, just so I wouldn't shame myself by being scared; and though Rimet and I *were* scared in a general sense, we'd done nothing very dangerous yet. Even this mission was considered routine. That mine was a complete surprise.

I wonder if I should say a prayer, or if I'm being influenced by the surroundings. I feel a little drunk. Through the silence, the echoey whoosh of traffic below the ha-ha, a sound like waves. The moon slips back behind a cloud, the night is dark again, and I decide to pray something that's not a prayer so much as an imagined wish; and I wish the first thing that bubbles into my head. I wish for Ryan to be well loved his entire life. That's the key to happiness, I think. I wonder what Sylvia wishes for Ryan; then my mind is pulled from my prayer, and I think that for a few weeks he was well loved by all of us, and we were loved in return. I was loved by Sylvia once — I'll always believe that — and I was loved more than I deserved by my mother and dad. And I loved them. I wonder what kind of tally this makes for one life, but I have my excuses. I'd have loved more people if I hadn't been injured.

I never knew why I survived, but I was glad I made it. I didn't imagine any other way to feel. There's the period to be proud of, too: years of autonomy, sobriety, and endurance. Why does nothing stand out?

But I can remember every instant of these last months. Every instant with Ryan, of course, but also moments when he played no part, moments with Robin or the Mesks, with my band of pipsqueak catchers and throwers, with Laurel and Nit and Harrison. For a while I awakened to all that was denied me — me and Timothy and the lieutenant and the rest of us — but now, as I contemplate that drab, fine life I'm so proud of . . . Well, I can't.

Time to go. The John Deere is the king of equipment, and as I climb aboard, it's hard not to think of when Ryan rode with me. That was my last day, too. The roar of the engine is deafening inside the shed, and as I pull out I see the clouds have cleared. Stars twinkle around the convent's silhouette, and I drive across the lawn, looking up at all the tiny, bright jacks. I've always liked stars. When I was a child I used to lie out with my dad and wait for meteor showers, just this time of year. My mother always preferred the moon, and Sylvia preferred sunsets, as far as I know. At least, when we were out together she didn't care about watching stars. I suppose everyone's fascinated by some aspect of the heavens, and lying on our backs to stare at the sky is something Ryan and I never did. One for the Buzzard's View camping trip, I think dreamily; then I catch myself.

Upstairs in the convent, a light goes on. Better hurry. Driving past the Contemplation Garden, I realize I never finished my prayer, and I say *amen*. I don't care about noise now, and I shout as loud as I can over the churning mower: "Unn-*mmah!*" I do it again, then I feel foolish. I feel queasy, like the wait time before the kick of a drug, and I could use pleasant thoughts to calm my nerves. I try picturing Ryan's face and come up with the Indians cap; then I run through everyone else in my life, and all the faces are jelled over. Maybe I'm rushing. I swallow hard and take a breath, and I see my dad with his arms outstretched and remember how gray his lips were that day in the snow, and his strange, sick expression, a little like indigestion. But I don't want to be seeing this. I want the *living*. I try to remember Dad in the warm mornings of my childhood, setting off to sell suits and neckties at Hanran's and looking pretty spiffy himself, since that was how you showed off the merchandise. But the picture eludes me in the clarity I want, and instead I see Timothy stretched flat in the road. Frantically, I conjure my parents' wedding photo, and there's Mom in a veil that puffed over her thick hair. But that was years before I was born, before my own time with her began.

Running up the slope, the John Deere purrs smoothly. I can see headlights down in the abyss, and I wonder who those people are. Late-night travelers, drunks heading home, people on strange quests. An ambulance flashes, and I'm ready for the floater feeling. But maybe I'm *too* ready, because as soon as I've got it, it slips away. In the past, I grew expert at hugging the steepest angle of the slope, but my aim was to push it and at the same time stay safe. Now I'm doing what I've only practiced for, and I hit the gas. The blade strikes a rock with a *ting!* and on instinct I let up. False alarm. I press again and ask myself if this is it. Is this it, is this it, for real? It is. I take a breath and look at the stars and think of the tropics, when I was young and the orange air raised me over the forest path, and the dirt sparkled like bits of stardust in the golden air, and the leaves were soft, soft fabric. *Here I go!*

I don't know why I don't go through with it. I think I'll always feel it was cowardice, and I'll wonder forever if my decision was correct. But my hands turn hard at the last moment, and the John Deere stalls with a wheel spinning out in space. And suddenly I'm afraid to move. I sit for a lifetime, my head on the steering wheel, and I could finish what I started, but I know now I will not. Perhaps it was the ambulance, flashing with dire urgency, or perhaps I really want to toast Ryan at his wedding. Maybe I'm a gutless sissy, trying to prove life is purely my own choice — and maybe I choose this life more than I thought. Here's another question I'll ponder for the rest of my days.

Perhaps it's not even very long that I sit there, because when Sister Amity reaches me she's out of breath. She grips my arm so hard that she must think I'll topple over, and when I open my mouth she whispers, "Never mind." I stare at her without moving and see wire glasses clipped to her nose, a glint of sweat on her lip. She's not in her wimple or habit, just a nightgown bunched into bright pink sweatpants, and she looks like someone in a fat-lady costume. "Don't ogle my clothes, Howard," she says severely. "You know I'm a nun. Can you get down?" She peers at me a little longer, then gently adds, "Come on, dear. You can do it." Her cropped hair stands stiff on her skull.

I climb down gingerly from my perch. My joints are stiff, and I feel as though I've been cramped in position for a very long time. I can't help considering how idiotic it would be if I and the mower and the claptrap of all my foolishness were to pitch suddenly down into the roadway, but the John Deere's ground its wheels into the hillside and doesn't budge. With Sister Amity's coaxing, my feet move from pedal to step and finally to the dry, mown grass.

But as I take my place by the side of the mower, something else remains aloft. I haven't awakened yet, and Sister Amity hasn't released my arm. I look down from a spot high in the orange air, and I can see us on the ha-ha, she in her bunched-up clothes, one hand on my elbow, me unsteady on my feet. I can see the dark night — or early morning — of summer in the great North American Midwest, and for a moment the whole world freezes in place. Nothing breathes, nothing moves. And then, as if from some great distance, comes the roar of waves, and one by one each sound is turned on. The cars on the highway resume their oceanic murmuring, and a nearby owl gives a lonesome hoot. There are peepers, too, and the general rustling and pulsing of the summer night, and as all this revs into a song of being I feel myself float down, like a kite Sister Amity slowly reels in. I float to earth and settle in my skin, and I can feel my shoes and my terrible sweaty T-shirt and the fabric of the shorts I put on long ago for baseball practice. I settle into my skin and give a shiver, and Sister Amity says, "Steady."

We start across the lawn, walking very slowly. This is all I can manage. Sister Amity says she's going to make tea and dabs her face with a tissue. I can sleep in a spare room on the first floor, she says. "I'll stay right outside, in case you need me." Halfway to the big building she lets go of my elbow, but it's not clear I won't float off again once I'm released, and to tell the truth, I want to be held down. All around us, the peepers sing joyfully of life, and the moon casts its lacy beams on the convent grounds. I hear a siren pass through the subdivision where I parked my truck; then it veers off into silence, like the close call it is. There's a plop from the reflecting pool. Something's broken the surface. As the stars circle slowly over us, I take Sister Amity's hand.

59

THIS HASN'T BEEN EASY. Years ago, when I first came home injured, I felt conspicuous above all else, and I could see the components of my old life being trundled out like theater scenery to prove that nothing had really changed. I feel that now, too. Every morning, at Laurel's instigation, I make breakfast for the household, and Harrison and Nit read the paper aloud. Almost always the day is gorgeous, and we take our waffles or eggs Benedict to the picnic table. From up and down the yards come the cries of kids and the roars of early morning mowers, and lately a yellow mastiff has been hanging around Ruby. Sometimes Ms. Monetti is here, too. Then breakfast ends, and the boys, like good citizens, take care of KP. It's terribly, determinedly, familiar. When work time comes, my housemates carefully tell me goodbye, Laurel brushing a hand down my arm or lately even offering a kiss. Nit and Harrison are more hail-fellow-handshake oriented, but just as sincere; once, unaccountably, Nit hugged me, and I was so startled I hugged him back. Then we climb into our vehicles and go to work. I'm back at the convent, of course, though on reduced hours because Jim, the heavyset guy I glimpsed once as he mowed the Long Field, is there now, too. Sister Amity prefers I keep clear of the John Deere, anyway, and she's shown some ingenuity in finding me other chores. "What we need is some good male *muscle!*" she'll say exultantly, and send me off to load peat moss for Robin. Or she'll decide two dozen bentwood chairs in the nuns' dining room need refurbishing and set me to a week of painting and gluing. I've even been enlisted to peel potatoes for Sister Margaret, and the unorthodoxy of giving this task to me instead of a novice only underscores the artificial structure that keeps me occupied. There's my old friend the underbrush, too, out past the isolation cabins, when I'm angry or uptight; but under Sister Amity's eye I'm seldom alone.

I have a second job now, too, because Laurel insists I need income. Nit saw a notice at the gym he and Harrison belong to, and before I knew it I was handing out towels. Three hours a day I'm holed up below street level, and the climate of shower steam and perspiration, cologne, baby powder, and moist flesh, plus the varieties of abashed and strutting and oblivious nudity and my own shadowy presence as a clothed person, all make me appreciate my time outdoors. When three hours are up I rush outside, and though it's only a parking lot next to the boulevard, I spend several moments just relishing the air. One reason I keep this job is for that sense of emergence, and often in these moments I think of Timothy.

I go right home after work because Laurel's waiting for me, at least these first weeks. Usually, she's shopped for dinner and puts me to work in the kitchen, but sometimes we go bowling or to a movie, just the two of us or with one of the housemates. It's not clear how much she's corralled them into monitoring me, just as it's not clear whether I truly need the second job at the gym or just have to be kept busy. In fact, I don't look closely at what's happening. Between Laurel and Sister Amity I'm on a pretty tight lead, and whether their efforts are coordinated or coincidental is another thing I don't look at. Things happen without my choosing, and I let myself drift.

Years ago, I accepted the charade of well-being because I believed it myself: I believed I'd get better. This time I see through everything, but I give in anyway. The self-consciousness I felt when

I came home from the war has been replaced by shame at how I handled myself recently, and if the likes of Sister Amity and Laurel and even the two dudes who live here feel like kinder souls for watching my ass, I can submit.

And there's not much choice. Saturday morning after my incident at the ha-ha, I slipped off early to take Ryan to baseball. I had my doubts, of course, but I went anyway, and from the end of the block I could see him and Raymond in Sylvia's front yard. Raymond had on a complete soccer getup from Spain or Puerto Rico or somewhere — bright shirt, brief yellow shorts, shin guards, special shoes — and they were kicking that soccer ball back and forth. I watched Ryan take it downfield, over the brown lines my wheels had laid in the grass, and I realized he'd learned to dribble. I'd brought a piece of screen as an afternoon project, but instead of continuing toward the house, I turned in an empty driveway and went back the way I'd come. That afternoon, Ed Mesk called and said he hoped we'd return to the Snakes. "I hope there weren't, uh, hard feelings after our last game," he said to the answering machine. "Juliana and I both thought Ryan was a big asset, especially as one of the younger boys. Unfortunately, the Twins pretty much outmatched the Snakes in all categories, as it turned out. But regarding the fighting, I felt the team had to draw the line. Nothing personal, I hope you agree."

A week later he calls again to say he learned from Robin that Ryan's no longer with me, but he hopes I still consider myself a Snake. "As umpire, coach, however you see it. A lot of these kids could use a positive role model." After this I almost go back, but while I'm dithering Ed calls a third time and says no one realized the official Little League season ended in midsummer, and with no opponents, the Snakes have disbanded. "Juliana wants to have a party for the kids, though, in the fall. You should all come to that." He says he counts on me for next year, but his voice is wistful, and I wonder if there will be Snakes another year. So July gives way to August, and the mornings remain cool and the afternoons temperate. Night after night we watch marvelous sunsets, and everyone says it's the most beautiful summer. Miraculous, they call it on television. If the miracle of a few golden evenings proves no match for my own deep blue longing, I'm not expecting much anyway.

It's not all bad. Sometimes Sister Margaret and I take our scullery duties to the goldfish pool, and sometimes I work out for an hour at the gym. I have powerful shoulders. I wait for Laurel to let up on her vigilance, but she doesn't do that, and one night she buys us tickets to the ballet. To my amazement, I enjoy it, and we go again three nights later, my treat this time. There's a ballerina in blue that everyone's excited about, and midway through one fiery number, Laurel takes my hand. Her long fingers are soft in my palm, and when the program ends I hang on a moment before applauding. But as Laurel continues night after night at my side, I figure I must be worse off than I realize. Meanwhile, we eat plenty of sweet corn and sit outside in the evenings, and I learn to make scones. The morning glories thrive, and little rocketlike buds appear amid the heart-shaped leaves.

Occasionally I look in the guest room closet, where the only thing hanging is that blue choir surplice from the elementary school. I don't sniff it or press it to my cheek because, as Laurel's pointed out, no one has died. But sometimes I lie on the futon with that choir thing spread out over my chest. The room is cool with the curtains drawn, so it's a place to relax, and I've got no illusions about staying in this spot forever. I even leave the door open. I close my eyes and fold my hands over the blue garment, but it's okay. I'm just lying here.

60

I DON'T HEAR FROM SYLVIA until after Labor Day. I'm upstairs when the phone rings, and I go to the top of the steps and listen. "Hi, Howie, it's me," she says. "It's been a while." In the pause that follows I hear dogs barking, and I touch my head to the patterned wallpaper of the stairwell. Sylvia says, "Since the middle of summer, I guess, and — Look, this isn't my idea. That whole scene when I came home was just so chaotic and . . . and damaging at a time when I really only — But Ryan was thinking he'd like to see you, so maybe you'd come over for dinner." She gives a date and says they're eating early these days, and I settle on the top step and contemplate not going. But Sylvia says to bring Laurel, so I'm committed. I could never resist, anyway.

Sylvia's front windows could use a wash, and as we peer through the screen I see stray toys and a sweater at large in the living room. I wonder if Sylvia needed those binges to keep the place just so. Laurel knocks, and when there's no response I have an urge to cut out: catch a movie or dinner or drive out into the country, just the two of us. I want to see Ryan, but Sylvia and Raymond may be more than I can handle. Then Sylvia calls cheerily, "Come on in," and I step in hesitantly, thinking of the last time I was here, and of the time before that, on her bed.

We find her in the kitchen, dressed in office clothes: pink skirt, nice blouse. She's letting her hair grow. She gives Laurel an effusive kiss and says, "We're running a *bit* late because I'm just in from the old temp racket. What I wouldn't give for a genuine job! But can I get you a Diet Pepsi? I don't keep beer or liquor in the house now . . . Hi, Howie." A peck for me and a small squeeze I'm too stiff to return.

Ryan shuffles in, looking bigger than I remember. Broad in the shoulders, too; could that be? He puts out a shy hand, and Sylvia says, "Give 'em a hug, ya goofus." When I put my arms around him, he's his familiar self, long and lean. A bit rigid 'til he softens against me, but this, too, is familiar. It's eight weeks now since he left my house, just the time he was there.

Something strikes me — no Indians cap — and I run my fingers through his curly hair. He looks balefully at his mother. "New rules. Not in the house," he says.

Sylvia says if she has to live by the law, then everyone has to live by the law. "Though Mama's on probation, isn't she, darlin'? And you're not."

Sylvia's mom was famous for a round, Bisquick-based hors d'oeuvre she called sausage puffs. She'd make up a giant batch and store them in Jiffy bags in the freezer, and though they were reserved for company, whenever Syl and I were alone in the house we'd heat up a dozen or so. Once those were gone, I'd start scheming for more. I suppose it's been years since I last thought of sausage puffs, but when Sylvia opens the oven I smell them again. "I bet you don't remember these, Howie. Ryan calls them sausage planets." Sylvia may not have promoted this get-together, but she's making the best of it.

We sit on the patio, drinking our sodas and munching the sausage planets. Fartin' Martin's Rottweilers woof at us when we step outside, but Sylvia silences them with a word, and I'm glad the backyard neighbor isn't around. It's enough that I'm waiting for Raymond to make an entrance. Play a little soccer, check out the phone line, use one of those tools he's got hanging from his waist. But either he's no longer on the scene or Sylvia's told him to make himself scarce. She doesn't mention him, though she does all the talking.

When she goes inside to check the dinner, Ryan and Laurel and I stare at one another. Ryan asks how Steve is, and I nod. *Fine.* He asks about Harrison, and Laurel says he's okay, under the circumstances. Losing a parent is a big deal, she says, and Ryan nods sympathetically. Laurel asks him what he's been up to, and he says, "Not much. You know, playing." Then she tells him I'm back at the convent, and I nod again. Ryan bites his lip, and I suppose he's forgotten how I allowed him to steer, or how we cut the borers from the pines. But I bet he recalls his terrified fall and the slap Sister Amity gave me. This must not seem like a job to go back to, but he blinks again. "Sounds good," he murmurs.

I feel myself blushing. I can't explain my life, and what, in any case, does a child know of compromise? Ryan takes another planet and asks how Ruby's doing, but I've already lost patience. I'd rather stare at the flagstones. Once, I think, our conversation was useful. We shared ball games and mountain views, and we planned activities. We accomplished plenty by gesture. But nothing important was ever built out of social chatter, and as we all sit nicely on Sylvia's wrought-iron furniture a gulf is evident, and what we had grows increasingly small. Inquiring after Ms. Monetti, Ryan's only doing what well-behaved kids do to talk to adults, and it feels like that first morning, when I drove him away from here.

Laurel keeps glancing at me, and I suppose I seem sulky. At last she announces she's going to offer Sylvia a hand, and we let her go. The Rottweilers whimper as she steps toward the house, and in the silence that follows I watch some small ants sneak from the grass to the slate. Ryan says, "What about Shawn? He still got his blue hair?" I shrug. "Hey!" he says. "And the Snakes! How was their season?"

I raise my hands. I have no idea. Ryan looks quizzical, then says, "You didn't keep going?" *Of course not*, I want to say, and I'm amazed he doesn't realize this. But he doesn't, and as he sorts through it his dreary manners evaporate. "You oughta go, man," he says with a touch of outrage. "You're on the team. Who you think's umping first?" He cogitates a minute longer, then asks, "Is Harrison still pitching coach? Harrison doesn't go either?" *Nope.*

Ryan gawps at me, then smiles sneakily. "You guys are *pussies*," he says. It's a forbidden word, and his eyes dart toward the house.

But I don't care. Hell, maybe we are pussies. I think of Ed's phone calls, of Harrison withdrawing to that colorful sheet. "Neep!" I say, but Ryan just shrugs. A handful of planets remain on the plate, and I pick one up and toss it at him. It bounces off his front teeth.

"Pussies, man," he murmurs mischievously. He picks the planet from the ground and eats it, then waggles his fingers at me. "Come on, tough guy. Your best shot." I toss another, and this time he catches it. "Mom's best, yum, yum. Okay, now you, Howie. Are you ready?" I catch it easily, nothing but mouth.

I'm not sure who gets the point in each round, but according to Ryan it's 3–2 when Laurel appears at the sliding door. She tells us to wash our hands, and as I step past her into the house, she murmurs, "Is she always this weird?"

And with dinner, the tyranny of talk resumes. Sylvia tells us how hard it is temping and wonders if she should repaint the house. "Or — oh, I don't know," she says brightly. "Sometimes I think we should just pack up and move. *Really* start fresh, doesn't that sound exciting? If we went to Chicago? My sister Caroline would lend a hand, and though my sponsor's here, honestly, I am just so weary of doing everything on my own. But I go back and forth. There are good things for me here, but some bad associations, too, which I've been warned about. *More* than warned. Though I don't say it to sound resentful. All lessons learned." She pokes a fork at her rice pilaf and adds, "Of course, Ryan wants to stay here. Friends, school, other things. Isn't that so, baby?" He nods.

While Sylvia speaks, Laurel and I sit quietly, eating our dinner. I'm accustomed to sitting quietly — it's what I do — and I'm used to Sylvia damming every lull with words. But Laurel can speak, so I'd expected customary dialogue. It's strange to see Sylvia rumble past her as she does me.

Laurel asks if she sees a lot of her sister, and Sylvia says, "From time to time. We're very different."

"I never had a sister," says Laurel. "Always thought it would be nice. And my brother's much older." She grins at Ryan. "Kind of grew up a singleton, like you."

"One thing I learned in my time away is the value of a support system," Sylvia announces. "Which I never, ever, ever had. I mean, there were people. There are always *people*, and in some way people provide a framework. But in the most basic sense I was alone, ever since childhood. I was alone, and coke was my support." I glance at Ryan, but he looks bored as shit; perhaps he's heard this before. Suddenly it strikes me that Sylvia's not speaking to him, or even to Laurel and me. She's speaking to herself, and with great determination. The frank talk, the mulling things over aloud, the maintenance of a chipper attitude: all these are for her. Of course, she's recently out of rehab and perhaps attitude is on her punch list, but still, this is *me* here, not some support group. Does she think I'm a stranger?

I eat my salmon, which is delicious, and wonder if she was always this way. Certainly in the old art-room days Sylvia was no conversationalist. She kept busy with projects, and there were other people and a radio, and the potter's wheels would be whirring. I was the one who kept up a running commentary. Sylvia had rare, sweet bursts of effervescence but didn't depend on talk.

When I first came home injured, Sylvia was in school. I didn't see her often, but occasionally she'd show me her paintings, and we'd look at them for a long time without speaking. She'd wait for me to respond. At last, I might gesture at a blue area, for example, and then, hesitantly, she'd talk about the blue. I remember her tentative and sincere at this time. Only later did her talkativeness manifest, and it was the coke that did it. I guess her cruel side emerged then, too; why didn't this bother me? Because she was always Sylvia? Remembering the shy B student I loved in high school, I realize how overjoyed she must have been to assert herself. It's always wonderful to be able to speak. If coke fueled her gregariousness, that must have been one thing she loved about it, and perhaps she vowed not to return inward as she dried out. Or perhaps now she can't help herself.

Laurel looks thoughtfully at a dark painting on the dining room wall. "Is that yours? Ryan told us how his mom was an artist."

Sylvia sniffs. "Oh, that whole — I don't know. Yes, I do, and yes, it's one of mine. But the whole 'being a painter' was such a dodge of responsibility. It was a fairy tale, a way out of reality, a fantasy about myself and my, I don't know, *vision*. What a waste of time, of decades! I'm so invested now in putting my energy into other things. In being a success, for example — I should say for a change! Just getting my act together, making *some* contribution! I think Howie knows what I mean, don't you, Howie? You've dealt with recovery." She looks at me, and I scratch my head. I know lost time, but creativity was Sylvia's strength.

Nevertheless, this *is* still Sylvia, looking healthy and attractive in pink officewear. *Isn't it?* Having us in for a perfect dinner, feeding us optimistic chat. The things she's saying may mean a great deal to her — health and prosperity and a better life for her and Ryan — and I don't begrudge that. I want her to be happy! But it sounds so conventional, and I've lived in a box for a long time, myself. There must be a margin for divergence, I think. For invention, for surprise. Just as there must be Snakes as well as Twins. I wish Sylvia were kidding — I wish this were a wicked imitation of Paula or Big John or some other rehab character — and though it may be perverse of me, I really don't care if she's a productive member. Success? I don't know what that means. I liked the Sylvia who didn't police herself, who knew she liked painting and her kid and, often enough, me. Is there any of *that* Sylvia still in evidence? To think I loved sad-addict Sylvia better than this sleek, improved model! Or that after all these years — these decades! — I'm less besotted. Could that be?

I'd like to go now. I'm still shaky from my own travails, and I can't sit any longer, peeling the layers from the motivational onion. I stand up and pat my stomach, and Sylvia says, "Thank you, Howie. We're eating lighter these days," then returns to her meditations. "Of course, there's so *much* to starting fresh. I wouldn't know anything about selling this house, for example. Caroline could get me an apartment in her building, and maybe a job. She really wants us living nearer." I look to see if she's gauging my reaction, but she's not; she's just talking. I wonder if I mind if she goes away. No more than she minds leaving me. But I don't dare look at Ryan. Sylvia says, "I think moving can be fun! New home, new school, new friends." She strokes Ryan's cheek, and he asks to be excused. It's the first thing he's said since we sat down.

I have a gift for Ryan: a photograph Ann took of us in our Snakes shirts that last day. He's on the bleachers, with an arm over my shoulders, and he's waving his cap against the blue, blue sky. Tearing the paper from the package, he says, "Whoa! Thank you, Howie!" Then he's silent a moment, running a finger over our two shirts. "I'm-a put this by my bed."

We troop down the bedroom hall, and Sylvia says, "Of course, part of reordering priorities means giving up pointless obsessions. Don't *look* at this mess of a room!"

Ryan sweeps a cluster of action figures into a drawer and sets the photograph on the bedside table. "Looks good," he says, and I agree. I have this photo by my bed, too. Sylvia gives him a look, and he says, "I *said* thank you," and Laurel masks a snicker by stooping to scratch Bindi's neck. Ryan watches with bemused dignity, then leans against me, resting his head on my stomach. I squeeze his shoulder. "Even if we do move away," he says, "I wanna visit you guys."

"Well, heck, cowboy, why wait? You can come anytime," says Laurel. "We hope you come soon." He says he will.

We're all quiet. The room is in shadow, and a beam of light

rakes in from the window. I can see Sylvia in the mirror, and for a moment her profile seems cast in gold. Then she turns, takes a stack of folded laundry from atop the desk, and slides it in a dresser drawer. Suddenly, this is no one I'm acquainted with. Bindi flops down on the carpet, and I hear her purring as Laurel scratches her ears. Ryan goes on leaning against me; then he turns, pressing his face to my belly. I pull him toward me, and he puts his arms around my waist. He steps away, picking up the Indians cap.

He asks if he can go play. Sylvia says, "Say a nice goodbye." We watch him head down the street, and she says, "You'll never guess. The kids play kickball at the empty lot. There's a construction light that shines all night long, and it's a big, big deal to go there around dusk. That's why he wants to eat early these days. But can you imagine? *Kick*ball!" She asks if we'd like coffee, but when Laurel runs a hand down my spine I know she's ready, too. Truly, I wish Sylvia the best, but outside, the air is fresh.

I drive down Sylvia's street and hang a right. A small jog, and there's the big light, with all the little figures arranged in formation. The bases are squares of junk cardboard and other detritus, and it's only kids, dozens of them, just like that go-cart run. Kids who aren't playing are spread out across the lot, some involved in other games, skipping rope, even dancing. Not a parent in sight.

I park under a tree, where we won't be noticed. No rushing in to officiate this time! Daylight is fading from the sky, and the cab is cozy. I have the radio on low, but the windows are open and we can hear shouts from the game and the croakings of evening creatures, and even a jet plane somewhere high in the clouds. Laurel slides over and leans against me.

It's getting dark quickly now, and the boys' and girls' shadows merge with the scrub at the edge of the field and with the unfin-ished houses beyond. A stray fluff of Laurel's hair tickles my cheek, and I smell the shampoo she uses and remember that she showered before we drove over here. Her body is soft and comfortable against my own, and I sit quietly, not daring to budge. Under the harsh, bright construction light, the kids dart around their makeshift playing field, almost all of them in baseball caps, so our guy could be anyone. One parent strolls by, then another, to take the younger ones home, but nobody pays Laurel and me any heed. I think of the neighborhood games of my own childhood, and I remember just this time of day, when the sky was slowly turning black and the trees were blackened silhouettes against it. We older kids stayed into the darkness as a skeleton team, and I thought I was growing up. How happy I was!

Laurel asks, "Are you asleep?" I lift a hand to show her I'm not. She tucks a strand of hair behind her ear. I put my arm around her, and she snuggles against me, nice and warm. I can feel the ribbing of the cotton sweater she's wearing. At my fingertips, her smooth forearm.

In the center of the diamond, someone stoops and rolls a red rubber ball, and a kid in a cap kicks and runs. A catch, a tag, a close play at first. A few voices raised, and it takes a minute to settle the dispute. Then they return to their places. The runner remains on, and the ball goes to the pitcher. In the outfield, a girl sings a snatch of a popular song.

Laurel says, "You know, if you think about it, we've been kind of — Oh, wait!" She breaks off, and as she sits up, her hand falls on my thigh. "Is that . . . Oh, wait, Howard, there he is! I didn't *see* him before!" Turning, she smiles suddenly at me. Ryan steps to the plate and does a funny little warm-up leg swivel, very showboaty. When he's ready he signals, and the pitcher rolls the ball. Ryan takes two steps and sends it flying through the infield. He's always had power. A moment later he's jumping up and down at first, his arms raised and his T-shirt flapping. We can hear him cheering.

A new runner steps up to kick the ball, and I suppose Laurel's forgotten what she started to say. It doesn't matter. She murmurs, "Good feller," and snuggles against me again, and I feel very conscious of her hand on my thigh. In fact, I can barely breathe. Ryan makes his way around, one base at a time, and when he reaches home he celebrates again, then looks up and spots my truck. He strolls over, a big grin on his face, and he doesn't seem surprised to find us curled up together.

"See me kick?"

Laurel says, "You're the man, babe."

Ryan looks satisfied. Casually scratching his neck, he asks again if he can visit. Laurel says of course. "Like when?" he says.

"This weekend, if you like, comrade. I'll call your ma, and we'll dream up an outing. You know, I've had a yen lately to go hiking."

"But a sleepover," he says. "I wanna stay in my room." We both nod. *Sure thing.* I give the bill of the old cap a tug, and he looks up, showing those bright, square teeth. I tickle his earlobe with one finger.

Ryan runs back to his game, and the autumn night grows a tiny notch darker. It looks like the kids will soon be calling it quits, and I suppose we should be moving along, too. I'm not sure what I'm doing with my arm around Laurel, and I'd be willing to bet Laurel's not sure either. But how long has it been since I took a chance? Come to think of it, not long. Still, I can't risk getting set in my ways. The world has shifted, and one more something has switched open within me. I recognize the feeling because switches have been opening inside me for decades. Meanwhile, under the darkening trees, a world is blossoming, and what once seemed beyond my grasp feels suddenly possible. Hesitantly I run my fingers through Laurel's smooth, soft hair, and she inclines her head to my touch. "Seriously, Howard," she says, barely loud enough for me to hear. "If you think about it, we're pretty lucky."

ACKNOWLEDGMENTS

Because this is my first published book, I'd like to thank several people who contributed to my development as a writer, if not overtly to *The Ha-Ha*: Melvin Jules Bukiet, Patty Dann, Amy Hempel, Catherine Hiller, Marie Ponsot, and Nahid Rachlin; also the late Jed Mattes and Fred Morris of Jed Mattes, Inc. Thanks to the Ragdale Foundation for the time to write, and to Jack Doren, Muriel Manuelian, Dana Aliger, Ben Michaelis, Judith Rosenberger, and Roy Shapiro for help and guidance. Thanks to my family and friends and to my partner, Frank Tartaglione: in fact, it's heaven that is other people.

I thank my professors at Columbia University's School of the Arts: April Bernard, Magda Bogin, Lucie Brock-Broido, Nicholas Christopher, Alfred Corn, Michael Cunningham, Richard Howard, Fenton Johnson, Stephen Koch, Jaime Manrique, Richard Peña, David Plante, and Alice Quinn; and my thesis readers, Marina Budhos and Mark Slouka;

the members of my thesis workshop at Columbia: Marika Alzadon, Kevin Chong, Scott Conklin, Darren Hayward, Alec Michod, and Eric Zelko;

my writing group, several of whose members read multiple drafts, and whose input and encouragement have been immeasurable: Mark Alpert, Jennifer Cohen, Johanna Fiedler, Steve Goldstone, Melissa Knox, Eva Mekler, Cheryl Morrison, and Emily Platt; and three final readers, Nalini Jones, Alec Michod, and Laura Miller, who provided crucial close commentary on the penultimate manuscript.

I thank Izaak and Saskia Bunschoten-Binet, Joshua, Jason, and Elizabeth Clark, Peter Matchette, Marlena Paulson, Morgan Rose, Kate Thompson, Desi Tomaselli, and Eric Wagner for inspiration.

I thank my agent, Kim Goldstein, whose intelligence, ingenuity, and friendship have taught me so much; my editor, Michael Mezzo, whose commitment to this novel made everything happen; and the extraordinary Michael Pietsch and a remarkable team at Little, Brown for bringing dedication, resourcefulness, and heart to the process. Publishing this book has been a joy and an education. Thank you all.